THE CTHULHU CASEBOOKS

SHERLOCK HOLMES
and the Shadwell Shadows

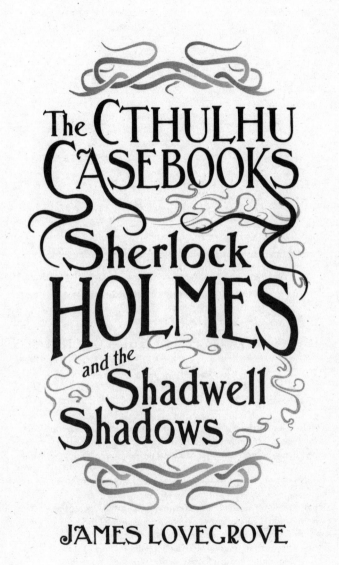

The Cthulhu Casebooks

Sherlock HOLMES and the Shadwell Shadows

JAMES LOVEGROVE

TITAN BOOKS

The Cthulhu Casebooks: Sherlock Holmes and the Shadwell Shadows
Hardback edition ISBN: 9781783295937
Paperback edition ISBN: 9781785652912
Electronic edition ISBN: 9781783295944

Published by Titan Books
A division of Titan Publishing Group Ltd
144 Southwark St, London SE1 0UP

First edition: November 2016
Paperback edition: September 2017
6 8 10 9 7 5

A CIP catalogue record for this title is available from the British Library.

Printed and bound by CPI Group (UK) Ltd, Croydon, CR0 4YY

This book and its sequels are dedicated to Miranda
Jewess, who not only instigated them but edited the
hell out of them – or should that be *into* them?

PREFACE
BY JAMES LOVEGROVE

IN THE SPRING OF 2014 I RECEIVED AN EMAIL OUT of the blue. It was from a firm of lawyers based in Providence, Rhode Island. At first I thought it was spam and nearly deleted it. As I scrolled through, however, I realised the email was bona fide, and I read on with curiosity and a growing bemusement.

The sender was Mason K. Jacobs III, a senior partner at Laughlin Jacobs Travers LLP. The subject heading was "A Legacy", which was why I'd been suspicious about the email, thinking it might be one of those scams where some Nigerian princeling wants to use your bank account to stash several million dollars temporarily, with you getting a percentage cut for your trouble (and in no way will your account details be stolen).

The text began as follows:

Dear Mr Lovegrove,
You are likely unaware of the recent passing, at the age of 82, of Mr Henry Prothero Lovecraft. This

individual was a lifelong resident of Providence and a longstanding if not regular client of Laughlin, Jacobs, Travers. Unmarried and without issue, he succumbed to heart failure in the fall of last year, leaving behind an estate worth in the region of $75,000.

As part of our due diligence in probate we have been chasing down relatives who might be in line to inherit part or all of his legacy. Mr Lovecraft was a solitary man and died intestate. He lived in a modest condominium in Smith Hill, which as you may or may not know is one of our city's less favored areas. The bulk of his estate accrues from the sale of his apartment, said property amounting to a $95,000 capital value. After taxes, various other duties and our fees have been deducted, we arrive at the residual $75,000 figure mentioned above.

By this point my heart had started to race. I was beginning to infer that I was in line for a cash windfall equivalent to roughly £50,000 sterling. The email certainly seemed to be heading in that direction. Ker-ching!

My hopes of a new car and a reduced mortgage, and perhaps a Caribbean holiday, were dashed by the next paragraph.

We have managed to track down a grand-niece of Mr Lovecraft's in Kennebunkport, Maine. To her – a Ms Rhonda Lachaise – goes the legacy, and to her it has been accordingly disbursed.

Curse Mason K. Jacobs III and his lawyerly punctiliousness. He'd never intended to mislead me. He'd just set out the facts of the matter in order, failing to appreciate that the reader – me – might imagine his preamble was heading in one direction when it was actually heading in another. He inadvertently led me up the garden path, only to slam the front door in my face.

Nonetheless, there were certain items among Mr Lovecraft's effects to which Ms Lachaise wished no claim. He was, it seems, an inveterate hoarder of books, papers, exotic paraphernalia, and sundry pieces of statuary and handicraft whose purpose appears to be religious but whose provenance is hard to determine and, frankly, baffling.

These have been disposed of, on the grounds that they have no obvious useful function and in some instances constitute a public hygiene hazard. The books and papers were of little value, according to representatives of both the public library and the John Hay Library at Brown University, while the majority of the objects – figurines, effigies, fetishes and such – were fashioned from organic materials such as hide and hair and were rather moth-eaten and sordid. I would not be surprised if Mr Lovecraft had made them himself. They had a kind of homespun crudity about them.

One particular item stood out, however, and seemed worthy of preservation. It is about this that I am contacting you.

During our researches we ascertained that you,

Mr Lovegrove, are a distant relative of the late Mr Lovecraft. The connection is attenuated, dating back some three hundred years, but real enough.

Furthermore, a junior partner in our firm is an avid consumer of genre fiction and is familiar with your work. It was he who suggested you were the appropriate candidate to receive the item in question.

The artifact, the nature of which you are no doubt eager for me to divulge, is a book manuscript. To be precise, three typed manuscripts which together tell a single tale. They are of some antiquity, perhaps a century old, and at a cursory glance purport to have been written by none other than Dr John Watson, a literary figure with whose oeuvre you have a more than nodding acquaintance, to judge by your own recent published output. They were discovered at the back of a closet in Mr Lovecraft's bedroom, inside a rusty strongbox.

Now my heart was racing again, but this time with a mixture of excitement and incredulity.

To cut a long story short, we believe these manuscripts to be nothing more than forgeries, at best some kind of pastiche. They center around Sherlock Holmes, naturally enough, given the purported author. The adventures they narrate, though, are like none to which aficionados of the character are accustomed. In point of fact, with their emphasis on strange and uncanny events they seem utterly antithetical to the spirit of rationalism which to my (admittedly limited) knowledge typifies the Holmes canon.

You, Mr Lovegrove, deserve to take possession of the manuscripts, by virtue of your familial association with Henry Lovecraft. You are also the best person, we feel, to adjudge their quality and authenticity, by virtue of your professional experience in the fields of fantastical fiction and, if I may use the term, "Holmesiana."

I am therefore dispatching them to you by international courier and they should arrive within the next two weeks. If by any chance you are able to make something of them, and perhaps even deem them publishable in some guise or other, we would of course be more than happy to represent you in whatever legal or executive capacity we are able.

Yours sincerely,
Mason K. Jacobs III

I spent the rest of that day visiting genealogy websites, frantically trying to establish how Henry Lovecraft and I were related. At the back of my mind lay the thought that this Lovecraft must be a descendant of the noted author Howard Phillips Lovecraft (1890–1937) whose horror fiction has been so seminal and enduring. There was the coincidence, or not, of the two men's identical initials. Of more relevance was the location, Providence, which was the birthplace and, for most of his life, home of the more celebrated Lovecraft.

I soon discovered that the three of us were indeed linked by bloodline. It turns out that our ancestral roots lie with Bavarian nobility, the Von Luftgraf family. The word *Luftgraf* translates loosely from the German as "high count". The Von Luftgrafs owned a large swathe of Upper Franconia, up until the 1760s when they experienced some sort of financial calamity and lost their estates and castles. As far as I could work out, one scion of the dynasty became involved with a cult of demon-raising black-magic practitioners, went mad, and essentially bequeathed his fellow acolytes all his worldly wealth, thereafter living out his final days in an insane asylum, the proverbial gibbering wreck.

To escape the shame and penury caused by this incident and seek a fresh start, the remaining handful of Von Luftgrafs emigrated in two directions, some north to Great Britain, others west to the United States. Both groups shortened and anglicised their surname on arrival in their new homelands, the British contingent adopting the spelling Lovegrove, the American contingent Lovecraft. Henry Prothero Lovecraft belonged to a different branch of the family tree that spawned Howard Phillips Lovecraft, the trunk of which was from those first mid-eighteenth-century arrivals in New England. All the same, he seems to have shared his relative's keen fascination with the occult and the arcane.

What this meant was that I was, in fact, a cousin about a hundred times removed from H.P. Lovecraft himself, whose stories I had devoured in my teens. That was fairly thrilling to learn, I can tell you. Lovecraft's facility for evoking the eldritch and for imparting a sense of creeping dread is unparalleled, but also anchored by a cool, cerebral reportage/memoir/diary technique and by fleeting winks of black comedy. His less wholesome personal attributes – principally his racism, a disgust for non-Anglo-Saxon cultures often expressed in his journalism and private correspondence – were unknown to me when I first discovered his work. Awareness of them blights it now to some extent, as does the occasional imprecision and over-baked ungainliness of his writing style, the latter more noticeable to me in middle age when I am an author myself and, I like to think, conscious of what does and doesn't constitute decent prose.

All the same, *the* H.P. Lovecraft. He and I had an affinity that was more than the simple fact that both of us eked a living from our pens. This was the man who explored and codified that amalgamation of ancient elder gods, forbidden knowledge, hostile supernatural forces and cosmic indifference which has come to be known as the Cthulhu Mythos – and he was family. We shared DNA. I even became aware of a vague physical resemblance between us, especially around the eyes.

The manuscripts arrived at my house a fortnight later, and I unsealed the package straight away and got to reading. The paper was yellowed and brittle, the text faint in places yet still perfectly legible.

The contents were, to put it mildly, remarkable.

I'm not going to say much further. The books should speak for themselves. I've had the paper checked by an expert, who tells me that the watermark and the high rag content denote that it is exactly the sort of bonded foolscap which someone in the 1920s might have used. Another expert confirms that the typewriter employed is an Imperial Model 50, judging by the font, the width of the carriage and the strike depth of the characters. That particular make was popular in Britain between the wars, which is when Watson, according to his foreword, wrote the books. In other words, on the face of it the manuscripts seem to be the real deal.

At the same time, I can't help wondering if they're a monstrous hoax (and I use the adjective advisedly). Reams of the right paper and a typewriter of suitable vintage are readily purchaseable. I've checked on eBay. For a few hundred quid, they could be yours. That and a bit of skill with literary mimicry is all you'd need to make the deception look credible.

I've spent a year or so, on and off, studying the manuscripts, rereading them, evaluating their worth, trying my very best to decide whether or not they genuinely are the work of the esteemed Dr Watson and do, in his own words, present "an alternate history of the career of Sherlock Holmes".

A part of me, for my own sanity, hopes that they don't; hopes that someone else, not Watson, perhaps Henry Prothero Lovecraft himself, is their creator, and they are just some abstruse metafictional joke, something designed to fascinate and bamboozle the world, that's all.

Because otherwise, almost everything we know about the great detective – his life, his work, his methods, his accomplishments – has all been a big fat lie, a façade concocted to mask a deeper, darker, more horrible truth.

I'm submitting the three manuscripts in published form under the umbrella title *Cthulhu Casebooks*. The individual volumes bear the titles Dr Watson gave them – *Sherlock Holmes and the Shadwell Shadows, Sherlock Holmes and the Miskatonic Monstrosities* and *Sherlock Holmes and the Sussex Sea-Devils* – and the central events in each take place at fifteen-year intervals, in 1880, 1895 and 1910 respectively. All I've done to the original texts after scanning them into my computer is correct a few solecisms and grammatical errors, resolve the continuity glitches for which the author is famous (some might say notorious), and weave in a sentence or two of explanation here and there to shore up an otherwise obscure reference.

I leave it to you, the reader, to make up your own mind about the books. You can decide if they effectively rewrite the Holmes canon, skewing it through the distorting prism of the Lovecraftian one, or if they are just the fevered outpourings of some reclusive, semi-anonymous scribbler exploiting the popularity of not one but two iconic figures of our times.

Call it crossover. Call it mash-up. Call it cash-in.

Or call it a revelation.

It's up to you.

J.M.H.L., EASTBOURNE, UK
November 2016

I AM AN OLD MAN. A TIRED, FRIGHTENED OLD MAN. I have lived a long time, done much, seen much. Now my eyesight is fading, my body is gnarled and weak, and I feel my life ebbing with each passing day. I am a trained medical practitioner. I know senescence when I see it, and the mirror habitually shows it me in all its greying, decaying glory, ever more blurred, ever more saddening.

That is when I can bear to look in the mirror at all. For the reflections in mirrors do not reveal only remorseless corporeal collapse. They also, potentially, expose things hiding in corners, things lurking at the periphery of one's vision, things that, once glimpsed, start to titter or whisper or else sometimes simply sit silent, watching.

I have written at length about the best and the wisest man whom I have ever known, a man I was proud to call friend and by whom I was proud to be called friend. I refer, of course, to Mr Sherlock Holmes, and to the dozens of narratives, all well received, in which I have recounted his adventures. I have expatiated on his deductive powers, his ratiocination, his peerless ability to penetrate to the truth of a matter, uncover malfeasance and bring wrongdoers to justice. His analytical methods, by my auspices, are known worldwide and have indeed been adopted and emulated by representatives of several international police forces. I flatter myself that in bringing his exploits to the attention of the masses, I have contributed significantly to the science of detection and improved the lot of law-abiding citizens everywhere, and by extension vitiated the efforts of the less law-abiding.

I can now, in the twilight of my life, confess that I have not told the whole story. Far from it. I have in fact told one sort of story in order to deflect attention from another, which strays into realms most ordinary people are incognisant of and are all the better off in their ignorance. I have constructed a shell of artifice around a dark, rotten kernel so as to protect civilisation from certain facts that would throw its cosy self-assurance into drastic and lasting disarray.

The time has come to unburden myself of secrets I have kept long after Sherlock Holmes died. At his express request I have buried the truth, but its grave has been unquiet and disturbances from it have since troubled me in the night. I would not go to my own grave without just this once, at last, exhuming the undecaying corpse and exposing it to scrutiny.

Hence I have decided to write three last books about Holmes, a final trilogy in which I shall lay bare all that he really did, all that he really achieved over the course of his life. They make up, for better or worse, an alternate history of his career, one that has the benefit of being unimpeachably true.

I do not expect them to be published. On the contrary, it is imperative that they never see the light of day. I plan to entrust them to the care of an American author, name of Lovecraft. His work is garnering repute in the pages of the so-called "pulp" magazines across the Atlantic – an offshoot of the penny dreadful and the shilling shocker, no less sensationalist, yet now and then, almost by accident, the repository for some fine creative endeavours – and, more pertinently, he seems well versed in the blasphemous and often perverse material that these books cover. Lovecraft and I have been corresponding of late – his letters are lengthy and detailed, and arrive with a frequency I cannot hope to match – and he is as intimate as anyone with the esoteric territory mapped herein (although a couple of his peers, Robert E. Howard and Clark Ashton Smith, are almost equally adept). He and I are kindred spirits and fellow travellers, his writings revealing as great an understanding as my own of the uncanny forces that hover at the very edge of reality, trying to break in.

Lovecraft will know what to do with the books, which is to lock them in a strongbox and throw away the key. I do not need him even to read them. I merely want them out of me, as it were, in the manner of a diseased organ removed by a surgeon. Before I die I wish to be rid of their accumulated weight, the plague of their presence in my soul. This, then, is a kind of literary exorcism.

My fingers are swollen with arthritis, pecking at the typewriter keys like twisted bird beaks. It aches to write, it *hurts*. Yet write I must. I keep the electric lights burning in my study, to banish the London gloom outside. To banish the shadows, too, for I know all too well what shadows may hide within their dark folds.

Holmes, my erstwhile companion, wherever you are, I trust that you will forgive me this shriving of my inner self, even if it goes against your recommendations. At the very least you will look on me with those sharp grey eyes, utter a fond chuckle, and declare that I am a foolish, blundersome oaf whose intellectual incompetence is equalled only by his lack of observational acuity – which, from you, amounts to a declaration of absolution.

J.H.W., PADDINGTON
1928

CHAPTER ONE

A Study in Scar Tissue

"THE MOST MERCIFUL THING IN THE WORLD, I think, is the inability of the human mind to correlate all its contents."

So has written another author, one H.P. Lovecraft, and it is a sentiment to which I, Dr John H. Watson, subscribe more wholeheartedly than most. Indeed, never was I so glad of being unable to make full sense of certain experiences as in the autumn of 1880 when I returned from Afghanistan to England sound in neither mind nor body. The physical injuries I had sustained during an expedition to a lost city in the Kandahar Province and an encounter with the dwellers therein were unpleasant enough. Worse, however, far worse, was the damage inflicted upon my psyche. Memories of the incident plagued me with the garish intensity of a nightmare. In order to dilute the power of those memories and preserve what was left of my sanity, I retreated into what I can only describe as a madness of self-denial. I swore blind to myself that the events of those days had never taken place, that I had succumbed to a delusion, some feverish aberration of the brain. None of it had been real.

The belief sustained me, and saved me from a spell at Netley, the very institution where I had trained as an army surgeon two years earlier. There is a certain ward at that military hospital in Hampshire, tucked away in a side wing, which is designated for those returning from warfare affected by no great bodily impairment but rather by mental traumas brought on by the horrors of the battlefield. The beds are fitted with restraints and occupied by men who, when their sedation wears off, are apt to resort to incoherent babbling and sometimes screaming. I, but for my half-conscious, half-instinctive decision to refuse to accept the evidence of my own senses, might well have been amongst their number.

As it was, I could not always reconcile what I wanted to accept as the truth with the plain facts. No alternative scenario I might concoct, however logical I tried to make it, would account for the deaths of the half-dozen members of the Fifth Northumberlands whom I had accompanied into the remoter reaches of the Arghandab Valley, amongst them Captain Roderick Harrowby, instigator and first victim of the ill-fated excursion. Nor was it a simple matter for me to forget the anguished cries of the soldiers as they were beset by the inhabitants of that subterranean city, and the yet more hideous sibilant ululations of the inhabitants themselves as they went about the slaughter of an armed platoon with fiendish glee.

All I could do was maintain the pretence to all and sundry that I had been wounded by a bullet from a Jezail rifle during the Battle of Maiwand, a clash from which I was in fact one of the lucky minority of British combatants to emerge unscathed. This fabrication, first devised as I was recuperating at the base hospital at Peshawar, allowed me to escape any further probing from interlocutors, who hailed my service to my country and accorded to me a valour I hardly felt I warranted. In time, with repetition, I almost came to believe the story myself.

Nonetheless, in the weeks after I set foot back in London I remained a hollow shell of the man I had been. I bore the stoop and haggardness of the invalided campaigner, along with the miserly and temporary pension; I also carried a dark knowledge in my eyes, whose gaze I could seldom meet in the shaving mirror of a morning: a knowledge of things commonly unseen, things that should remain commonly unknown.

That same mirror would show me the other, more tangible mark I was doomed to carry for the rest of my days. It was an ugly gouge scooped out of the meat of my upper left shoulder, and in certain lights it might have passed for a rifle bullet wound. Equally, it could be taken for the result of a crooked talon raking my deltoid muscle, furrowing through the flesh clean to the bone. The injury ached more or less constantly and somewhat impaired my use of that arm. Still, I was aware that I had escaped lightly. During my sojourn at Peshawar the wound had become infected, and the surgeons had debated whether or not to amputate the limb. Luck had favoured me, and the sepsis had abated as rapidly as it had flared; but it was a close-run thing.

Time and again I would examine the puckered scar tissue, and would try not to think of the repugnant creature that had inflicted it. "A bullet," I would tell myself, in the manner of a chant. "A bullet from a Jezail. A bullet." Thus, like a mesmerist enthralling his subject, I endeavoured to implant one idea in my consciousness so that it superseded another.

The cold, wet winter of that year set in, and my funds

were running perilously low, when I bumped into an old acquaintance, Stamford. As I have stated in the novel *A Study in Scarlet*, this fellow had been a dresser under me at Barts. Everything else that I have said about the meeting, and its repercussions, is false, and I present the accurate version herewith.

Stamford and I did not chance upon each other in the respectable, opulent environs of the Long Bar at the Criterion Restaurant just off Piccadilly Circus. Rather, the location was a much less salubrious drinking establishment, a pub in a back alley somewhere amid the labyrinth of rookeries off the Commercial Road. I shall not dignify its name by giving it in these pages. Suffice to say it was the type of tavern where those with little money find ways of spending it on the many vices that life has to offer and will encounter no few individuals of low morality and even lower standards to engage in facilitating those vices. Games of dice, dominoes and cards were conducted in the saloon, cock-fighting in the back room, bare-knuckle boxing in the basement, and more besides. Everywhere within, the dregs of society could be seen swilling the dregs of their ale, and the songs that every so often burst forth spontaneously from this assembly were of the lewdest sort.

I fetched up there mostly because of the light and noise emanating from its windows and doorways. To one traipsing the chilly byways of the capital on the first day of December, ankle-deep in slush from the previous day's snowfall, it seemed a haven of warmth and life. Once inside, I was drawn to a table where Nap was being played, close by a roaring fire. I was – am – an inveterate gambler, fond of a flutter at the bookmakers', only too ready to chance my arm when a deck of cards is in sight. It is my one abiding vice. As I watched the game unfold, the lure of money to be won worked its irresistible wiles on me, and soon I had joined in and was betting with what little remained of my pension. I fared relatively well, too, at least to begin with. In one memorable hand I bid a Wellington and managed to take all five tricks as declared, leading with my lowest value non-trump. That is no mean feat. But alas, subsequent hands were less propitious, and an hour or so later I had squandered all my winnings and was a couple of pounds the poorer. It dawned on me that my fellow players might be conspiring against me, but since they were a rather rough-hewn lot – full of Cockney menace, their language pure Billingsgate – I refrained from voicing my suspicions. I merely made my excuses and rose from the table, preparing to leave the premises.

I might not have noticed Stamford at all in the midst of that fuggy, overcrowded space were it not for the fact that, just as I was making for the door, he became embroiled in an argument with a pair of Lascars over the price of a girl whose services he wished to procure for the evening. The Lascars were acting as the girl's agents, so to speak, and what had started as a negotiation escalated into an altercation.

Heated exchanges of opinion were evidently far from unusual in this pub, for the other patrons displayed little or no interest in the goings-on. Even the publican, a thick-necked, lavishly mutton-chopped cove with a world-weary face that had seen all the less savoury behaviours of men, was content to polish glasses with a bar cloth and pay no heed. Everyone seemed to think that the row would surely blow over, and if it did not, then they could weather it by keeping their heads down and their involvement minimal.

Stamford averred angrily that two shillings was his final offer, a generous one, and the Lascars could take it or leave it. They demanded five, not a penny less.

"I do not like your attitude," Stamford declared. "Your sort should really mind their manners. Did you learn nothing at sea? When a white man orders, you obey him, with all the respect he is due."

The larger and swarthier of the Lascars responded with a grin that was equal parts amusement and contempt. "Oh, we learn how to take orders all right," he replied in a thick subcontinental accent. "We take them up to here." He held his hand level with his nose. "And then we don't take them no more."

"The bosun's whip teach us respect," the other chimed in. Two of his upper incisors were capped with gold. "So do the first mate's fists, and everyone else's boots. Lascar is dog of the ship. Captains trade Lascar from ship to ship like barrel of grog. Lascar is nothing. We know how white man treats us, so now we treat him the same. Fair play."

The first Lascar raised five fingers. "Five for her. Pay up or go."

The "her" under discussion was a pallid, frightened-looking waif dressed in clothes that were one step up from rags, although with their flounces and frills they aimed at coquettishness. I estimated her age to be thirteen at the

most. Her pinched face was smudged with dirt and her
eyes bore dark rings around them, whilst knock-knees and
a slight curvature of the spine suggested she had suffered a
bout of rickets during infancy. Life and her fellow human
beings had, it was clear, maltreated this girl from the very
start. She was a pitiful sight even in such shabby, sawdust-
floored surroundings, a stunted rose surely destined never
to grow to full bloom.

"For the whole night," Stamford said, "three shillings."

The Lascars, however, held out resolutely for five.

It was at this point that I elected to intervene. I
remembered Stamford as a jolly, exuberant sort, an
exponent of the macabre humour that is often the recourse
of the medical man, especially in the operating theatre
where blood and offal are part and parcel of the daily
grind. He did not seem of a cheerful disposition any longer.
He seemed, rather, to be under considerable nervous strain,
sweating, sallow-cheeked and bleary of eye. I feared he
was making a spectacle of himself. I was loath, too, to see
the unfortunate girl hired out to anyone, but least of all to
a fellow of whom I had affectionate memories and who
ought not to be stooping to this lowly practice.

"By Jove!" I exclaimed, as though I had only just
entered the pub and noticed him. "It's Stamford, isn't it?"

Stamford twitched, then turned round and peered at
me. "Do I know you, sir?"

"You may not recall me well, but know me you do.
John Watson. We were students at Barts together."

His eyes evinced a flicker of recognition, and a trace of
evasiveness which I took to be born of shame. "No," he lied.

"Sorry. You are mistaken. We are strangers, you and I."

"Yes, you go, sir," said the larger Lascar to me, sounding almost polite. "The gentleman and we do business. Business that is none of your business."

"Come, come, Stamford," I persisted, ignoring the Lascar. "Don't be silly. Stop joking about. Depart with me. We'll find somewhere pleasanter to share a pint or two and a few reminiscences."

I yoked an arm round his shoulders. In hindsight, this was a tactical blunder. Not only did it make Stamford stiffen with resentment, it gave the Lascars a clear signal that I was laying claim to their client. If they lost the transaction, I would be to blame, not he. In retrospect I should have handled the situation with more finesse. But, as I have already made plain, I was not at that time in the rightest of minds. Recent history had bred a recklessness in me, a sense that civilisation was a fragile, essentially meaningless construct, forever at the mercy of hostile undercurrents. Why else would I have been in that dingy pub with its no less dingy denizens in the first place? Humanity was brutish, I had come to believe, a mere step away from its animal ancestry. Here, one could see that fact in all its grimy splendour, and revel in it.

Yet I could not bear to watch Stamford descend irredeemably into degradation. Perhaps, in attempting to save him from his baser urges, I was hoping to save myself.

Be that as it may, Stamford had no wish to be rescued, and shook off my arm. The Lascars, meanwhile, were affronted by my temerity in interfering in their affairs. The gold-toothed one, from a pocket of his naval pea coat, produced a sailor's jack-knife, the kind that is five inches long when closed and nearly double that when opened, and which as well as a cutting blade sports a marlinspike for ropework. In a swift, well-practised motion he clicked open the blade and aimed the point at me.

"Back away, friend," he advised – and seldom can the word "friend" have sounded quite so bereft of its meaning. "Now. While you still can. Otherwise things not go well for you."

"I might say the same for you," I answered, balling my hands into fists.

I realised that this, or something like it, was what I had been after all along, the reason I had been out wandering in such dismal conditions. I had not been looking for respite in drink and gambling but for a confrontation of some sort, a way of venting the anxiety and anger that had taken hold of my life and made it nigh on unbearable. My earlier pusillanimity at the Nap table seemed a distant memory. That I was unarmed and the Lascar was not, that he and his companion outnumbered me and, in the case of the larger, outweighed me by a good thirty pounds, did not trouble me. I could fight. Perhaps I might even win.

Then the old man appeared.

He emerged from a far corner, having sat concealed in a snug nursing a bottle of gin. Said bottle was now in his hand, held by the neck, its contents sloshing merrily as he staggered across to us, weaving from side to side in the classic manner of the heavily inebriated.

His age I reckoned at sixty. He was hunched of shoulder, grey-headed, thickly and wirily bearded, and clothed in a threadbare tweed jacket and a flat cap with a collarless shirt and a grubby blue neckerchief. He looked for all the world like a man from whom the tide of early promise had receded, leaving him stranded in regret, forever down on his luck. The red webs of broken capillaries on his cheeks attested to a fondness for alcohol even more than did his unsteady gait; likewise the bulbous, dimple-textured nose he sported, the badge of the veteran imbiber.

"'Ey up, what's all this then?" he slurred in broad Yorkshire tones. "You lads should calm thissen. Nowt to be gained by skrikin' and fratchin'. No call for any of thee to bray any of thee either, if us can just settle down and be nice. What dus't tha reckon?"

The gold-toothed Lascar turned his knife on the new arrival. "What that language you talking? That English?"

"English as she is proper spoke," said the Yorkshireman.

"So you say. You better do like I just told this other one." By which he meant me. "Back away. This nothing to do with you."

"Mebbe so, mebbe not. But do thissen a kindness and put that knife away. 'Appen as there's nowt I like less than some lairy tyke brandishin' steel in my face."

The Lascar, apparently provoked beyond endurance and preferring to use his weapon rather than sheathe it, made to stab the old man.

What happened next was breath-taking both in its execution and its unexpectedness. The Yorkshireman ducked the blow, and at the same time, with a speed and agility that belied his age and drunkenness, launched a counter-attack. The hand clutching the gin bottle swung up and round, smashing it hard against the gold-toothed Lascar's temple. Glass shattered, gin sprayed, blood spurted, and the Lascar reeled. The other hand caught the wrist of the hand in which the Lascar was holding the knife and twisted it sharply sideways, so that the Indian had no choice but to let the knife go. Thus, in the space of a few heartbeats, the Lascar was both disarmed and disabled, for as the knife dropped to the floor, so did he, semi-concussed, with blood pouring from a deep gash in his scalp.

His bulkier companion lunged for the old man with an infuriated, tigerish growl, and promptly found himself with his right arm wrenched up behind him and rotated from the shoulder at such an angle that he was bent double and could scarcely move. The Yorkshireman, having deftly sidestepped the assault, now had the Lascar fully under his control, like a lassoed bull. However much the Lascar struggled, he could not turn around or break free. He swore as saltily and lustily as only a sailor knows how, both in English and his native Bengali, but his invective had no more effect than his bodily straining.

The Yorkshireman then dealt a savage punch to the Lascar's midriff. His fingers were half bent and rigid, so that his fist was less like a pugilist's, more like a blunt-edged axe. The blow landed on the right-hand side of his opponent's ribcage, just above the liver, and I could tell that this was no accident. He had struck precisely at the point for which he had been aiming, and the resultant shock to that organ left the Lascar breathless, sickened and helpless. He swooned, collapsing to his knees beside his associate. Both men were ashen-faced and close to insensibility. The fight had definitely gone out of them.

"Well," said the victor of the brief contest, straightening up. "That's those two dealt with." He no longer sounded like a native of Yorkshire; rather, his voice had the crisp, clipped resonance of a well-educated product of the Home Counties. "And you, my girl," he said to the Lascars' unfortunate living merchandise. Around us the pub patrons, briefly diverted by the fracas, had returned to their pursuits. "Quick now. While your abusers are incapacitated. You will never get a better opportunity than this to escape. There is a Salvation Army shelter on Hanbury Street in Whitechapel. Seek refuge there. Young as you are, you may yet put your miserable formative years behind you and make something of yourself. Here." He slipped a half-crown into her hand. "That ought to see you on your way."

The girl secreted the coin in a pocket of her skirt. "Bless you, sir."

"Don't thank me. Just go."

She turned and made for the door. One of the Lascars grabbed feebly at her heel, but she skipped past him, and then was gone.

"As for you," the Yorkshireman said, turning and fixing me with a pair of grey eyes whose glittering brightness was in stark contrast to the ruin of the rest of his face, "you too can redeem yourself by helping me pursue your friend Stamford. It's your fault that I've lost him, so you owe me the courtesy of joining me in the act of recovering him."

"Lost…?"

I looked around. Stamford was nowhere to be seen.

He must have fled while the old man – who was clearly much more than he seemed – had been giving the Lascars a drubbing.

"Yes, lost. Dr Stamford is the reason I am in this den of iniquity, passing myself off as a ne'er-do-well. If not for you, I would still be observing his activities, unseen, and he none the wiser. Now, come. We must hurry if we are to pick up the scent again."

And that, in all honesty, was how I first met Sherlock Holmes.

CHAPTER TWO

A Private Clarence

MY THOUGHTS WERE RACING AS I FOLLOWED THE bogus Yorkshireman out of the pub. At that precise moment I had no idea who he was, what his game was, why he was in heavy disguise, or what motive he had for shadowing Stamford. He had not even volunteered his name, or enquired as to mine.

I was intrigued. I felt that I had been dragooned into an enterprise whose nature I could not fathom, and by rights I should have baulked. But there was something compelling about this stranger; his manner was so authoritative that I was unable to resist. I went along in his wake, meekly, but not reluctantly. I had been stirred out of my dejected torpor and for once I was not brooding on the disturbing implications of all that had befallen me in the Arghandab Valley. I was clear-headed again, with a plain and appreciable goal before me: to catch up with Stamford. Everything else was immaterial.

That said, I did not lack concern for my erstwhile dresser. Stamford seemed a desperate, more troubled soul than the young man I remembered. He had refused to acknowledge me and the helping hand I had extended. He was under surveillance by this enterprising and quick-witted individual who had passed himself off as an elderly son of the Dales. What, I could not help but wonder, had he done to get himself into such a fix? What had gone so dramatically awry in his life?

We burst from the pub into the frigid night air. The

alley was empty save for the girl, of whom we caught a last fleeting glimpse before she vanished round the corner. Now it was just the two of us. Of Stamford there was no sign whatsoever. I could not even hear any fading footfalls, owing to the racket coming from the pub and the adjacent tenements.

The bogus Yorkshireman went down on one knee and began examining the many shoe prints in the slush. With questing, birdlike movements of the head he directed his gaze from one to the next, until at last his focus alighted on a single impression which he declared, with no apparent fear of contradiction, to be Stamford's.

"How can you be so sure?" I asked.

"It is a ten and a half, Dr Stamford's size. It is the imprint of the sole of a pointed-toe, elastic-sided ankle boot, exactly of the kind Stamford is wearing. It has, if one looks closely, a hole in the sole, as does Stamford's. Added to that, the imprint in general is smeared rather than sharp-edged, and deeper at the toe end than the heel, suggestive that the wearer is not walking but running. And see? Here is another, matching imprint, a stride's length away. Thus we have the direction in which Stamford is heading, and the assurance that he is proceeding at some pace. This way! No time to waste."

He set off along the alley at a fair lick, and I fell in beside him.

"You run fast," he said as we reached the junction at the end of the alley.

"I'd run faster if the going were firmer." The slush was treacherous underfoot. It would have been all too easy to slip and end up with a twisted ankle.

"Nonetheless you move with the intrepidity and alacrity of a military man, ever ready for action."

"I have seen service."

"I know. You have paid the penalty for it, too. The way you favour that shoulder of yours, the stiffness with which you hold it. A war wound."

"You are observant."

"I am that at the very least. An army surgeon in Afghanistan?"

"Good heavens!" I ejaculated. "How did you work that out?"

"Simple. I overheard you addressing Dr Stamford, reminding him of your time together at Barts. Couple that with your history with the military – it was the most logical inference. You have lately spent time in the tropics, to judge by the darkness of your skin – a suntan, because it does not extend past your wrists, which are pale. Afghanistan it must have been, for there is hardship etched into your features, and those qualities abound in that country for the Englishman as nowhere else."

All this he expounded as we continued to dash through the maze of alleyways. He was not in the least out of breath, while his eye continually searched for, and identified, the spoor of our quarry in the slush.

"I could tell a great deal more about you," he went on, "were you to hand me a personal item and allow me to peruse it for a minute or two. A pocket watch, for instance. But this is neither the time nor the place for a full practical demonstration of my methods. Keep up, Dr Watson!"

I had started to flag. My shoulder was giving me gyp, and the weeks I had spent bedridden in Peshawar and subsequently idle aboard the *Orontes* from Karachi to Portsmouth had taken their toll on my stamina.

"You know my name," I panted. "Of course. You must have overheard that too when I announced myself to Stamford. But I, sir, am ignorant of yours."

"Holmes. Sherlock Holmes. I would say it's a pleasure, and under more relaxed and congenial circumstances would shake your hand into the bargain. Let us consider ourselves formally introduced, and at a later date we can—"

He broke off, his brow creasing into a frown. We had come to a halt under a gas lamp, a rare feature in that seamy, warren-like part of London. By its light I could see that the greasepaint that lent Holmes an aged pallor was now streaked with perspiration. One corner of his false beard was peeling away from his cheek, the heat from his exertions having loosened the grip of the spirit gum. I was able to perceive, moreover, that his dipsomaniac's nose was nothing more than a cunning confection of putty.

"Dr Stamford is cleverer than I gave him credit for," he said tightly. "Look. We are at a main road, and his tracks end on the pavement here, close by this set of wheel ruts in the roadway itself."

"A cab," I said. I bent and braced my hands on my thighs, winded and glad to be able to catch my breath. I fear I could not have continued the pursuit much longer. "He flagged down a hansom."

"No," Holmes replied. "Not a hansom. There are two parallel sets of ruts in the mud, indicative of a four-wheeled carriage rather than a two-wheeled one. The narrow gauge of the axle leads one to deduce a clarence rather than a brougham."

"It could still have been a cab. Plenty of growlers are used as hackney carriages."

"But no jarveys ply this area of town at such a late hour. The dearth of fares makes it not worth their while, and the prevalence of dragsmen, who'll rob their cash boxes as well as their passengers, is an even greater disincentive. No, this was a private clarence – 'growler' if you must – hired or borrowed by Dr Stamford for the express purpose of spiriting him away with the young lady whose services he intended to acquire."

"That is all supposition," I said. "Guesswork."

"I never guess!" Holmes expostulated hotly, his eyes flashing in the lamplight. "If you should know anything about me, Doctor, it is that. I make inferences based solely on analysis. When I say Stamford absconded in a clarence, that is because he did. He came to the pub on foot. I know, because I followed him in similar wise. All along, the carriage was strategically positioned nearby, a provision so that he could make a quick, clean getaway."

"If you say so."

"I most certainly do." Holmes cast a forlorn glance along the street. "Well, anyway, we have no chance of overtaking him now. Had he enjoyed less of a head start, the outcome might have been very different. As it is, Dr Stamford has truly eluded us. But the night is not a complete loss," he added. "That poor girl has, unless I am much mistaken, been spared a terrible fate."

"Might I ask what your interest in Stamford is?" I phrased the question carefully, wary of sparking a fresh outburst of vituperation. "Why have you been impersonating an aged Yorkshireman in order to follow him? What is all this about?"

"Ah, Dr Watson, thereby hangs a tale. If you enquire out of mere idle curiosity, I am not sure I can be bothered to explain. If, on the other hand, your eagerness to know is sincere, I believe I can accommodate you."

Holmes studied me closely, and I had the impression I was being tested, undergoing some sort of audition. Somehow my integrity was on approval, and if I passed muster, I would be initiated into a great mystery.

I bristled at that. I did not care for such shenanigans. The person before me, this Sherlock Holmes, struck me as the type who enjoyed feeling superior to his fellow men. Even if it was only through the masking of his identity by a theatrical disguise and an assumed regional accent, he relished being in on a secret to which others were not party. I sensed that he had the propensity to be insufferable, and I was not in the mood, either on that night or at that general period in my life, to put up with anyone possessing such a character trait.

I was more than a touch surprised, then, to find myself saying, "Actually I am very keen for answers, sir." Not only saying it but meaning it.

"And accordingly," said he, "I shall furnish them. But not here. We can repair to somewhere warmer and drier than this, a place perhaps forty-five minutes' walk away, no further. Baker Street. I have rooms there. Just moved in. Can't afford them, to be honest. Decent, well-priced lodgings are so hard to find in London nowadays. If you would be willing to accompany me...?"

CHAPTER THREE

To 221B

HENCE TO THE ROOMS AT 221B BAKER STREET, which at that time, in the winter of 1880, were much as I have portrayed them elsewhere. Later on they were to become shabbier, messier, a magpie's nest littered with more books than would fit the available shelf space, alongside hosts of parchments in loose-leaf folders, the odd scroll, and numerous leather-bound incunabula of venerable antiquity whose Latin titles I cannot recall without a shudder. These, in their heaps and piles, would vie for space with tribal masks sporting anguished expressions; rune-etched stones; intricately carved locked wooden boxes whose keys never left Holmes's side; marble busts and clay bas-reliefs depicting a host of nightmarish beings; display cabinets full of talismans, amulets and totems; and sundry other handcrafted objects the origin and nature of which one might do better not to consider and which our landlady Mrs Hudson was under strict prohibition not to touch even with a feather duster, let alone her bare hands.

Let me enshrine the sitting room here, this once, recalling it just as it was back then in what I have come to regard as a more innocent time. Holmes's chemistry bench was *in situ*, scarred with acid already, but the various pieces of equipment perched on it looking neat and not yet well used, nor yet subjected to the various gruesome substances, mainly organic fluids, that would stain them indelibly. The Persian slipper stuffed with his tobacco was on the mantelpiece, flanked by his two favourite pipes, the clay and the cherry-wood, and overlooking the coal scuttle where he kept his cigars. His encyclopaedias, dictionaries, gazetteers and other reference works sat in neat rows, thus far not supplanted by a plethora of grimoires and similar occult tomes. His scrapbooks and clippings collections were in their infancy and therefore did not occupy much room. His Stradivarius sat in pride of place on the table by the front window, resting athwart sheet music for a selection of Mendelssohn lieder. There was the comfortable if worn furniture, the bearskin hearthrug spread before the fire, the drinks cabinet – all the humdrum domestic features familiar to my readers from my prose and from Mr Paget's illustrations in *The Strand*.

So the place presented itself to me after Holmes and I had ascended the seventeen steps from the ground-floor hallway and entered; and so, in many ways, I prefer to remember it, before subsequent addenda transformed it into a shambolic museum of macabre curiosities, forbidden texts and ghastly relics.

As for Holmes himself, after he returned from his bedroom having removed all his make-up and prosthetics and changed into a quilted smoking jacket, he was every inch the suave, spare-framed gent I have depicted time and again. In 1880 he was a mere six and twenty years old, with smooth skin and a firm jawline. His widow's peak was not so pronounced as it would become, but his aquiline nose and domed forehead were as prominent as they would ever be. His grey eyes shone with an austere, lofty intelligence, and there was self-confidence in his every gesture.

He kindled a fire in the hearth, and offered me a glass of cognac, which had much the same effect on my person as the fire had on the room.

"I promised you answers, Dr Watson," he said, sitting and sipping a cognac of his own. "Very well. How much do you know about Stamford?"

"That is a question, not an answer."

"Indulge me."

"Well, what can I say? I know that he was perfectly competent when it came to the dressing of lesions and bandaging of wounds. I know that he ran with a fairly rowdy gang of contemporaries at the hospital, a fraternity whose principal bond was that they all came from a wealthy background. I know that he was something of a prankster and was responsible for gluing scurrilous speech balloons onto the Hogarth murals in the Great Hall which cast aspersions on the probity of the hospital's main benefactors, the Hardwick family, and also for dressing the statue of Henry VIII on the gatehouse in a nurse's uniform, although he was never caught and censured for either misdeed. I know that his Christian name is Valentine. Apart from that, not much."

"Did you know that he is an opium addict?"

I was taken aback. "No, I did not. That would account for the pastiness I noted in his complexion tonight, though, and the redness of his eyes. What a wretched come-down. He was always boisterous but still, I felt, level-headed beneath it all, likely to mature into a responsible citizen.

But I suppose a lot can change in a couple of years."

"Yes," said Holmes, "Dr Stamford has become a slave to the poppy, and his habit takes him often to a den in Limehouse run by a Chinaman called Gong-Fen Shou. This in itself is a tragedy, but what makes it more terrible, by any judgement, is that I have divined a connection between your former colleague and a string of grotesque murders."

Now I was flabbergasted. "See here, Mr Holmes," I said. "That's quite an accusation to be bandying about. Who are you anyway? What is your profession? You act somewhat like a policeman, yet with all that disguise folderol – your imposture as a Yorkshireman – not to mention those unusual fighting techniques of yours, and above all your self-styled 'inferences', you are unlike any policeman I have ever met."

"That is because I am the superior of any policeman you have ever met, or are likely to meet." Holmes spoke with calm equanimity, as though this were no boast but an unambiguous statement of fact. "I am, my dear doctor, something else altogether. I like to refer to myself as the world's first consulting detective."

"The world's first *what*?"

"Consulting detective. Not merely the first but, I suppose, the only one."

He launched into his lengthy disquisition on the science of deduction with which my readers will already be familiar and so does not need to be reproduced here. I confess that I glazed over somewhat in the middle, but when I later came to set it down in *A Study in Scarlet* Holmes assisted me, rewriting that section of the book himself and fine-tuning many of the sentences so that his words read as a smooth and cogent elucidation of his empirical approach to criminal investigation.

The irony is that by the time I began work on *A Study in Scarlet*, seven years on, virtually everything about his worldview had altered, so that he was propounding in print a manifesto to which in life he no longer adhered. This is so with all my published chronicles of his adventures. Together, over the course of fifty-six short stories and four novels, Holmes and I colluded in an extravagant scheme of misdirection, in order to offer reassurance to the public at large and allay any suspicions regarding the true, unsettling nature of his cases. I feel no guilt about this. It was the politic thing to do, a fraud perpetrated in the service of the greater good.

"You have heard, of course, about the recent spate of deaths in the East End," Holmes said after I had been made thoroughly *au fait* with the intricacies of his unique vocation. We were each on our third drink, and I was finding myself developing a grudging fondness for the man sitting opposite. Brash and abrasive as he was, I intuited a noble heart beating within that wiry physique and knew that I was in the presence of a powerful force for good. Not only that but, since we were drinking Boutelleau, he served a decent cognac.

"Regrettably, I have not been keeping up with current affairs," I allowed. "I have been... preoccupied."

"The yellow press has made some noise about it. See for yourself."

He tossed a newspaper across to me from a small stack on the floor by his chair. It was a month-old edition of the *Illustrated Police News*; the sight of the masthead made me chuckle.

"I never would have pegged you as the kind to read this sort of twaddle, Mr Holmes. It appeals to the lowest common denominator, a readership with an insatiable thirst for gore and scandal."

"Yet the *Police News*, *Famous Crimes*, the *Police Budget* and their ilk prove an invaluable resource for someone like me. Therein lies coverage of the crimes and misdemeanours that more highbrow periodicals are wont to shun. In many respects they paint a more authentic portrait of British life − violent, unrefined, occasionally outrageous − than do the daily broadsheets. At any rate, for the price of a penny a week, it is an investment I am willing to make. Turn to page two, if you will, and read the second lead article."

It was a short piece headlined "Another Emaciated Body Discovered!":

An appalling and grisly sight greeted residents of London's Tarling Street on the morning of November 3rd. A man's body was found lying in a back yard at the foot of a passage leading to a boarding-house in said thoroughfare. The body was withered and shrivelled in a manner suggesting extreme starvation, and was identified by those residents of the neighbourhood who saw it first-hand as belonging to a Jewish vagabond notorious in those parts, rejoicing in the sobriquet Simple Simeon. No other name for the individual is known.

The cause of Simeon's demise is adjudged to have been heart failure brought on by a chronic lack of sustenance. This would seem to accord with his itinerant existence and lack of gainful employ, yet fails to jibe with reliable accounts, which aver that only a few days prior he had appeared in reasonable health and comparatively well-nourished for a man of his indigent status, owing to the charitable ministrations of a local baker, another Israelite, who had been known to spare him a loaf every so often.

The death brings to four the total number of corpses that have turned up in the vicinity in a similar condition of abnormal gauntness. Furthermore, there is the unnerving fact of the expressions on the faces of the deceased, which were uniformly fixed in a position of what more than one eyewitness has described as "abject terror".

No connection has been descried between the various victims beyond their state of significant carnal diminution. However, it may be wondered whether the deaths are not unrelated to the sightings of strange "shadows" in the Shadwell area, predominantly around Cable Street, St George Street and Cannon Street. For the past few months natives of the district have been claiming to have seen patches of darkness at night-time which appear to move in a most unnatural manner and which elicit feelings of debilitation and dread in any who stray into their propinquity. It is impossible to dismiss outright these stories, however implausible and extraordinary they may sound, by dint of the fact that descriptions of the "shadows" and their effect on the beholder vary little from one account to the next.

Might the aforementioned shadows be some malign influence stalking the streets of Shadwell and environs, depriving inhabitants of their lives? We can but speculate.

Accompanying the article was a neatly engraved picture showing how the mortal remains of Simple Simeon may have looked. The artist rendered him skeletal, like a bundle of twigs wreathed in tattered garments, and did not neglect to include the expression of "abject terror" on his face. This was echoed in the faces and indeed the postures of the small crowd of onlookers depicted in the background, their eyes and mouths wide, rearing back, halfway between ghoulish fascination and fainting.

"Well?" Holmes said. "What do you make of it?"

"Personally, I think there's nothing more here than the mundane tragedy of a tramp perishing on a chilly late autumn night. This Simple Simeon's constitution cannot have been the strongest. It is no surprise that he might succumb to sudden cardiac arrest. I'm sure the same thing happens on almost any given night somewhere in the land to someone living as he did."

"Agreed, but what about the emaciation?"

"What about it?"

"Does it not strike you as singular that the corpse was quite so markedly shrunken? Especially when Simeon was alleged to have been in fine fettle before he died."

"We have only the word of one or two local residents to vouch for that. Besides, you are ascribing an accuracy to the journalist that seems out of keeping with the shoddy tenor of his work and the nature of the paper he is writing for. Take this 'look of terror', for example. That is a frequent misconception about corpses. I have seen many a cadaver whose face might be described as looking horrified, even though I know the person to have died peacefully in his sleep. A rictus of the mouth is a normal by-product of rigor mortis, sometimes giving the illusion of a scream. Also, the skin tightens and recedes post mortem due to desiccation, meaning the lips pull away from the teeth and the eyelids from the eyes. To the layman that might denote terror in the deceased's final moments, but it is all perfectly natural, trust me. Merely an initial phase of the process of decomposition."

"I bow to your professional expertise, Doctor," said Holmes. "I imagine the penultimate and last paragraphs likewise meet with your disapproval."

"As to that," I replied, "it would be easy to discount this talk of sinister 'moving shadows' as pure superstitious bunkum."

"I discern a certain hesitancy in that avowal."

"No. No. You are quite wrong."

"Really?" He looked at me askance. "'It would be easy to discount…' That is hardly a comprehensive rejection. It is as if you are saying what you think I should hear rather than what you would like to say."

"Then you misinterpret me grievously."

Holmes was silent a moment, then nodded. "I shan't press the point. In the event, I too am of the opinion that it is, as you put it, superstitious bunkum. The stews of the East End are a breeding ground for legend and phantasmagorical rumour. Vampires haunting rooftops, spectres loitering at crossroads where criminals were once hanged, humanoid beings with blazing eyes able to leap about like kangaroos, all such kinds of absurdity. It is as though some people's lives are incomplete without a dash of fantasy, and the mania for such woolly-headed nonsense is fuelled by papers like the one you're holding, which see their circulation increase the more credence and column inches they give to it. No, the world is big enough for us, Watson," he concluded with finality. "No ghosts need apply."

I observed that he had dropped my title and addressed me by surname alone, a sign that we had travelled some way down the road to amicableness. Automatically I reciprocated. "If we discard the supernatural aspects of the matter, Holmes, then what are we left with? The phenomenon of four people dying in superficially similar circumstances in a corner of London that is both heavily overcrowded and rife with disease and dissipation. I remain to be convinced that it is anything more than grim coincidence. And somehow Stamford is bound up in all this?"

"You have not listened to the full narrative yet," said Holmes. "Lend me an ear, be patient, then give your verdict."

CHAPTER FOUR

The Four Deaths

HOLMES SETTLED HIMSELF DEEPER INTO HIS CHAIR and commenced his account.

The first of the deaths had passed him by altogether, he said. He failed to register it, even though since setting up his practice as a consulting detective some three years earlier he had become quite diligent about trawling the newspapers for reports of unusual and unexplained fatalities. Only once the subsequent deaths had begun to occur did he go combing back through earlier editions for articles about other incidents that fit the same pattern. The first body was that of a street pedlar selling spices and dried fruit, and was found huddled in a doorway on Juniper Road. A police statement mentioned that it had been "in a parlous condition" but did not explicitly allude to the kind of emaciation that had befallen Simple Simeon.

That was in August. The second body cropped up a month later, that of a crossing sweeper, a boy barely in his teens. Opinion had it that he had been suffering from consumption or some other ailment that causes wasting and atrophy of the flesh. Given that he was a mere sweeper, the illness would have been neither diagnosed nor treated. Stoically and uncomplainingly he had endured his symptoms until such time as he collapsed.

October brought a third body, that of a match girl, and the general consensus was that she had succumbed to phosphorus poisoning. That particular affliction tends to blight the lives of those who work in the match-making factories, manifesting as "phossy jaw", the rotting of the mandible that first causes tooth loss, then abscesses and creeping necrosis, and is invariably fatal if left unchecked. Presumably even one who only sells matches, as opposed to one involved in their manufacture, might not be immune to it. Thus it would come as no surprise that the lass was rail-thin when she died, riddled and hollowed out by her disease.

"Now what unites these three unfortunates, Watson?" Holmes said. "What is the binding thread that ties them?"

"Other than that they died alone and in misery?"

"That is some of it, but what else?"

I pondered. "They were hardly pillars of society, any of them. Quite the reverse."

"Indeed. Indeed!" Holmes clapped his hands, clearly delighted by the scintilla of intelligence I had shown. "They were nobodies. A street pedlar, a crossing sweeper, a match girl – anonymous individuals, whom the average citizen pays barely any heed. I doubt there is a Londoner who saw any of the three on a daily basis and knew his or her name."

"The same can be said for Simple Simeon, save for the name."

"Yet his surname was a mystery to all. His only appellation was that slightly derogatory nickname. These, the four of them, were people who might pass unnoticed and" – his look turned sly – "whose passing might go unnoticed."

I let that sink in for a moment, as he no doubt wished me to. He was enjoying leading the conversation, drawing me along, letting me be Plato to his Socrates. I saw no harm in indulging him.

"You mean they were specifically selected for murder because their killer knew no one would make much of a fuss about their deaths."

"That is what I mean, in a nutshell. And the conjecture is borne out by the evidence."

Holmes resumed his narrative; each of the four was buried in an unmarked pauper's grave at the municipal cemetery, accorded the bare minimum of respect and rights in death just as they had been in life. No one thought to perform an autopsy on any of the bodies. No one was prompted to suggest that the cause of death in each case had been anything other than some illness, whether specified or not. Had the victims been in some way prominent or publicly renowned, it would have been a very different story. But who is going to care about one less crossing sweeper? Who is going to miss a match girl?

Even the police failed to link the deaths together. The officials of the Met seemed quite happy to treat them as discrete and isolated and to overlook the telling detail that all four corpses appeared unnaturally starved.

"Why wouldn't they?" I said. "We have established that the four were all impoverished and very likely in bad health."

"Quite so."

"In point of fact, the only person to have drawn the same conclusion as you, that the deaths share commonality, is the nameless author of the *Police News* article."

"I can reveal his identity, if you wish. He sits before you right now."

"You? I may hardly know you, Holmes, but I would

lay a thousand to one against that."

"And you would lose your money, something you can ill afford after your run of bad luck at the card table earlier this evening," my interlocutor said with a wry smile. "I am, on my honour, the journalist whose literacy and accuracy you so roundly impugned. I placed that article myself, posing as a neophyte freelancer. Papers like the *Police News* aren't too fussy about the identity of those from whom they accept a submission, as long as it accords with their editorial policy of offering the most lurid take on a subject."

"Why did you want it published? And why yoke the deaths to this bizarre business about shadows, which you yourself have just denounced as nonsensical?"

"I shall come to that shortly. In the meantime, let me spin my yarn a little further."

*

Holmes's career as a consulting detective had not got off to a flying start, he admitted. There had so far been a mere smattering of clients, bringing with them some "pretty little problems" such as the Tarleton murders, the case of Vamberry the wine merchant, the singular affair of the aluminium crutch, and Ricoletti of the club foot and his abominable wife. There had also been the altogether more intriguing conundrum involving Reginald Musgrave, a contemporary of Holmes's at university, and the strange observance known as the Musgrave Ritual. And how could he forget the queer adventure of the mummified hand in the Gloucestershire attic? These had provided him with enough income to keep body and soul together and give him cause to feel that he was justified in pursuing his chosen livelihood. Each successfully concluded investigation was a notch in his belt and a feather in his cap, promising greater things to come.

Yet there were fallow periods in between. Weeks and sometimes months would go by without a visitor calling at his former rooms on Montague Street, and when not occupying his time furthering his researches into scientific fields and deepening his knowledge of various practical skills such as singlestick and an Eastern martial art called baritsu, he was constantly on the lookout for anomalous events that might merit enquiry. If clients failed to come to him, he would be his own client, appointing himself to solve crimes that were of no interest to anyone else. It was all practice, grist to the mill.

Hence, having read in September about the death of the crossing sweeper and the following month about that of the match girl, Holmes cross-referenced them with the death of the street pedlar back in August and divined the possibility of an association between the three and a human agency behind it all. That inspired him to delve further into the matter.

With scant evidence to go on other than a handful of brief news reports, he decided his best approach would be to pinpoint the precise locations where the three bodies were discovered, then scour the surrounding areas for clues and interview local residents for whatever information he might glean. This he duly did.

On learning that the deaths had all taken place in the district of Shadwell, Holmes became more convinced than ever that the three were related. On perceiving that they had occurred at regular monthly intervals, he discerned the hand of someone with an interest in the calendar. On working out that each death had fallen squarely on the night of the new moon, he distinguished a ritualistic sense of calculation on the part of the perpetrator.

"The darkest night of the month," I said.

"The better to conceal dark deeds," said he.

"Might the timing be in some way related to the lunacy that is said to coincide with the phases of the moon?"

"The lore has it that certain states of madness are at their peak when the moon is at its fullest. This is the opposite of that and seems to belong at the other end of the scale, a deed perpetrated with cold, artful rationalism."

It was by that time late October, and the moon was fast waning, due to disappear from the night sky on November 2nd. Conscious that that date marked the next scheduled death – a deadline in more ways than one – Holmes redoubled his efforts. He took to roaming the bystreets and backwaters of Shadwell in various guises. He had been a keen exponent of amateur dramatics during his undergraduate days and had been commended in several reviews for his ability to submerge himself into a role, altering not just his face and voice but his very posture, his every mannerism, so as to make the performance seem utterly alive and authentic.

"In consecutive terms I played a fresh-faced Hamlet, a hoary Lear, and a blustering Othello," he told me, "and not one bore a shred of resemblance to either of the others. I was hailed as a chameleon of the stage."

In Shadwell, he manifested over the course of five successive nights as a decrepit seaman, a French workman, an Italian priest, an amiable Nonconformist clergyman, and a harmless old crone. He loitered and patrolled, doing all he could to ferret out potential victims and protect them.

"But I failed," he said. "As is obvious."

"Simple Simeon."

"He slipped through my net."

"Do not berate yourself. You were just one man, watching over thousands. You could not hope to keep an eye on them all."

"I know, but nevertheless..." He exhaled a sullen sigh. "I saw nothing untoward on the night in question. Whoever is responsible for the deaths eluded my vigilance and struck again, precisely according to his predetermined timetable, and I was powerless to prevent it."

"Might I ask why you didn't involve the police? Did you not go to them with your theory about the deaths and recruit their aid? The addition of several dozen constables would have made your 'net' that much broader and more tightly meshed."

"Ah, the police," said Holmes. "There are a couple of Scotland Yarders with whom I have forged promising but as yet tentative bonds: a Tobias Gregson and one G. Lestrade. The 'G', I believe, stands for Gabriel, so it is perhaps unsurprising that he prefers to be known by the initial. I plan to cultivate those relationships to my advantage, for the two of them have displayed an intelligence signally superior to that of their brethren – although that is not saying much, given the dull-wittedness of the average copper. They are also excessively rivalrous of each other, which amuses me. But to answer your question, I tried and was rebuffed. I knew I was right, but to the police I seemed to have only a theory, as you say. And a theory without hard evidence to back it up is as substantial and credible as a fairy's gossamer wing."

All was not lost, however, because the following day, after Simple Simeon's body had been found and removed and the attendant hue and cry had abated, Holmes was able to visit the scene and make a thorough search. He went over the back yard, the passage and the ambit of the boarding-house on his hands and knees, scrutinising them with a tenacity that would have done a terrier proud. Lo and behold, he unearthed what he was certain was a clue left behind by the killer: a gold cufflink that had been trodden into the mud between two cobblestones. He knew it could only have been deposited there in the preceding twelve hours because the weather had been dry for over a week beforehand. Rain had fallen during the small hours of the morning of the 3rd, but until then the mud would have been hard and the cufflink would not have become embedded in it. It would have lain on top for all to see, and being gold – twenty-four-carat gold, no less – it would not have remained there long; a passer-by would have snatched it up and taken it to a jeweller or pawnbroker.

"Not handed it in to the Lost and Found at the nearest police station?"

"In Shadwell? I hardly think so, Watson. The cufflink was the property of a gentleman, that much was clear, which ruled out its belonging to a Shadwell native. Not just any gentleman, either, but a doctor."

"How the deuce could you tell?"

"Elementary, my dear Watson," Holmes said, uttering that now celebrated phrase for the first and last time in my hearing. "It consisted of two oval discs connected by a short chain, and once I had wiped the mud off, I could see that on one of the discs was engraved the Rod of Asclepius, the symbol of your calling."

This gave Holmes the occupation of his potential suspect. Better yet, on the other disc was engraved a pair of initials: V.S.

"I have the very item here, should you wish to take a look at it," he said, and he went to his writing desk and retrieved the cufflink from a drawer. It was just as he had described it, and seemed to me exactly the sort of thing Stamford might have worn, although I could not profess for certain that I had ever seen such cufflinks on his person. Perhaps they had come his way after graduation. I could imagine his father bestowing them on him, a gift from a proud, moneyed parent to commemorate his son's success in obtaining his degree.

So now, Holmes went on, he knew he was looking for a doctor with the initials V.S. Thereafter it was merely a case of consulting the register of licensed medical practitioners held by the General Council of Medical Education and Registration. Within a short while, having gone through the "S" section of that thirty-thousand-strong list of entries, Holmes emerged onto Soho Square with a handwritten list consisting of half a dozen names and their respective work addresses. These he whittled down by excluding any who lived a significant distance outside London. He doubted someone would commute a hundred or more miles into the capital purely to commit murder.

By that expedient he narrowed the sphere of focus to three candidates, whereupon he set about reconnoitring each one, stalking him like game. He was able to eliminate a Harley Street clinician specialising in disorders of the digestive tract. The fellow was in his sixties and frail in physique and bearing. To Holmes's mind the killer was young and healthy, the sort unafraid to brave the wilds of the East End where danger lurked round every corner for the unwary and the vulnerable. Similarly, he discounted a surgical resident at St Thomas' Hospital in Lambeth. Although the man was only in his early thirties and a keen golfer and swimming enthusiast, very much fitting the image that Holmes had formed of the culprit, never once did he wear cufflinks. He favoured button-cuff shirts exclusively.

Just one prospect remained, the likeliest of them all: Valentine Stamford.

Stamford's history in the time since I had known him at Barts might kindly be termed a chequered one. He had carried on at the hospital after I left, but increasingly he had fallen foul of the administration. His work became lackadaisical, his attendance irregular, his manner often petulant. In the end, after a patient in his care died from gangrene of the bowel following an appendectomy, the board of governors had no alternative but to discharge him. The complication itself was not unusual or wholly avoidable after such an operation, but the death would have provided the governors with a legitimate excuse for dismissal.

It cannot be confirmed that Stamford's opium addiction had already started around this point, but on the balance of probabilities it seemed likely. The poppy, Holmes opined, could ruin a man and destroy all nascent promise as surely as a bullet to the head.

With a black mark against his name in the records of the General Council, Stamford was unable to find employment at any of the main accredited hospitals, and wound up plying his skills at a voluntary hospital attached to a workhouse in Mile End, St Brigid's House. That charitable institution offered treatment to the destitute at no cost, funded by donations and subscriptions from wealthy, philanthropic benefactors. Its staff were badly paid, their ranks bolstered by doctors from other hospitals giving up their free time and some fulltime staff like Stamford of independent means – in his case, a small income from a family trust – who could for that reason survive on a negligible salary. St Brigid's House could not afford to be choosy about whom it hired, and so even a disgraced doctor was welcome within its walls.

Evidently Stamford was trying to redeem himself by continuing to heal the sick, even if it meant living in straitened personal circumstances and working in unsanitary conditions with patients from the undesirable end of the social spectrum whose primary complaints were typhus, consumption and venereal disease. Yet the lure of opium must have persisted, and now, with his relocation to the East End, temptation was right on his doorstep. Gong-Fen Shou's opium den lay but a short walk from the hospital, and Stamford began making that journey all too frequently.

This much Holmes was able to extract from a nurse at St Brigid's, an Irishwoman with a penchant for stout and a tongue that loosened further with every pint he bought her. She recognised the signs of addiction to opium, having seen them in enough patients, and although many times she tried to persuade Stamford to abandon the narcotic, her pleas fell on deaf ears. He was tethered to the pipe and the entrancing dreams it brought as tightly as a dog to its master. Even had he wanted to slip the leash, his physical craving and the pangs of abstinence would not let him.

As of August, Stamford had relinquished his post at St Brigid's and disappeared from view. Holmes had the devil of a time tracking him down and spent most of November engaged in that task, but eventually, as the month was in its final throes, he found him. His home was now a shabby two-room apartment under the eaves of a terraced house on York Road, backing onto the Blackwall Railway line. From there he went out only to eat, visit the bank to withdraw money, and go to Gong-Fen Shou's.

"I began keeping careful watch on him," Holmes said, "monitoring his comings and goings, traipsing after him night and day. The new moon was fast approaching, and I planned to intercept him in the commission of his next attack, red-handed."

"Which you would have done tonight," I said, "had I not unwittingly interfered."

"It was damnable luck. The girl at the pub was sure to have been his fifth victim, but now I have no proof of it. He was importuning her, of that there is no doubt, but short of actually seeing him attempt to inflict harm on her,

I cannot aver that his intentions were anything other than those that men customarily harbour towards her kind."

"She did not end up like the other four," I said. "That is something."

"But there is another potential victim out there somewhere, Watson. There must be. The new moon is upon us, and Dr Stamford must make his offering to it, pay his obeisance to it, or whatever his obscure purpose is, even if he is delayed by a day."

"What does he do to his prey?" I asked. "What kind of death does he wreak on them, that renders them so emaciated in appearance?"

"I have no idea," Holmes said. "I do not have sufficient data concerning the method of murder, although I do have some thoughts in that direction."

"Won't you share them?"

"Not yet."

"What, then, was the purpose of your article in the *Police News*? How did that further your aims?"

"Ah-ha. I was trying to unsettle Stamford, that's all. There he was, reckoning he was getting away with his crimes, secure in the belief that his pattern had not been detected. I hoped he might read the piece, or get wind of it from an acquaintance, and it would rattle him. It would make him clumsier, less assured. It might even provoke him into precipitate action, meaning he would be easier to catch *in flagrante*. I'm not sure I didn't accomplish that goal. The girl at the pub was, unlike his previous targets, a known quantity in the area. She had friends, if you can call the two Lascars that. She was not quite as solitary and indigent as the others, and moreover he sought her out in public, before dozens of witnesses. That smacks of a recklessness he has hitherto not shown."

"And the shadows you wrote about? They, I take it, are pure fiction."

"Yes and no. During my peregrinations around Shadwell I have heard about them more than once. They seem to be a recent addition to the folklore of the place, and therefore are often talked about by virtue of their sheer novelty. I included them in the article simply to add colour and spice and make the piece as a whole more intriguing, as well as more attractive to the editor. There is no correlation between them and Stamford's activities, I can assure you of that, mostly because he is real and they are not."

"What's next, then?" I said. "Presumably your pursuit of Stamford continues."

"Naturally, but not tonight. It is late and he will have gone to ground. If he has any sense – and he is, if nothing else, cunning – he won't have returned home to his lair. He will be somewhere else. Where, I cannot say. But I shall pick up the scent again tomorrow. And you, Watson, are exceedingly tired."

I could not deny it. I could not restrain an enormous yawn.

"That or I have bored you unduly," he added.

"Not at all. But I ought to be on my way. It's getting on for two o'clock and my digs in Norwood are some distance from here."

"Why not stay the night? There is a second bedroom, and Mrs Hudson insists on keeping the bed made up in case I have a guest. It's modest but comfortable. You would be more than welcome. I can even lend you a pair of pyjamas."

I did not much fancy sallying forth into the dark at such an hour. The cognac had made me groggy and slothful. More relevantly, after my failure at the nap table I had no money left for a cab. The second bedroom sounded enticing, and I accepted Holmes's offer.

As I lay beneath the covers, I mused on the evening's events and the stranger into whose fantastically complex life I had strayed. I felt like some explorer who has stumbled into uncharted territory, with no map to guide him. At the same time, in that small, cosy room, I felt quite contented, almost as if I had come home.

CHAPTER FIVE

Gregson of the Yard

I AWOKE TO THE SMELL OF A DELICIOUS COOKED breakfast and came out into the sitting room in a borrowed dressing gown to find a compact, fastidious-looking lady of a certain age decanting said meal from tray to table.

"You must be Mrs Hudson," I said.

"And you Dr Watson," she replied. "Mr Holmes informed me that he had an overnight guest of that name. I trust you slept well."

"Like a log," I said with mild surprise. A full night's sleep had lately become a rarity. All too often, troubled dreams would rouse me from my slumber and leave me sweating, with a palpitating heart, wakeful until dawn. Plainly the cognac had had a sedative effect on me, but perhaps so too had the alarms and excursions of the night before, wearing me out. "Where is Holmes? Is he yet to rise?"

"Oh no," said Mrs Hudson. "Up and abroad long since. I heard him leave by the front door shortly after seven."

It was now nearing nine.

"Do you know where he has gone?"

"He didn't say. He seldom does. He simply left me a note telling me about you and asking me to extend you every courtesy."

"But he'll be back soon," I said. "Hence the breakfast."

"No. I have no idea when Mr Holmes is returning. He keeps all manner of peculiar hours. I have grown accustomed to that, if not tolerant. The breakfast is for you."

"For me?" I eyed the fried bacon, poached eggs,

buttered toast and steaming coffee with unalloyed greed. I could not think just then of a better way to start the day.

"Yes, so sit down and eat up," Mrs Hudson said, and I gladly did as bidden. There was even *The Times* to read, neatly folded by my place setting. It was a kind of heaven.

Holmes came in whilst I was finishing my toilet in the bathroom, using supplies furnished by his redoubtable landlady. He revealed that he had been to Stamford's apartment on York Road in order to ascertain that he was correct in his supposition that Stamford had not returned there last night. He had not. None of his fellow tenants in the house recalled hearing his tread on the stairs, and his rooms were empty, the bed made and unused.

"How do you know that?" I asked. "About the state of the bed?"

"How else?" Holmes said with a nonchalant shrug. "I picked the lock on the outer door and had a look for myself."

"Picked the—? But that's a felony, surely. Breaking and entering."

"The commission of a minor offence is justified if it is part of an attempt to thwart another, far more serious offence, Watson. You must see that."

"Well, yes, I suppose. All the same…"

"You had a pleasant breakfast, I trust?" he said, changing the subject as abruptly as a signalman changes points on a railway track.

"Very pleasant. I ate with gusto."

"The crumb of toast still adhering to your moustache testifies to that. I myself have not breakfasted yet. Mrs Hudson!" he called down the stairs. "Two kippers and a boiled egg, if you will. There's a good woman."

While waiting for the food to arrive, Holmes slipped a hand into his pocket and took out a gold cufflink. It was the twin of the one he had produced last night, right down to the engraving on both discs.

"Holmes," I said, aghast. "You didn't…"

"Afraid so," he said, setting the second cufflink down on the writing desk beside the first. "I shall have to add larceny to my catalogue of crimes. I found it on Dr Stamford's bedside table."

"Well, that would seem to clinch it. He was at the scene of Simple Simeon's death." I said this reluctantly. A part of me was clinging vainly to the hope that the Stamford I had known, the raffish student, had not degenerated into a monstrous murderer.

"At the very least it confirms that he lost the other cufflink there," Holmes said, "although he may have done so after, not during, the event. What if he was amongst the crowd that gathered to view the body? What if that is his only connection with the death? One must at least consider these possibilities."

"You seem unwilling to give them much weight, though."

"Very little. The odds in favour of Stamford's guilt are overwhelming."

Presently Holmes's breakfast was brought in, and not long after he had set to work on the kippers there was a knock at the front door and we heard Mrs Hudson go to answer it. Only a few moments passed until she bustled into the room, ushering before her a tall, white-faced, flaxen-haired man with fat hands and a gallant, capable air.

"Inspector Gregson," she announced, and withdrew.

I recalled Holmes mentioning a Gregson last night. Here was one of the two Met policemen he rated marginally above the rest, the pick of the herd.

Holmes greeted the official cordially, inviting him to sit. "I would enquire if you would care to partake of coffee, but you appear already to have had your fill of it for today."

"What makes you say that?"

"Coffee leaves distinct traces on the breath, of course, and I am picking up a strong aroma of it on yours, suggesting you have drunk at least two cups so far, if not three. Then there is the small brown stain on your shirtfront, which looks comparatively fresh and is unmistakably coffee-coloured."

Gregson glanced down at his chest. "Ah."

"Yes. To have spilled coffee on yourself is a sure sign that you have overindulged. The hand begins to shake as the caffeine takes hold. Cup misses lip. Sartorial besmirching ensues. I would propose a glass of water instead. Your stomach will thank you for it."

"I shan't, if it's all the same to you, Mr Holmes." Gregson looked at me. "I don't believe we've met. Mr...?"

"Dr Watson," I said, shaking his hand.

"Pleasure."

"The pleasure's all mine. And now, with the utmost respect to the both of you, I shall take my leave. You have some matters to discuss which can be none of my affair, and I must not impose on Holmes's hospitality any longer."

"Tut, my friend!" Holmes declared. "You must stay.

Unless I miss my guess, the inspector is here on the self-same business in which the pair of us were caught up yesterday evening."

"If you mean Dr Valentine Stamford," said Gregson, "then yes, I am."

"That is exactly what I mean."

"How did you know?"

"Stamford was the main topic of conversation between the two of us when last we met, and I cannot think why else you would have come to me with such urgency, first thing in the morning, if not to convey some fresh development in the case. You have not visited before. You are not, as it were, here in the capacity of a prospective client. Thus I can only infer that it is Stamford that brings you to my door."

"Harrumph. Yes, well, I ought to be used to your deductions by now, but they always still seem like magic."

"It was hardly a deduction, more a statement of the obvious."

"Man can't take a compliment," Gregson muttered under his breath.

"So anyway," Holmes said, affecting not to have heard the remark, "I'm hoping your news is positive. Stamford is in your custody."

"As a matter of fact, he is."

"Hurrah!" Holmes was in a transport of delight. "You cannot know how glad I am to hear that." His expression turned sombre. "Please tell me he hasn't added a fifth victim to his tally."

"No. To the best of my knowledge, this series of murders you are convinced Dr Stamford has been committing has not claimed another soul."

Holmes brightened again, and it occurred to me that he was of the most mercurial temperament, his moods switching from one to the next with ease. This, I concluded, must be a by-product of having such an alert and fast-moving brain.

"Then that is all the greater cause for celebration," he said. "Pray enlighten me as to how he has come to be under arrest. What were the circumstances?"

"It's… ahem, a somewhat irregular state of affairs," said Gregson. "He is highly dishevelled and not what one might call in full possession of his faculties. We're not even completely sure it *is* Dr Stamford. We found calling cards in his wallet identifying him as such, but who's to say the wallet is actually his own? It might have been stolen, its present bearer a pickpocket or an opportunistic thief. At any rate, since I have never clapped eyes on the man before and since he is behaving in so startlingly obtuse a manner, I thought it would be best if you were to come to the Yard with me, Mr Holmes, and corroborate that he is who he appears to be."

CHAPTER SIX

A Horribly Familiar Language

THUS IT WAS THAT, NOT HALF AN HOUR LATER, WE were at 4 Whitehall Place and had entered Scotland Yard. Prior to leaving Baker Street I had again made my excuses and offered to absent myself from the proceedings. Holmes, however, would have none of it. He said that I was as much involved in the Stamford affair as he was; and besides, from the sound of it, the opinion of a medical man might be needed. The more I cavilled, the more adamant he became, until all I could do was give in. I felt browbeaten but at the same time flattered and even a little honoured. I was also, without question, curious to see Stamford once more and discover what had befallen him between last night and this morning. The mystery had its hooks in me. More to the point, I had nothing else to do, certainly nothing better.

Stamford had been consigned to a holding cell in the basement of the building, and we heard his voice even before we reached that long, dank corridor lined with cast-iron doors. He was sending forth a stream of guttural vocalisations that barely sounded like words, much to the annoyance of prisoners in the other cells, who shouted oath-peppered imprecations, inviting him to shut up and promising dire retribution upon him should they ever get the chance.

"He's been ranting like this, on and off, since we took him in," Gregson said.

"And when was that?" Holmes asked.

"Around five. Couple of constables coming to the end of their night-time rounds nabbed him on Aldgate. He was acting erratically, they said, yelling and trying to do himself mischief. They restrained him, but not without difficulty. One of them received a broken nose for his pains."

As we neared the cell, Stamford's cries dwindled, subsiding into silence.

"Thank God for that," came a gruff voice from the berth opposite. "Peace and quiet again. Long may it last."

The officer whose job it was to supervise the detainees and escort visitors into this underground domain produced his impressive ring of keys and unlocked the door. He remained outside the cell while the rest of us went in.

Stamford sat on a wooden cot in the corner, wrists and ankles manacled. At the sight of him I could not withhold a gasp, for he was barely the same man I had encountered the previous evening, and if I had not happened to meet him on that occasion, I might not have recognised my former fellow student.

He was wild-haired, mad-eyed, with a froth of saliva on his lips and a ribbon of mucus dangling from one nostril. His skin had gone so pale it was almost grey, and his clothing was ragged and sodden. My sense of smell told me he had soiled himself recently, but even more arresting than that fact were the multiple abrasions and contusions on his face. His forehead was a lumpen jigsaw of black and blue bruises, and his cheeks bore the marks of having been raked by fingernails.

Holmes was only somewhat less taken aback than I.

This was undoubtedly Valentine Stamford, and we both affirmed as much for Gregson's benefit – yet he was radically changed. In a mere few hours he had been transformed from a still apparently sane human being into a raving lunatic who looked as though he belonged in Bedlam.

He scarcely registered our presence in the cell. He was staring at his hands, murmuring to himself in low tones.

"His injuries…?" said Holmes.

"All self-inflicted," Gregson was quick to assert. "Well, nearly all. My boys were as gentle as they could reasonably be, under the circumstances. He may have sustained a scratch or two as they bundled him into the wagon, but the noteworthy bumps and scrapes you can see were already there. They caught him hitting his forehead against the Aldgate Pump, as like to dash his brains out. Then, when they remonstrated with him, he started dragging his nails down his face. They think he may have been trying to gouge out his eyeballs."

I shuddered. "This is appalling. What do you reckon, Holmes? Do you think he is suffering symptoms of opium withdrawal?"

"Is that your view, Watson?"

"I am no expert in such things, but it is at least a feasible explanation. Normally there is shaking, convulsions of the limbs, excessive sweating, hallucinations. I daresay, though, that more extreme reactions can occur, and one such sits before us. I would have to consult the literature to give a more definitive diagnosis, but…" I shrugged to indicate that I had pronounced on the topic to the best of my ability.

Holmes nodded. "You are proving a useful companion. Our meeting is beginning to seem highly fortuitous. Perhaps—"

He was unable to finish the sentence, for at that moment Stamford sprang abruptly to his feet with a clank of chains and began screaming.

"*Fhtagn! Ebumna fhtagn! Hafh'drn wgah'n n'gha n'ghft!*"

The three of us – Holmes, Gregson and myself – took an involuntary step back.

Eyes bulging, spittle flying, Stamford repeated the incomprehensible outburst. "*Fhtagn! Ebumna fhtagn! Hafh'drn wgah'n n'gha n'ghft!*"

"What is that?" I breathed. "Is that even a language?"

"Search me," said Gregson. "He's been spouting similar mumbo-jumbo all morning. Someone thought it might be some Cornish dialect, or Gaelic. Someone else thought it might be Welsh, but I brought along our resident refugee from the valleys, Inspector Athelney Jones, for a listen, and he says not."

Once more Stamford gave vent to the string of sounds, and then again, and again, without cease. Reiterated over and over, the words gained the rhythmic insistence of a chant or incantation. I found it hard not to want to stop my ears. There was something eerily familiar in their formulation. They pricked a memory in me, stirring the recollection of an incident that I had done my level best to suppress, and I felt a nauseating dread begin to well up inside. I smelled ancient dust and damp. My skin prickled as though in proximity to walls carved out of cold subterranean rock. I heard voices lost in cavernous echoes, and glimpsed scaly skin, slit-like pupils, flickering forked tongues…

Oh dear Lord, it *was* a language, one that I knew only too well and would have recognised sooner had I not spent several months trying intently to forget it. This was not the first time dark, clotted syllables like these had wormed their way into my ears. It was as though a shovel were being dug into the earth of my mind, disinterring a buried horror.

"Watson? Watson!"

Holmes's voice sounded above Stamford's, clear as a bell, fraught with concern.

"Whatever's the matter with you, man? You've gone white as a sheet."

He reached out a hand, grasping me by the shoulder to steady me. Without it I might very well have fainted. As it was, his grip – which was strong, exceptionally, indeed painfully so – restored me to my senses. My thoughts sharpened and the wave of light-headedness that had come over me receded. I was myself again.

My stomach continued to churn, however, and my heartbeat to race.

"I'm fine," I said, brushing off Holmes's hand. "Fine, I tell you." And then, to myself, I added: "A Jezail bullet. Only that. The bullet from a Jezail."

"Hold up!" Gregson cried out, leaping forward. "Stop that!"

My vision regained focus in time to see something that will remain with me to the end of my days. Even now, nearly fifty years on, I can conjure up the image as clearly as though it were yesterday. I have been exposed to many a shocking sight in the interim, and I ascribe several of the white hairs on my head to those experiences, but this particular one is imprinted more deeply and ineradicably than most.

Both Holmes and Gregson had been diverted by my sudden queer turn, and their attention had not been on Stamford. He, perhaps taking advantage of their momentary distraction, or perhaps simply deciding now was the time to do what he had intended all along, bent his head to his forearm…

…and began to chew.

His teeth dug hard into the soft skin, and with a wrench of both neck and arm he managed to excise a significant chunk of his own flesh. Even as the blood began to flow, he spat out the lump of meat onto the floor and brought forearm back to mouth in order to take a second bite from the wound.

That was when Gregson sprang into action, but he was too late. This time Stamford had his teeth around tendons and veins, including amongst the latter the radial and ulnar arteries. He tugged and gnawed, snapping both in twain. Gregson fought to disengage the arm from his jaw, but his efforts succeeded only in helping Stamford complete the ghastly self-mutilation. Blood jetted from the roughly-severed ends of the rubbery tubes in thick, pulsing streams, and Stamford beheld his handiwork with a gleam of awe and amazement in his eyes, his gore-smeared mouth gaping in a weirdly serene grin.

"It's over," he said, and it was akin to a sigh. "I'm

done. There's only peace now."

He collapsed back onto the cot, and I rushed to his aid. Unstrapping my tie from my collar, I wrapped it round his bicep and fastened it with a tight knot. In this way I fashioned a tourniquet, closing off the brachial artery, the supplier of the two lesser vessels.

Blood continued to pour from the edges of the gash itself, and I had every certainty that the injury Stamford had done himself was fatal. Yet I could not have stood by without at least trying to save him.

He began to go into shock. Tremors ran through his body, deepening into spasms. I slapped his cheeks. "Stamford," I urged. "Stamford, stay with us. Stay conscious. Don't pass out."

But his blood pressure was plummeting, and I did not have my medical bag so I could not inject him with a stimulant. Nor could I bind up the wound with cotton wadding and carbolised bandages. I would have needed to do either or both of those things within the next couple of minutes to guarantee a good outcome, and that was time Stamford did not have.

He rested his gaze on me and said wanly, "You're a decent chap, John Watson. I always thought that about you. Solid old Watson. By-the-book Watson. I regret that we could not have been better chums." He glanced at the makeshift tourniquet. "Thank you for this. A sterling effort, if futile. In return, a piece of advice. Forget about Shadwell. Steer clear of the place. Never go back there. There are forces at work… Men who would be more than men… They consort with the Great Old Ones. They seek power from where they should not, and God help us if they succeed. God help… usss… allll…"

His voice faded. His eyes clouded. His breath crackled in his throat.

He was with us no more.

CHAPTER SEVEN

A Moveable Feast

"WELL, BLOW ME DOWN," SAID GREGSON, KNUCKLES pressed to brow in bewilderment, staring at Stamford's lifeless remains. "That's… That's not what anyone would have wanted."

"Anyone but Stamford," Holmes pointed out. "It took some willpower to do what he just did. An iron determination."

"He must have been quite mad."

"Or else horribly sane. Did you not hear him at the end? His address to Watson? Those were the words of someone entirely lucid. It was as if a fog had lifted and in his final dying seconds he saw everything with perfect clarity."

"Are you quite sure?" said Gregson. "What I got from it was pure babble. I mean, 'Great Old Ones'. What's that about? 'Forget about Shadwell.' 'Men who would be more than men.' Lunacy not lucidity, if you ask me."

"Gentlemen," I said sharply, "a man has just died. Someone I used to know. I would appreciate it if you didn't straight away set about forensically analysing his mental status, and would instead, if only for a moment or so, accord his passing some respect."

Chastened, both Holmes and Gregson apologised.

I would not perhaps have spoken to them with such asperity had I not been so thoroughly discombobulated by the turn of events. From Stamford's use of that strange language to his grisly suicide and his grave warning, everything about the episode had impinged on my nerves.

Compounding my agitation was my failure to keep him in the land of the living. He had slipped through my fingers like water.

"You are right of course, Watson," Holmes said. "We were insensitive." He withdrew the grey horsehair blanket from beneath Stamford's body and draped it over him, covering his face. "There. Inspector? Let us repair to your office, where we may partake of a restorative nip of whisky. Watson needs it, and I could do with some myself."

"Whisky? I don't—"

"The hip flask I can see forming a bulge in your left jacket pocket – it doesn't contain lime cordial, now does it?"

Shortly we were ranged round Gregson's desk, which was heaped with manila folders. His in-tray was overflowing with cases pending, while his out-tray was almost empty. Gregson tended to be busier than the average detective inspector, mostly because he was more conscientious than his peers and less apt to leave stones unturned and avenues of enquiry unexplored.

A few sips of his whisky did something to revive me, but I still remained dazed and detached as he and Holmes argued over the implications of Stamford's untimely demise. As far as Gregson was concerned, the matter had been resolved. If Stamford was responsible for the murders as Holmes claimed, then with his end came an end to his homicidal campaign. Gregson liked to think of himself as a thorough man, keen to see things through all the way, but surely in this instance a case had tied itself up with a bow, all nice and neat, no further attention required. A killer now lay beyond the capacity to kill again, and whilst he may not have faced trial and undergone the due process of British justice, the outcome had been much as it would otherwise have been, presuming his guilt was never in doubt.

"Mind you," he added, "the paperwork on this one is going to be hellish. I hope I can call on both of you to sign affidavits swearing that Dr Stamford took his own life and was not a victim of police violence. This is just the sort of thing the liberal reformers will jump on and use as a stick to beat the Met with, if I don't square it away properly."

"Do you genuinely think the affair is over, Inspector?" said Holmes.

"Isn't it? It appears to be. Taking your own avowed belief that Dr Stamford is a repeat murderer, and factoring in the lack of a fresh victim in Shadwell, can we not draw the obvious conclusion?"

"There are still unanswered questions."

"Such as?"

"How did Stamford commit his crimes?"

"You mean what method did he use to dispose of his victims? It was starvation, no? Judging by the emaciation of the bodies. Isn't it as simple as that?"

"I see. You are saying he held them captive without food or water until they perished."

Gregson spread out his hands. "Wouldn't you agree that's the logical assumption?"

"'Logical assumption' is, in my view, an oxymoron. The words do not even belong in the same sentence. But let us parse your proposition anyway."

"Oh dear," Gregson groaned, with the weariness

of a man knowing he was about to watch his newborn brainchild be coolly and mercilessly dissected.

"How long does it take to starve a person to death? I would estimate a fortnight. Wouldn't you concur, Watson?"

"Much depends on the individual's general state of health beforehand," I said, "but yes, it would be two weeks, give or take, before death occurred from catastrophic organ failure or myocardial infarction. Three at the utmost if he was strong or had significant reserves of fat to draw on."

"Stamford would thus have had to select and abduct each victim a substantial period of time in advance, then hide the poor wretch somewhere, unfed, unwatered, and wait for nature to take its course. What that fails to allow for is the precision of his timetable. Each body showed up the morning after the night of the new moon. How could he guarantee that cessation of life would take place precisely on schedule? It is not possible, not when death by starvation is, as we have ascertained, a moveable feast."

"He held them captive, starved them, but then slew them himself," Gregson countered. "Lack of sustenance left them thin and weak, and Stamford finished the job off by his own hand at the time he needed to."

"And through such means adhered to the demands of his lunar agenda. Very well. I grant you that, Inspector."

Gregson bowed his head with a measure of grace and a larger measure of sardonicism.

"Had a coroner assessed the bodies," Holmes continued, "he may have been able to determine whether their ends were violent. There might have been visible evidence of strangulation, say, or suffocation."

"We have that 'look of terror'," said Gregson. "It would seem to suggest that the deaths came suddenly and were far from tranquil."

"I shall refer you to Watson on that subject."

I regaled Gregson with the same discourse on the early effects of bodily decomposition that I had given Holmes.

"Furthermore," Holmes said, "the whole business of starving the victims might have led to death striking too soon. What if one of them had expired within the first day or so of captivity? Then Stamford would have had to keep the body while it gradually rotted until the desired date arrived, with all its astronomical or astrological or practical significance. None of the corpses, as far as I am aware, was anything but fresh. I'm certain that signs of bloating, skin discolouration or putrefaction, had there been any, would have been noticed and remarked upon. The smell alone would have drawn attention to the fact that the body had decayed somewhat."

"So he was fortunate in that respect," said Gregson. "The victims all lived long enough."

"Indeed so, but there is one final hole I can shoot in the hull of this whole forced starvation thesis that will sink it outright. Dr Stamford was scouting for his next victim *only last night.*"

"I didn't know that."

"I didn't tell you, so I don't hold you to blame for your ignorance." Holmes gave a brief summary of our doings at the pub in Shadwell and after. By careful omission he avoided revealing that I had participated in gambling there, leaving it implicit but unsaid that he and I had been tailing Stamford together all along. I nodded discreetly to him, acknowledging his tact.

"But," said Gregson, "perhaps he already had this new moon's victim on hand, trussed up and dead. Perhaps this girl whose saviours you became was to be his *sixth* victim."

"Then he would have been kidnapping her far too soon," Holmes said, "would he not?"

Gregson shook his head, conceding defeat. "All the same, Mr Holmes, it seems cut and dried to me. However Stamford did it, he did it, and now he won't be doing it any more. If you wish to pursue the case further and clear up these peripheral details, by all means go ahead. You have my blessing. I personally shall devote myself to the many other demands on my time." He patted one of the stacks of case folders, much like a father absentmindedly patting the head of one of his offspring. "But do keep me apprised of your progress."

*

The day was brilliantly bright, the air as cold as the sky was blue. Holmes and I picked our way east along the Embankment, with the Thames sliding by on our right, sleek and uninviting, and traffic clattering to and fro on our left. We cut up to Trafalgar Square and thence to Oxford Street, and all the while Holmes was mired in thought, brooding silently. I sensed that any intrusion upon his meditations would be given short shrift, so I refrained. Already I was getting the measure of the man.

With Advent just begun, the shops on Oxford Street were parading gaily towards Christmas. The windows of almost every one were glittering wonderlands, magnetically attractive to passing children and their mothers, nannies and governesses. There were displays of merchandise festooned with cotton wool to emulate snow, trees garlanded with baubles, sweets, tinsel and paper chains, and wax mannequins of angels, elven toymakers and good old Father Christmas himself. A brass band struck up on Oxford Circus, parrumping their way through a succession of carols and other seasonal tunes. The traffic was not so heavy that they could not be heard above the clatter of wheels and hooves. The festive spirit was everywhere in abundance. Yet it touched neither Holmes nor me. We were insulated from it by Stamford's horrendous self-assassination and the knowledge of his crimes.

"Watson," Holmes said eventually, as we began tramping north through Marylebone, "I do not intend to ask why you froze the way you did in Stamford's cell, when he started speaking in that alien tongue."

"I appreciate that."

"It appears you have secrets you would rather keep, and it is not my place to pry into them. I shall restrict myself to commenting that, whatever they are, they must be daunting, to have so stalwart a fellow as you in their thrall. Perhaps one day you will see fit to unburden yourself of them to me."

"Perhaps."

"In the meantime, I hold you under no obligation to continue with me in the investigation into the murders. I should, however, like to enquire whether you would be willing at least to consider assisting me in another sphere, namely the maintenance of my tenancy at 221B. I like the rooms very much. They suit me, and I want to keep them, but I am currently somewhat more impecunious than I would wish, and financial assistance from your good self, as a fellow tenant, would be invaluable."

"You're asking me if I would move in with you and go Dutch on the rent."

"I am."

"Then why not just say so? I would be more than happy to, Holmes. My current accommodation is nowhere near as comfortable as yours, nor as conveniently situated, and you and I seem to rub along. If you have any bad habits, I am sure they are nothing I couldn't live with, and I in turn am a fairly regular and dependable sort."

"That is exactly what you are, and exactly why I am extending you this invitation."

"As to the other issue, the investigation – well, I can't say I'm not intrigued. It's like a story missing its final pages. I should like to know how it turns out."

"Splendid!" He held out a hand to me, we shook, and the deal was sealed. "I have gained a colleague and a fellow lodger in one fell swoop. Now come, there is much to be done, starting with fetching your belongings from Norwood."

"I shall have to give my landlord notice."

"Do, but I still want you ensconced at Baker Street today. By early afternoon, if possible."

I was unable to fathom why there was such a rush, but I nodded assent.

"Oh, and, Watson? As an ex-serviceman, you wouldn't

happen to be the owner of a firearm, would you?"

"I would, as a matter of fact. A Webley Pryse top-break revolver, taking Eley's No. 2 .450-calibre cartridges."

"Excellent. Of all your personal effects, that is the one that will be the most essential in the near future."

"Whatever for?"

Holmes regarded me evenly. "My dear fellow, Dr Stamford may be no longer with us, but there is more going on here than his death. You heard him. 'Forces at work. Men who would be more than men.' Stamford and his trail of emaciated corpses are part of something larger. It cannot be otherwise."

"You never said so to Gregson."

"Why would I? He has so much else on his plate, and I, I have only a host of loose ends which as yet I am unable to tie up. My instinct is that I will eventually do so, if only I can follow them to their extremity. My instinct, too, is that wherever they lead, we may find grave danger."

CHAPTER EIGHT

The Lair of the Dragon

NIGHT HAD FALLEN OVER LONDON, BRINGING WITH it one of those "particulars" for which the city is renowned: the yellowish fogs that turn every street into a miasmic tunnel and reduce visibility to a few yards during daylight hours and even less after dark. The residue of the snow had begun to melt away, leaving the cobblestones and pavements glossily slick, with ridges of ice here and there. It was still bitterly cold, and the chill and the fog in combination made the notion of venturing out of doors undesirable. The warmth and safety of the hearthside were more than usually alluring.

Yet venture out Holmes and I did, into the noisome, icy breath of the fog, and our footsteps were directed towards Limehouse, specifically towards the opium den owned and run by a certain Gong-Fen Shou.

En route, Holmes filled me in on all he knew about the Chinaman. Gong-Fen had been resident in Great Britain since the late 1850s, emigrating from his land of origin in the wake of the Second Opium War, the flight of the Emperor and the burning of the Summer Palaces. Nothing was on record about his past before he came to these shores, but he had in the subsequent couple of decades built up a considerable business empire based on the importation of silk and rice. He had cornered the market in England for those two commodities almost entirely, such that an estimated ninety per cent of the trade in them passed through his hands, allowing him to cream a handsome profit off the top.

He was, then, an immigrant success story, rising from nothing to become the model plutocrat, one who paid his taxes, gave generously to charity, and had a Belgravia mansion and a manor house retreat in the Surrey countryside, each with an army of servants, to show for his entrepreneurialism.

But darker rumours swirled perpetually around Gong-Fen Shou, linking him to at least three East End opium dens. The same steamships out of Shanghai and Hong Kong that brought over his bolts of silk and sacks of rice also carried chests of raw opium hidden in secret compartments below decks, or so it was alleged.

Since the restrictions on the sale of opiate-derived drugs imposed by the Pharmacy Act of 1868, addicts often found it easier, and preferable, to visit opium dens and partake of the pure stuff there rather than purchase the watered-down versions that were commercially available in the form of morphine, laudanum and various patent preparations. There were fortunes to be made smuggling and illegally supplying the narcotic, and Gong-Fen was said to be London's foremost purveyor of it. Nothing had ever been proved to that effect. There had been not a whiff of a criminal prosecution against him. He was to all appearances virtuous, his reputation spotless. Still, it was common currency in the area that he ran those dens. He was the *éminence grise* behind them, their unseen sponsor and beneficiary. He sat deep at the heart of them like a dragon in its cave, a zealous, quasi-mythical presence.

Tonight, Holmes and I were going to beard that dragon in its lair.

The plan was simple. We were posing as a pair of gentlemen, one of us a regular user of the pipe, the other a willing aspirant who was keen to be inducted into its delights. Holmes, of course, was the former, and he had tricked himself out accordingly, adding a touch of sallowness to his complexion with make-up and introducing a dab of salted water into his eyes to lend them a suitable pinkness. I was the latter, under instruction merely to be myself and let Holmes do most of the talking. Our goal? To behave in a manner that would ensure us an audience with the man himself, Gong-Fen.

This would not be without its risks and rigours, and I was not a little apprehensive as we entered that section of Limehouse that had become a predominantly Chinese community, a network of half a dozen streets where every other mercantile premises was a laundry or a tobacconist and where bobbing Asians in coolie hats outnumbered white westerners five to one. Shop signs were almost all written in Chinese logograms, as were the banners which overhung the roadway announcing who-knew-what in that elegant yet baffling script.

The buildings were rickety and tawdry, and the smells that emanated from many a basement grating were redolent of foreign climes and exotic cuisines − spicy, fragrant, sometimes repellent. The residents themselves, as they passed us in the fog, spoke to one another in the liquid, songlike intonation of their mother tongue and aimed looks at us that strove to be incurious but bore a hint, or so I thought, of animosity. It was as though they knew we had every right to be there, as native-born Englishmen, yet still resented us as intruders in their realm.

I cannot say that our country's behaviour in their homeland over the preceding few decades, alternately swaggering and bullying, would have endeared us to any of their nationality, and of course the situation in China would later come violently to a head during the Boxer Rebellion, the inevitable outcome of British imperial intransigence and the Qing dynasty's inability to rein in dissent amongst its subjects. All the same, I did not care for being regarded as an interloper in my own city. It put me on my mettle.

The opium den of which Stamford had been a habitué purported to be an ordinary if rather run-down hotel. Called the Golden Lotus, it was sandwiched between a shop offering herbal medicines and a butcher's with pigs' heads and whole duck carcasses hanging on display. A notice posted in the window, in English, promised A WARM WELCOME, ENVIABLE TARIFFS, AND ALL POSSIBLE COMFORTS. As we approached the front steps, the door opened to permit someone to leave. He emerged with his hat brim low and the collar of his ulster drawn up, and hastened past us with scarcely a glance in our direction. No sooner was he out of earshot than Holmes chuckled and, when I asked what was amusing, said, "Did you fail, Watson, to recognise a peer of the realm? A prominent Liberal who sits in the House of Lords, no less?"

"I barely saw his face."

"As he intended. But the features he could not help but expose were sufficient. A man of the utmost probity in his public deeds, yet a noted libertine in his private life. Little wonder that Gong-Fen Shou has remained untroubled by the law, if he can count such illustrious legislators amongst his clients."

"How very dashed cynical of you."

"Cynicism is simply realism with a veneer of irony."

So saying, Holmes climbed the steps and pushed through the door. Inside, in a modestly appointed reception area, we were greeted by a tiny and very old Chinese woman clad in a tight-fitting mandarin gown decorated with flowers. Her hair was coiffed in a tight, glossy bun, which was secured by a pair of chopsticks inserted crosswise. She bowed to us with exemplary courtesy and enquired in broken English what we required.

"The very best that you have," Holmes replied. "We have heard great things about your establishment, madam, and are eager to sample its fare for ourselves. I myself am no stranger to the kind of hospitality on offer, while my friend, though unversed, anticipates becoming a frequent caller."

Briefly the old woman appraised us both with a wizened, expert eye. Seeming satisfied, she bowed again and said, "Of course, good misters. We would be honour to have you stay with us at Golden Lotus Hotel. We have many, many fine room. You stay for just short time or maybe longer. Maybe upstairs we have just what you looking for."

"Upstairs, yes. Somewhere nice and quiet, where no one is likely to disturb us."

She beamed toothlessly. "No disturb. No. Much quiet, and sweet dreams."

"Sweet dreams. That sounds ideal."

"This way."

We followed her delicately quick-stepping form up a flight of narrow wooden stairs, and soon were in a low-ceilinged room with shuttered windows and a score of low bunks pressed close together. The atmosphere was filled with smoke so dense it was almost as impenetrable as the fog outside, and richly, beguilingly aromatic. Oil lamps gleamed like faint stars, and on almost every mattress lay a human figure, each with a pipe in his hands or lying nearby him. Some of these people were inert, utterly limp, as though drained of all energy. Others moved restlessly, limbs twitching, throats emitting mumbled snatches of monologue. Now and then a dim, lacklustre eye fluttered open and caught mine, but I did not have the impression of being seen but rather of being looked through, as though I were a phantom, evanescent and unreal.

A couple of Chinamen dressed in long shirts, loose trousers and close-fitting caps glided amongst the smokers, checking on them as solicitously as nurses making their ward rounds.

"Li. Zhang." The old woman beckoned the pair over. "You take good care of these two gentlemen." She patted one of the chopsticks in her hair, adjusting its position slightly. "You understand?"

Li and Zhang both nodded.

Holmes slipped the old woman a shilling for her pains.

She accepted the coin with yet another tidy bow before disappearing back to her post at reception.

Both of the Chinamen were young, and the one I took to be Li wore a moustache consisting of two lengthy tendrils that hung down on either side of his mouth like the barbels of a sturgeon, while his companion, Zhang, was clean-shaven but sported a foot-long pigtail queue. With gestures and soft murmurs they directed us to a pair of adjacent vacant bunks. They barely had a word of English between them, but the language barrier was immaterial. They needed to communicate only where we were to lie and how much money we should give them. When Holmes produced a crown, Zhang shook his head ruefully and held up two fingers. Holmes duly doubled the price to a half-sovereign, which was graciously accepted.

So far, so civilised.

Holmes stretched himself out on his bunk with a louche, experienced air. I followed suit, in my own way. Li and Zhang departed and returned shortly with long metal pipes, the bowls of which they stuffed with tarry brown wads of opium. They handed us one each, then placed small oil lamps on stools next to us. They invited us to roll onto our sides and made a dumb show of placing the pipe bowl over the lamp flame and sucking air in through the mouthpiece at the other end. Holmes nodded impatiently, as though an old hand at the practice, and shooed Li and Zhang away. The two Chinamen retreated into the wreaths of smoke, leaving us to our own devices.

"How far are we meaning to go with this?" I asked

Holmes in a whisper. "You don't really expect me to ingest opium, do you?"

"Play along," came the reply. "Pretend. Make it look good. Just remember not to inhale."

Easier said than done. I was already woozy and fuddle-headed from the fumes in the room alone. I feared that I might inadvertently take some of the smoke from the pipe into my lungs and this would be enough to tip me over into a state of full-blown narcotic delirium. In a gingerly fashion I heated the opium over the lamp until it began to sizzle, then drew on the pipe until hot, smooth smoke flooded my mouth. I kept it there for a few seconds before breathing it out in a plume. I saw Holmes do the same on the other bunk. He made the subterfuge look more convincing than I believe mine was. After several further puffs he let his head sink back on the pillow, pulled his legs up, and laid the smouldering pipe across his chest. I copied him, adding what I hoped sounded like a satisfied moan, an expression of pure contentment.

Holmes had not vouchsafed what his next move would be, telling me only that I should be ready for anything. When I had asked why he was unable to divulge that portion of the plan, his answer was that my surprised reaction must be as authentic as possible, in keeping with the roles we had adopted. I had already learned how Holmes relished theatrics. This looked as if it would be another of those occasions where his knowledge of what was afoot, and the ignorance of others on that score, gave him a small thrill.

If I had only known in advance what he had in mind,

I almost certainly would have refused to go along with it.

"I say!" Holmes yelled all of a sudden. "Hullo! Li. Zhang. Whatever your names are. Come here. I want a word with you."

Zhang appeared instantly at his bedside, forefinger pressed to lips, mutely indicating that Holmes should keep his voice down.

"No, you devil, I will not be quiet," my companion declared haughtily, louder than before. "Look here. This opium you've sold us – at great expense, I might add – is a very shoddy specimen. I believe you've thinned it with something, probably tree resin. I'm a connoisseur of the poppy. I know my stuff. This diluted muck barely passes muster. Do you understand what I am saying?"

Whether he did or not, Zhang insisted Holmes calm down, making a flattening motion with both hands. Li was now beside him, looking every bit as agitated and as desirous of Holmes's quiescence.

"How dare you waft your hands at me like that," Holmes thundered, working himself up into a thorough-going lather of indignation. "Haven't you even learned the Queen's English? You come to our country and don't have the decency to pick up the lingo. Damn you, you impertinent Oriental rascal."

He was laying it on a bit thick, I thought, but his tirade was undoubtedly having an effect. Not only did it discomfit Li and Zhang, it disturbed the papaverous slumbers of the addicts. They were stirring, some sitting up, others calling out, wanting to know what the fuss was about. It started as a few grumbled complaints but rapidly became a din of protest as Holmes continued to berate the Chinamen about the poor quality of the product they had sold us and their non-existent grasp of our language.

It culminated in his striking Zhang on the arm with the end of his pipe. That was a step too far for the Chinamen, and together they hauled Holmes roughly off the bed.

"You ruffians, take your filthy paws off me!" Holmes objected, trying to wrestle free of their clutches. "Do you know who I am? You'd let me go in a flash if you had any idea how important a personage it is you're manhandling. I could have you hanged for this. I could!"

Evidently Li and Zhang had been subjected to verbal threats before. Even if unable to comprehend the actual words, they were familiar with the tone of expression, and it bothered them not at all. With a grim set of the lips they began frogmarching Holmes towards the exit.

Over his shoulder he addressed me: "Are you just going to lie there and let them get away with this, old chap? It's rank effrontery, that's what it is. They ought to know better, and we're the ones who should be teaching them the lesson."

The room was in full uproar by now, opium addicts on all fours on their beds or standing on their feet, bleary but angry, shaking their fists, incensed to have had their blissful reveries so rudely interrupted.

I stumbled after Holmes, wondering what "teaching them the lesson" might actually entail. I found out the next moment as he gave an almighty wrench and managed to pull free of both his captors.

What ensued was one of the most balletic fights I

had ever witnessed. It made the previous night's clash between Holmes and the Lascars look like a clumsy, cack-handed brawl. That confrontation had been hopelessly one-sided. This was altogether a better matched and less asymmetrical battle, and the more elegant and spectacular for that.

Holmes aimed a sharp, savage punch at Li, and seemed not at all startled when his opponent blocked the attack with a swiftly raised forearm. The Chinaman responded with a pivoting sidelong kick under which Holmes ducked by bending backwards from the knees. His retaliation came in the form of a stiff-fingered thrust to the solar plexus which connected solidly and left Li winded.

While Li was doubled up, choking, Zhang came at Holmes, hands aloft like a pair of broad-bladed knives. There followed an exchange of blow and counterblow that was almost too fast for the eye to follow. Fist wove around fist, kick succeeded kick, elbows and shins were deployed as offensive weapons. Conducted by anything but Marquess of Queensberry rules, it was hypnotic in its ferocity and speed, like watching two cobras vying over territory. Both Holmes's face and Zhang's were fixed in masks of absolute concentration. Each man's gaze never left the other's. They were fighting, it appeared, as much on the mental plane as the physical, a contest of intellects as well as bodies.

I roused myself from my fascinated absorption only when I saw Li rise up behind Holmes, clasping a short dagger. Without further thought I launched myself across the room at him. Even as I ran I was tugging the revolver out of my pocket. Li had produced a weapon, and so I quite justifiably felt that I should too.

Li saw me coming and spun towards me, at the same time flipping the dagger up to catch it by its point. He drew back his arm for a throw. I at last managed to extricate my Webley. I knew I had only a second in which to act, otherwise that dagger would be hurtling my way. I raised the gun, cocking the hammer with my thumb, and fired.

It was a wild shot. There had been no time to aim. The bullet missed, embedding itself in the wall behind Li, but he recoiled anyway, shrinking out of its path. That gave me the opportunity I needed. Still at a run, I covered the last few paces between us, and used the revolver to club the dagger out of his hand.

I levelled the barrel of the gun at his head and told him to stay still. "Or I'll blow your brains out," I added. My intention would have been crystal clear to him, even if the specifics of my threat were not.

Not just the room but now the entire building was in upheaval. The gunshot had panicked everyone, and the addicts immediately around us were stampeding for the door while elsewhere, from other rooms, other floors, there came drumming footfalls and cries of alarm. Holmes and I had succeeded in creating pandemonium, just as we had meant to.

Holmes was still engaged in combat with Zhang. Out of the corner of my eye I observed the ebb and flow of their battle, the repeated exchanges of thrust and parry, strike and evasion. Perspiration glazed Holmes's brow, while Zhang's expression spoke of thinly veiled disbelief, as though he could not wholly countenance the idea that his opponent was giving as good as he got. The Chinaman was skilled in some form of Oriental martial art, but he was clearly surprised to find a westerner who was similarly adept. Holmes's baritsu presented a different style of fighting from his own, but one that was no less effective and, in the hands of a master practitioner, every bit its equal. It seemed possible Zhang might even come away the loser, for Holmes stood a head taller and had a concomitantly greater reach. Zhang's only response was to bring himself in close so that the height advantage was mitigated. This, however, served Holmes well, for baritsu – as I would later come to learn – incorporated elements of wrestling and judo, and could be employed in the clinch as devastatingly as in separation.

Thus Holmes, spying his chance, seized Zhang by the lapels and attempted to upend him. Zhang struggled to keep his balance as Holmes tried to swipe the legs from under him and send him crashing to the floor. Some fierce, precise punches to Holmes's abdomen almost bought Zhang his freedom, but my companion clung resolutely on and persisted in his attempt to gain leverage over the Chinaman.

His grit and determination paid off in the end. Though Zhang's blows were undoubtedly hurting him, he finally managed to manoeuvre himself into a stance whereby he could hook his leg around the backs of both the Chinaman's knees. Zhang was toppled, and Holmes bore down, slamming him onto his back.

Ever so briefly the fight went out of Zhang. He lay

dazed. Holmes, bent over him, raised a fist to deliver the *coup de grâce*. It looked as though victory was his.

Alas, I had neglected Li. I had thought I was covering him with the revolver, but little by little my focus had strayed. The clash between Holmes and Zhang had become increasingly the centre of my attention. How could it not, when it was so desperate? Having become a rapt audience to it, I gave Li an opening which he did not hesitate to exploit.

All at once his grip was around my gun hand, my fingers were bent back, and the Webley was plucked from my grasp with almost insouciant ease. Then Li had the revolver pressed to my temple and an arm encircled round my neck. In the space of a heartbeat I went from subduer to hostage.

Li barked something in Chinese to draw Holmes's attention. He, seeing my predicament, straightened up and backed away from Zhang. The blow that would have put Zhang firmly out of contention never landed. The downed Chinaman sprang to his feet with a triumphant grin, while Holmes dropped his arms and hunched his shoulders in a posture of submission.

"Fair enough," he said. "You have won. Please do not harm my friend. We will leave peaceably."

Li seemed to understand the terms of surrender Holmes had set, but nonetheless he ground the barrel of the Webley hard into my skull, the better to emphasise his superiority and my helplessness. He shoved me forward by the collar, and the four of us went in procession down the stairs to the reception area.

Here, the patrons of the Golden Lotus were milling about in an angry throng, remonstrating with the old woman. She in turn was attempting to allay their concerns. "Is nothing worry about. Please to be calm. No problem. Go back to rooms. All is under control."

It did not help her cause that a burly Chinaman was stationed at the front door, barring anyone from leaving, and that another two were standing guard sternly in front of her, a human bulwark. The assembled addicts were unhappy at being corralled and had no qualms about voicing their discontent. Jolts of adrenalin had dissipated the palliative influence of their opium intake. Pleasant intoxication had been replaced by outrage and vituperation.

"What on earth's going on?" one of them growled. "Shouting. Gunfire. A right royal ruckus. This is insupportable!"

"You cannot coop us up like cattle," said another. "I demand that you give us our liberty."

"Is it a police raid?" asked a third anxiously. "Only, I can't afford to be caught here. If my wife were to find out, there'd be hell to pay."

Others were less articulate in their reproach, directing obscenities and insults at the woman and her associates, including many a racial slur.

There were gasps as we appeared from the staircase. The sight of Li with a gun to my head provoked shock and deeper fury.

Zhang spoke to the old woman in rapid-fire Chinese, after which she announced to the mob: "Here are troublemakers. We make them go and not come back.

See? All safe now. You not need worry. We look after."

Li pushed me ahead of him, and the crowd parted to allow us through. At a command from the old woman, the burly Chinaman at the door made way.

As we were on the point of being ejected, Holmes spoke up.

"Gong-Fen Shou," he said.

"What?" said the old woman. "What that you say?"

"Gong-Fen Shou. You know full well whom I'm talking about. The 'respectable' businessman whose dirty secret this place is. Tell him I'm on to him. Tell him he won't be able to maintain the façade of respectability much longer. He's not as untouchable as he thinks he is. I'm going to dethrone him. His life of luxury is about to come crashing down around his ears."

"You mistaken, mister," said the old woman, blank-faced. "No Gong-Fen Shou here. Nobody have that name. You speaking foolish. You are crazy man. Now go! No return. We see you and your friend here again, you will not like it. We not be so nice to you next time."

Li booted me unceremoniously through the doorway, with such force that I lost my footing and slithered down the front steps. I fetched up in a heap on the pavement, and cried out in pain, but it was my pride that was damaged more than my anatomy.

Zhang dished out the same treatment to Holmes, who made an altogether more dignified descent than mine, catching himself on the railing before he could fall.

Li waved my revolver at me with a mocking laugh. Then, in a move calculated to offend, he slipped the gun into his trouser pocket and patted it, as if to say, "Mine."

I scrambled to my feet and started back up the steps, bent on retrieving it from him. Holmes stopped me.

"Don't, old man. It's not worth it. It's just a gun. You can always buy another."

I began to remonstrate, but then saw sense and yielded. He was right. I stood no chance against Li, whose martial arts prowess was, from what I had seen of it, the equivalent of Zhang's. To try and wrest the Webley from him would be to invite a beating, and perhaps worse.

In order to salvage what was left of my dignity, I sneered and flapped a dismissive hand. I said I hoped Li would have fun with it. I wouldn't miss it.

This was an arrant lie. The revolver was amongst my most treasured possessions. It had saved my life more than once, not least in the Arghandab Valley. To it I owed a debt as great as I owed any man.

With a sore heart to match the rest of my sore body, I resigned myself to never seeing it again.

*

Bruised, battered, bedraggled, Holmes and I put the Golden Lotus Hotel behind us. I was despondent. I had acquitted myself poorly, I felt. If not for my carelessness, Holmes would have won his bout with Zhang outright and we could have left the place with our heads held high rather than at gunpoint, in a condition of humiliation.

However, when after several minutes I aired these thoughts to Holmes, he pooh-poohed them.

"Don't be downcast, my friend, and for heaven's sake don't apologise. We have had a refreshing and singular evening. I feel quite enlivened by it. And furthermore, it has not been in vain."

"You think so?"

"I know so. We achieved exactly what we set out to. Gong-Fen will hear about us. We have disrupted the well-ordered running of a business that relies on discretion and anonymity to thrive. We have made a nuisance of ourselves, in a way that is hard to excuse or overlook. If one of his minions from the Golden Lotus is not following us right now, I should be very surprised. All in all, a job well done."

"Following us…?"

"Don't turn round," Holmes hissed. "I don't want to give away that we know."

"But is it really true?" I said, lowering my voice. "There's a Chinaman on our tail?"

"One or more. I cannot say so with any great degree of certainty, but it would be the sensible strategy on their part. They will want to know where we are going. If we head for a police station, they will make a move to intercept us, and likewise if we accost a passing constable, they will make sure he is either bribed off or otherwise neutralised before he can bring trouble to their door. Gong-Fen has not kept his opium dens in business for this long without being a shrewd operator. Even if he is not actively co-ordinating the day-to-day running of the places, he will have employed underlings who are as wily as he needs them to be. That old crone, for instance, is no fool. Don't let her poor English lead you to underestimate her. She is as crafty as they come."

"Yes, one could see it in her eyes."

"Could one? Or are you simply being wise after the event?"

"Perhaps," I allowed.

"You failed to notice her signal, then?"

"Signal?"

"She was on to us from the start. She sensed we were impostors, and alerted Li and Zhang accordingly."

"How? She said only a handful of words to them."

"But she also touched the chopstick in her hair. Tapped it briefly, three times."

"To adjust it."

"To send a coded message. Zhang arrived at my bedside the moment I started to kick up a hullabaloo. He responded with such promptness because he and Li had been warned that they might expect trouble from us and were ready. That triple tap on the chopstick was far more than it seemed. I imagine she assumed we were plainclothes police officers conducting an undercover operation. Now, thanks to my bandying about the name Gong-Fen Shou, she will know we are something else and want to learn more about us."

We walked on, and I had to resist the urge repeatedly to glance over my shoulder. Were there footfalls behind us? Could I hear them, muffled through the fog? Or was it simply the echo of our own footfalls rebounding off the buildings? It was an eerie sensation, knowing there was the possibility one was being stalked. The thick billows of fog made it all the more so. Our shadow might be a scant few paces behind us, and we should never see him. Even in the event that Holmes was wrong and no one had been despatched from the opium den to keep track of us, the idea of an unseen pursuer still set my nape hairs prickling. We traipsed from one nimbus of lamplight to the next, and the gaps between these oases of illumination seemed unfathomably long and unnaturally murky. Now and then a fellow pedestrian would loom before us – a grandee in top hat and opera cloak wending his way home from his club, a shuffling tramp looking for somewhere to bed down for the night, a midinette in search of one last customer for her wares – each a silhouette that would briefly assume three-dimensionality and detail before dissolving back into hazy nothingness.

In due course we reached our destination, but only when the front door of 221B was shut securely behind us and locked did I allow myself a deep sigh of relief. I tended to the many contusions left on Holmes by the fight with Zhang, daubing them with liniment of turpentine oil. Then he and I bade each other goodnight and retired to our bedrooms. I was so keyed up with nervous energy I thought I might never fall asleep, but in fact I was out almost the moment I extinguished my bedside lamp.

I was awoken a while later by the sound of someone moving stealthily about in the pitch darkness of my room: the tiny creak of a floorboard, a stifled breath barely audible above the ticking of the mantelpiece clock.

Then a hand was pressed to my mouth and I heard the voice of Sherlock Holmes, at a whisper, saying in my ear: "Watson. Not a word. Get up. Quiet as you can. *We are not alone.*"

CHAPTER NINE

The Trespasser in the Night

ELECTRIFIED, I DIVESTED MYSELF OF THE BED-covers and rose as noiselessly as I was able.

"Someone is in the sitting room," Holmes confided. Beyond him the door that connected our two chambers stood open. "Whoever it is, they are making only a poor effort to be surreptitious. They have even turned a light on. The glow is visible under my bedroom door."

"Mrs Hudson?" I queried. I looked over to the door that connected my own bedroom to the sitting room beyond, and sure enough, could see a chink of light.

"Hardly. She would not enter my lodgings without permission, and certainly not at three o'clock in the morning. Besides, her room lies directly above mine and I have been listening to... Well, at the risk of being unchivalrous, let us just say the good lady is not the silentest of sleepers."

"Who, then? A burglar?"

"That is what we must go and find out. I wish you still had your revolver."

"Not as much as I wish it. Do you not have a gun of your own?"

"In the sitting room."

"Confound it. Is there no household object we can put to use as a weapon?"

"None to hand. We shall simply have to depend upon our own wherewithal. Are you ready? Follow my lead. If we both rush the intruder at once, we shall have the best hope of catching him unawares and subduing him."

We approached my bedroom door. At that moment a shadow moved across the light that shone from beneath it, accompanied by a soft tread, shoes on the bearskin hearthrug. My stomach curdled with the sense of anger that one rightfully feels when the sanctity of one's home is violated. On the other hand, I was very afraid, my pulse thumping like timpani in my ears.

"On the count of three," Holmes said, grasping the doorknob. "One. Two."

With "Three!" he thrust the door open and charged through. I was hot on his heels.

Our trespasser was standing with his back to the fireplace, where the embers of a blaze we had set the previous evening still radiated a faint heat. He looked entirely unsurprised when we burst in, as though he had been expecting both us and our somewhat brutish mode of entry. His stillness, his air of complete unflappability, brought the pair of us up short. We had been braced for startlement, fear, an attempt to flee, even fisticuffs; not a quiet nod, a wry smile, and eyes that twinkled with aloof amusement.

He was Chinese, tall for his race, with fine angular cheekbones and neatly combed, receding hair. His attire was immaculate, from the wing collar and gold tiepin to the felt spats covering the uppers of his patent leather shoes. His double-breasted Newmarket coat and grey Angola trousers, although I have never been good at judging such things by sight alone, looked expensively tailored, a product of Savile Row. It fit his spare, lean frame with bespoke precision. A Chesterfield overcoat, also of high quality, had been folded in half and draped over an armchair, with his hat and muffler placed on top. This gesture and the lit desk lamp gave the impression that the visitor, notwithstanding his lack of invitation, had succeeded in making himself quite at home.

"Forgive my calling by unannounced," the man said in perfect English without a trace of an accent. "I had no wish to disturb your landlady at such an ungodly hour."

"Never mind our landlady," I said. "What about us? State your business, you blackguard. Unless you want to leave by the window rather than the front door."

"Watson," said Holmes, "save your breath. His presence here is not entirely unsolicited."

"You know the fellow?"

"Know *of* him. Is it not obvious who he is? Can you not tell?"

Until Holmes said those words, I had not paused to consider the Chinaman's identity. Now I realised it could be none other than...

"Gong-Fen Shou."

At his name, the trespasser clasped his hands together. "The very same. Mr Holmes I have no trouble distinguishing, but you, sir, have me at a disadvantage."

"This is Dr John Watson," said Holmes, "my friend and ally. As to how you are able to put a name to my face..."

"You are beginning to garner a reputation in certain circles," said Gong-Fen. "It is becoming widely known that, for the resolution of problems which the legal fraternity either will not or cannot attend to, Sherlock

Holmes of 221B Baker Street is your man. A 'consulting detective', is that not right? You advertise in the Help Available columns of several newspapers, but you also benefit from word-of-mouth recommendation."

"Look here, this is all very nice and polite," I said, "but how did you even get into the house?"

"Ah, there I must plead for clemency. I have some facility as a picker of locks."

"You broke in!"

"Calm yourself, my boy," said Holmes.

"Calm? How can I be calm?" I exclaimed. "Holmes, the man is a drug lord. A scoundrel. He has just confessed to a crime. We should haul him down to Scotland Yard forthwith, that's what we should do."

"You did not offer me the same treatment when I told you yesterday that I had broken into Stamford's lodgings."

"Yes, but dash it all, this is different."

"Not so different," Holmes said with equanimity. "What you are forgetting, or choosing to overlook, is that we set out to engineer this very outcome: that Gong-Fen Shou should notice us. Here he is, in person. Mission accomplished."

"All the same…" I could have blustered on, but I doubted it would have got me anywhere. Holmes seemed almost enchanted by Gong-Fen's audacity, as if sheer insolence were a virtue.

"Allow me to make up for any nuisance I may have caused," the Chinese millionaire said. "I have a gift for you, Doctor."

From his pocket he produced a gun. I was on the point of diving for it before he could turn it on us. There was no question in my mind that he was about to shoot us. I *had* to seize it from him.

He, however, held it out with the grip towards me, the barrel in his hand. His fingers were nowhere near the trigger.

That was when I perceived it was my very own trusty Webley Pryse.

"I believe this is yours," said Gong-Fen. "Please accept it as proof of earnest and a sign of goodwill. Li Guiying ought not to have confiscated it. It was ill-judged of him. Ungracious."

I snatched the revolver out of his grasp. It looked in good order. I noted, though, that there were no bullets in it.

"Yes," said Gong-Fen, seeing me check the cylinder, "I did take the precaution of unloading it. I mean you no harm, but I was not certain you would reciprocate the sentiment."

"You would be correct," I muttered.

"So," he said, "now that you have in effect summoned me, Mr Holmes, and I have come, what is it you want? I am told you took my name in vain at a certain premises in Limehouse in which I may or may not have a financial stake."

"There's no may or may not about it. You do. That opium den, thinly disguised as a hotel, is yours. How else would you have come by Watson's revolver?"

"I am a prominent figure in London's Chinese community. Their spokesman, some would say. Their leader, according to others. Perhaps it was passed on to me by Li with a request for it to be returned to its rightful owner."

"Perhaps," said Holmes, the word salted with doubt. "Certainly someone must have followed us home from Limehouse tonight, else how would you have known to come here?"

"Again, my standing in the Chinese community means I am privy to every item of intelligence the community gathers."

"I'll take that as a yes."

"Take it how you will. At any rate, you were heard to utter dire prophecies of doom against me and attribute malfeasance on my part. Such assertions, especially of the latter variety, I do not take lightly. I am a subject of the Crown just as you are, Mr Holmes, and prepared to abide by the laws of the land. Anyone who says otherwise had better have hard evidence to back up his claims."

A flinty spark came into Gong-Fen's eyes as he spoke the last sentence, a glint of something cooler than the amicability that had hitherto typified him. He was serious. He was not a man to be trifled with.

"My interest in your affairs stems from the activities of the late Dr Valentine Stamford," said Holmes.

"The name is unfamiliar to me."

"I believe that statement to be an out-and-out falsehood."

"You may believe what you like, my good sir. Again, without evidence—"

"I have evidence," Holmes said, cutting in brusquely. He nodded to the window. "Through the gap in the curtains I have spotted a clarence parked at the kerb outside. Yours, clearly. And it was a clarence that whisked Dr Stamford away from Shadwell in the early hours of yesterday morning."

"Of what consequence is that? I am not the only person in London to own such a vehicle."

"You did not allow me to finish. I was about to say, whisked him away after he failed to acquire the next in his procession of murder victims."

"Murder…?"

"Stamford having been a regular patron of the aforementioned 'premises in Limehouse', the Golden Lotus Hotel, it is hardly difficult to extrapolate a direct relationship between you and him."

"It may not be difficult for you, Mr Holmes, but for anyone else…"

"Stamford was acting as your errand boy. That is my conclusion. He was choosing and fetching the victims on your behalf."

"Errand boy? This is preposterous. Why would I employ him as such? I have more domestic staff than I know what to do with, Mr Holmes. One snap of my fingers and they jump to it. If I want anything menial done, I simply ask one of them."

"But this was no menial task. This was something else altogether. You cannot send just anyone to roam the East End looking for lost souls to kidnap. You would need someone on whose discretion you can count and whose loyalty is beyond question. Someone over whom you have an unshakeable hold. That would be Stamford, whose enslavement to the poppy would have made him, by extension, your slave too."

As Holmes said all this, I could see that it made a

grim, dismaying sense. Stamford had been working for Gong-Fen, no doubt in return for free opium. To him it would be an invaluable recompense for his vile labours; to the Chinaman, relatively paltry.

"You are on thin ice here," Gong-Fen said, his face still serene but his voice now devoid of its earlier warmth and magnanimity. "To bandy about such accusations is to risk provoking my ire, and I am not a man with whom you would wish to cross swords, trust me."

"Where the chain of reasoning leads from that point on," Holmes continued, unabashed, "is into the realm of pure conjecture. I do not at present have the data from which to build a solid deduction. What I do have is a workable hypothesis."

"Would you like to share it?"

Holmes debated inwardly. "I am loath to, but since you asked... Dr Stamford and you, I would submit, have been collaborating in an experiment."

Gong-Fen arched an eyebrow. "Go on."

"You have been testing out some powerful new narcotic on a selection of unsuspecting innocents snatched off the streets. Stamford, with his medical knowhow, was aiding you in its design. You have been conducting trials of this exotic drug, but so far the results have not been positive – anything but. Its effects are instantaneous, dramatic, and lethal. It robs the user of his vigour, his physical robustness, his very essence. It rapidly saps the life from him, leaving him a husk. You have then had to discard the depleted bodies at random around Shadwell, passing them off as discrete, unconnected deaths, the results of malnutrition or sickness or both. You have done this on a monthly basis, leaving adequate intervals between experiments so as to prevent your endeavour looking too much like what it is, a rash of killings. Were the deaths to occur too close together, the bodies to begin to pile up one on top of another, even the beef-witted blockheads at the Met might sit up and take notice. Timing the abduction and disposal of each victim to coincide with the arrival of the new moon is simply a practical expedient, darkness affording the best cover for your degenerate nocturnal undertakings. All in all, you and Stamford have developed into a latter-day Burke and Hare, the distinction being that Burke and Hare had the decency to visit their abuses on the already dead, at least to begin with, while the doctors to whom they sold the corpses were engaged only in dissection for the purpose of teaching anatomy rather than the kind of fatal torment through which you have put your 'laboratory mice'."

I was hoping to see astonishment on Gong-Fen's face. I thought the accuracy of Holmes's surmise would hit him smack between the eyes like an arrow.

As it was, he merely laughed and slowly applauded.

"So near, Mr Holmes," he said, "and yet so far."

Gong-Fen's derision had the same effect on Holmes as a slap might have. He flinched, then tried to cover up the reaction.

"As I said, a workable hypothesis only. Perhaps you would be so decent as to tell me where I have gone amiss."

"I am under no obligation to tell you anything. You are young, Mr Holmes, and slinging mud around to see if any sticks is something only youngsters do. It would be of benefit to you, and to your sidekick, to leave well enough alone. You have strayed into a world about which you know nothing, and if anything comes of this meeting it should be the realisation that life is infinitely more complicated and more precarious than it seems."

"That sounds to me like a threat."

"Take it how you will. What you must understand is that we are all at the mercy of forces we cannot control, let alone comprehend. This Valentine Stamford, if I interpret what you say correctly, had a taste for opium. Addiction rode roughshod over him. Now, like many a man before him who has fallen under the drug's spell, he is dead."

"How do you know he is dead? I did not say so."

"You referred to him as 'the late'. You spoke of him in the past tense."

"You did, as a matter of fact," I said.

"Yes, all right, Watson. Thank you," Holmes said testily. He had been wrong-footed by his own inattention. Thinking he had bowled on the wicket, he had watched the ball go wide, and he liked it not a bit. "Be that as it may, Gong-Fen, I am convinced his death arose from his connection to you."

Gong-Fen waved slender fingers airily. "Another baseless accusation. All I am saying is that death is an easy thing to come by, and some deaths have greater meaning than others."

"Again, a threat. Only those who are cornered or have something to hide issue threats."

"You misconstrue me. I am explaining more than I

should, more than is safe for you to hear. I am, in a manner of speaking, trying to help you."

"Very well." Holmes drew himself up to his full height. "Then, as you are in such an informative mood, tell me what is meant by 'the Great Old Ones'."

Now it was Gong-Fen's turn to flounder, if only briefly. His aura of refined urbanity evaporated and I glimpsed something beneath it: a level of primal fury all the more incongruous in a man so polished, so much an avatar of modern civilisation. The fury was born not of displeasure, or so I judged, but of dread. It was there and gone in a fraction of a second, so quickly concealed one might not be sure one had seen it at all. Yet it lingered in my recollection, and made me think that Gong-Fen Shou was both more and less than he wished everyone to assume.

"Where did you hear that phrase?" he enquired.

"Dr Stamford himself uttered it, shortly before he committed suicide in a most ghastly fashion."

"You were with him before he died." It was less a question than a realisation. "That is interesting. And perhaps regrettable. What else did he say?"

"He was far from sane at the end. He spoke in a peculiar language that may simply have been gibberish but was probably not. He also mumbled something ominous-sounding and apocalyptic. It was all most peculiar and rather horrible."

"I can imagine."

"I think you can do more than imagine, Mr Gong-Fen. I am of the view that you were one of the last people to see Stamford before he was reduced to a state of maddened incoherence, and that you were actively responsible for it."

"Again you sling mud. Were the good doctor here anything like an impartial witness, I might have you up in front of a judge for slander."

"How quick you are to resort to vague menaces. You never repudiate explicitly."

"That would be to give credence to your claptrap."

"Such tact. Such defensiveness. Mr Gong-Fen, let me be frank."

"Oh, please do."

"I have developed a surprising liking for you while at the same time being convinced that you are one of the wickedest villains in London. If I could only prove the latter beyond reasonable doubt, we would be holding this conversation with bars between us. You on the wrong side of them, of course."

"Of course."

"It might be best if you were simply to confess. Make a clean breast of it. You would save us both a great deal of time and bother. In the absence of that, you will find me a dogged and relentless pursuer, a veritable bloodhound. I shall not rest until you are brought to justice."

Gong-Fen acknowledged this with a slight tilt of the head. "So be it. You are after answers. You seek definitive solutions."

"I do. It is my *modus vivendi*."

"In that respect you are typical of your era and your milieu. A pre-eminent Victorian. For you and your peers, everything is explicable. Everything can be rationalised through logic and science. Everything must bow before the might of industry, the miracles of technology and the march of progress. You British have built an empire on empiricism. You pay lip service to religion and the mysteries of the divine, but it is cold, hard fact that you really worship. You look upward with your telescopes and downward with your microscopes, and there, in space and water drops, the stars and bacteria, do you find God."

"A pretty sermon."

"Wasn't it? Thank you. Yet you, Mr Holmes, and you, Dr Watson, are ignorant. Quite blinkered. You think you know so much, and you know so little. It is rather sad. The universe is far larger and far deeper than you can possibly suspect."

"These metaphysical maunderings of yours are becoming tiresome," said Holmes. "I am aware that your race has a long tradition of mysticism. The Taoist philosophy. The eternal struggle for harmony embodied by yin and yang. Alchemy. Meditation. Confucianism. *Neidan. Qigong*. All of that. I find it bizarre that a man such as yourself, so inherently contemporary and westernised, should start making reference to practices he left behind in his homeland years ago."

"Ha ha. I do not refer to China at all, as it happens, but to a cosmology more ancient than that country's, than any country's – one that has lain long dormant, hidden from view, known only to a handful."

"Elucidate."

"I wonder…" Gong-Fen fixed Holmes with a steely gaze. "What if I were to give you the opportunity to learn everything you need to? To discover all the answers you could conceivably want?"

I sensed that the interchange between the two men was arriving at its climax. The conversation had been somewhat like a chess match – full of feints, gambits, sacrifice and forced moves – and now the endgame was upon us. Perhaps this was where Gong-Fen had intended it to wind up all along. He had been manipulating the board cunningly, arranging his pieces to leave Holmes in a position of checkmate, with no alternative but to capitulate.

"What precisely are you offering?" Holmes said. He was wary but obviously more than a little intrigued.

"A form of enlightenment. Come with me, today, right now, this moment, and you will be given the chance to see things as they really are."

"Don't listen to him, Holmes," I urged. "It's a trap."

"I swear I will not harm you," said Gong-Fen. "That is a solemn promise. On my honour."

"A quality you signally lack."

"On the contrary, Dr Watson, I am a man whose word is his bond. Ask anyone who knows me. Well, Mr Holmes?"

"These answers – they will include the truth behind Stamford's fate and the emaciated corpses?"

"The revelation will be all-encompassing. You will emerge from the experience with a broader, profounder appreciation of how things are than ever you had before."

So does the witch in the fairy tale entice Hansel and Gretel into her gingerbread cottage, by blandishment and the lure of sweetmeats galore. So does the spider weave its web, waiting for the fly to buzz by and ensnare itself.

"All right," said Holmes. "I accept."

"No!" I said. "Holmes, what are you doing?"

"Taking steps to solve the case, Watson."

"You have no idea what he's offering. This is hazardous beyond reckoning. He will whisk you away and no one will ever see you again. There will be an ambush and you will end up like Simple Simeon and the others. No, worse, like Stamford."

"I cannot turn down an opportunity like this."

"You jolly well can, and you will," I said. I braced him on both arms, as though to pin him to the spot. "I forbid it. We have not been friends long, but I feel I have earned the right to tell you that you are acting rashly and I cannot countenance it. Having only just met you, I would consider it a great misfortune then to lose you almost immediately."

"This is very touching," said Gong-Fen.

"Keep quiet, you," I said, jabbing a forefinger at him. "Holmes, if you insist on going through with this, at the very least let me come along. I can protect you. I can watch your back."

"No," said Gong-Fen. "Just Mr Holmes, alone. That is my one stipulation, and it is not negotiable."

"Then…" I lunged for the poker that lay beside the grate. "Drastic measures. I will brain you, Gong-Fen." I brandished the implement above my head, fully as though I was about to bring it down with force on his cranium. "That will render the whole issue moot. How about that?"

The Chinese millionaire regarded me levelly, maintaining the same damnable imperturbability with which he greeted almost everything. If I intimidated him at all, he gave not the least outward indication of it.

Out of sheer spite, I swung the poker. It was not my intention to strike him. I merely wanted to see him blink and perhaps cringe – to wipe that smug look of imperviousness off his face. But if the poker were to connect by accident, would that be so terrible? I thought not.

In the event, my hand was stayed by a powerful grip. Holmes, moving with astonishing speed, intercepted the blow, catching my wrist and at the same time wresting the poker from my clutches.

"Enough, my boy," said he. "I am going with Gong-Fen, and that's final. And in case you get it into your head to try that little stunt again…"

He grasped the poker at either end and, by sheer muscular force of his arms, bent it, first into a horseshoe shape and then further until the ends crossed and it resembled a lower-case Greek alpha. He accomplished this with very little apparent effort, yet a circus strongman might have struggled to replicate the feat. Angry as I was, I could not help but be impressed.

"There we have it." The now-useless poker clattered to the floor. "My mind is made up. Gong-Fen? Allow me to wash, shave and dress, and then I am all yours."

*

Twenty minutes later, Holmes was ready. Meantime Gong-Fen and I had sat in awkward silence, I glaring at the Chinaman, he purporting not to notice whilst flicking idly through a copy of *Blackwood's* which happened to be lying around.

They departed together, with an extraordinary kind of genteel bonhomie, and I was left impotent and fuming. I fully anticipated that Holmes would never return. He was putting his head in the lion's mouth, and the creature would snap its jaws shut.

It may seem surprising to readers of this chronicle – not that there will be any, save its author – that Holmes would so readily put himself in danger. I have characterised him elsewhere as a cerebral calculating machine, never one to head off into the unknown without carefully assaying the pros and cons first.

But the Holmes of 1880 was still a young Holmes, with a young man's streak of recklessness and impetuosity. In later years his dynamism would be tempered somewhat by intellect, although it would never fade completely. In the early days, however, he was prone to going out on a limb without necessarily ascertaining first whether it would support his weight.

After Gong-Fen's clarence had clattered off into the night, all I could do was pace and fret. Come dawn, I dressed and continued to wait. Mrs Hudson brought up breakfast for two and then lunch for one. I touched not a morsel of the food. My appetite was gone. Afternoon shaded into evening, with still no sign of Holmes. My anxiety only deepened. Night fell around five o'clock. In the wake of an overcast day, rain set in. All was dismal.

I may have slept, but if so it was only in snatches, a fitful few minutes here and there, ensconced in an armchair, restless, unhappy. At dinnertime Mrs Hudson lay a plate of delicious-smelling hot stew in front of me and took it away cold a while later, with a cluck of disapproval.

At last, as the hour was closing in on midnight, a key turned in the front door. I sprang to my feet and took the stairs three at a time down to the hallway.

The man who staggered across the threshold was Sherlock Holmes, of that there was no doubt.

But it was not the same Sherlock Holmes who had left the house almost twenty-four hours before.

CHAPTER TEN

The Box Hill Barrows

HAGGARD OF FACE, BLOODSHOT OF EYE, HOLMES all but collapsed into my arms. I helped him up to our rooms, noting the mud that caked his boots and trousers and the extensive grass stains on his jacket. Scratches criss-crossed his cheeks, forehead and hands, and he was shivering almost uncontrollably. I coaxed the fire to a searing burn, sat him before it, and plied him with brandy. His clothing, damp from the rain, steamed as it dried. His shivers abated, although not completely. Some colour returned to his cheeks.

"What did that monster do to you?" I asked.

In response, his head lolled and he moved one hand listlessly, holding up a finger, begging patience. Eventually, collecting himself, he spoke. The voice that issued from his mouth was scarcely a croak.

"He was right, Watson. Gong-Fen. When he said that the universe is far larger and far deeper than I could possibly suspect. Damn him, he was right."

"I don't understand."

"Neither did I. But now I think I do."

Holmes reached for his pipe with a trembling hand. He selected the cherry-wood rather than the clay, but when he tried to fill it, shreds of tobacco tumbled everywhere, despite its broader bowl. I had to perform the task for him, and apply the match as well. It was distressing to see so able a man reduced to such febrility that he was incapable of carrying out the most basic of actions.

After a few restorative puffs, he gathered enough strength to begin recounting his recent exploits.

*

At first Holmes had presumed Gong-Fen would be taking him to Limehouse, until the clarence turned right on Marylebone Road rather than left. Thence they drove across Hyde Park, so that Gong-Fen's Belgravia townhouse seemed their likeliest destination. This too proved not to be the case, for the carriage continued southward, bypassing that district and crossing the river. Holmes settled back in the seat. It seemed he was in for a long journey.

All the while, Gong-Fen talked about himself. He described his upbringing in Qinghai, a remote highland province of north-west China close to the border with Tibet. His family were farmers, scratching a living from the harsh, arid soil, all but penniless. Young Shou always had ambition, a dream of bettering himself, and in due course, when he was old enough, he left home and worked his way south to Peking.

There he found employment in various lowly occupations, from emptying chamberpots at a house of ill repute to vending dumplings and rice balls from a street cart. He rid himself of his rustic accent and dialect, which made him sound like a country bumpkin and often elicited mockery. He learned to emulate the more elaborate and refined speech patterns of the Pekingese until he could pass for one of them. He discovered a chameleon-like talent for fitting in.

In the capital he saw at first hand the extent to which

the opium trade was ravaging his country. There were addicts everywhere, men and women forced into ragged penury, selling everything they had, even their children, in order to feed their dependency on the narcotic. There were only two classes of people who benefited from opium: representatives of the British East India Company, which grew the poppies in India and shipped the drug to China, and the local middlemen who sold it on. By this means the East India Company was managing to claw back much of the money that had flowed into China from Britain since the mid-1600s, when the country had opened up the market for its goods – predominantly silk, porcelain and tea – to the wider world. The opium trade was imperialism by underhand means, a way of subjugating a nation without a shot being fired, so it ought to have come as no surprise when China decided enough was enough and the Emperor took action, confiscating and destroying large quantities of the drug. Britain retaliated with gunboats, and so the fuse was lit for the First and Second Opium Wars.

Gong-Fen had by then risen to become one of those middlemen himself, doing business with the East India Company, meeting their ships off the coast in a double-masted sampan, paying for their cargo with silver and transporting it back to the mainland for distribution. He hated what opium was doing to China, but his survival instincts told him this was where the money was and so he was able to swallow his moral indignation in the name of turning a profit. By the time he was twenty-five, he was fairly wealthy. By thirty, he was unquestionably rich. He achieved this through being more ruthless than his rivals and at the same time undercutting them. He expanded his sphere of influence from Peking down to Shanghai, and then on to Hong Kong and Macao, shouldering aside anyone who stood in his way. He became fluent in English, the better to make his deals with the British, and they in turn favoured him because he was courteous and articulate. One of the East India Company's sea captains referred to him, to his face, as "the whitest yellow man I have ever met", meaning it as a great compliment.

After the Second Opium War ended, the Convention of Peking was signed, its provisions including the legalisation of the opium trade. China, in the view of most of its inhabitants, had been thoroughly humiliated. Emperor Xianfeng exiled himself to the north and died there not long after. The country was forced to cough up crippling indemnity payments, and now stood exposed to all manner of foreign influences, some civilising, some rapacious. As far as Gong-Fen was concerned, his homeland was dead. The outside world beckoned.

"So you came to England," said Holmes. "You decided better the devil you knew."

"Just so," said Gong-Fen. "The future did not lie in China. It lay here, in the embrace of those who had defeated China. Here I could apply the lessons I had learned and excel at being 'the whitest yellow man'. Tolerated by the establishment, feted without being approved of, something of a novelty in polite society, I have risen tirelessly and smoothly to the top – or at least, as far as someone of my race may go."

"Yet you still harbour a simmering resentment of us.

Hence your opium dens. Your little revenge on the British Empire."

"Can you blame me for that? When I see an Englishman brought low by opium addiction, wracked by cravings, spending all he has until he owns nothing but the shirt on his back, abased by the same drug that brought so much misery to the land of my birth, can you not begrudge me a secret smile of satisfaction?" Gong-Fen no longer feigned innocence about his less savoury practices or his baser impulses. The time for pretence, it seemed, was past.

Onward the clarence rumbled, weaving through the slumbering suburbs of Wandsworth, Wimbledon and Morden, and Holmes now surmised that it was Gong-Fen's Surrey residence for which they were making. The Chinaman owned a fifty-acre estate on the fringes of Dorking, his Regency manor house nestling amid gardens designed by Capability Brown.

Again my friend was proved wrong, although this time only partially so. The carriage did halt outside the house; it was merely a stopover. Holmes was invited to remain in his seat while Gong-Fen went indoors. Dawn broke, mistily, and the coachman fetched fresh horses. Gong-Fen returned carrying a small, iron-banded chest, and the clarence rolled back up the drive, out into the countryside.

"Not far now," said the Chinaman, sitting with the chest perched across his knees. "You won't have to wait much longer."

*

"At that point," Holmes admitted to me, "I was feeling some trepidation."

"Only some?" I said. "If it were me, I would have been quite unmanned by my apprehension."

"I doubt that," said he. "Stout fellow like you? Never."

*

As they wove their way through the wilds of Surrey, Gong-Fen started to talk about religion and how the conventional faiths misinterpreted the nature of the divine.

"A god," he said, "is not some benevolent, omnipotent being who created us as an expression of his love. That is an anthropomorphic fallacy, brought about by man's craven desire for an ineffable father figure to pat him on the head every so often and tell him he is doing well. It is a modern affectation that has grown to be the orthodoxy in an age when we have tamed the wilderness and circumnavigated the globe and appointed ourselves masters of all we survey. The further one goes back in history, you'll find, the more hostile and uncaring the gods become. I don't just mean the Jehovah of the Old Testament, smiting His enemies and sending plagues and demanding that people suffer in His name. Nor do I mean the pagan pantheons with their endless debauchery and chicanery, no better than those who worshipped them and offered them libations and sacrifices. I am referring to a time before that, when mankind was freshly out of the cave and one step up from pure savagery, and civilisation, such as it was, consisted of warring fiefdoms ruled by barbarian kings. A dark antediluvian age, an age of stone and steel and fire, of which almost nothing remains for archaeologists to dig up and ponder."

That age, Gong-Fen said, was the age of the first gods, and its gods were those it deserved. Gods who were a true reflection of the violence and chaos that lay at the heart of every man then and still does, buried but alive, even today. Gods who desired nothing more than conquest, rapine and slaughter. Gods who revelled in carnage and considered men to be on a par with cattle, or at best pets.

To illustrate, he pointed to the field they were passing, where a shepherd was prodding sheep out from a barn to nibble on the frosty grass. "Those gods possessed as little sympathy for our lives as that man does for the lives of his flock. To him, his sheep are merely a source of food and wool. They furnish him with a livelihood, and he will hobble them, lop off their tails, castrate them where necessary, and kill them for meat when the time comes, all without the least pricking of conscience."

It was only when he arrived in England that Gong-Fen became aware of the existence of these ancient deities. Before then he had been blissfully oblivious. The folk religion of his childhood, with its dragons and nature spirits and countless propitiatory rituals to bring luck and prosperity, was something he had left behind when he moved from Qinghai to Peking. After that, nothing had taken its place. He had lived in a religious vacuum, and was content with that, if he ever gave it any thought at all – a state of apostate grace.

London, however, was where he discovered the truth: that the gods are amongst us, and want only our lives and our destruction. Up until then, gods had been a fanciful delusion as far as he was concerned. Let simpletons and the unlearned believe in them. In England's capital, of all places – that peerless urban jewel, heart of empire, epicentre of the modern world – this presumption of his was rudely shattered.

"There is more to London than the average Londoner realises, Mr Holmes. Far more. It is a city resting on primordial foundations, with neglected and forgotten corners where the old interpenetrates the new. London was there well before the Romans came and built a settlement. Long, long ago, the tribes of primitive Britain camped at a confluence of rivers large and small, and erected their temples and shrines, and paid brutal tribute to the entities they venerated by offering them the lives of captured foes and of the undesirables from amongst their own number. Do you know how the city gained its name?"

"Surely from Londinium, the name the Romans gave it."

"So the history books tell us. But the etymology of 'Londinium' itself is uncertain. According to Geoffrey of Monmouth a semi-mythological pre-Roman king called Lud was the actual founder of the city and 'Londinium' derives from *his* name, but scholars dispute this, and it has lately been suggested that the word is a corruption of a Celtic term, *lowonida*, meaning a river too wide to ford."

"That would describe the Thames, certainly."

"However," said Gong-Fen, "in a small number of little-read texts you will find associations between the capital and a god going by the name of Lobon."

"Can't say I've heard of him."

"Few have. Lobon was one amongst several deities whose influence was strong in the area at that time, three or four millennia BC. A warrior god, his followers were belligerent and ferocious even by the standards of the day, and thus came to dominate the neighbouring tribes. From 'Lobon', by a long and winding path of translation and mutation, we arrive at 'London'."

"This is all very fascinating, I'm sure, but…"

"But what is the relevance? Merely to lay the groundwork for what lies ahead, Mr Holmes. I have had my own mentor in this process of gnostic revelation. Now I feel it is my turn to don the mantle of mentor and impart what I have learned to one whom I deem a worthy recipient."

Holmes bowed to Gong-Fen as if flattered, which I think he was to some extent. He had noticed that the clarence had begun an uphill climb, and the gradient of the road was growing ever steeper and the horses' efforts more laboured. His knowledge of the geography of the Dorking area was not comprehensive, but to his mind they must be ascending the slope of the North Downs, that ridge of chalk hills which stretches all the way from Guildford to the White Cliffs of Dover. In fact, they were travelling to one of the highest points on the North Downs, Box Hill.

When the road petered out and the clarence could go no further, Holmes and Gong-Fen disembarked. They continued the rest of the way to the top on foot, with the mysterious chest suspended between them, each of them holding one of its handles. They must have looked, Holmes said, for all the world like a couple of friends setting out on a picnic. The chest was heavy, however, and although he had no idea what it contained, he heard objects click and clank inside it as they walked.

They gained the summit, and a vista of Surrey and Sussex stretched away at their feet, twenty miles or more to the South Downs. On a brighter, less cloudy day this would have afforded a breathtaking prospect, rural England in all its forested, hedgerow-parcelled, gently undulating glory. Even on a gloomy December day, with the ploughed fields brown and the trees leafless, it had its charms.

But they were not there to enjoy the view. Gong-Fen led Holmes to a set of pillow-shaped mounds which he identified as burial barrows, the resting places of prehistoric dignitaries – kings, chieftains and high priests. They set down the chest and Gong-Fen unbuckled the leather straps that secured it. From its interior he brought out a large, worn, aged book, some jars of powder, and a hypodermic syringe filled with a brownish liquid. He spent the next half hour shaking the powder carefully out onto the grass, describing a large circle with it and then drawing peculiar ornate symbols at points equidistant around the perimeter, all the while consulting the book for reference.

Holmes looked on, stamping his feet and rubbing himself to stave off the cold. He could not determine the nature of the powder other than that it was pale grey stuff, some kind of ash perhaps, clumpy and feathery. As for the book, the gold leaf lettering on the spine was so rubbed and worn as to be almost illegible, but he managed to make out the author's name, one Ludwig Prinn, and construed that the title was *De Vermis Mysteriis*, or something close to it.

The clouds loomed very low overhead, sending down opaque tendrils to brush the caps of the bare-branched trees which stood in a semicircle overlooking the spot like the audience at an amphitheatre. All was quiet and seemed to grow quieter as Gong-Fen worked. The occasional croak of a rook or clap of a woodpigeon's wings were the only sounds to disturb the hush, and these soon dwindled and died out, until all that remained was the sough of a soft wind, like a continuous, wavering exhalation of breath.

At last Gong-Fen declared that everything was ready, and instructed Holmes to roll up one sleeve.

"What preparation is that?" Holmes asked as the Chinaman tapped the syringe to dislodge any air bubbles, then depressed the plunger to expel a few tentative droplets of the liquid from the needle's tip.

"A concoction of my own devising," came the reply. "An amalgam of various substances – one might call it a cocktail – the main constituent ingredients being opium and cocaine, added to which are various extracts of herbs known to grow only in mainland China."

*

"And you let him inject it into you!" I said, aghast. "Holmes, are you mad? Do you have any idea how rash that was?"

"I hardly had a choice. Without the drug, Gong-Fen said it would be all for naught. Nothing would happen. My 'dream-quest', as he termed it, would not occur. I might as well just stand there twiddling my thumbs. If one wished to draw down lightning, one needed a lightning conductor, and such was the drug."

"Still, old man…"

"Nag me later, Watson. For now, keep listening. I have to relate this while it is still fresh in my mind. Later, I may come to believe it was all just some feverish delusion."

*

With Gong-Fen's "cocktail" circulating through his veins, Holmes stepped into the powder circle. The Chinaman himself stayed outside. He instructed Holmes not to disturb any of the markings.

"The powder with which you have drawn them," Holmes said. "It appears to have a high calcium content. Would I be correct in thinking…?"

"Bone ash," Gong-Fen confirmed.

"Ah. And I hazard that it is not the animal bone ash used in the manufacturing of bone china."

"Its source is the ossuary beneath St Bride's Church on Fleet Street. Not easy to obtain, nor cheap. The crypt keeper drove a hard bargain. Now kindly sit down and make yourself as comfortable as you can."

Holmes seated himself cross-legged on the ground, trying to ignore the chilly dampness that seeped through the seat of his trousers; trying to ignore, too, the proximity to his person of a significant quantity of pulverised human bone.

Gong-Fen reopened the book, flicked through to the page he sought, and began to read aloud.

The words were unknown but the language was not. Holmes recognised it as the self-same tongue used by

Stamford in his cell at Scotland Yard. All those rough agglomerations of consonants, the glottal stops within the individual words, the awful snarling cadences – it could be no other language, because no other language resembled it.

As the words insinuated themselves snakelike into his ears, he could simultaneously feel the drug swirling through his bloodstream. The sensation was akin to tiny ice-cold fingers crawling beneath his skin. He felt fear and curiosity both at once, a weird kind of eager calm, as though there were an unavoidable rightness about this experience, a necessity. In time he no longer listened to Gong-Fen's voice. He heard the ungainly rhythms of the sentences and knew them to be an invocation of some sort, an appeal to an otherworldly power, but they seemed to be receding behind a veil, becoming distant and insignificant. He blinked, and suddenly perceived that he was alone on the hilltop. Gong-Fen was gone. All was still. Even the breeze had dropped.

Then the dream-quest began.

CHAPTER ELEVEN

The Dream-Quest of Sherlock Holmes

TO BEGIN WITH, HOLMES THOUGHT THAT THE EYE-blink must in fact have been a brief period of insensibility, during which Gong-Fen had taken the opportunity to slip away. It occurred to him then that the Chinaman must have been playing an elaborate prank on him. All that talk of occult matters in the clarence, the magic circle of powder, the invocation – it was simply a big build-up to nothing, a crescendo followed by a resounding anti-climax. The powder was not human bone ash but only animal. The so-called drug had merely been tinted water. The disconcerting physical sensations he had experienced had been no more than psychosomatic. A hoax, and he had fallen for it wholesale.

He was quite incensed by the notion, and resolved that Gong-Fen would not get away with making a fool of him.

Then he noticed that the wind had stopped blowing. This in itself was not remarkable, but far more so was the silence left by the wind's absence. Holmes had never encountered a silence so total, so all-negating, so deadening. From near and far there came not a single sound. The countryside is never truly quiet. There is invariably the chirrup or chatter of some woodland creature, a cowbell, a birdcall, the yell of a farmhand, the trundle of cart wheels, *something*. But now Holmes was enveloped in absolute noiselessness. Even when he shifted a foot on the grass, it generated not the least rustle. All he could hear was his heartbeat and his breathing.

The clouds were not moving. This was possibly even more unnerving than the silence. They hung as though painted, the backcloth to a stage play. The world seemed in stasis, frozen in a moment in time.

Or between moments in time. That was how it felt: as though he had slipped into the gap between the tick and the tock of the clock. Holmes took out his hunter watch to confirm the supposition, and sure enough it had stopped. The second hand was stationary. He wound the side-winder, but the watch refused to go. Either it was broken or the world had somehow come to a complete standstill.

Then a man appeared.

Holmes was not aware of seeing him approach. The man was not there; then all at once he was, right in front of him, within arm's reach.

He was clad in a kind of kilt, with fur boots on his feet and a cloak draped across one shoulder, secured by a finely wrought copper clasp. Gold armlets encircled his biceps and a gold torc his neck. Bright blue markings zigzagged across his skin; Holmes took them to be daubings of woad, the plant dye. His hair was shoulder-length and shaggily cut, and his complexion overall was weatherbeaten and swarthy.

He was muscular in the way that no modern cultivator of the physique is. His lithe, sinewy body was that of one who has known hardship and strife in abundance, for whom life has been a battle on every front. He was carrying, as if in illustration of this, an axe with a double blade. It hung from his hand, haft clasped loosely, head near the ground. Both of its cutting edges were nicked and pitted, and Holmes could not help but think that these marks indicated that the axe had struck both armour and bone, and often.

The man eyed Holmes speculatively, then grunted, although it was not obvious whether this signified approval or the opposite. It may have been a greeting. When he finally spoke, it was in gruff tones, and somehow Holmes knew it was in an unrecorded, unremembered language, although he could understand it perfectly and the man in return could understand him.

"You have come. Who are you?"

"I might ask you the same question. I am Sherlock Holmes, and either you are real and Gong-Fen has gone to a lot of trouble getting you all dressed up like some sort of Celtic warrior, or I am dreaming you and you are little more than a figment of my imagination. Whichever it is, I would judge that you represent some ancient ancestor. That is what you are supposed to be, or actually are, depending on how one looks at it."

"I am ignorant of any Gong-Fen," said the man. "Is he a druid? A wizard?"

"He may well fancy himself as such. I still am not cognisant of your name."

"My name is immaterial. Know that I was a chieftain once, leader of a great tribe. We came from the north, from the harsh mountainous lands where the winters are long and the winds blow hard and cold. We fought our way southward through year after year, generation after generation, expanding our domain, absorbing the tribes who allowed themselves to be absorbed, eradicating those that would not. We reached this far, almost to the white coast, and the majority of Britain belonged to us. That was when I erected my fortress by the banks of the great Tamesas river and called it home. There I held sway with my iron axe and my iron will. I had paid tribute to the gods in blood and pillage, and for a time I reaped the rewards, mighty and uncontested."

"No doubt you were. But all good things come to an end, eh? Reading between the lines, that is my impression."

Holmes evinced a rare sanguinity before this imposing stranger. Despite the man's rugged, surly demeanour and sizeable battle weapon, he sensed that he had nothing to fear from him. Their meeting had been engineered for his benefit, to bring only edification, not destruction.

"The gods," said the nameless chieftain, "are not always appeased, and are easily disappointed. They demand souls released in the tumult of armed combat or on the altar stone by the priest's sacred blade. Usually that is enough to sate their appetites and ensure they do not awaken fully from their slumbers. Sometimes it is not, and then the world of men had best beware."

"You can keep them docile by feeding them. Is that it? Rather as a mother contents a fretful infant in the night by suckling."

The chieftain laughed balefully. "They are not the infants. We are. The gods are old, older than time. They came here from the stars, from other worlds, while the Earth was still young and unformed. Some say they were banished, others that they left of their own free will, seeking pastures new. They rode across the cosmic gulfs on the backs of comets, arriving here in their hordes. They were not one race but many intertwined. They made this world their own, dividing it up between them. But they were not at peace. It is not in their nature."

"They fought amongst themselves."

"Over millions of years, these star-spawned creatures of nigh limitless power and fearsome knowledge clashed and clashed again. Son rebelled against father. Servant battled master. Brother warred with brother. They ravaged continents with their competition. Their weapons were terrible, of a nature and magnitude hard to comprehend. They razed mountains and fissured canyons. It is reckoned that all the land masses of the world were one, until the gods' hostilities broke them up and set them moving apart."

"There are geologists – Antonio Snider-Pellegrini for one – who would offer an alternative explanation for the phenomenon of continental drift."

The chieftain glared at Holmes.

"But do go on," Holmes said.

"In time, the more powerful of the gods established themselves as the rulers of the Earth," the chieftain said. "The lesser ones withdrew, some underground, others beneath the sea. Many were imprisoned for the crime of being on the losing side, and their dungeons were not always on Earth but elsewhere, in other realms, within folds in reality. A kind of truce was agreed and enmities were put aside, although not always forgiven. Between Cthulhu and his half-brother Hastur the Unspeakable, for instance, there will never be anything other than hatred."

At those two names, particularly the first, Holmes succumbed to a shudder that was involuntary, deep-seated, almost atavistic. Although he had never heard them before in his life, it was as though some inner part of himself, some embedded race-memory, knew to be frightened at their mention. Cthulhu. Hastur. The words spoke to him of dread and rage and horror.

"Slowly," the chieftain went on, "the gods sank into sleep, as the bear hibernates for winter. Their conflicts were done, and it was time to rest. There are cycles in the cosmos, just as there are seasons in the year. Even immortals, with all their power, must perforce close their eyes and dream. In their far-flung cities, in their caverns, in the spaces between worlds, they now lie dormant. Yet they are watching us still. They have always watched us, observing mankind as we emerged from a state of animal ignorance and awakened to self-knowledge. The Great Old Ones and their kin are aware of us, and now and again call to us, wanting whatever we can give them."

"You, I take it, did not give them enough. That was your downfall."

The chieftain nodded sombrely. He cast a look backwards at the barrows. "There my bones lie mouldering. My flesh became food for worms. I was an acolyte of Lobon. My forebears were from Sarnath originally, where Lobon was the ruling deity, and when that city lapsed into ruin, his faith travelled with the populace in their exodus out of the land of Mnar. I am a direct descendant of those that came to these islands, and to me, as king of my tribe, fell the duty of maintaining Lobon's favour. Since he is a warrior god, the blood and hearts of our enemies were sufficient for that."

"'Were'. What changed?"

"I changed. I wearied of strife. As age encroached, my taste for battle waned. I wished only to preside over the lands I already had gained, not to acquire fresh territory. Hence our inexorable southward march stalled. Lobon was displeased. He came for me in the night, in the form of an ivy-crowned youth bearing a spear. We fought in my bedchamber, he and I, but there could be only one outcome." The chieftain sighed. "I wielded my axe bravely and with vigour, but who can win against a god?"

"Who indeed? At least your people buried you in a pleasant spot, an exalted position for the grave of an exalted ruler."

"This? This was done at Lobon's bidding, the final insult. From here, one looks out over the region of the country I refused to conquer, the last corner of Britain which, in my aversion to further bloodshed, I left untouched. This is not an honour. This is punishment."

"You are sure, though, that it was Lobon himself you fought? Might it not have been some usurper, a young upstart with pretensions to your throne?" Holmes was keen to propound a rational interpretation of the chieftain's death. He was a detective seeking a murder rather than an act of divine retribution.

"Even if it was merely that, it makes no difference. He was an aspect of Lobon regardless. A killer who appears in the guise of a god is a god by any other name, doing that god's work."

"I see."

"I fear you do not see," said the chieftain. "I fear your field of vision is still far too narrow."

"Well, how would you go about widening its scope?"

The next instant, Holmes regretted posing the question. For, in answer, the chieftain hoisted his axe and brought it whirling round. Before Holmes could duck, before he could even move, one of those chipped blades was scything towards him and...

*

...failing to make contact. But not missing either. The axe passed through him. He felt it, a silvery *swish*, an intangible thread of ice entering and exiting. Yet he knew he was unhurt, intact. It was a kind of severance, but not of head from neck or trunk from legs. Instead, a severance of soul from body. All at once his intellect was free from its corporeal shell. He was thought, pure essence of being. He was everything that was Sherlock Holmes save the fleshly frame that carried him around.

He flew. Up from Box Hill, up from Surrey, up from England. Out over the Channel, over Europe, Arabia, India, Asia. He flew across the face of the planet like a streak of light. And, from a birdlike vantage, he saw sights. Such sights.

He flew to an island in the heart of the Pacific, a speck of volcanic rock littered with rotting fish carcasses and topped by a white monolith. Nearby, in a seabed crevasse, a bulbous, scaly creature – part fish, part Cyclops – was stirring, rising to the surface.

He flew to another, larger Pacific island where stood a lost city with buildings whose contours and angles were irregular and seemed to fold away when looked at, as though their makers were privy to a branch of geometry unknown to other mathematicians. Here, in slimy-walled vaults, lay human-sized monsters, all of them fast asleep and clustered around a much larger bat-winged behemoth, also slumbering, whose visage Holmes only glimpsed and was glad not to view more closely.

He flew on, out across the snowy wastes of Antarctica, down to another abandoned city, this one a place of massive walls and deep-dug catacombs. He saw animals that resembled nothing so much as albino penguins six feet tall, waddling along the streets, their eyes vestigial slits, quite blind. He saw, too, a black protoplasmic mass somewhat like a jellyfish, its gelatinous surface writhing with tendrils and sensory organs that had no direct analogy to any that he knew of from his studies in biology.

Onward he flew to the southern states of America, to witness a hellish voodoo rite in the swamps of Louisiana, and thence to Greenland, where an all too similar rite was in progress. Whether in the humid heat of the bayou or the frigid cold of the Arctic Circle, whether the participants were half-naked seamen of West Indian origin or fur-clad Eskimos, the chants and dances were more or less identical, and the object of frenzied reverence in each case was an effigy of that vast bat-winged beast he had spied earlier asleep amid its minions, the one whose tentacle-adorned face he had shrunk from scrutinising.

He flew next to New England, where in that most civil portion of the United States there proved to be more sites of lurking horror than there were stars in the sky. He perceived them as warts on skin or cancerous growths on an otherwise healthy organ, a disease blighting the deep green valleys and cosy small towns and bustling cities and endless forests and rolling farmland, clusters and speckles of corruption arising in the unlikeliest, most apparently innocuous of places.

Whereas his audience with the swarthy chieftain had seemed to occur within a single unending moment, Holmes was conscious of time passing at extraordinary speed during his back-and-forth grand tour of the globe's darkest corners. Night and day alternated, flickering like a guttering candle flame, and the interchange between the two grew faster and faster still. He felt himself accelerating, whirling through the air with such velocity that in the end gravity lost its grip on him and he was projected outward, flung headlong from Earth's atmosphere into space. Like a living rocket he shot across the universe, past stars, past galaxies, through the vast emptinesses between. Somewhere at the very edge of creation, so far from our solar system that our sun was comparable to a mote of dust, he arrived at a place where dozens of planets stood joined together by bridges of incalculable size. These worlds pivoted around one another in carefully preordained orbits, like some cosmic orrery, and as a whole revolved in a continuous, steady circuit around the periphery of space.

Their inhabitants were many and bizarre. Some were dark and formless, others incandescent balls of energy. Some were humanoid, others animalistic. Some walked proudly, wreathed in mist or flame, whilst others crawled or slithered or oozed. They were beings of such omnipotence that they had almost forgotten what it meant to have needs or desires. They wafted through their endless existences, occasionally encountering one another for a desultory exchange of conversation, otherwise dwelling in splendid, stately solitude. Somehow Holmes knew them to be the Elder Gods, the forerunners of the Great Old Ones, creatures who had ignited into life shortly after the universe itself was birthed. After a billion epochs they no longer cared about anything, not even themselves. They simply *were*, and that was enough for them.

From the limits of space Holmes was abruptly drawn back, reversing his trajectory as though attached to an India-rubber band that had suddenly been released. He was whisked from the frontier of all-that-is to the very centre, the core around which the cosmos spun.

Here lay chaos, a churning maelstrom of light and dark, in the midst of which floated a number of strange citadels that spiralled and twirled, utterly at the whim of the titanic currents around them. One resembled a snowflake, another was composed of polyhedrons, while a third had walls that rippled and flowed like water. No two were alike.

They were the abodes of yet another pantheon of gods, but these, the Outer Gods, were uniformly avaricious and malign. They were things of fog and stone and jewel and flesh, and they waited. They waited to be summoned. They waited to be called upon with all due obeisance. They waited for the invitation to traverse the void and commit hideous, heinous acts. They could span immeasurable distances with but a thought, and would go anywhere as long as they deemed the journey worth their while. They emanated nothing except loathing, depravity and contempt. Even those that were creatures of light shone only so as to cast shadows and, in the shadows they cast, to slake their foul lusts.

Proximity to the Outer Gods instilled in Sherlock Holmes such terror that he thought he might go instantly, irredeemably mad. Nothing any human villain could do could compare to the evil of these deities. They were horror incarnate.

Holmes wished only to escape their presence, and particularly their notice, for he sensed that if any of these monsters were to turn its gaze on him, he would be lost forever, dragged into some howling pit of pain for all eternity, without hope of surcease. He had no idea how to engineer a retreat from that dire place other than to persuade himself that it was all some awful hallucination. Its reality, he said, was beyond question, yet if he could only convince himself otherwise, if he could be certain that he was perched atop Box Hill in Surrey and merely imagining everything he saw…

*

"My intellect saved me, Watson," he said. "The science of analytical reasoning in which I have trained myself rigorously since adolescence was what brought me back to myself. Without the power of my brain, my soul might even now be the plaything of some Outer God while my body would be discovered on that hilltop, bereft of sense and wit – something to be locked up and studied in vain by alienists, a drooling, incontinent wreck."

*

Through sheer force of will, Holmes denied the evidence of his eyes and insisted that he was on Earth, in his body, in a trance, nothing more. He was aware that several of the Outer Gods were becoming curious. They had detected an interloper. A creature made of quicksilver was extending an amoeba-like pseudopod in his direction. A blind, pustule-covered spider flung out an exploratory strand of silk from its web home, as though casting a line. On a balcony, a thing that might be mistaken for a beautiful woman began to sniff, raising her nose like a cat catching an odour on the breeze. If he did not leave immediately, he never would.

He thought of the chill North Downs air. He thought of the damp ground he was sitting on. He thought of the murky layer of cloud not far above. He thought of all these impressions, the sights and sounds and smells of the Surrey countryside in December, the mundanity of them, the hallowed ordinariness. They were facts. Data. All else – Great Old Ones, Elder Gods, Outer Gods – was mere conjecture and fancy. He did not deal in conjecture and fancy. Only that which could be proved by observation and logic was acceptable. He refused to countenance any other truth.

So it was that bit by bit, slowly but surely, Holmes came to. No longer did he hover at the centre of the universe, at the rim of an Olympus that was also a Hades. He had returned to his body, and he was cold all over, stiff of limb, aching, famished. He prised apart his eyelids, which felt so heavy it was like opening a set of rusted doors, and saw that twilight had come and night was all but fallen. He fumbled for his hunter, which was working once more and showed the hour to be past five.

When he attempted to stand, his legs failed him. He had spent the entire day in that cross-legged posture, exposed to the elements, and lack of circulation had left his lower half numb and inflexible. He had to resort to crouching on hands and knees until feeling had returned sufficiently to his extremities. Then he staggered out of the bone-powder circle and down the hill.

Gong-Fen was long gone. So was the clarence. Holmes was quite alone; and without even a dark-lantern to light his way, and the moon and stars occluded by cloud, he had to proceed with the utmost care. The road was little better than a rutted lane, and he stumbled often. Low-hanging branches slapped his face. Rocks tripped him. He was effectively blind.

To compound his woes, it started to rain. He considered finding a dry spot under a tree and sheltering there for the night, or at least until the downpour passed, but he suspected that if he halted, he might never set off again. So he forged on, until at last the lights of a cottage hove into view. Holmes knocked on the door, only to be greeted by a double-barrelled shotgun wielded by a less than friendly provincial. There followed a brisk exchange in which the householder encouraged the visitor to depart while the visitor begged succour from the householder. They were at an impasse, and then the man's wife came to the rescue, who scolded her husband for not recognising a gentleman when he saw one – a gentleman in distress, what was more – and invited Holmes inside and furnished him with a serving of hot, invigorating rabbit pie. Thereafter the woman prevailed upon her spouse to hook up the horse to the dog-cart and drive their guest into Dorking, which the man grudgingly did, and in short order Holmes was deposited at the railway station in time to catch the last train to Waterloo. Thanks to his dishevelled, besmirched condition, none of the other passengers wanted to ride next to him. They took one look and moved on to another compartment. It was a small blessing.

*

"And here we are," Holmes concluded. "I am keen to think that all that I underwent was a drug-induced mirage. There was no chieftain. There are no gods; old, elder or outer. All fantasy. Myriad are the ways Gong-Fen might have manufactured it. Perhaps, while I was under the influence of his 'cocktail', he remained with me, crouching by my side, whispering suggestions into my ear. My subconscious mind took these verbal cues and transformed them into heady visions. And perhaps the chieftain was, as I initially surmised, merely a man dressed up in costume, some penurious actor paid to play the part. That would certainly account for my being able to understand his tongue and he mine. The whole thing, then, was a rigorously stage-managed charade, a mystery play put on for my benefit alone, and I in my narcotised stupor was incapable of distinguishing make-believe from reality."

"To what end?" said I. "Why would the man go to such trouble?"

"To disorientate me. To bewilder me. Punishment for the disruption I caused at the Golden Lotus Hotel. And yet, Watson…"

"Yes?"

"Would that I could dismiss it so readily. Something inside me, deep in my marrow, is telling me that it all happened just as I have related. You must reckon me mad for saying so, and possibly you would be right. Yet, try as I might to rationalise the experience, I cannot. Gong-Fen's rite was not intended to drive me to the brink of insanity, although it very nearly succeeded in doing so. It was intended to open my eyes to the way things truly are. It has brought about a dreadful epiphany!"

I was tempted to offer him some form of consolation. I could have reassured him that, no, he was mistaken; it *had* been a delusion. I could have said that after a good night's rest, he would be able to put it all in perspective. By tomorrow he would be his old self again, and he would remember the events of today only as a kind of vague delirium. By the time the scratches on his face and hands had healed, he might not even remember anything whatsoever.

This, though, would have been a lie, and I could not have convincingly delivered it. Instead, I found myself saying this: "Holmes, I realise you are exhausted and no doubt looking forward to a bath and bed and nothing else. I would beg your indulgence, however, for I have something to tell you. It is something I have long wished to get off my chest, and I can think of no more apposite moment than this."

Interest brought a glint to his dulled eye. His curiosity was piqued. "Yes?"

"I too have experienced a 'dreadful epiphany', as you so aptly put it. I have for months been hoping for an opportunity to unburden myself of it to someone — anyone who might be able to understand. I believe you are that person and now is the time. After what you have been through, what you have witnessed, we have more in common than before. You are of course acquainted with the line in *Hamlet*, 'There are more things in heaven and earth, Horatio, than are dreamt of in your philosophy.'"

I leaned a fraction closer to him.

"I," I said, "have seen that for myself. In the earth. Under the earth. More things. Terrible things. I am the living proof."

CHAPTER TWELVE

The Lost City of Ta'aa

IN HINDSIGHT, PERHAPS I SHOULD NOT HAVE inflicted an account of my adventures in the Arghandab Valley upon Holmes, not that night, not while he was still recovering from the trauma of his own rude awakening. It was self-indulgent of me. In my defence, I was wrung out with tiredness and tension. It had been a more than trying day. My natural reticence had been eroded, my inhibitions lowered. Holmes had just become a fellow wayfarer on a road down which I had thought I walked alone. No wonder I was eager to confide in him.

*

It began on the retreat from Maiwand. The forces of Ayub Khan, Emir of Afghanistan, had routed ours. Although the Afghans had taken the greater casualties, we had been trounced nonetheless. After a three-hour artillery duel, the Ghazis rolled over the ranks of Indian infantry on our left flank and swung right to do the same to the 66th Berkshires, the regiment to which mine, the Fifth Northumberland Fusiliers, was attached. The Royal Horse and the Bombay Sappers and Miners stood firm, fighting a rearguard action to cover the retreat of the rest of the company, and paid the ultimate price for their bravery, almost to a man. It was an unmitigated disaster, the credit for which must lie with Brigadier-General George Burrows and his inexperience and lack of tactical acumen, but also with the air of overconfidence with which we approached the battle. Following a string of resounding victories at Peiwar, Kabul, Ahmed Khel and elsewhere, we in the British Army had begun to assume we were invincible and the Afghans would continue to fall before us like wheat before the scythe. Ayub Khan comprehensively disabused us of that notion.

We tramped away from the Maiwand Pass in a demoralised, straggling column. Bad though it was, it could have been much worse. For some reason the Afghans did not pursue us to finish us off. Once they had triumphed on the battlefield, they seemed to lose interest, and so we were able to depart unmolested. I, not amongst the wounded myself, did my duty as physician towards those who had sustained injuries. As we limped back to Kandahar, I applied salves, reapplied bandages, extracted bullets, and even carried out a couple of emergency amputations by the roadside. A relief force met us the next morning at Kokeran, and it was during the course of that same day that Captain Harrowby proposed a small side excursion.

Roderick Harrowby was an amateur field archaeologist, an ardent aficionado of the work of Heinrich Schliemann and Sir Arthur Evans. He had taken a military commission at the insistence of his father, a veteran of the Crimea, but longed to pursue his passion for digs and ancient relics. During the campaign he had often spoken about the many sites of great archaeological interest to be found in Afghanistan and elsewhere in the Hindoo Kush, and lamented how he should be exploring them while he was here, rather than spending the time skirmishing with the natives, all for the sake of controlling a country which was of little strategic importance to Britain and of which our government sought control only because they were unwilling to cede it to Russia, just another square on the board of the Great Game to tussle over and occupy.

Despite the occasional seditionary turn of phrase of that kind, Harrowby was an engaging raconteur, and his talk of long-lost cities secreted in deserts, on uncharted islands and in hidden valleys, the legacy of dead civilisations, struck a romantic chord in me. Time and again around the campfire he would conjure visions of a pre-Sumerian age when densely packed stone metropolises housed people of surprising sophistication whose knowledge of sciences such as astronomy and medicine was at least the rival of ours. He mentioned Atlantis and Lemuria as though, far from being mythical places beloved of philosophers and theosophists, these were genuine sunken continents beneath the waves, awaiting rediscovery. He spoke of other civilisations from that time – Commoriom, Uzuldaroum, Olathoë, Valusia – whose names, though I had never heard them before, elicited a prickle of wonder and unease. He talked of a global cataclysm, perhaps a great flood, that had wiped away almost all traces of this era, leaving only rare pockets of it still extant.

One of those "rare pockets" was situated not far from the region in which we were fighting. Harrowby knew of the location of a subterranean city in the northern reaches of the Arghandab Valley, where the valley shaded into the lower foothills of the Himalayas. He had read about it in a book called *Unaussprechlichen Kulten*, or *Unnameable Cults*, by

Friedrich Wilhelm von Junzt, a copy of which, published in English in 1845 by Bridewall, he had chanced upon in a second-hand bookshop just off Charing Cross Road. Somewhere in the book's one thousand pages was a description of a defile leading to a cavern wherein the city, known as Ta'aa, lies spread out, inviolate, the streets and houses perfectly preserved, untouched by wind or rain. Von Junzt had not seen this place for himself; he was merely citing reports found in other sources, obscure texts in ancient tongues. However, he was convinced of its existence, and so was Harrowby.

As we were preparing to resume the march to Kandahar, escorted by the relief force, Harrowby came to me with a proposal.

"Look here, Watson. We're all footsore, battle-weary and deserving of respite. I've had an idea. We should return to Kandahar, of course, but what if we were to take a little detour along the way? A few of the men are up for it. You're a solid, dependable chap, good in a pinch, and it'd make sense to have a sawbones along with us, just in case."

"What are you suggesting? That we desert?"

"Keep your voice down. It won't be desertion, it will be… diversion. Shouldn't take us more than a week, if my calculations are correct. Ten days at the most. We can say we became detached from the main body of troops. We were disorientated and got lost. We'll trundle into Kandahar the Sunday after next, looking suitably shamefaced and sorry for ourselves, and no one need be any the wiser. If the brass come down on us, I'll take it all on my shoulders. Dad's a chum of Field Marshal Roberts, so if we get into serious trouble I can always pull that particular string and have it all smoothed over. What do you say?"

"I suppose I should like to know why. Where will this detour of yours take us?"

"Can't you guess?"

I could. It was obvious.

Ta'aa.

And I said yes. I have no idea why, other than the fact that Harrowby had enchanted me with the yarns he had spun, particularly about Ta'aa. To be so close to the city and not take the opportunity to look for it – this struck me as little short of perverse.

Thus, at the potential risk of court martial, a group of us held back as the column set off again. We lingered at the van, dragging our feet, until we were thoroughly engulfed in the dust cloud thrown up by the horses' hooves, the men's boots, and the wheels of the wagons and artillery caissons. By the time it cleared, the rest of the column had moved so far ahead as to be out of sight.

Leaving the fertile banks of the Arghandab river behind, we sallied forth into ragged, bare hill country. We had water and provisions and a faith in Captain Harrowby's researches and orienteering skills. The July sun was ferocious, the air thin as a razor blade, and after a mere three days our eager little escapade had turned into a trudge. The men from the ordinary ranks started to grumble, and even I was beginning to have my misgivings. Harrowby exhorted us onward, as bouncy as a springer spaniel, but his enthusiasm for the expedition was shared less and less by those he was leading. Perhaps, we were thinking, this was all a bit of a mistake. Harrowby seemed confident about where we were going, but really! Lost underground cities. Books about long-defunct religious cults. Books by German authors, moreover. Who was to say the captain wasn't taking us on a wild goose chase? There was precious little concrete proof that this Ta'aa had ever existed, beyond a few lines in a tome whose very title gave one cause to doubt the veracity of its contents.

By dawn of the fifth day the mood had turned mutinous. The men, all half-dozen of them, were tired, dispirited, and full of dark mutterings. I tried to rally them but my heart wasn't in it. Even Harrowby himself seemed crestfallen, as though on the point of admitting defeat. We had climbed hill after hill, crossed valley after valley, and seemed no nearer our destination. There was a signpost, according to von Junzt, a marker that indicated unmistakably the entrance to the defile that led to Ta'aa. It was a granite pillar, standing some one hundred feet from base to apex, crowned with a weather-worn figure. Once we found that, we should know we were only a short journey from the city.

A passing goatherd proved our salvation – or, arguably, our damnation. Harrowby addressed him in clumsy Pashto, enquiring if he knew the whereabouts of said pillar. The man at once became very agitated. He pretended not to understand, but Harrowby pressed him, even going so far as to threaten him with a pistol, although I like to think he would not actually have stooped to using it. The goatherd, his wrinkled walnut face fixed in alarm, his gaping mouth showing toothless gums, confessed that he knew of the pillar. He gave us directions. We could be there in half a day. He added a proviso, which Harrowby was unwilling to translate for the rest of us until we badgered it out of him. It was this. The goatherd had said that we should turn back and not even think of looking for the city. No Afghan went near there. Any who did came back quite deranged, or else failed to return at all. It was an evil place but, more than that, it was deadly.

By the time we had extracted this warning from Harrowby, we were almost halfway to the pillar. We chose not to let it deter us. Silly native superstition. Ignorant heathens. The Moslem could not be relied upon for common sense. We were British. We were soldiers. We had guns. Any perils we might encounter we were well able to meet.

The pillar towered on the horizon. When we reached it, each of us took a turn with Harrowby's binoculars to inspect the figure that surmounted it. A hulking, crouching thing with the body of a man, the wings of a bat and a head like a squid, the statue was a forbidding sight. It seemed designed to make the casual visitor think twice before entering the mouth of the defile where it stood sentinel. Yet who would be a casual visitor to this remote, desolate spot? We were miles from anywhere. The last village we had passed, early the previous forenoon, had been a tiny cluster of huts only a quarter of which were tenanted. We were truly in no man's land, with nothing around us but scrubby ochre slopes and yawning blue sky. The statue's minatory mien was not intended for the likes of us, who had not wandered here by chance but had actively sought out this location.

Into the defile we went, Harrowby at the fore. A pebbly path wound between sheer rock walls, often becoming so narrow we were forced to go in single file. It ran for at least three miles from one end to the other, and as we walked we became subdued. There was something oppressive in the atmosphere of the place, the very geography itself. One felt hemmed in and at the same time vulnerable. The path inclined downward, the walls grew higher on either side, and the impression one gained was of being inside the jaws of a vice while the screw was being turned. The further one went, the more trapped one became.

Eventually, to our relief, the defile opened out, and across a kind of natural courtyard stood the entrance to the cavern, a cleft surrounded by extensive carvings. These, of remarkable quality and intricacy, depicted the same bat-winged creature that surmounted the pillar, lording it over men with the heads of lizards, who cowered cravenly before it. Elsewhere the lizard-headed men were seen slaughtering normal human beings, slitting their throats and cutting out their hearts and entrails with their clawed hands. In several of the images, the eviscerated innards were offered up to the bat-winged thing on dishes, as food. In others it was the lizard men themselves who feasted upon them, and on limbs and lesser organs as well.

Harrowby spent nearly an hour admiring the carvings and making sketches of them in his journal. He declared that this was one of the great archaeological finds of the decade, if not of the century, and we were all a part of it. He promised that when he returned to England and made an official announcement about it – to the Royal

Society, where else? – each of us would receive our due share of the credit. I myself did not mind much whether or not I was one of the first westerners ever to clap eyes on the carvings, or for that matter on the city of Ta'aa. As fascinating as Harrowby found the illustrations, I found them repugnant and intimidating. And I was not unique in that. The men were full of bravado, commenting crudely on this or that aspect of them, not least the nudity of all the figures shown and the grotesque *Grand Guignol* detail of the killings. Their voices trembled a little, however. Beneath the ribald jeering there was disquiet. Whoever had made these illustrations, one did not wish to be associated with those people in any way. The images attested to a sick, deviant temperament.

At last it was time to go in. Harrowby lit a lantern, we followed suit, and our wary procession passed through the cleft and down into the bowels of the earth.

*

For an episode I once tried my hardest to forget, it remains sharp in my memory, even today. In my dotage I have trouble remembering where I have left my reading spectacles and the name of the maidservant who draws my evening bath for me, yet the journey into Ta'aa and the flight out of it I can recall as clearly as though it happened yesterday.

A long tunnel, seemingly endless, suddenly gave onto a broad shelf of rock, an escarpment from which we looked out over a vast, sprawling cavern large enough to swallow a score of cathedrals. Lumpen sedimentary columns lent their support to its roof, the slenderest of them at least a dozen yards in diameter. At the further end a cataract glistened, fed by some aquifer and filling the air with its churning echoes. All this was visible courtesy of the eerie, eldritch light shed by a luminous fungus that clung in huge clumps to various surfaces.

Dousing our lanterns at Harrowby's instruction, we let our eyes adjust to the purplish glow, and in its lambency perceived the outlines of buildings on the cavern floor. They were little more than rough-hewn, slab-built cubes, with hollow rectangular apertures for doors, arranged in a higgledy-piggledy street formation. At the very middle of them was a single larger structure whose size and centrality, along with its domed roof and colonnaded flanks, suggested religious or political significance: a temple or meeting-house. Dwarfing and outclassing the surrounding edifices, it seemed the purpose of them, their *raison d'être*. They existed to service it, like a colony of ants their queen.

Our trepidation notwithstanding, we gasped at this vista. All of us, that is, save Harrowby, who wore a look of pure self-satisfaction. He was no doubt ranking himself with his heroes Schliemann and Evans, and likening his achievement to their discoveries of the sites of Troy and Knossos. I see now that, though charismatic, he was an arrogant, vain man, perhaps even foolish, albeit not so foolish as the rest of us who blindly, blithely accompanied him.

There were steps hacked out of the face of the escarpment, and we descended them, with Harrowby naturally in front. Soon we were parading through Ta'aa, blinking around us at the remains of a city that was old when dynastic Egypt was young. Aside from the carvings at the entrance there was little sign of cultural or domestic life. We saw no potsherds; no decoration around or in the houses, the few of them we looked inside; nor any open spaces that might have been marketplaces or squares. The temple, if temple it was, appeared to be the only place where the inhabitants were likely to have gathered and communed in numbers. That, consequently, became our goal. At Harrowby's urging we navigated the mazy streets, making turns at junctions only if this served to bring us closer to it. All the while, the great waterfall hissed, muting the shuffle of our footsteps and forcing us to speak at normal volume when we would much rather have whispered, for whispering felt more appropriate and somehow safer. It was as if we had no wish to be overheard – and yet who could be there to eavesdrop? Ta'aa was a dead city, so long unoccupied that the bones of its denizens had crumbled to dust. We were alone. Surely we were alone.

The central building proved to be a place of worship after all, a shrine to the same loathsome hybrid monstrosity who perched on the pillar and dominated the carvings outside. Its likeness was etched onto all four external walls, and inside atop a large plinth stood another statue of it, this one a representation some thirty feet in height, wrought from black marble shot through with veins of a golden mineral. The idol's bulbous head and plump, squat body I can recall only with a thrill of horror, and likewise the moment when, gazing up from by its feet, Harrowby gave voice to a word.

"Cthulhu."

Initially I thought dust must have got up his nose and

he had sneezed. Then he repeated the word, louder and with a kind of awe.

"Cthulhu."

"What does that mean?" I asked.

"Mean?" said he. "It means him, Watson." He pointed up at the idol. "It is his name. Cthulhu. One of the Great Old Ones. The greatest, some say. Son of Nug. Half-brother of Hastur. Husband of Idh-yaa. Father of Ghatanothoa, Ythogtha, Zoth-Ommog, Cthylla and Shaurash-Ho. Grandfather of Yogash the Ghoul. Great-grandfather of K'baa the Serpent. If von Junzt is to be believed, Cthulhu's influence stretches far and wide across the globe. Haiti, Louisiana, the South Pacific, Mexico, Siberia, Greenland – you'll find peoples that worship him still in all those places, and countless more. But it's here, in Central Asia, that the faith has its heartland. It may be that this city is its nucleus – its *sanctum sanctorum* – or even its *fons et origo*. I can't imagine there being a monument to him anywhere else that rivals this one. We have found the Cthulhu cult's Westminster Abbey. All other shrines are mere chapels by comparison."

I was minded to chide him for expressing such a blasphemous notion, but I doubted he would have cared. The bumptious lad was too caught up in the excitement of his discovery. Nothing could ruin the moment for him, not even when one of the men, Private Edginton, drew our notice away from the statue to an altogether more prosaic but no less sinister feature of the temple.

"Captain, sir, are those what I think they are?"

He was pointing to various heaps of bones that littered the floor of the shrine. I myself had not registered them upon entering the place. None of us had. The idol had commanded our attention to the exclusion of all else.

Harrowby bent to examine the nearest of the bone piles. He extricated one of the larger specimens and held it up for me to look at.

"What do you make of that, Doctor? Unless I am much mistaken, it's a human femur."

I could not help but concur. "There are characteristics to it that are unusual. It is inordinately curved, for one thing. The owner would have been very bow-legged. But it is human nonetheless."

The men did not take this revelation well. They were even less happy when one of them, Lockwood, pointed out that the femur bore certain tell-tale scrapes and grooves on it. Lockwood had been an apprentice butcher back in Dorchester before signing up with the Fifth Northumberlands, and knew what a hambone looked like after it had been given to a hungry dog.

"Them's gnaw marks, them is," he said, "and no mistake."

"Wild animals, opportunistically taking advantage of carrion," Harrowby asserted confidently. "Wolves, or jackals. Hyenas maybe. There are even bears in these parts, I'm told."

To my eyes, the gnaw marks were too blunt to have been made by the teeth of any of those creatures. Incisors and molars were responsible, not the canines of carnivores. Teeth that may well have been human. I kept the thought to myself, however. The men were already jittery. No point in unsettling them further.

Not that my reticence availed us anything, for another of the privates, Smythe, had picked up one of the many skulls that lay around us. At a cursory glance it might have passed for human. There were certainly a few undeniably human skulls amid the osseous detritus in the temple. Yet the cranium of this one had an elongated dome, and the frontal and occipital bones were both etiolated. The maxilla, meanwhile, was oddly elongated, and Smythe produced a separate mandible that matched, fully half as long again from ramus to chin as the human equivalent. The finishing touch was a broad, underdeveloped nasal aperture, suggestive of a flat, recessed nose.

All in all, though human-like, it was not a human skull, not in the conventional sense. The only conclusion any of us could draw was a chilling one.

"The lizard-headed people from the carvings," I said. "They exist."

"Existed," said Harrowby, correcting me. "A species of reptilian hominid hitherto unknown to science. These are the last corporeal relics of them. Gentlemen, we appear to have made not only archaeological but paleontological history today. Our names are going to be celebrated down through the ages. I can just hear them now at the Royal Society, the wisest heads in England cheering us to the rafters."

"I'd settle for a bit of coin for my trouble," said Lockwood.

"There'll be riches aplenty," Harrowby assured him. "The statue of Cthulhu alone is priceless. Assuming we can devise a means of getting it out of—"

"Hsst!" said Edginton. "Anyone else hear that?"

We listened hard. The only sound was the susurration of the waterfall, still dimly audible through the temple walls.

"It's nothing," Harrowby said at last. "Doubtless what you're hearing is a fore-echo of the applause to come as our finds are unveiled before an audience of dignitaries at the British Museum a few months hence."

"Doubtless it isn't," Edginton said, adding a belated "sir" for fear of coming across as insubordinate.

"Then what did you hear?"

"Sounded to me like… voices."

"In which case your ears are playing tricks on you, Edginton. There's no one around but us."

Smythe then put into words a question that I myself had been pondering. "Captain, if this civilisation is as ancient and defunct as you say it is, how come these here lizard-head bones don't look all that old?"

Harrowby had a ready answer to that. "The last few members of the race must have survived until relatively recently. As to how they managed that, there's a constant supply of fresh water from the waterfall, and their other dietary needs would have been taken care of by consuming, say, bats, the occasional rodent or other small mammal, possibly a wild boar now and then. Hunting parties would not have had to forage far from the cavern to find game."

"I think, Harrowby, you're avoiding one other somewhat obvious source of sustenance," I said. "The tooth marks on the bones would indicate to me that, *in extremis*, the lizard men resorted to breaking the ultimate taboo."

"Cannibalism," said Edginton, and chased the word

with an oath. "This temple – it doubled as their dining hall."

One of the other privates, O'Connor, an Irishman and a staunch Roman Catholic, crossed himself, while Smythe touched the carbine on his shoulder, deriving a more tangible comfort from the weapon's wooden forestock.

"This be the Devil's realm," said Lockwood in his thick Dorset drawl. "'Tain't for us to be here. This be an antechamber to Hell, is what it be."

"I won't abide that sort of talk," Harrowby snapped. "We are not children. We are grown men, and we mustn't behave as though—"

Someone let out a cry that was halfway between a gasp and a scream.

"Lance Corporal Fielding," Harrowby barked. "What was that in aid of? Explain yourself."

"I saw…" said Fielding. "I thought I saw…" He was staring at the entranceway to the temple. "Someone out there. Moving. Looking in. He had a face. Wasn't no ordinary face. More like…"

"Like what?"

"All scaly. Long snout. Bulging eyes. Like one of them lizard men would look like for real."

"If any were still alive," said Harrowby, "which they are not. They are long extinct. I want you all to listen very closely to me. You are letting your imaginations run riot. You need to get a grip on yourselves, every man jack of you. Remember who you are: subjects of Her Majesty the Queen. Remember what you are: soldiers of the British Army, the greatest fighting force on the planet. Remember what that means: you are not a bunch of mithering, lily-livered poltroons. Got that?"

There were nods all round, some more avid than others.

"Now," Harrowby continued, "let us concentrate solely on the matter at hand. We are standing in a place of worship where a long-dead race, quite possibly the missing evolutionary link between *Homo sapiens* and the dinosaurs, paid tribute to—"

Those were Roderick Harrowby's final words, rudely truncated by the appearance of a man-shaped beast which sprang out from behind the idol's plinth and lopped his head off with a single swipe of a taloned, reptilian hand. One moment Harrowby was standing there pontificating. The next, his head was rolling across the floor while his decapitated body sagged to its knees and keeled over.

His assassin absconded before any of the rest of us could do a thing about it. The culprit was one of them, the lizard men from the carvings. He clambered swiftly up the side of the wall, using his talons like a climber's pitons, and disappeared into the shadows of the ceiling.

Somewhat after the event, wits were collected, shock overcome, rifles unshipped, bolt actions worked, rounds discharged; but the perpendicular volley of bullets resulted only in cacophony and a hail of stone fragments, none of the shots finding their target in the gloomy recesses overhead.

As the firing petered out, I assumed command. Being the highest ranking after Harrowby, it fell to me to order a withdrawal.

"Where there's one of those things, there may be more," I said. "We fall back in an orderly fashion. We make for the tunnel."

"You heard the man," said Lance Corporal Fielding, giving my authority the subaltern stamp of approval. "Move!"

The troops hurried from the temple, reloading their rifles as they went. I took a last look back at Harrowby's corpse, a pitiable sight, death having come for him unexpectedly at what he believed was his moment of crowning glory, the accomplishment that would set him up for life. The eyes in his severed head looked startled and just a little chagrined, as if he acknowledged now, too late, his own hubris and folly, but also recognised the injustice of his fate.

Then I turned and ran.

*

Our journey back from the temple to the escarpment began as an organised retreat but became a shambles. In many ways it was Maiwand all over again, although in this instance our enemy did not leave us be. Rather, we were harried the entire way. The lizard man in the temple was far from being the only exemplar of his race. There were, as we rapidly ascertained, scores of the reptilian hominids still resident in Ta'aa, and they did not take kindly to intruders in their midst. No, that is not strictly accurate. In some respects they welcomed us in their city, for had there not been human remains, human skulls, amid the bone piles in the temple? Had the carvings not told the story? The lizard men were not merely cannibalistic but anthropophagous, and we were their next meal.

They leapt at us as we scuttled along the streets. They

pounced from the rooftops. They sprinted out from between the houses. They were naked and smoothly scaly. They were bandy-legged, with powerful thighs, which made them fast, disconcertingly so. They were, above all, ferocious.

They hissed as they attacked, and sometimes their hisses formed speech. One phrase in particular stood out, a set of words they reiterated again and again in their foul, inhuman voices, as though it were a war cry.

"Ph'nglui mglw'nath Cthulhu R'lyeh wgah'nagl fhtagn!"

I would not have been able to represent it accurately here in text form if not for later studies conducted by myself and Holmes. Only during the course of the events that comprise the main body of this narrative did we garner a working knowledge of the language known as R'lyehian, or occasionally Aklo. Likewise, I could not have understood then, as I do now, that the lizard men were reciting the principal line of a chant they would have used in their rites of worship, a paean of praise and fealty to their obscene god: "In his home at R'lyeh, dead Cthulhu waits dreaming."

The hominids uttered it as they besieged us, their forked tongues a-flicker, their lipless mouths seemingly fixed in grins of ecstasy. They shared it with one another as a rallying cry, calling up more of their number from wherever they lay in wait. Ambush followed ambush, all accompanied by lizardly throats chorusing the words in unison or antiphony.

One must thank the Lord, and the manufacturers of small arms, that our guns were able to cut down the lizard men. Else none of us would have made it even halfway to the escarpment. A well-placed round from rifle or pistol could stop one of our squamous assailants in his tracks. They were as vulnerable in that regard as any living thing.

But, although we had the firepower, the lizard men had the superior numbers. They also knew the layout of Ta'aa, whereas we were fumbling through the city, having long abandoned all hope of retracing the exact route we had taken on the way in. One jagged, house-fringed street looked much like another. Our sole point of visual reference was the temple. The more distance we put between us and it, the likelier that we were going in the right direction. The escarpment was not visible in the fungus-lit gloom, not until we were fairly close to it.

By that point we were running low on ammunition and one amongst us, Lockwood, had fallen prey to the lizard men. The Dorset native had stumbled mid-run and gone sprawling, and hominids had caught him and dragged him off. His piteous screams were abruptly cut short, and we knew there was nothing we could do for him. The apprentice butcher had himself been butchered.

On we went, and then a massed horde of the lizard men attacked from front and rear at once. Still hissing that ugly chant of theirs, they closed in. We felled as many as we could at long range, then when every last round had been fired, engaged them hand-to-hand. Those of us who had knives and bayonets used them. I myself raided my medical kit and retrieved a bone saw and a scalpel, both of which performed respectably well in an offensive, non-surgical capacity. We cleaved through the lizard men's ranks, matching their talons with our manmade claws. We spilled plenty of their blood, but so they did ours, alas. By the time we were clear of them, we were down to three: Smythe, Edginton and me; by the time we gained the foot of the escarpment steps, that total had been reduced to two. Smythe had sustained a terrible leg wound during the foregoing fracas, and Edginton and I carried him between us as far as we could before realising that he was no longer able to assist by propelling himself along with his good leg and had become so much dead weight. His femoral artery had been nicked and he had died of blood loss, slipping away silently in our embrace.

The lizard men were still in hot pursuit. Dropping Smythe's lifeless form, Edginton and I scrambled up the crude steps, near frantic in our efforts to escape. Our mob of assailants followed, some using the steps too, others crawling up the sheer face of the escarpment. By God's good grace we reached the summit before any of the hominids, and then we were in the tunnel, racing through it with all the ebbing strength in our bodies. Not having had the time to light our lanterns, we were more or less blind in the dark. So were the lizard men. Yet we made no attempt to be cautious. Better to hare along, arms out, feeling our way, and receive the occasional bump on the head or knock to the knee, than to proceed with prudence. We did not have that luxury.

Ahead, a dim golden glow began to waver. It meant the cleft, the natural courtyard, the defile. On no account did it guarantee sanctuary, but at least we would no longer be underground in the lizard men's domain. They would be in ours, and in broad daylight we might stand a better chance. At the very least the cleft was so narrow that they would have to exit it one by one, and the two of us could then deal with them accordingly. The numerical advantage would, for a change, be ours.

A yelp from Edginton, at my rear, made me halt and turn.

"Private Edginton?" I said, peering. I could just about make him out, a dozen yards behind, canted against the tunnel wall, one leg drawn up. "What is it? What's the matter?"

"Tripped on my own ruddy bootlace, didn't I, Dr Watson. Only gone and turned my damn ankle over."

"Let me help you."

"No, sir. I'll only be a burden. Can't put an ounce of weight on my foot. You go on."

"Don't be daft, man. Together we can still—"

"All due respect, but that's rot and you know it."

"I'm not leaving you to the mercy of those monsters." I could hear the lizard men fast approaching, the clatter of their feet, the murmuring of their prayer to Cthulhu.

"Not your choice to make," said Edginton adamantly. "I have my bayonet. I can take a couple of them with me. Get out of here alive, and tell everyone about this hellhole, and make sure somebody comes back with dynamite and seals this tunnel. Promise me."

"I'm not—"

"Promise me, Dr Watson. On your word."

So I solemnly made the promise – a vow I was not to keep – and Edginton, brave Edginton, wished me godspeed, then about-faced, raised his bayonet aloft, and hobbled to meet the lizard men head-on.

"Come and get me, you beauties," was the last I heard from him, not counting the long, protracted scream that issued along the tunnel a few seconds later.

I all but flung myself out from the cleft, falling prostrate to the dusty ground. Heaving for breath, I tried to get to my feet, but I was weak, scarce able to move. The horrors I had seen overwhelmed me.

Just as control over my body returned to me, the foremost of the lizard men appeared, framed by the cleft. A hand grabbed for me, bent on hauling me back into the darkness, to my certain doom. I reacted quickly but not quickly enough. The hand seized my shoulder. I wrenched away from it, and one of the talons tore deep into my flesh. With a shriek of pure anguish I lunged forward, heading for the defile.

Upon reaching it, I dared a glance back, fully expecting to see the thwarted lizard man lumbering after me with a swarm of others hot on his heels.

It was not so, however. The hominid had shrunk back into the cleft, one hand shielding his eyes. He wanted to continue the chase and finish what he had started, but was incapable of doing so. The same was true of his fellows, who were congregated behind him in the tunnel. None of them was able to go any further. They could not leave the tunnel's shade.

It dawned on me as to why. The dazzle of the sun, which was just past its zenith, was too much for them. A lifetime spent in Ta'aa, with only the pale purple luminescence of the fungus to see by, had left their vision unable to adapt easily to a much brighter light source. Even indirect sunshine was as torturous to their optic nerves as the flare of burning magnesium is to ours. Previous generations may have been more frequent visitors to the outside world, judging by the presence of the carvings; that or they had engraved them by the light of the moon alone. Whichever it was, no lizard man of the present era could leave Ta'aa during the daytime.

I did not hesitate to seize the advantage this afforded me. I scurried into the defile and along it. Sometimes I was reduced to going on all fours when the path became too tortuous and uneven and my legs could no longer be relied upon to support me. Having passed the pillar with its perching Cthulhu, that brooding demonic scarecrow, I tottered onward into the wilds of Afghanistan, never once looking back.

*

Some Afghan villagers found me, half crazed with pain and thirst and caked in blood, not all of it my own. In a rare fit of charity towards one who represented their foreign oppressor, they treated me with kindness and decency. At their headman's insistence, my shoulder was bound up and I was transported by mule-drawn travois to the nearest hill station. Thence I was borne by wagon to Kandahar and onward by train to Peshawar.

I neglected to fulfil my promise to Edginton mainly because I had resolved already to treat the entire incident as though it had never happened. I managed to persuade myself that there had been no Ta'aa, no bone-strewn temple to Cthulhu, no lizard men. It was the only way to salvage what little sanity I had left. I had been shot by a sniper during the march back from Maiwand, the bullet passing clean through the top of my shoulder. That was the received opinion, based on the dimensions and nature of my wound. Unbeknownst to the main body of the retreating troops, some cowardly Ghazi had fired on me from his hiding place. The same sniper, with his Jezail, had done for Captain Harrowby and a half-dozen other men as well. I, sole survivor of the sneak attack, had been left behind, forced to fend for myself, roaming injured and delirious through inhospitable terrain for days until my rescue.

It was a miracle I had lasted so long. I was lucky to be alive. So everyone insisted, and who was I to argue?

I was lucky to be alive.

CHAPTER THIRTEEN

Speaking of the Devil

THE FOLLOWING MORNING FOUND HOLMES AND ME in subdued mood. We exchanged hardly two words over breakfast, and Mrs Hudson, sensing the atmosphere between us but misconstruing its root cause, was prompted to remark, "I do hope you two haven't had a falling out already, so soon after Dr Watson moved in? That would be a shame. You seem, if I may be so bold, a most compatible pair."

Eventually Holmes said to me, "Well, my dear fellow, either we can pretend that we are both deranged, or we must accept that each of us, in his separate way, has pierced the veil of a great occult mystery. I use 'occult' in its literal as well as its figurative sense, meaning hidden as well as paranormal."

"You no longer question the content of your vision on Box Hill?" I asked. "You are certain it was fact, not fancy?"

"One might easily argue that Gong-Fen's drug did nothing more than cause me to experience wild hallucinations. Vivid and disturbing though they were, they had no more substance than De Quincey's laudanum-induced dream of silvery seas paved with upturned human faces."

"And yet...?"

"And yet, immediately after I described my vision to you, you took it upon yourself to relate your adventures in the city of Ta'aa, where you too encountered evidence of this Cthulhu entity. You saw with your own eyes religious iconography pertaining to him, along with a breed of half-human beasts who worshipped him. I myself saw, with the eyes of the mind, the god-creature himself in his Pacific fastness, surrounded by his servitors. You provided independent verification for something which I would otherwise be quite happy, in the cold light of day, to reject as delusion."

"You doubt nothing I said?"

"Not a bit of it. You are far too stolid and unimaginative, Watson, to invent a tale like that."

I took umbrage at the remark. Stolid and unimaginative? But Holmes seemed to mean it as a compliment.

"No," he continued, "none of it can be dismissed as mere coincidence. The overlap is too great, the details too consistent. Much though I wish it were not so, it would seem that this god Cthulhu was known and venerated by the ancients. Worse" – his expression became pained – "that he was and is real. And if he is real, then everything else I saw is real too."

"There is the unknown language as well," I said. "We both heard Stamford use it. The lizard men also spoke it."

"Hence your queer turn at the Yard. Stamford's utterances must have transported you straight back to the cavern and the gruelling ordeal you underwent there."

"They did. Very much so."

"And that is another plank of evidence shoring up the veracity of your experience, and by extension mine."

"But what are we to make of all this?"

"I do not know, but I suspect you and I can never be the same again. I suspect we have been changed irrevocably by what we have learned, and to some extent damaged by it. The challenge before us is to try to carry on as before."

"As though nothing is different? I'm not certain I can do that, especially now that I no longer have the excuse of being able to tell myself that none of it was real. Ta'aa *was* real. So were the lizard men. So are Cthulhu and his ilk. Your dream-quest has put that beyond doubt, as far as I'm concerned, just as my account of Ta'aa has put your dream-quest beyond doubt. I have never felt so small, Holmes, so unsteady. Never has the ground beneath my feet felt so liable to give way at any moment."

"The remedy," said Holmes, "would be to throw ourselves back into the fray."

"What fray? You mean the Shadwell murders?"

"One way to rid the mind of unwanted tenants is to occupy it with something else, something practical."

"But the matter is almost resolved, is it not?" I said. "Gong-Fen Shou is the guilty party, Stamford his puppet. You were right about the two of them manufacturing a new and dangerous drug. Never mind that Gong-Fen denied it when you accused him. Of course he would. The same goes for Stamford's death. The Chinaman must be responsible for that as well. All that remains for us is to compile compelling evidence against him and present it to Inspector Gregson. He can do the rest."

"It is not so simple, I'm afraid, Watson." Holmes waved a hand at that day's *Times*, through which he had been distractedly leafing while I toyed with a poached egg. "There has been a complication."

"Pray tell."

"The spate of deaths by emaciation has claimed a

fifth victim after all. Look here."

The piece was short and to the point. Since I neglected to make a clipping of it, I cannot reproduce it verbatim here, but the gist was this. Stevedores arriving for work at the London docks the previous morning had happened upon a body on Tench Street, propped against the back wall of a wharf building. The victim was of Chinese descent and appeared to have starved to death. There was the suggestion that he had been a stowaway on a ship from the Far East and had perished during the long voyage. His body having been discovered by the crew on arrival in London, it had been dumped overnight. Police, apparently, were chasing up all possible leads.

"Or so they say," Holmes said, "but I doubt the Met will pursue the investigation aggressively. One dead stowaway will not rank high on their list of priorities."

"The article does not link the death with the others," I observed.

"So far the broadsheets have been wholly oblivious to the goings-on in Shadwell. Reportage of same has been confined to the pages of the yellow press. A paper like *The Times* will have noted this death simply because of the morbid and somewhat exotic overtones: the foreign fugitive wasting away unknown in the hold of a merchantman, then tossed out like so much bilge water. Well!" Holmes rose to his feet, buoyed by a sudden surge of energy. "We who know better, who are aware of connections overlooked by others, must do our duty. The game is afoot, Watson. Grab your overcoat and come with me."

"Where are we going?"

"To the East End, of course, to make a tour of the area's hospitals. Specifically, their morgues."

*

Holmes and I spent a dreary few hours traipsing from hospital to hospital, including my alma mater Barts. My medical credentials secured us access to the morgue of each, until in the basement of the London Hospital on Whitechapel Road we found what we were looking for.

The Chinaman's cadaver was brought out for us and laid on a marble slab, covered with a sheet. As the morgue attendants left, Holmes commented to me that this was to be his first chance to view one of the emaciated corpses. From anyone else the remark might have sounded ghoulish, but his interest stemmed from genuine forensic curiosity. Before, only the accounts of others had been available for him to go on. Now he could examine a victim for himself and perhaps glean fresh data.

At his invitation I drew back the sheet, to reveal the head and bare torso of what appeared to be a frail, wizened old man who had somehow avoided the indignity of his hair going grey. His cheeks were sunken, his chest hollow, with the ridge of his clavicle and every rib prominent. There was virtually no muscle on him. His veins and tendons stood proud against his skin, which had the colour and texture of parchment. He looked to weigh no more than five stone, half the average for someone of his height.

Then there was his face.

The eyes were wide. I imagine someone at some point must have tried to close them, only to find the lids stiff and unresponsive, and hence left them as they were. The same went for his mouth, which gaped in a rictus, exposing his buccal cavity all the way to the uvula. Rigor mortis would have locked it in that position by now.

For all the world he looked as though he was screaming.

In that cold, glazed-tiled room below street level, with our breath emerging as wisps of vapour, Holmes and I were hardly at our warmest. Yet the sight of the dead Chinaman's face sent a shiver through me that had nothing to do with ambient temperature. There was I, a doctor, having only a couple of days earlier spoken dismissively, with the disdain of an expert, about the so-called "look of terror" on a dead body; how such a thing was a misreading of a perfectly unremarkable physiological phenomenon. Yet now, confronted with that self-same phenomenon in the flesh, my immediate response was that of the unlettered layman. All I could think was: yes, this was just that – a look of terror. The Chinaman had died in a state of hopeless, cringing fear. I might even have gone so far as to aver that it was terror that had killed him, rather than malnutrition. Whatever he had seen in his last moments on Earth had been sufficiently horrendous to stop his heart.

"Oh, Watson, Watson," said Holmes, running his eye over the cadaver, "this is fascinating. Quite fascinating. One would say, would one not, that the poor fellow had eaten and drunk nothing in many days, to judge by his condition."

"It would be the logical conclusion."

"Yet you and I both know that that is impossible."

"How so?" I lowered my voice, even though we were alone, with no one to hear us but the Chinaman himself and the other unclaimed dead. "Because of Cthulhu and suchlike? Because we are both now aware that the impossible is all too possible? I don't know about you, Holmes, but I am not going to go around seeing the inexplicable everywhere, in everything. That is not how I wish to live my life, not if I can help it. My sanity, such as it is, is too precious to me."

"I am not asking for that. I am asking you merely to observe. Observe the cadaver's face."

"I have done so, and would prefer not to have done."

"Observe his moustache, then."

The man had long strands of hair hanging down on either side of his mouth.

"What of it?" I said. "That style of facial topiary is not rare amongst the Chinese. We met someone just the other night who wore exactly the same…"

My voice trailed off.

Holmes smiled thinly. "Now study the face itself closely. Granted, he is much altered. He is not the man he was. But the bone structure remains. Note, too, the small discoloured patches on his left forearm and his solar plexus. That is not livor mortis. Those are bruises inflicted ante mortem. I can be sure of that, since I myself was the cause of them."

I could not deny what he was asserting, much though I might have liked to.

Holmes and I were looking at the body of one of the

employees at the Golden Lotus Hotel. The one who had held me hostage with my own gun. The one named Li Guiying.

*

"But he was in perfect health when last we saw him," I said to Holmes as we left the morgue and threaded our way back through the hospital. "There is no way he could… In the space of a single night… I mean, it's…"

"Impossible?" said my companion, his eyebrows arched. "The very thing you have resolved not to look for. Yet here it is, rearing its ugly head once more. I hate to say this, but 'impossible' would seem to be the path we are destined to follow, my friend, at least in the foreseeable future."

"Did you know in advance that the dead man would be Li Guiying?"

Holmes nodded. "Gong-Fen appeared irked by him. 'Ill-judged' and 'ungracious' were how he described his behaviour in taking your revolver. I imagine the reward for those who earn Gong-Fen Shou's displeasure is a harsh one. In addition, a fifth death was required to perpetuate the model already established – one murder a month. This time Gong-Fen chose not a random stranger but someone closer to home."

"But the new moon was two nights ago."

"Better late than never."

We emerged from the main entrance and started down the front steps.

"Well, if nothing else," I said, "we now have a solid foundation upon which to build a case against the fiend. Li was a known associate of his."

"Li worked at an opium den which Gong-Fen is only alleged to have ties with," said Holmes. "That is not a hard-and-fast link between the two of them."

"Gong-Fen admitted to knowing him when he broke into 221B the night before last and handed back my gun."

"Hearsay. Inadmissible in court. The same goes for everything he told me on the journey to Dorking, which was all but a confession to his involvement in opium smuggling. If it came up in a trial, he could simply deny saying anything of the sort. It would be my word against his, and although a jury might not be favourably inclined towards a wealthy Oriental businessman, they might equally look askance at an impoverished aspirant sleuth, even if he were of English origin. Any decent lawyer – and Gong-Fen can afford the best – would tear my testimony to shreds."

"Dash it all, the man's laughing at us," I said. "Mocking us openly. He's getting away with murder, and daring us to prove otherwise, knowing we cannot. He's the Devil himself, Holmes."

"And speaking of the Devil…"

A carriage was pulling up beside us, a four-wheeler, and as it halted its door opened and from its interior issued the voice of the very man we had just been discussing.

"Mr Holmes, Dr Watson," said Gong-Fen Shou. "A moment of your time, if you will. Please step aboard. It's urgent."

CHAPTER FOURTEEN

Not Prey but Guests

I HAD NO DESIRE TO ENTER GONG-FEN'S CLARENCE.
I would much rather have walked barefoot into a nest of
vipers. I did not even have my Webley on me, which might
have offered me some reassurance. There would then
have been the option of simply shooting the scoundrel if
all else failed.

Holmes, by contrast, showed little hesitation about
climbing into the carriage, which left me with no
alternative. I could not allow him to face Gong-Fen alone,
unaided. I had done so once, to my regret. Not again.

Gong-Fen rapped on the front window, the coachman
whipped the horses, and we were away. The Chinaman
now presented a somewhat different figure from the
confident, serene sophisticate who had invaded our home.
There was a marked perturbation about him. His hand
showed a tiny but distinct tremor as he drew the curtains
at the front and the blinds at the sides and back, cocooning
the carriage's interior in shade. He was trying to behave
like his usual self, and failing.

For all that, I could not help muttering to Holmes, as
an aside, "I do not feel that this is wise. Now we cannot
even see where he is taking us."

"Tut, Watson. Think it through. Mr Gong-Fen wants
us here, in his carriage."

"Of course he does. To kidnap us."

"Perhaps I spoke inaccurately. He *needs* us here. Why
did he pick us up? Did he simply happen to be driving by

the London Hospital, look out, spy us passing, and decide to make good on an opportunity presented by fate? He did not. He knew we were likely to visit the hospital at some stage, because he knew we would be looking for Li's body and he knew it had been taken to this very morgue. Hence he waited for us outside."

"So it was a trap, and he has sprung it. Li's body was merely the bait."

"A singularly poor trap, in so far as we have entered it willingly, knowingly."

"*You* did."

"And we could quite easily overpower our trapper, could we not? If it came to that. Am I not correct in my surmise, Gong-Fen? We are not prey but guests."

The Chinaman nodded. "I see you are as perceptive as ever, Mr Holmes. You have come through your dream-quest unscathed."

"More or less."

"I knew you could endure it. A lesser mind might have cracked."

"Like Stamford's, you mean?"

Another nod, this one slightly rueful. "It was his choice. I might have counselled against it, had he not been quite so insistent. An addict of any kind is always on the lookout for newer, more intense experiences. After a time he builds up an immunity to the rush of sensation he receives from his addiction. He seeks greater heights, higher stakes. In Dr Stamford's case, opium no longer fulfilled his needs. He was smoking it in ever-increasing quantities but still becoming inured to its effects. He wanted more, and knew I could provide it."

"That was the incentive for him, no?" said Holmes. "That was how you got him to perform abductions for you. You dangled before him, like a carrot before a donkey, the promise of an even more powerful narcotic than opium – the same narcotic you gave me atop Box Hill. Your 'cocktail'."

"Stamford knew I had the knowledge and the wherewithal to make it. He had heard me speak of its dizzying transformative properties. He was so far sunk in desperation that he would have done anything, agreed to anything, for a taste of it."

"Was he aware how dangerous it was?" I said. "How it might warp the user's mind and bend him towards madness?"

"If he did, he did not care. He yearned for a more sublime state of alteration than opium alone could offer. He paid little heed to the potential consequences."

"Five victims," said Holmes. "That was your price."

"A fair one, he thought."

"Yet in the event Stamford furnished you with only four. That is odd. You strike me as someone who does not like it when a purchaser welches on a deal, and who does not hand over goods unless the invoice has been paid in full."

"Again, so perceptive."

"Stamford came up short. He let you down. You needed a fifth body on the night of the most recent new moon. He failed to provide one, thanks to us. You gave him the drug anyway. This was not generosity on your part. It was a punishment. You had a fairly good idea it would tip him over the edge. If what he saw was half as devastating as what I saw, it was likely to destroy him. Ravaged by opium use, he was already clinging on to mental equilibrium by his fingernails. You gave him a last little push, and he was gone."

"My God," I breathed. "You truly are evil."

"I am… pragmatic," said Gong-Fen. "I weigh up the pros and cons and make my decisions accordingly. I cannot make allowance for sentiment or ethics. Those are lifebelts by means of which others may keep their heads above water, whereas I swim. Besides, Doctor, compared with some I am a veritable saint. You have not yet met true evil."

"On the contrary, I believe I have," I replied, thinking of the lizard men of Ta'aa. Yet were they actually evil? Were they not merely bestial primitives, with little concept of morality, doing whatever they must to survive?

"Trust me," said the Chinaman. "There are beings on this Earth – one in particular – whose hardness of heart and commitment to self-interest even I marvel at."

As he spoke, he seemed to quail inwardly. The trembling of his hands became more noticeable than ever. It occurred to me this might just be some pose, a pretence of fear in aid of making some obscure point; but it appeared that Gong-Fen was riven with a genuine dread of someone – or something.

"You refer to a god, perhaps?" said Holmes. "A Great Old One such as Cthulhu?"

"Ah, I see your education was thorough," said Gong-Fen. "What else did you encounter on your dream-quest?

The ancient chieftain, perchance?"

"I did."

"He appears as a spirit guide to some, the lucky few. He serves as a kind of intermediary between this reality and others. His presence eases the transition. I took you to Box Hill, his burial place, precisely in the hope and expectation that he, as a *genius loci*, would come to you. That is a token of the esteem in which I hold you, Mr Holmes. I would not have gone to all that trouble for just anyone. I certainly did not for Dr Stamford. Him I left simply to wander the streets after I had injected him with the drug."

"You left me to fend for myself in the backwoods of Surrey. It is not so dissimilar."

"I was not exacting a penalty from *you*. Far from it. Having heard of your activities at my 'hotel', I was already forming the opinion that you were a man of rare calibre. I was told you fought with skill, utilising an unusual martial art. Jujitsu, from the description Zhang and Li gave."

"Baritsu."

"A close relative, deriving many of its holds and disciplines from jujitsu. An arcane choice, especially for an Occidental. I became even more intrigued by you when I called on you at home that same night. Your reputation was all it was proclaimed to be, and more. I saw in you a potential member of an exclusive club, one which only the best, brightest and most deserving are invited to join."

"The club of Cthulhu."

"So to speak. I acted, then, as I thought fitting."

"You took me to Box Hill, performed a ritual, dosed me with your drug, subjected me to a spiritual baptism of fire," Holmes said, "all in order to recruit me. To induct me into some elite cadre."

"Such was the intent. We are few, we who know of the true gods, we who understand their power and would wish to partake of it. In the civilised world, that is. I am not talking about the many savages who genuflect before idols and mindlessly ape the rituals handed down to them through innumerable generations. They are of no consequence. We" – Gong-Fen indicated himself and Holmes – "are men of consequence. We *matter*. We are capable of reaping so much more from knowledge of the existence of the Great Old Ones than simply being their vassals."

In all honesty, I was not offended to be excluded from Gong-Fen's category of "men of consequence". I cannot speak for Holmes, but to me it was not a grouping to which I wished to belong if the diabolical Gong-Fen Shou was amongst its ranks.

"We," he continued, "are the ones who may change the world, shape it to our liking, if we so choose. And with the gods behind us, we may do it all the more readily."

"If you say so," Holmes said with diffidence. "I personally am of the opinion that my own abilities will suffice in that sphere. Nor do I have any great desire to change the whole world. I work only to make my own small corner of it a place where honest men may prosper and wrongdoers the opposite."

"That is much as I suspect. It seems I should have known better. It seems that, in attempting to enlist you to our cause, I have erred."

This to me sounded like a threat, or at any rate the

precursor to one. I half rose, my hands raised.

"God help me, Gong-Fen," I snarled, "I am prepared to throttle you if need be. Stop the carriage at once and let us out, else you'll regret it. You are a self-professed murderer, a villain of the highest order, and—"

"Watson, Watson." Holmes pressed me gently back down into my seat. "Forgive my friend's hot-headedness, Gong-Fen. He regards himself as my protector, amongst other things, but he sees peril where perhaps there is none. I note that you have dressed in some haste this morning. You are normally a dapper man, concerned about neatness of appearance. However, your shirt is misbuttoned and your hair less neatly combed than on the last occasion we met. That is indicative of distress, almost as much as the way your hands are shaking. All in all, I am led to the conclusion that the upshot of your error is not that *I* am in dire straits, but rather that *you* are."

Gong-Fen heaved a quavering sigh. "I come to you as a supplicant, Mr Holmes. A client, indeed. Far from wishing you ill, I seek your help. I hate to say it, but I need you to save me."

CHAPTER FIFTEEN

An Anonymous Admonition

THE CLARENCE ROLLED ONWARD, ITS CAB SWAYING, its wheels emitting their distinctive growl on the cobblestones. Where we were, I could not judge. So far, we had gone a couple of miles and made more than several turns. I reckoned we had not travelled north, since we had climbed no significant gradients, nor south over the Thames, since a carriage crossing a river bridge makes a far different noise – lighter, hollower – than it does on a solid roadway. We had gone east or west, then, but beyond that I was in the dark, in more ways than one.

"I have transgressed," Gong-Fen said. "I have been, it is implied, intemperate and rash. I was acting on my own initiative and it seems I should not have."

"Who has told you so?" Holmes asked. "Whom have you offended? Is it Cthulhu or one of his brethren?"

"No. In many ways it is worse. Permit me." Gong-Fen drew a folded slip of paper from his pocket. "This was posted through the letterbox of my Belgravia house this morning."

It was a quaint note. All it said was:

Dear me, Mr Gong-Fen. Dear me!

"A singular epistle," said Holmes. "No superscription. No signature." He passed the note back to Gong-Fen. "Yet I sense it is no mere anonymous admonition. The sender is not being cryptic. He knows you know who he is, and knows you will not misinterpret his meaning."

"No superscription or signature are needed. I recognise the hand. It belongs to someone of whom I have been a close associate for some while."

"On our drive to Dorking you mentioned having a mentor, before anointing yourself in a similar role for me. Unlike Watson here, I am not a betting man, but I would wager good money that this mentor and your 'close associate' are one and the same."

"You would be correct in that surmise," said Gong-Fen. "He and I have been, I suppose you could say, coevals. He is a highly charismatic individual, and one with great ambition and aspirations. A true 'man of consequence'. It was he who gave me my first inkling about the terrible powers that lurk at the fringes of our world. It was he, too, who proposed that those powers might be invoked for personal gain. He spoke to me of transcending mortal constraints, of becoming rich beyond riches, mightier than kings."

"Fine talk."

"It was. You have no idea. He was a complete stranger when he approached me out of the blue one day early last year. He invited himself into my home without a by-your-leave, sat himself down in my drawing room, and in minutes had me... the only word I can think of for it is *captivated*. There's something about him, about the way he speaks, his voice..."

"What about it?"

"I cannot explain. He told me about a project he had, a scheme that would enable him and anyone he favoured to rise above the rest of humanity and, in his own words, 'walk amongst the stars'. He did not strike me as merely some deluded fantasist. Even when he began talking about the Old Ones, the Elder Gods, Cthulhu, the kind of discourse I would normally have derided as utter nonsense, he was utterly compelling. I asked for proof of his outlandish claims, of course, and he said he could not furnish it, not yet. What he wanted from me was the one thing he himself did not have: money."

Holmes let out a droll laugh. "So all this clever, intriguing fellow was after was cold hard cash. Such high-flown talk, and yet he was coming to you cap in hand like a common beggar."

"It was little money, by my lights. Enough to enable him to travel abroad in search of various esoteric materials and artefacts. I wrote out a cheque, and thereafter did not see or hear from the gentleman again for several months."

"All the while thinking, no doubt, that you would never see or hear from him again at all," I said.

"Oh no, Doctor. Somehow I knew he would come back. And when finally he did, he showed me the proof I requested."

"Took you to Box Hill?" said Holmes.

"No. Somewhere closer by than that. There I saw for myself that men are but fly-specks, tiny and insignificant. Everything we strive for is as nothing. Our lives are meaningless when held up next to the awesome, chilly majesty of aeons-old gods. But my newfound friend and mentor persuaded me it could be otherwise. And once I was fully won over and committed to the cause, together we set about putting his scheme into action."

"The killings in Shadwell."

Gong-Fen nodded. "Which was what brought you, Mr Holmes, onto the stage. When I learned of your exceptional talents, you struck me as well suited to joining us. But my colleague, now that he knows you are involved, is not best pleased. In his eyes, I have erred, and by erring put myself beyond the pale. The consequences will be severe."

"And can you not, with all your affluence and resources and your self-described pragmatism, defend yourself against this gentleman's malignancy? Why must I be involved?"

"Because, alone, even I might not prevail," said the Chinaman. "With the aid of one such as you, however, I stand a chance."

"What if I am not predisposed to help you? What if I find you despicable and feel that your current plight is entirely your own doing and a well-deserved comeuppance?"

"Hear, hear," I said.

"I can appreciate why you might think that way," said Gong-Fen. "Obviously I have failed to endear myself to you. I can, however, make it worth your while to swallow your antipathy and come to my aid in my hour of need. Very much so. Name a figure. Double it. Treble it. Add a nought. I can set you up comfortably for life, Mr Holmes. You need never work again."

Holmes chuckled. "That would be tempting, were not the money you speak of gained largely from illegitimate activities. Tainted money."

"Do you know how desperate I am? I would have to be, to throw myself on another's mercy like this."

"Perhaps you ought to tell me who your foe is," said my companion archly. "Honour him with a name. He sounds fascinating and I should like to meet him."

"You would not say so if you knew him. You think I am ruthless? Not compared with him. That note might as well say 'Fear me', not 'Dear me'. The sense is much the same. In hindsight, I should have known better than to act independently of him. Now he is—"

That was when the clarence slowed, the wheels' growl and the horses' hoofbeats diminishing into silence.

"What is this?" Gong-Fen said. "I gave the driver explicit instructions to keep going until I told him otherwise." He rapped on the front window, addressing the coachman outside. "Why the hold-up? Bad traffic?"

Answer came there none. There was a creaking of springs, and the cab inclined somewhat to one side. Then it bounced back to the horizontal and we heard the sound of footfalls – the coachman's – proceeding away in some haste.

Gong-Fen wrenched back the front curtain. The driving seat was empty, the whip laid across it. The horses stood with their heads bent, idle. He thrust the door open.

"Wherever are you off to?" he called down the street. "Hullo! Thacker! How dare you! I shall have your licence for this. When I'm through with you, you won't be fit to lead pit ponies at a coal mine!"

The only response from the coachman Thacker was a mumbled "I'm sorry, sir. Sorry to you all." This was delivered from some distance away, after which his already rapid pace accelerated to a run.

"He's bolted," said Gong-Fen. "Left us here. The

impertinence of the fellow. That's not like Thacker at all. What can have got into—?"

Then something seemed to click in his head, like the final piece of a jigsaw falling into place. "Oh no," he moaned, subsiding into his seat. Gone, suddenly, was every last trace of his self-assurance. "Oh no, no, no…"

"Stop whimpering, Gong-Fen," I said. "Collect yourself. What in heaven's name is the matter?"

"Not heaven's name. No. Not heaven. I can't believe it. This is not right. Not fair."

"Watson," said Holmes, suddenly tight-lipped, "I am of the opinion that we are in considerable danger."

"How?" I said. "Where are we anyway?"

I peered outside. We had fetched up beneath the arch of a bridge, where a railway line traversed an alley between rows of faceless factories. Above us and on either side was nothing but a tunnel of dark, dank brickwork, the mortar ribbed here and there with moss. No living creature was within view save a mangy black cat which, as soon as I looked at it, hissed, turned tail and fled. A train thundered overhead, wheels squealing, rolling stock clanking.

A lonely spot, but I could think of worse places to be marooned than on a backstreet in the heart of a metropolis of some six million souls. We could not be more than a few hundred yards from a main road. We were hardly in the middle of nowhere.

Gong-Fen remained agitated, almost beyond consolation, certainly beyond the level that our predicament seemed to warrant. To Holmes I said, "If we are in danger, it is far from apparent where it is likely to come from. We are quite alone. All one of us need do is climb out and take control of the carriage. I'm happy to volunteer for that—"

"No!" Gong-Fen cried. "Stay in the cab. It can only be safer inside."

"Don't be ridiculous," I told him. "If we are about to be set upon in some sort of ambuscade, then it makes no sense to stay put, not when there is the recourse of getting mobile again. Besides, I do not see where any likely assailants could be hiding."

"That is because they can hide anywhere," said Gong-Fen. "Anywhere there is darkness, there they may be. That is why we have stopped here, of all places."

"Absurd." Over the Chinaman's protests, I clambered out.

A hand grasped my arm, staying me. The grip was so strong it could only be Holmes's.

"Perhaps we had better do as Gong-Fen suggests," he said.

"Not in the least," I declared. "I will not pander to that man. How is it safer to sit still than to move? If I learned anything during my time in Afghanistan, it is that to be stationary is to be vulnerable."

I shook off Holmes's hand, irritated that he was opting for passivity over action. As yet I still could not descry any immediate menace. The tunnel was barely fifty feet in length, and we were at its midpoint. The road at either end was empty. The shadows beside the bridge's buttresses were too slender to conceal a man. Nor were we overlooked directly by any windows, where a marksman might lurk. Once I goaded the horses to a canter, we would be swiftly in motion and back on the public highway in next to no time.

As I grasped the arm of the driving seat in order to haul myself up, I glimpsed movement out of the corner of my eye. It was a flicker of blackness low near the ground, by the tunnel wall. I presumed it was the stray cat, ambling insouciantly back, having overcome its wariness of the carriage. Something uncoiled and coiled again, very much like the tail of a feline.

A second look, however, showed me that the cat was nowhere in sight. If I had seen anything, it was merely the movement of some innocuous object. A piece of litter perhaps, caught up by a breeze.

Ensconced in the seat, I gathered up the reins. The horses were suddenly very nervous, whinnying and pawing the cobbles with their front hooves. I clucked my tongue and made soothing sounds. "I know I am not your usual driver," I said to them. "Just bear with me. I will do my best."

Ears pricked, the horses turned their heads this way and that. They seemed eager to be under way. I picked up the whip, all set to give them a light tap on the hindquarters.

Then Gong-Fen screamed, a shrill, almost hysterical wail. "They're out there," he said. "Can't you feel it? Dear God, they're out there."

I looked around. I could not fathom what he was talking about. There was nobody nearby. I had an unrestricted view fore and aft, and we were quite alone. How could he see something from inside the cab that I could not from outside?

Then, quite distinctly, one of the buttress shadows shifted.

It seemed to extrude from the tunnel wall, articulating tendrils of itself towards the clarence. Ribbons of darkness reached for the carriage, and all at once I was conscious of a kind of torpor creeping up on me, a lassitude that was as much of the spirit as the body. Strength left my limbs. Light-headedness washed over me. I could not move, nor see the point in moving. The whip hung in my hand, inert, heavy as a lead pipe.

The horses themselves were similarly afflicted, no longer keen to quit the spot, seemingly content to stand in the traces with their heads drooping. A part of me knew I must rouse myself, must resist the temptation to linger. But why bother? It was a futile effort. Better to watch the shadow continue to grow and spread. There was something fascinating, mesmerising, in its flower-like blooming, a hideous beauty. Pure void had come to life and was stretching out to gather me up in an octopoid embrace.

A second shadow oozed out from the opposite wall, and a third began to descend from the tunnel roof, extending thin black fingers of itself downward like strange stalactites. Now I was doubly, triply, disinclined to make any attempt to escape. Everything was unfurling with a kind of weary inevitability. I felt that the touch of one of these shadows would be strangely welcome. They radiated a coldness, but that coldness would numb and anaesthetise, like ether. As when one steps into an icy lake, there would be an initial shudder followed by blissful insensibility.

In my enervated state, I was only dimly aware of anything else that was happening. There was no one but myself and the ambulatory, encroaching shadows. I did not perceive, until he climbed into the seat beside me, that Sherlock Holmes had managed to exit the cab. His every movement spoke of exertion and exhaustion, as though he had just run a ten-mile steeplechase. His teeth were clenched tight, his brow furrowed in concentration. The shadows were sapping the life out of him, but he refused to succumb, resisting them with every erg of energy he had left.

He took the reins and the whip from me. He raised the latter and brought it down on the flank of the right-hand horse. The beast flinched at the sting of the whip's tip. It seemed to recollect its purpose in life, connecting the pain with the imperative to advance. Its legs stirred. Holmes lashed again, and the horse moved. Its counterpart, remembering its duty as half of a pair, did likewise.

In this manner, with excruciating slowness, the clarence pulled away.

The shadows, however, were upon us. Their black tendrils were stroking the sides of the cab acquisitively and creeping up around Holmes's legs and mine. I did not want to look directly into their darkness, yet somehow I was unable to help myself. My eye was drawn irresistibly to a shape that was visible in their depths. Faintly, as though through a fathom of brackish water, something could be discerned – something multifarious and kaleidoscopic, something awful. It had no fixed form. It churned and billowed like smoke. Yet it was solid, too; glossy, fleshy. It seemed to remake itself with each passing second, rippling, constantly evolving. Eyes. It had eyes. Dozens of them. They blinked and revolved and stared. They were watching me. They could see me.

They hungered for me. They ached to devour me.

At that moment I may well have shrieked. I do not clearly recall. What I do recall is Holmes repeatedly inciting the horses to go – go faster – switching at them again and again with the whip, and they striving forward as though into a powerful headwind. The whole episode had taken on the atmosphere of a nightmare, one of those in which you are trying to escape from a horror but your feet are mired in quicksand and you cannot budge.

In the cab, Gong-Fen was in a frenzy. The shadows on either side had permeated through the gaps around the doors. He was howling and throwing himself about. I could imagine him enfolded in their nebulous clutches, vainly struggling to break free.

The clarence crawled ever closer to the tunnel's end, ever nearer the blazing daylight. Meanwhile, I strove to wrench my gaze away from the *thing* that lurked inside the shadows, even as my eyes kept returning to it remorselessly, helplessly. It was their progenitor. They were extensions of it, limbs it could project into the world. It was controlling them and using them to ensnare its prey. Its appetite was as foul as its appearance. It possessed no mouth and did not need one. It imbibed. It absorbed. It subsumed. To be ingested by it was to know one of the most horrendous deaths imaginable, as one's emotions, one's essence, one's very self were decanted into it like blood into a leech.

The heads of the horses cleared the tunnel gloom. Light spread along their toiling backs, down their tails, now arriving at Holmes's feet and mine. The shadows shrank back from it as though it were scalding hot. For us, it was cleansing, like a warm spring zephyr. The more the light spread over us, the more like ourselves we felt. The shadows were repelled by it, just as the lizard men of Ta'aa had been by the sunshine outside their cavern home. When one of the dark tendrils extended past the tunnel's shade, its tip evaporated to nothingness and the stump withdrew as though in pain.

Then, at long last, Holmes and I were fully free of that accursed tunnel, and the horses found a new quickness of pace. All at once they were trotting enthusiastically, fired with a zeal to be away from the bridge. The whip was no longer necessary. Holmes had only to snap the reins to encourage them to keep going.

I peered over my shoulder. Some shreds of the shadow tendrils still clung to the clarence, but they were dissipating, vanishing into thin air. Within the tunnel the shadows themselves were retracting back into the dark niches whence they had been spawned. Even as I watched, the railway bridge reverted to being nothing more than it was, a brick-built structure supporting a section of the Great Eastern Line not far from its terminus at Bishopsgate Station. It could not, from any objective viewpoint, have looked more ordinary.

We had escaped. We were free.

So why was Gong-Fen still screaming?

Holmes hauled back on the reins, bringing us to a standstill again. The cab rocked back and forth, Gong-Fen ululating in his native Mandarin. I saw him through the front window. Shadow tendrils wreathed him. Even detached from their source, there were still enough sunless spaces in the cab for them to thrive.

Holmes and I dismounted with alacrity. As one, we flung the cab doors open on either side, letting more light in. This destroyed the remaining shadows, leaving Gong-Fen writhing on the seat, unencumbered by their sinister black embrace but still afflicted by dreadful paroxysms.

I seized him and dragged him out, Holmes assisting. We laid him supine on the roadway. He weighed no more than a child might, and the reason for that was perfectly apparent. He was shrunken, reduced by half. His suit, formerly so well-fitting, now hung about him in baggy folds. His shirt collar was several sizes too large for a neck that had become as scrawny as a vulture's. His teeth seemed too big for his mouth, his eyes for their sockets.

He groaned and mumbled, wild-eyed, raving. He was alive, but to my mind not for much longer. His pulse was feeble and intermittent. Cardiac arrest was imminent, and there was nothing I could do to forestall it.

"Gong-Fen," said Holmes. "Gong-Fen. Speak to us. You must help us. What were those shadows? Where did they come from? Who sent them? Who laid that trap? If you want the malefactor brought to justice, you have to tell us."

"Holmes, he is past that," I said. "He can't hear you. He has but moments left."

Holmes was not to be deterred. "Gong-Fen Shou, I demand that you listen to me. Focus on the sound of my voice. You are going to a place where you are beyond risk of reprisal. You have nothing to fear from your friend-turned-enemy any more, and so nothing to lose by naming him. Quick, man! Out with it, while you still can."

The shrivelled, dying creature that had been Gong-Fen Shou strove to articulate a response. Lips and tongue attempted to form words around gasped exhalations from failing lungs. Holmes put his ear close, but it was all in vain. There was to be no revelation from Gong-Fen, no identification of his murderer. There was only one last wavering aspiration, and then Gong-Fen was gone.

CHAPTER SIXTEEN

Students of the Unusual

"SO THIS IS IT, IS IT?" SAID INSPECTOR GREGSON, having been fetched from Scotland Yard by a constable whom Holmes had collared on the Mile End Road. "This ties it all up nice and neatly?"

Holmes and I, standing on the opposite side of Gong-Fen's body from him, both nodded.

"Gong-Fen," Holmes explained, "was the mastermind behind the entire scheme. He inveigled Dr Stamford into acquiring victims on his behalf for experimentation. Together they had devised a new kind of drug, a potent form of opiate which happened to have deleterious side effects."

"Highly deleterious," said Gregson, "given that it killed any who used it stone dead. A drug lord wants to create addicts, not corpses. The money lies in repeat custom."

"Gong-Fen and Stamford persevered nonetheless in their attempts to refine and improve the drug, believing it could eventually be made safe and therefore profitable. At what location they performed the tests on their human subjects, I can only speculate. Gong-Fen must surely have warehouses all over the East End, any one of which could be put to use as a laboratory."

"I will have my men perform a search."

"One wonders how long that would take. There must be better allocations of manpower than to hunt for a makeshift laboratory, which is now of no importance anyway, given that the two men who operated it are dead."

"It would yield evidence, if found."

"Well, Inspector, if that is your wish," said Holmes airily. "But it strikes me that you would be on a hiding to nothing."

Gregson shrugged, seemingly half persuaded by Holmes that the task was not worth undertaking. "Can you at least tell me why I am looking at Gong-Fen's dead body?"

"Aware that my investigations were bearing fruit and the net was closing in, Gong-Fen opted to take the easy way out, rather than face the inevitable scandal and ruin which a conviction for multiple murder would entail."

"The easy way out?" Gregson eyed the withered, gape-mouthed corpse at our feet. Around us a small crowd of onlookers had assembled. Uniformed policemen kept them at bay. "Doesn't look all that easy to me, from the state of him."

"Death on his own terms," said Holmes, "without a trial, the resultant public opprobrium, the hangman's noose. To a man of his standing, this counts as a kind of victory. Not for him the undignified end of a common-or-garden killer."

"And how did he actually do away with himself?"

"The method is obvious, surely: a fatal dose of the same drug he and Stamford administered to their victims. He took it right before our eyes. We rushed to prevent him, but alas we were too slow. The good doctor here tried his hardest but could not vitiate its effects."

Gregson looked at me sympathetically. I tried to radiate an aura of medical virtue, as though I were at that very instant mentally reciting the Hippocratic Oath. In truth, my thoughts were scattered, barely coherent. I was struggling to digest all that we had just been through, and wishing I had even half of Holmes's remarkable powers of dissimulation.

"And, let me get this straight," Gregson said. "The two of you were passengers in his coach up until the final, fatal moment?"

"We were," said Holmes.

"How did that come about? My guess would be that you cunningly engineered a rendezvous, Mr Holmes. You waylaid and boarded the carriage, with a view to bearding Gong-Fen. You planned to confront him with definitive, inescapable proof of his culpability."

"That is exactly what happened."

"But unbeknownst to you, he had an escape route secreted on his person: the drug."

"That too, alas, is so. Gong-Fen Shou was the sort of man to plan ahead for every eventuality, even for his own defeat. You cannot be as successful as he was without putting a great deal of forethought into all that you do."

Gregson returned his gaze to the corpse, specifically to the hypodermic syringe which protruded from its neck. The needle was embedded in the carotid artery, the plunger was fully depressed, and the clear barrel showed smears of a sinister-looking yellowish liquid inside. He could not have known that, before Holmes sent for him, he had despatched me to the nearest chemist's to procure both the hypodermic and measures of various poisons, nostrums and potions. We had mixed the liquids together to create a concoction which would have killed Gong-Fen as surely as the marauding shadows did, then injected it into the still-warm corpse before disposing of the excess materials, bottles and all, down a drain. A coroner examining the contents of the hypodermic would conclude that they were responsible for Gong-Fen's death, and, although hard put to account for the corpse's emaciation, would be unable to rule out the possibility that the injection had caused that too.

"And the coachman?" Gregson turned his gaze to the clarence and its stationary, dully nodding horses. "What of him? Where is he?"

"He fled the scene the moment he realised something was amiss," Holmes said. "We were too busy attending to Gong-Fen to intercept him. I wonder if he feared he would be implicated in his employer's demise."

"Or, more to the point, in his murderous activities."

"Indeed."

"Would you happen to know his name?"

"I would not."

"Never mind. I'm sure he'll turn up if we look for him. His testimony would be useful in corroborating everything you have just told me. Not that I doubt your word in the slightest, Mr Holmes," Gregson hastened to add, "or yours, Dr Watson. I am simply the sort who likes all the i's dotted and the t's crossed. Thorough, that's me. Meticulous."

"And we would have it no other way, Inspector," said Holmes. "Now, if we're done here…?"

Gregson deliberated, then nodded. "Yes. This would seem to put the lid on it all, wouldn't it? Once again I am indebted to you, Mr Holmes. You have managed to lighten my caseload on a couple of occasions lately, and here, now, you have done so again. Congratulations, sir."

*

The fluency and readiness with which Holmes – and to a far lesser extent I – had lied to Gregson disturbed me. Yet we had needed to, for expediency's sake. As Holmes himself put it that afternoon, when we were settled once again in the cosy confines of our lodgings, "What alternative was there? To give him the uncensored, unvarnished truth would be to risk incredulity at best, at worst out-and-out ridicule. Gregson and his ilk are simply not equipped to deal with the implications of the *mare incognitum* upon which your barque and mine are now sailing."

"I'm not sure I am either," I said. "Living, moving shadows that can suck the very life force out of a man? The inhabitants of Shadwell have been right all along. Those reports that seemed to some so much bunkum are true. It is incomprehensible. Not to mention ghastly."

"Come now, Watson! Straighten that spine. Stiffen those sinews."

"Had you but seen what I did in the thick of those shadows, Holmes, you would not find that such an easy command to obey."

"I did catch sight of something myself, as it happens, and I grant you, it was not pretty. Where we must count ourselves lucky is that neither of us viewed it fully, in all its unfettered glory."

"I pray I never shall. I doubt I would survive."

"You are made of sterner stuff than you realise, Watson. One of your great virtues is that you do not know quite how courageous you are. To take an example, if you had not climbed up into the driving seat of the clarence when you did, I might not have followed. You showed remarkable pluck. Do not forget that."

"It was more foolhardiness than pluck," I said, "but I shall accept the compliment. So, what now? Having all but perjured ourselves to a senior police officer, how are we to proceed? Is it too much to hope that, with Gong-Fen Shou out of the picture, these 'shadow' deaths will cease?"

Holmes shook his head with a kind of whimsical regret. "I fear not. Gong-Fen, after all, did not instigate the attack on the clarence. Rather, he was the victim of a betrayal."

"What makes you say that?"

"Come, come, Watson! It's obvious. Do you not recollect his words when it dawned on him that Thacker the coachman had abandoned us, and not at random but in a deliberately chosen location? 'I can't believe it,' he said. 'This is not right. Not fair.' It is also quite plain, from Thacker's behaviour, that the coachman was either browbeaten or bribed to do as he did. So by whom?"

"The author of the note to Gong-Fen, I would hazard."

"As would I. His former mentor, the singularly persuasive gentleman whose foreign expeditions he sponsored and whose willing acolyte he became. It is evident that this personage can command those eldritch shadows to do his bidding, which makes him a threatening proposition indeed."

"I'll second that," I said, with feeling.

"The question is, was Gong-Fen the sole intended victim of the ambush, or were we targets as well?"

"I hope the answer is that he was and we were not, but I fear otherwise."

"Indeed. Chasing down Thacker would seem a profitable course of action, and I shall take it, although I do not see much prospect of success. Thacker was prepared to be disloyal to Gong-Fen Shou, no doubt fully cognisant of the treatment his employer is liable to mete out to those who offend against him. That would imply that the person with whom he has thrown in his lot – our unnamed master of shadows – is someone he knew would be able to shield him from retaliation if things did not go according to plan, someone whose power and influence are the rival at least of his late master's."

"Someone, too, who if need be can shield him from the long arm of the law."

"Yes, I would not be surprised to find that Thacker is already many miles hence, possibly even at sea, bound for the continent. Wherever he fetches up, there he will be established rather nicely, in splendid seclusion, incognito, incommunicado, hard to reach."

"That, or he is dead."

"Yes. It is a possibility. Our unknown foe appears just as coldly callous as Gong-Fen. He might not want Thacker to remain alive, for fear that he might be found and made to turn evidence against him. At this juncture, however, I think our energies are best directed towards divining as much as we can about Cthulhu and company. This last incident has put beyond all doubt the reality of such startling, powerful monsters, as far as I am concerned. If any last shreds of scepticism had been still lingering in my mind, they are now most unequivocally dispelled."

"What do you propose we do?"

"I have had various thoughts on that score already. We need to put our thinking caps on, you and I, Watson. We must become scholars again – students of the unusual – and take a course in a whole new field of research. A university beckons, one without colleges or professors, and we are to enrol as undergraduates."

CHAPTER SEVENTEEN

Sequestered Volumes

OUR "DEGREE", IF I MAY CALL IT SUCH, WAS conducted in the basement of the British Museum, in a dusty, remote archive set well apart from the rest of that venerable institution and known by a somewhat euphemistic soubriquet: Sequestered Volumes.

Our guide and helpmeet in this rarefied realm was a woman by the name of Miss Chastity Tasker, a doughty little spinster of advanced years who combined fastidiousness with garrulousness, as free with her talk as she was severe in her habits and sententious about the behaviour of others. A librarian by trade rather than a curator, she bucked the trend of her profession by not insisting on silence, at least not from herself, but she was also adamant, as any good librarian ought to be, that the books in her care be treated with respect by those reading them.

The Sequestered Volumes collection was kept under lock and key in a vaulted chamber with a cage-like door. Miss Tasker instructed us to handle the books as though they might crumble at the slightest touch, which more than one of them looked liable to do.

"A lot of these are considered dangerous," she added, waving a small, gnarled hand at the mouldering spines on the shelves around us. "For their content, I mean. According to certain individuals, they aren't simply books, they are portals to knowledge which some deem forbidden and others profane – knowledge which can forever alter one's perception of the world. Now, many would take that claim with a pinch of salt." The light sniff with which she accompanied the statement suggested she was amongst their number. "But there's no accounting for the fragility of some people's minds. Those of a sensitive disposition, prone to neuroses and depressive fits or afflicted with an excess of imagination, might be recommended to steer clear. The illustrations, especially in the medieval texts, often border on the gruesome."

"We appreciate the advice, madam," said Holmes. "Rest assured, my friend and I are of a sufficiently robust constitution to cope. Nothing we find in a mere book will rattle us."

"I am quite certain that's true," Miss Tasker said, eyeing us up and down. "I feel duty-bound, however, to deliver the warning to any and all who come this way. We have had, on occasion, a visitor depart Sequestered Volumes ashen-faced, looking very much as if he might be ill. Helena Blavatsky herself dropped by one afternoon. She was over briefly from America, where I believe she lives now, and was conducting research for her *Isis Unveiled*. She spent less than an hour here, leafing through various of the more obscure texts. Something she read left her quite offended, disgusted even, and close to fainting."

The librarian chuckled, amused at the idea of the notorious and cantankerous spiritualist displaying such infirmity.

"Perhaps what she found was confirmation of the fraudulence of her absurd beliefs," she said. "At any rate, she didn't return. Not many do."

Under Miss Tasker's aegis, Holmes and I spent the next fortnight poring over old works of often obscure provenance and authorship. On each visit, the librarian locked us into the chamber with an enormous brass key and sat at her desk outside, ready for us to call her in when we needed to return a book to its rightful place or request another. The security measures were a safeguard against theft, since many of the books were priceless and a number of them so rare that each was believed to be the sole extant copy of that title.

Seated at carrels, of which the chamber boasted only four, Holmes and I leafed through book after book, taking reams of notes. I can safely say that much of this literary arcana was pure drivel, the ramblings of deranged or depraved minds. Some of the books were concerned with black magic and ancient hermetic traditions which had little or no bearing on the subject matter that provided our focus. Others, such as *Malleus Maleficarum* – or *Hammer of Witches* – by German Inquisitor Heinrich Kramer, took a steadfastly Christian approach to manifestations of the supernatural, and thus seemed irrelevant also. The same applied to such medieval treatises on necromancy as *The Sworn Book of Honorius* and *The Key of Solomon*. Nowhere did any of these incunabula contain mentions of Cthulhu, Hastur and the like.

We were likewise able to discount books like the *Grimorium Verum*, a fraudulent text purporting to have been written by an Egyptian, one Alibeck of Memphis, in the early 1500s, but in fact the work of some unknown

European author a couple of centuries later. We flirted with discourses on alchemy and matters qabalistic, but found that they too had little useful to offer us.

Soon enough we were able to winnow out the books that were truly pertinent to our needs. These included *De Vermis Mysteriis*, the compendium of spells and enchantments which Gong-Fen had used on Box Hill. Its author, Prinn, was a thirteenth-century Crusader who had been taught by wizards whilst being held captive in Syria and had also studied at the Library of Alexandria. Holmes addressed himself assiduously to this particular work. Another such volume was the unexpurgated edition of *Unaussprechlichen Kulten*, the book from which Roderick Harrowby had divined the location of Ta'aa. I would look up frequently from my own studies to see Holmes transcribing long passages from it, sometimes page after page, and making copies of its illustrations too.

There were more: the *Book of Iod*, the *Book of Eibon*, the *Cultes des Goules*, the *Pnakotic Manuscripts*, *Thaumaturgical Prodigies in the New-English Canaan*, the *Liber Damnatus Damnationum*. These often made references to other texts of which no copies were known to have survived into the modern era and to scriptures, such as the *Seven Cryptical Books of Hsan* and the *Tablets of Nhing*, which had never been seen on Earth and were thought to reside only in the palaces of the dark gods themselves.

Day upon day, we entered the basement and immersed ourselves in the books. Where our understanding of French or Middle English was deficient, Miss Tasker stepped in to assist. She was one of the most educated women I have ever met, having eschewed the customary feminine pursuits of wifeliness, motherhood and domesticity in favour of a life of scholarship. Her grasp of Latin was likewise invaluable to us, who had both learned the language as boys but had found little use for its conjugations and declensions since then and had allowed our familiarity with the intricacies of its vocabulary to lapse. Often she would upbraid one or the other of us for failing to make sense of a line which she regarded as simple to translate, much as though she were a schoolmistress and Holmes or I a dull-witted pupil. Yet she developed a fondness for us, and we for her. The archive was not a frequented spot, and she, queen of this lonely domain, was glad of regular company.

It was a period of intensive labour, and it took its toll. One could bear only so much exposure to all that abstruse lore and convoluted cosmology before one's head began to reel. For respite, Holmes and I would enjoy long, restorative strolls round Regent's Park or apply ourselves to more worldly tasks, such as tracking down Gong-Fen's errant coachman.

In that enterprise we drew a blank. Holmes took out advertisements and interviewed various members of the carriage-driving fraternity, while I spoke to as many of Gong-Fen's remaining domestic personnel as I could locate. Since their employer's death, his dual sets of household staff had gone their separate ways, taking up new posts wherever they were able. To a man and woman, they swore they had no idea what had become of Thacker. They had said as much to the police, and they were saying it to me, and I did not doubt their word.

Time and again I would see Holmes with the enigmatic unsigned note that had been sent to Gong-Fen and that had effectively been his death warrant. He had appropriated it from the Chinaman's pocket shortly after he expired, and was wont to scrutinise it in a spare moment as though its scant six words – "Dear me, Mr Gong-Fen. Dear me!" – might yield up a trove of secrets. The cursive handwriting was neat but nondescript, the paper a high-quality bond but one that might be purchased from any good stationer's. If he hoped the note a Rosetta Stone which would somehow miraculously unlock the identity of the sender, he seemed doomed to disappointment.

After a while my brain became so crammed with mind-boggling newfound knowledge that there seemed little room for more. Many of the phrases and images I came across in the books at Sequestered Volumes stayed with me long after I left the museum, and haunted me in my dreams. I was, in addition, not sleeping well. Our encounter with those creeping shadows and the formless being that lurked within them had left me with an abiding wariness of the dark. I had adopted the practice of keeping a lamp burning by my bedside the whole night through, habitually waking up to replenish its oil reservoir whenever it ran low. Even passing a patch of dim shade outdoors during the daytime would be enough to make me cringe and cavil. Darkness, I had learned, was no friend. It is a phobia I have retained into old age. The sort of fear that children are supposed to grow out of, I grew into and still cannot wholly shake. And it is only one of many fears I have, and none of them exists without good reason.

*

Our continuing sojourns in Sequestered Volumes led us, with seeming inevitability, to the *Necronomicon*.

Or rather, would have, had the book still been there.

It was a source of some consternation to Miss Tasker when Holmes asked her to fetch down the museum's copy of the *Necronomicon* for him and she was unable to find it. She checked thoroughly, wondering if it had been misplaced, returned to an incorrect slot by some careless browser. She became flustered as she scanned every shelf in the chamber, to no avail.

"I… I cannot believe this," she said, both appalled and angered. "It is gone, quite gone. This should not happen. It is unheard of. I have never lost a book, never! My standards are most exacting. Who can have stolen it?"

The *Necronomicon* is the ultimate repository of information about Cthulhu and company, and was the book towards which Holmes and I had been building up in all those days of study and research – our final destination, the goal for which we had been sedulously shaping and preparing ourselves.

First set down around 730 by the Yemeni mystic and scholar Abdul Alhazred, it was translated from Arabic into classical Greek two hundred years later by Theodorus Philetas of Constantinople, and then into Latin in 1228 by Jutland-born Olaus Wormius. Various modern-language versions have appeared since, one in Spanish allegedly by Cervantes, another in English by the astrologer and occultist Dr John Dee.

Full of rites, symbols and formulae, the *Necronomicon* is considered crucial to codifying and understanding the nether gods, and to summoning them as and when required. Yet its history is littered with tragedy and horror. Not for nothing has Abdul Alhazred come to be known as the "Mad Arab", for madness is the fate of almost everyone who has encountered his book, and more often than not a terrible death too.

Alhazred himself was torn apart by an invisible beast on the streets of Damascus. In 1771 Joseph Curwen, a Rhode Island merchant and sorcerer who owned a copy, disappeared in mysterious circumstances after a raid on his farm in Pawtuxet by some of Providence's most influential men. In 1840 the luckless von Junzt, who published a German translation of the text, was found dead in his room, the door locked from the inside, his throat viciously slashed as though by talons.

Many copies were burned by the authorities. Pope Gregory IX placed it on the *Index Expurgatorius*. Incomplete manuscripts of translations were frequently lost, never to be recovered. The *Necronomicon*, throughout its long life, has seemed to attract nothing but misery and misfortune.

In many ways, I was rather pleased that the British Museum's copy had gone missing.

Miss Tasker went in search of it in another of the building's literary collections, reckoning that a classification error might have led to it being stacked with the medieval anatomical textbooks, although her tone of voice implied she thought this an improbable scenario. She returned downcast, but not empty-handed. She had with her the ledger in which were written the names of visitors to Sequestered Volumes and a list of the books consulted by each. She was punctilious about recording who read what and when. All of December 1880 was taken up with entries for Sherlock Holmes and John Watson, with our signatures against our printed names and the times we had arrived and departed each day, correct to the minute. She flicked back through the pages, looking for the last time someone had requested the *Necronomicon*. It had been in May of the previous year.

"Ah yes," she said. "I remember the man well. Courteous he was, and oddly charming, if somewhat lacking in looks and physical grace. He came just the once. He was interested only in the *Necronomicon*. He spent the morning absorbed in contemplation of it and then he..."

Her brow furrowed. She was perplexed.

"Do you know what? It is most strange. He came. I am clear about that. I remember him walking in and introducing himself and stating his wish to see the *Necronomicon*. But of his departure I have no memory whatsoever. He must have left, it goes without saying, and he would have had to pass by my desk to do so. But I cannot say I saw him go. And I am not a forgetful person."

"Besides," said I, "you would first have had to release him from this chamber. He would have been locked in, as is the case with us."

"It would have been no great feat for him to gain egress independently," said Holmes. "There is a keyhole on the outside only, but he could have reached his hands through the bars. The lock itself is old and of the kind that easily surrenders to jimmying with, say, a file."

"I would have heard him," said Miss Tasker. "Unless, maybe, I nodded off. But that is not my habit. Sleeping on the job? I would rather die."

"Still, somehow he must have let himself out and made his way past you, with the book concealed about his person. If I may be so indelicate, Miss Tasker, did you abandon your post at any time that day to answer the call of nature?"

"It is of course possible, but I am careful about such things. I feel a terrific burden of duty towards these books. They are my charges, I their custodian, and I am loath to leave them unsupervised. Oh, Mr Holmes, I am cudgelling my brains to recall the events of that day, but it was a year and a half ago, and I am not as young as I was. The details have become... well, foggy."

"Do not upset yourself, madam."

"I shall lose my job over this. I'm sure I shall."

"Not if I have any say in the matter," Holmes declared. Although he never evinced any romantic interest in the fairer sex – not even with respect to the bewitching nemesis he so admired, Irene Adler – my friend was unfailingly gallant towards females. Damsels in distress brought out a knightly streak in him. "Watson and I will find the fellow in question and, if he has the book in his possession, prevail upon him to return it. What, pray, is his name?"

"Now, what is it again...?"

Miss Tasker ran a finger down the column in the

ledger until she arrived at the requisite entry.

"Ah yes," said she. "Moriarty. That's right. Professor James Moriarty."

CHAPTER EIGHTEEN

Moriarty

THE NAME ITSELF HAD NO EFFECT ON HOLMES when he heard it that first time. Why would it? Moriarty was unknown to either of us, and to the public at large, back then. His name bore no associations, generated no particular frisson. It was merely a name.

The signature beside it, however, did pique Holmes's interest. He squinted at it, then extracted the note to Gong-Fen from his jacket, unfolded it, smoothed the creases, and laid it alongside the open page of the ledger. He examined the signature and the writing on the note for fully three minutes, before saying to me, "Look at that. Compare the hands. What do you see?"

"They are similar."

"Similar? They are identical! Consider the loop beneath the lower-case *g* in 'Gong-Fen' and the loop of the *y* of 'Moriarty'. They are of the same shape and dimensions, the tail on each overlapping the downstroke to precisely the same distance. The dot above the *i* in both cases is exactly the same height above the bulk of the letter. The capital M's of 'Mr' and 'Moriarty' have peaks and valleys of matching size, their internal angles alike almost to the degree. The two characters are twins."

"If you say so."

"I do say so. In fact, I insist upon it. The note to Gong-Fen came from the man who wielded his pen here on this ledger. This Professor Moriarty is the Chinaman's one-time ally, the mentor who then turned on him when

Gong-Fen displeased him by anointing himself mentor to me. I am certain of it. If you are still unpersuaded, take into account the fact that he appears to have made off with the *Necronomicon*, right under poor Miss Tasker's nose. The nature of the book, the urtext of nether god worship, puts the matter beyond doubt."

The more I thought about it, the more Holmes's supposition seemed valid.

Miss Tasker had been listening attentively to our exchange. Now she piped up: "The *Necronomicon* carries a formidable reputation. They say it is dangerous, capable of robbing a man of his reason. They say, in the wrong hands, it could destroy the world. That's so much hogwash as far as I'm concerned. However, this copy of the *Necronomicon* poses a risk to me personally, because it has been stolen while in my care. My professional integrity is at stake. I beg you, Mr Holmes, Dr Watson, for my sake, find the thief – Professor Moriarty, if it is he – and wrest the book from his clutches."

*

For the remainder of that day Holmes left me to my own devices in Sequestered Volumes while he went off to unearth as much intelligence as he could about Professor Moriarty. My current endeavour was compiling a lexicon of the language that was called R'lyehian by most and, by a few, Aklo. To that end I scoured various texts, jotting down every instance where a word or phrase of R'lyehian was used, and cross-referencing it with the appended translation if there was one. It was painstaking work but I found it strangely rewarding. Its methodical nature was refreshingly normal. My brain, schooled in the art of memorising the names of bones, organs and diseases, had an aptitude for it.

Facts about R'lyehian were scanty. It was held to be the tongue spoken by Cthulhu himself and his extended family tree, and was first written down by an unknown author on a set of clay tablets – the Black Tablets of R'lyeh – some fifteen thousand years ago. Traces of it are preserved in China in the form of scrolls from the third century BC. The glyphs used to represent it are akin to Chinese script but bear elements of Sanskrit as well, consisting as they do of characters suspended from horizontal bars.

From the Far East, knowledge of the language spread westward through Babylon and Persia. A Latin translation of the scrolls cropped up in Rome circa 200 BC, and latterly a German translation of *that* translation, entitled *Liyuhh*, surfaced in Heidelberg during the eighteenth century. The notorious rake and libertine John Wilmot, the second Earl of Rochester, is said to have produced an English version in spare moments when he was not composing bawdy poetry or bedding the wives of half the aristocracy, but no copies of that publication exist.

With a thoroughness that I hoped would do Holmes proud, I had gradually been amassing a decent working knowledge of the ancient tongue. It is not always easy to follow the sense of a sentence in R'lyehian since the language makes no distinction between parts of speech, and rules of grammar are all but non-existent. A noun can serve as a verb, an adjective as an adverb. Pronouns are optional. Verbs appear in only two tenses, the present and another tense which can be past or future, perfect or imperfect, and which can be parsed solely depending on context. Singular and plural have no meaning, word order is variable, and pronunciation is guesswork. All in all, R'lyehian seems tailor-made to perplex, frustrate and obfuscate. It has as little affinity with any human mode of speech as the roar of a lion does with the chatter of a monkey.

Holmes had reproduced from memory Stamford's reiterated R'lyehian outburst at Scotland Yard, and I now embarked on the business of using my lexicon to render it into English. Initially it was difficult to make head or tail of what he had said, but in the end, with persistence, I succeeded:

STAMFORD

"*Fhtagn! Ebumna fhtagn! Hafh'drn wgah'n n'gha n'ghft!*"

MY TRANSLATION

"He waits! He waits in the pit! The priest controls death in the darkness!"

I remained unsure about "controls". The word *wgah'n* does double duty, meaning "reside in" also. Under the circumstances, "controls" seemed the more logical choice, but the sentence could also be interpreted as "Death resides in the darkness with the priest!" Such is the imprecision of R'lyehian, a language in which perhaps only gods are meant to be fluent.

As to who it was who "waits in the pit", was that "the priest"? Or was it some personification of "death"?

"Your guess is as good as mine," I said to Holmes

when he returned from his excursion, having shared with him the fruits of my labour.

"Hmmm," was his reply. "Stamford was undoubtedly very keen to convey something. Was it the parroting of something he overheard? Or was he trying, in a befuddled way, to give us a clue? If only his brief period of lucidity at the end had lasted longer. Well, you have made sterling progress today, Watson. Would you care to hear about mine?"

"I would."

"Then let us get a restorative cup of coffee, and I shall tell all."

Having bade Miss Tasker a good evening, with Holmes renewing his promise to do everything in his power to retrieve the *Necronomicon* for her, he and I repaired to a coffeehouse on Great Russell Street.

"Professor James Moriarty is a queer fish," Holmes said. "He is our age, and a mathematician of high repute. Some in the field have even called him a genius. At twenty-one he wrote a treatise upon the binomial theorem, which has had a European vogue and earned him a chair at one of our smaller universities. His lecture on the dynamics of an asteroid, which he has subsequently expanded and turned into a book of that name, is deemed the *dernier cri* on the topic. It is also, I might add, the only work on the topic, and having scanned a copy upstairs in the mathematics section, I can safely say that no one could dispute its arguments, since no one but Moriarty can understand them, and perhaps not even he."

He chuckled.

"At any rate, what we have here, to all intents and purposes, is an academic who is destined for a stellar career. A permanent post at Oxford or Cambridge, laurels, a college chancellorship – it all awaits him. There is just one tiny problem."

"Namely?"

"Moriarty is in disgrace. A scandal has blighted him. Some heinous deed prompted his dismissal from the groves of academe, and now he resides in a purdah he may never escape."

"What deed was that?"

"Ah. There, we can discover some clarity, albeit not much. I have gone through the newspaper archives and have also spoken to dons at the University of London."

"A seat of learning of which I am an alumnus."

"Quite. Amongst the distinguished personages with whom I had audiences there, one alone was able to shed any light on the circumstances of Moriarty's downfall. He, the current incumbent of the Chair of Political Economy at King's College, was a contemporary of Moriarty's at that other university, somewhere in the Midlands. He left before Moriarty did but he had been aware, while there, of the rumours that swirled around the man. There was talk of diabolism, blasphemous practices, black magic rites. He averred, however, that Moriarty was never anything less than pleasant on the occasions they met. In the common room, our political economist found him erudite, interesting and quite convivial company."

"Did he know what precisely it was that Moriarty did to lose his position?"

"All he had to go on were oblique remarks in the letters of former acquaintances with whom he still corresponded. From those, however, and from a smattering of newspaper reports, I was able to compile a semi-coherent narrative. It would seem that Moriarty committed an act in his rooms one evening which caused a substantial commotion. Students and dons in neighbouring accommodation heard a roaring and a caterwauling as though of some enraged jungle beast, and there followed a loud cacophony of thumps, bangs and crashes, with Moriarty shouting to be heard above them. Knocks on the door brought neither an end to the ruckus nor a reply from the occupant. Eventually the noises ceased of their own accord, and Moriarty emerged a while later looking bedraggled and wan, like someone who had just gone several rounds in the ring with a heavyweight champion. The room itself was a shambles. Books had been tossed about, furniture smashed, the curtains torn to ribbons. It was as though a hurricane had passed through. When asked to give an explanation, he had none."

"Or refused to supply one."

"Just so. The only reasonable conclusion to be drawn was that he had indulged in a wild, unbridled tantrum, one most likely brought on by a less than complimentary critique of *The Dynamics of an Asteroid* which had just appeared in the Royal Astronomical Society's *Monthly Notices*. It was judged that Moriarty was not of sound mind and was potentially a danger to his peers and pupils, and so he was invited to tender his resignation by the board of trustees."

"Do you put any store by that 'tantrum' notion?"

"No more than you do. Something else occurred in the room that night. Moriarty essayed some sinister, arcane ceremony that got out of hand, and set something loose which he then struggled to banish back where it belonged. That was two years ago. The good professor is now in London, clinging to his title and the prestige that goes with it, if not the salary. He ekes out a living tutoring the scions of the wealthy to help them pass their British Army officer corps examinations. And..."

Holmes consulted his watch.

"He is expecting a visit from us at his home in three-quarters of an hour. He responded with creditable promptitude to my telegram requesting a meeting. He lives in Moorgate, so if we are to be punctual and not leave him twiddling his thumbs, we had best make haste."

CHAPTER NINETEEN

A Little Mesmeric Legerdemain

THOSE FAMILIAR WITH MY PUBLISHED CHRONICLES of Sherlock Holmes's exploits will be under the impression that I never met Professor Moriarty; indeed that I barely laid eyes on him. In the story titled "The Final Problem" I depict myself catching sight of a distant figure silhouetted against the verdure of the Swiss landscape who was more than likely, but by no means certainly, he. The only detailed description I provide of the man's physical appearance is one furnished by Holmes.

But meet him I did, this fellow whom I have dubbed a "famous scientific criminal" in *The Valley of Fear*, and he entered our lives far earlier than I have stated elsewhere. Eleven years earlier, to be precise.

In person, Moriarty was a most unprepossessing specimen. He was tall and thin, not unlike Holmes, but had an enlarged, bony forehead which beetled over a pair of deeply sunken, puckered eyes. His shoulders were rounded, suggesting too much time spent bent over books, and the pallor of his complexion likewise suggested an excess of time spent cloistered indoors, away from fresh air and sunlight. His smile betrayed an attempt to be charming and ingratiating but revealed an array of pin-sharp teeth and too closely resembled the leer of an angry dog.

His home was on the first floor of one of the shabbier houses on one of the shabbier streets in Moorgate. A smell of boiled cabbage and mildew permeated the entire building.

His mode was courteous and hospitable. He offered us dry sherry. Holmes accepted; I, filled with mistrust, refrained. He invited us to sit upon a creaking sofa whose threadbare upholstery doubtless played host to his students while he coaxed some semblance of scholarly prowess from them. He seated himself on a hard wooden chair and observed us for a time with his head jutting forward and oscillating queerly from side to side, a slow questing motion that put me in mind of a snake. I had once seen a king cobra sway in a similar manner in front of a petrified mouse, moments before delivering the fatal strike. Moriarty seemed only a fraction less deadly than that reptile, a fraction less sleek and venomous, for all his superficial geniality.

"Mr Sherlock Holmes," he declared. "It was inevitable, I suppose, that you and I should meet. However, I did not imagine it happening quite so soon. Indeed, I envisaged our first encounter taking place several years from now, once we were both better consolidated in our respective positions. It is a privilege and a pleasure nonetheless."

"Tell me," said Holmes, narrowing his eyes. "Have our paths crossed before?"

"They have not," came the reply. "Not until today."

"But your features are familiar, and I am not one to forget a face."

Especially, I thought, one as memorably ugly as Moriarty's.

"You must be mistaken," said the academic. "We are strangers. But I will confess I have been following your fledgling career with no little interest. Did you know that Victor Trevor and I were once acquaintances?"

"My old college friend?" said Holmes. "I did not."

"He embarked on a degree course in botany back in seventy-six, shortly after you and he came to a parting of the ways. I was conducting my postgraduate studies at the same university. He did not stick it out, and quit to become a tea planter in – Bengal, was it?"

"Terai," Holmes confirmed.

"He told me once about your little joint escapade. Something to do with his father and the part he had played in a convict uprising aboard a transportation ship bound for Australia, the *Gloria Scott*. He spoke of your acute observational skills and how you had deduced a great number of truths about Trevor senior simply from his ears, a tattoo on his elbow, and the walking stick he carried. Also, how you deciphered a coded message in a note sent to him. It is regrettable that your participation in the affair served to precipitate the old man's death. I suspect his heartbroken son never quite forgave you, hence the estrangement that arose between you. Victor spoke highly of you but in the somewhat bruised tones of a man trying very hard to find clemency in his soul."

"It was not I who caused Victor's father's stroke," Holmes said stiffly. "That was brought about by the re-emergence of a figure from his past, the author of the note which had such a calamitous effect upon his health. His own sins caught up with him. I was neither the agent nor the instigator of his terminal decline. I was only an interested bystander."

"Well, if that is how you choose to remember the events…"

Holmes bristled, then composed himself. Moriarty was needling him, but he chose not to give the man the satisfaction of knowing that he had been successful.

"Speaking of notes…" he said, but the other cut him off.

"Ever since Victor told me about you, I have logged your name in my memory, anticipating I might need to keep an eye on you. Such an unusual Christian name, too. Sherlock. How innovative of your parents. Your older brother's Christian name is no less unique. Mycroft."

I could not help aiming a sidelong glance at my companion. Holmes and I had not known each other long, but at no point yet had he alluded to an older brother, or to any sibling. What a closed-off fellow he could be, I realised. So jealous of his secrets and his private life, while so keen an enquirer into those of others.

"Mycroft is something in the government, is he not?" Moriarty continued. "It is hard to fathom his precise role, but he is much lauded by those in the know, rising fast and destined for great things, they say."

"I would like to be flattered that you know so much about me, Professor. There comes a point, however, when curiosity shades into obsession, and I fear you are veering close to that."

"Not at all, Mr Holmes. Not at all."

"It is especially worrisome to me – embarrassing, even – given that until today I was not aware of your existence."

"That is only because I wished it to be so," said Moriarty. "And it would have remained thus were it not for Gong-Fen Shou and his ill-advised attempt to make an ally of you, when he ought either to have ignored you or else disposed of you. He misjudged you, and it has set you on the trail that has led to this meeting. I blame his foreignness. He saw in you a man of great accomplishment and intellect, which you are, and it commanded his respect, to the exclusion of all other considerations. He did not discern, as a fellow countryman of yours would, your implacable streak of honour. He did not see one of those Englishmen who unthinkingly serve some spurious notion of decency, integrity, *heroism.*"

He spat the last word, as though it were an expletive.

"Gong-Fen was unable to read your character as I might," he went on. "I understood what manner of man you are the moment Victor Trevor mentioned you. It was reaffirmed when I caught wind of that case you investigated not so long ago regarding Mrs Farintosh and her opal tiara. You rode to that lady's rescue like a proper Sir Galahad. Such a scandal there would have been, had it become widely known to what purpose her husband had been intending to put the money he tried to claim from his insurers for the allegedly stolen tiara. You were there in Mrs Farintosh's hour of need, able to return the treasured family heirloom to her and even negotiate a rapprochement between her and Mr Farintosh, such that they are now hailed as one of society's most exemplary couples, the epitome of marital harmony. A miracle worker! And so keen to shun the limelight, too, often letting the dullards in the police force take credit for your successes. I can see, as Gong-Fen was unable to, that you are a shining incorruptible, and it was foolish on his part to have attempted to bring you into our little fold."

"A folly for which he paid the ultimate price."

"Tchoh!" Moriarty flapped a hand, as though swatting a fly. "He got no more than he deserved. Besides, he was on his last legs as far as I was concerned. For a time he was a good accomplice."

"His money made him so."

Moriarty acknowledged this with a nod. "He was useful in that regard. But lately he had become unreliable. I charged him, you see, with the task of finding fodder for the shadows to consume."

"Sacrificial lambs for the altar. The nobodies of Shadwell."

"Yes. The latest of them being one of Gong-Fen's own underlings, whom he volunteered for the role in retaliation for the man's having displeased him."

"You call them fodder. I call them human beings."

"As you wish. Those *human beings*, with the gift of their life force, have been sustaining a certain party whose influence I have been cultivating for some while. The monthly supply of nourishment, conveyed to him via the shadows, has been sating his appetite and currying me his favour."

"And that party would be…?"

"I cannot mention his name."

"Cthulhu?"

"Not he. That would be too brazen by far, even for me. I may be ambitious, Mr Holmes, but I am not mad. At any rate, Gong-Fen agreed to help. In truth, the man was so much in my thrall he would have done anything for me. But then he chose to farm out responsibility for the work to another."

"Stamford."

"Fancy doing that!" Moriarty exclaimed. "Delegating something so important to an individual of such questionable aptitude. Of course I can follow his reasoning. A well-spoken Englishman roaming the stews of the city would give a far greater impression of trustworthiness, and be far less liable to arouse suspicion and draw notice, than an Oriental. Stamford could merge into the background in a way that Gong-Fen could not. All the same, Gong-Fen ought to have consulted me first. I would have persuaded him that he was making a mistake. It was sloppy of him. Lazy, even. Perhaps his huge wealth had left him soft, made him careless."

"Then how good of you to relieve him of some of it."

"Money serves a purpose, but it is not the be-all and end-all. Look around you." Moriarty indicated his modest abode and gestured to his cheap, ill-fitting clothes. "Material goods matter little to me. All worldly trappings are ephemeral. There are greater and longer-lasting rewards to be had, and they do not originate from this earthly plane. At any rate, Gong-Fen then proceeded to attempt to draw you, Mr Holmes, into our little coterie – and that was the last straw, as far as I was concerned. I could overlook the Stamford matter, even forgive it. I could not, however, be so magnanimous about his decision to recruit a man who would inevitably, as anyone with sense might see, prove inimical to our enterprise. When I learned how he had overstepped the mark, how egregiously he had blundered, well… that was when I knew he had outlived his usefulness."

"In attacking Gong-Fen with those shadow creatures, you nearly killed Watson and me into the bargain," said Holmes. "I presume that does not trouble your conscience."

"A conscience is something I can ill afford. I admit I had no idea you two were in his carriage with him. In a way I am glad you survived, else we would not now be having this enjoyable little gathering, would we? On the other hand, had you *not* survived – well, I would have rid myself of a potential nuisance as well as an actual one. The proverbial two birds with one stone."

"And Thacker the coachman? He would be another 'potential nuisance' you have disposed of?"

Moriarty gave a quizzical grin. "Has the body not turned up yet? Maybe it never will. The Thames flows fast at this time of year. A man leaping from, say, Waterloo Bridge at dead of night, his pockets full of stones, might drown in a trice. With the high tide ebbing and the current running west, his corpse might be carried straight out into the German Ocean with no one any the wiser."

"A suicide?"

"A willing one. I can be very persuasive, you know, especially where lesser minds are concerned. The mental processes of a working-class menial are easily manipulable, until—"

I had had enough. I could take it no longer. Professor Moriarty's crowing, his wheedling tone, his sheer arrogance grated on me to the point of becoming unendurable.

"Dash it all, Holmes!" I exploded. "Do you expect

me to sit here and listen to this villain? We should be dragging him off to the police, making sure he is clapped in irons. He has openly confessed to two murders. He has attempted much the same on us. He is rubbing our noses in his wickedness."

"Ah, finally," said Moriarty. "The lapdog bares his fangs."

"Lapdog? Why, you…!"

Holmes restrained me from leaping on the man and giving him a thorough drubbing.

"Watson, calm yourself. Professor Moriarty knows, as I do, that we have no concrete proof of his involvement in any malfeasance. He can brag all he likes, secure in the knowledge that it is impossible to link him directly to Gong-Fen's death, or that of Thacker. Not in any way that will stand up in a court of law."

"The note," I said. "What about the note he sent?"

"A few words of wry disapproval. They hardly constitute an expression of malicious intent."

"Then… then… the theft of the *Necronomicon* from the Sequestered Volumes archive of the British Museum. How about that? There at least we have him. All we need to do is look for the book. It is somewhere close at hand, surely, in these very rooms."

I was clutching at straws. I knew it. Holmes knew it. So did Moriarty, who shook his head condescendingly and said, "It is not here, I assure you. But I see now how you picked up my scent. It was not Gong-Fen who gave you my name; it was Miss Tasker's ledger. In retrospect, I ought to have signed in under a pseudonym. However, my decision to take the *Necronomicon* was made on the spur of the moment. The idea occurred only after I realised how straightforward it would be, having seen for myself how lax was the security at Sequestered Volumes. A dusty, secluded section of the building, a superannuated crone as sole steward... It was all but an open invitation to larceny, and I could not refuse it. Impulsive of me, but there you go."

"So you jiggered the lock on the door and——"

"Oh tush, Mr Holmes! Jiggered the lock? Nothing so tawdrily practical as that. All I needed to do was summon Miss Tasker and convince her to let me out without checking whether I had returned the book to the shelves. She did so most obligingly."

"You bribed her, then?" I said. "To turn a blind eye?"

"Again, tawdrily practical, Dr Watson, and unlikely to have worked with someone like that, so dedicated to her vocation. No, again this was an instance of my persuasiveness. I have a knack of getting my way, when I wish it. I possess the silveriest of silver tongues."

"Professor," said Holmes, "much though I find this verbal joust entertaining, I feel we must get down to brass tacks."

"Do let's." Moriarty rubbed his hands together.

"I am of the view that you pose a great danger – to London, to the empire, perhaps to the world. You have begun trading with a being of immense power in order to accrue power for yourself. That is inordinately rash, and I am here to tell you to stop. Desist at once. Relinquish the *Necronomicon* to me, so that I may return it to its rightful place in Sequestered Volumes, and abandon all your dealings with whichever god you have attached yourself to. It is not too late. You can still turn back. This course you have embarked upon will lead only to your ruin, as it has for many others."

"Your concern is most touching."

"Did you not learn your lesson that night you conjured up a monster in your university rooms? Did that not frighten you into seeing sense?"

"You have been diligent, sir. Enquiring into my background. I should be flattered. But to answer your question, no, it did not. On the contrary, it gave me a glimpse of the limitless majesty of the Great Old Ones and their ilk, their sheer ineffable might. It gave me a taste of greatness. It was intoxicating!"

"Nothing will come of these dabblings except your destruction," Holmes persisted. "I know enough about Cthulhu and his kith and kin to know that with absolute certainty. You cannot master a force so ancient and deadly. You risk unleashing Hell in your efforts to command a god."

"Or," said Moriarty, "I risk becoming like unto a god myself. The game is then definitely worth the candle, wouldn't you agree?"

"That is your goal? Divinity?"

"Something close." Moriarty sighed, as though wistful. "I have studied asteroids – their orbits, their trajectories, their elemental composition. I have contemplated the stars and the endless gulfs of space. I started by looking out beyond Earth through telescopes, but as time wore on my astrophysical researches became more metaphysical. I turned from science to older disciplines, from the new orthodoxy to longer-enduring traditions. The more I learned, the less it seemed that we in the modern era, for all our advancements, know. Brute logic had told me that the cosmos is cold and inimical. I discovered that, at its birth, it spawned entities who bore those same traits, which made them perfectly fitted to their environment. They are gods, but not the kind that the vast majority of people worship nowadays. They do not love us. Neither, for that matter, do they hate us. They are supremely, supernally indifferent to us. They use us from time to time, as a beekeeper uses his bees; our souls are like honey to them, a side-product of our lives, a sweetmeat. Why should we not use them in return, if we can, if we are bold enough? Why should we not claw something back from them for ourselves?"

"I am warning you, Moriarty…"

"No." The head oscillated more intently than ever. The hooded eyes stared at us with a disconcerting fixity. "*I* am warning *you*. Both of you. The time has come for you to take a step back. I have indulged you so far, tolerated you. I will not do so further. Go and be a detective, Mr Holmes. Go and solve crimes, unmask murderers, recover stolen property. Help the heir who has been swindled out of a legacy, the woman who is on the receiving end of a blackmail demand over some past indiscretion, the innocent who has fallen prey to ruffians. That is what you are best suited for. Keep your friend Dr Watson by your side and devote your huge intelligence to a life of sleuthing.

It is likely to bring you riches and renown. There is no harm in that, nor any shame."

He leaned closer to us. Something in his tone of voice, in the glitter of his eyes, was making me feel ill at ease – but also strangely acquiescent, even docile. With his words he wove a kind of tapestry which, to me, seemed attractive and desirable. The future he depicted had nothing wrong with it that I could perceive. A life of adventure and public service, and no monsters, no gods, no hideous immortal beings from the ancient past. Why not?

"Yes," he continued, languidly, lullingly, "you know in your heart of hearts that that is what you want. You want certainties, not vagaries. Logic, not mysticism. The empirical, not the imprecise. Keep that in mind as you depart now. Leave alone what should be left well alone by a man such as yourself. It will go hard for you otherwise."

*

I recall nothing from that moment on until some while later, when I once again found myself seated opposite Holmes at Baker Street, the clock in our sitting room chiming midnight. I had no memory of leaving Moriarty's house, or of crossing London. It was all a blank.

Holmes was wreathed in a haze of pipe smoke, and was tapping out the dottle and refilling the bowl as I came to with a start.

"Ah, there you are, old chap," he said. "Back in the land of the living."

"I was not aware that I had been absent from it. And yet – when did we get in? Did we walk here? Drive?"

He shrugged his shoulders. "I cannot tell you. The past few hours have been like a dream, the sort one cannot recall upon waking. I myself only came around from the reverie at a little after eleven. You were clearly deeper under Moriarty's spell than I."

"Spell? As in magic?"

He barked a laugh. "Hardly. Hypnosis, more like. I daresay he employed an element of something less mundane and more eldritch in the process, but the basis of it was good old animal magnetism. A certain rhythmic vocal cadence, a compelling gaze, words that worm their way into one's ear and impinge upon one's subconscious… The same technique no doubt enabled him to ingratiate himself with Gong-Fen, pilfer the *Necronomicon* right from under Miss Tasker's nose, and cajole Thacker into hurling himself off the parapet of Waterloo Bridge. In a sense we were lucky. Moriarty could have done far worse than merely send us home. But perhaps, when all is said and done, he is right."

"Right? In what respect?"

"Perhaps we should do as he counsels and leave well enough alone." Sombrely, pensively, Holmes lit his pipe. "I quite fancy the idea of being a mere consulting detective. It is all I have ever wanted from life. The alternative presently before us is too… extreme. Too convoluted. I have a penchant for the outré, but there is outré and then there is…" He half smiled. "Outer God. It would seem wise to follow his advice and back out now, while we still can, before we wade in over our heads and begin to drown."

I nodded.

I shook my head.

Then I nodded again.

Then, with great vehemence and finality, I shook my head once more.

"Listen to yourself, Holmes. Is that you talking, or Moriarty?"

"It is I, of course."

"No. He has wormed his way inside your skull. He is preying on your qualms, your misgivings. You must not let him."

"You seem adamant about that. How so?"

"I don't know. No, I do." I undid the top two buttons of my shirt, then pulled my collar open to expose my wounded shoulder. "See? See this scar?"

Holmes surveyed the deep, puckered cicatrix. "Nasty," he opined with a wince. "The lizard man certainly took his pound of flesh."

"He did, and it still causes me pain. The ache has not yet gone away and possibly never will. Cold weather like this only seems to exacerbate it. The scar is a constant reminder of Ta'aa and Roderick Harrowby and our ill-fated excursion. It will be with me forever. I have at last come to terms with it and everything that it means, but only recently, since meeting you and becoming embroiled in these shadow-creature killings. If there is any redeeming feature in what I went through, it is this: I am ready to confront the inexplicable and the otherworldly. I may not like it, but I am the product of the trial I endured in the Arghandab Valley. And I have not reached this accommodation with myself only to give up now, simply because an unrepentant scoundrel like Professor James Moriarty has told me to. Neither should you."

Holmes regarded me through the smoke, then clapped his hands.

"Capital fellow! Well said. I was merely testing your resolve."

Was he? I had my doubts.

"You have passed with flying colours," he continued. "Moriarty cannot surely have thought he could deter us with a few well-formed sentences and a little mesmeric legerdemain. He was giving us a sporting chance, that is all. It was a demonstration, more than anything else, of his supreme self-confidence. He does not rate us as opponents."

His expression hardened.

"And that is a mistake," he concluded icily, "a great mistake, and one that he shall rue."

*

The following morning Holmes vanished after breakfast, without a word. He returned half an hour later looking grimly satisfied.

"Where have you been?" I enquired.

"The telegraph office. I could not leave our business with Moriarty unfinished, he believing that we had been swayed by his mesmerism. I have sent him a wire stating in no uncertain terms that we are worthy of his notice, and shall continue our investigation into the deaths in Shadwell. He was wrong to have dismissed us as if we were beneath his concern."

"That is tantamount to a declaration of war."

"Then so be it," said Holmes with a determination that I wished I shared. "Moriarty has made an enemy of us, and now must face the consequences."

CHAPTER TWENTY

Unhappy Christmas

THE NEXT NEW MOON WAS TO FALL ON NEW YEAR'S Eve. We had until then to stop Moriarty presenting another victim to the Shadwell shadows and thus cementing further his status with the demonic god to whom he had pledged allegiance, and whose power he hoped to exploit for his own gain.

That meant more hours spent in Sequestered Volumes. Miss Tasker was still willing to assist but a certain chilly gulf had opened up between her and us. Our failure to bring back the *Necronomicon* as promised had been a disappointment to her, and although she thanked us for trying, she was obviously demoralised. Holmes insisted he would recover the book eventually, and she consented not to tell her superiors about its purloining for another couple of weeks. She was too dutiful, however, to keep the fact a secret from them any longer than that.

Lacking a copy of the *Necronomicon*, we had no ready method of establishing what rites Moriarty might be using and with which particular god, out of the whole dark pantheon, he had forged a relationship. Miss Tasker knew of only two other copies of the book in public ownership and thus accessible to all. One was at the National Museum of Prague, but in order to view it an application had to be lodged at least three months in advance and a twenty-page form filled out, the enquirer then being subjected to a tortuous, labyrinthine bureaucratic process with no guarantee of success at the end of it. The other was all the way over in the United States, at Miskatonic University in Arkham, Massachusetts. In both instances, time was against us. It would take too long to secure permission to see the Prague *Necronomicon* and it was too far to travel to consult the Arkham *Necronomicon* and return before New Year. On that front, we were stymied.

It was not a happy Christmas for us. Church bells rang, families sat down to roast goose, gifts were exchanged and children were thrilled with their new toys – while Holmes and I felt a cloud hanging oppressively over us. Our rooms remained undecorated with festive ornaments, no evidence that the season of goodwill was upon us save for a single solitary Christmas card from Holmes's brother Mycroft perched on the mantelpiece. Holmes had not to my knowledge reciprocated the gesture, and this served to deepen my melancholy, for it made me think of my own older brother, who at that time was still alive but suffering one of his periodic bouts of indigence. With his finances straitened by his excessive expenditure on alcohol, and his conduct likewise impaired, he had been evicted from his current accommodation and was of no fixed abode. Would that I could have sent him, my only living family, a card, or better yet paid him a call, but his whereabouts were unknown to me.

On Christmas Day itself, Mrs Hudson invited us to join her and a few friends downstairs for a festive meal. We declined. We remained in our rooms, listening to the laughter and chatter below. Crackers snapped. Stemware clinked. Voices rose. Jokes were told. We could not have joined in the merriment had we tried. It was profoundly depressing.

A dreary Boxing Day was followed by that empty period between Christmas and New Year, that anticlimactic aftermath which is neither one thing nor the other, neither holiday nor the full resumption of routine. Snow fell in listless showers, enough to garnish the tree branches with white but not enough to settle and form a thick blanket on the ground; all it produced instead was a grey patina on the pavements and cold brown mud on the roads. That and a knifing north wind deterred one from going out. The British Museum was closed, besides, so we had nowhere we needed to go.

Holmes paced like an animal in a cage. He walked circles in the sitting room, his brow furrowed so deeply I feared he would be left with a permanently ingrained scowl. A pipe was never far from his lips. The delivery boy from the tobacconist's came daily with a packet of shag for him. He scraped at his violin from time to time, but distractedly, without conviction. It reached the point where he became so uncommunicative, I was lucky if he even grunted at me.

At one point I suggested that we should simply have done with it and go over to Moriarty's and thrash him into submission. This proposal received very short shrift.

"The man is hardly likely to give us the opportunity, is he? He has only to deploy that mesmeric influence upon us again to render us helpless. He might even use it to make us turn on each other this time."

"What if we were to lie in wait and ambush him? Fasten a gag around his mouth before he can speak? Failing that, the judicious application of a blackjack…"

"But even if we were to incapacitate Moriarty himself, there is another threat to consider. The god with which he has affiliated himself remains at large. The shadow aspects which this entity can assume are not necessarily going to go away even if Moriarty is taken out of the equation. They could well run rampant, making them as much of a present danger, if not more so, than our wayward academic. No, Watson, we are better employed trying to defeat both enemies – Moriarty and the deity – in one fell swoop. Would that I knew how."

Things thus stood at an impasse. Holmes, try though he might, simply could not think his way to a solution to the problem.

Then two events transpired in close succession which helped bring the entire affair to a head.

CHAPTER TWENTY-ONE

A Caller and a Telegram

IT WAS THE MORNING OF NEW YEAR'S EVE. IF Moriarty were to offer up another sacrifice to his chosen deity, he would surely do it that night, to coincide with the dark of the moon.

Holmes's mood, as a consequence, was itself of the darkest. He had reached a nadir of frustration and self-recrimination. When I went to bed the previous evening I had left him sitting in his armchair, knees drawn up beneath his chin, hands clasped around his bony shins, staring into the middle distance. When I came downstairs in the morning he was in the exact same pose. All that had changed was that the room reeked more strongly than ever of tobacco smoke and the ashtray beside him was full to brimming with stubbed-out cigarettes.

"Holmes, did you even sleep? If the pinkness of your eyes is anything to go by, I very much doubt it."

He twitched his head a fraction, like someone who had just heard a distant sound he could not identify. "Oh. What? Hum! Sleep? Perhaps. Possibly. Probably not."

"Well, at least get some food inside you. I shall call down to Mrs Hudson. I believe I can smell her cooking some of her excellent devilled kidneys."

"Not hungry. How can I be? Someone in London is going to die tonight, die in the most horrible manner, and I am powerless to prevent it. I have no way of telling who it might be, whom in this city Moriarty has set his sights on. Even knowing that the sacrifice will take place somewhere in

Shadwell is of no benefit. I cannot patrol an entire borough."

"Then bring in the police. Contact Inspector Gregson and enlist his aid."

"As far as Gregson is aware, the case is closed. We saw to that, remember? We bamboozled him into believing that Gong-Fen took his own life and the spate of deaths by emaciation is over. We cannot now go to him and confess that we lied, then hope that he will see fit to overlook that and offer us Scotland Yard's full support. We'd be lucky if he didn't throw us in jail. We are hoist with our own petard, Watson."

"How about the other fellow, then?" I said. "The one you also rate. What's his name? Lester?"

"Lestrade."

"Yes. We haven't perjured ourselves to him yet, have we? We can try him."

"Really, Watson!" Holmes snorted with disdain, as though he had never heard anything so nonsensical. "If you have no worthwhile suggestions to offer, you would be better off not talking at all."

"I say, Holmes, you have no right to speak to me like that. I am only trying to help."

"Then don't."

"What is wrong with the idea of engaging Lestrade rather than Gregson?"

"Everything. For a start, it would put us in exactly the same predicament as if it were Gregson. We would have to account for why Gong-Fen Shou's so-called 'suicide' has brought no end to the killings, and that would entail the risk of incriminating ourselves. Lestrade would want to know the reason we had omitted to tell Gregson the whole truth. We would lay ourselves open to the accusation of hampering the police in the course of an enquiry."

"We could lie again and say we made a mistake."

"That would hardly incline Lestrade to look on us with favour."

"What if we claimed it was Gregson who had made the mistake? You told me the two of them are rivals. Lestrade might leap at the opportunity to show his fellow inspector in a bad light."

"They are, I admit, as jealous of each other as a pair of professional beauties," Holmes said, "but they are also, all said and done, both Scotland Yarders, policemen to the core. Their loyalty to each other may be tenuous but their loyalty to the law supersedes all other concerns. Lestrade would check with Gregson first to see if our allegation held water. He would find it did not, and we would be back where we started, and perhaps even deeper in the mire. No, Watson, seeking police assistance is fruitless in this instance. As is, it seems, any other course of action. I fear that I have met with my first real failure – so early in my career, too – and an innocent life will be the price."

I could think of nothing further to say that might stir him from his torpor and rally his spirits. The outlook for him was as bleak as the grey sky outside which since dawn had been sending down a thin wintry drizzle onto the rooftops and streets. Breakfast arrived, and I ate desultorily and Holmes not at all.

Then, an hour later, came the clangour of the doorbell, and into our rooms stepped a lean, dark-eyed, ferret-faced little fellow who was known to Holmes but not to me. It was, it so happened, one of the two men we had previously been discussing. Inspector Lestrade cut an altogether more lugubrious figure than Gregson. The latter had a puppyish eagerness about him. Lestrade was subdued and serious, and spoke with a faintly adenoidal whine which carried more than a hint of officiousness.

After he and I had been introduced and my bona fides as Holmes's companion had been established, Lestrade said, "My apologies, Mr Holmes, for the intrusion. I'm loath to disturb you on—"

Holmes cut him off. "Out with it, man. Say what you have to."

Lestrade was taken aback by the abruptness, but soldiered on. "This is, strictly speaking, a police matter, but I felt you should be included, if only because you and the person concerned have an association."

"And also because, not to put too fine a point on it, you are stumped. I see the way you clutch the brim of your bowler and rotate the hat in your hands. It is one of your tics, Lestrade, a mannerism that invariably attends an admission from you that you have drawn a blank in an investigation. Then there is the dampness of the hat's crown, the extent of which tells me that you have been out in this inclement weather since first light. Why would that be unless you were scouring the streets on some protracted and ultimately unsuccessful errand? Finally, the very fact that you are here leads me to deduce that you need my help on a case on which you have made little or no headway yourself."

"Yes, well, there is all that." Lestrade looked somewhat shamefaced. "It's Inspector Gregson, you see."

Holmes straightened in his seat, his lethargy receding. For the first time that day he appeared to have some energy. "What of him?"

"He is gone."

"Gone?"

"He has not reported in at work for two days running," said Lestrade. "We have received no notification from him that he is ill or otherwise indisposed. I sent a constable round to his flat in Battersea first thing yesterday morning to see if he was home. The man received no answer to his knock, and when he managed to gain ingress to the property by shinning up the drainpipe and climbing in through an unlatched window – which was quite improper of him, I might add, and he shall be disciplined for it – he found the place empty. No sign of Gregson, but neither of anything untoward."

"You mean no indication that he had packed a bag, or that he had been abducted after a struggle."

"Just so. The flat was spick and span. The bed was made, the sitting room tidy, there was no unwashed crockery in the sink, nothing to suggest he had been forced to leave in a hurry or against his will."

Holmes unfurled his long legs and leaned forward, elbows on thighs, fingers steepled. "If he lives in a flat, then there must be other tenants in the building. Were they aware of any comings and goings?"

"The constable made the appropriate enquiries. The elderly couple on the ground floor said they had heard

Gregson leave by the front door on the morning of the twenty-ninth, Wednesday, at the usual time. The solicitor's clerk on the top floor confirmed it. It is as though Gregson stepped out to catch the omnibus to work… and vanished. I had men on the lookout for him all of yesterday, frequenting his known haunts, to no avail. It is most curious."

"Most curious," Holmes agreed. "And under the circumstances, not a little troubling."

"Ah-ha," said Lestrade. "Already you sound as if you know something I don't. Gregson was consulting with you on a case just before Christmas, was he not? One which culminated in the suicide of a certain Gong-Fen Shou. Do you think his disappearance might have some connection to that? Has he been kidnapped by Orientals, associates of Gong-Fen's, in revenge? Might it be the handiwork of one of their gangs, their – what do you call 'em? Tongs."

Lestrade looked optimistic. He was clearly hoping for a simple answer to the mystery, one which made logical sense, one he could act upon. And why not?

"If so," he went on, "I can have a score of men, a hundred, combing Limehouse. Just like that." He clicked his fingers. "They'll find him in no time."

"Inspector," said Holmes, "I cannot tell you that Gregson's disappearance has no relation at all to what happened with Gong-Fen. Nor can I tell you that it *does*."

"Oh." Lestrade was crestfallen. "Well, what *can* you tell me?"

"Not much, for now. Is it entirely uncharacteristic of Gregson to behave in this way? You know him better than I. There has been no prior absenteeism of this sort?"

"None. Gregson, if nothing else, has an exemplary attendance record. Whatever I think of him as a detective, I have to give him that."

"All the more concerning. I shall need to look over his flat, of course. Scour it for potential clues. One can only hope your constable did not interfere too much with the state of it and mar whatever useful evidence there might be. Policemen can be such clodhopping oafs."

"Now, now, Mr Holmes…"

"You know it to be true as well as I do, Lestrade. So his home will be my first port of call. Battersea, you say. I will need the address."

*

Lestrade departed 221B with more of a spring in his step than when he had arrived. He was obviously heartened by the knowledge that Sherlock Holmes was on the case.

Holmes himself seemed invigorated, but worried too.

"I would like to dismiss this as coincidence," said he as he gathered up his overcoat and muffler. I, too, was attiring myself against the dismal weather. "It may simply be that Gregson has had to respond to some dire family emergency and, in his haste, neglected to notify his superiors."

"But you do not think so."

"No, Watson, I do not. He is too conscientious, too punctilious for that. I think the timing, so close to the new moon, is all too significant. I think – I fear – that Moriarty has selected his next sacrifice. The question is, why Gregson, of all people? The usual victim each month has been a nobody. As a police official, Gregson is quite abundantly a somebody."

"As was Gong-Fen," I pointed out.

"Yes, but that was different. That was a reprisal, and occurred out of sequence, between new moons. I maintain that the choice of Gregson is inconsistent with Moriarty's pattern hitherto. It is a suggestive development, an escalation, and—"

He was interrupted by the doorbell ringing again. This time it was a messenger with a telegram, which read:

MR HOLMES

COME TO THE DIOGENES CLUB POST HASTE.

— WHITWORTH

"The Diogenes Club?" I said. "I have never heard of such an institution."

"Few have," replied Holmes. "My brother belongs to it – is one of its founders indeed. It is, simply put, the queerest club in Christendom. Its roster is a veritable *Who's Who* of oddballs and eccentrics, the kind of men no other club would take, the kind who have a particular genius for getting along with nobody."

"Oh." I nearly asked if Holmes himself was a member. "And who is Whitworth?"

"The secretary."

"What does he want from you?"

"That remains to be seen. But it is highly out of the ordinary for him to have cabled me, as we have nothing in common but Mycroft. One can only infer, then, that it is on the subject of Mycroft that he wishes to see me."

"What do you think the matter is?"

"I cannot say, but the terse and peremptory wording of the telegram does not lend itself to a positive interpretation. It seems more summons than request, and I must do as bidden."

"But Gregson… Battersea…"

"Can wait," Holmes said, lodging his opera hat on his head and making for the door. "Mycroft first."

CHAPTER TWENTY-TWO

The Queerest Club in Christendom

IN MY PUBLISHED OEUVRE I INITIALLY MADE reference to the Diogenes Club and the most distinguished of its members, Mycroft Holmes, in the story "The Adventure of the Greek Interpreter", which recounted events in the year 1887, seven years after the narrative set out in these pages. I stated in that tale that I had not known until then of Mycroft's existence, and had even come to believe that Sherlock Holmes had no living relatives.

That was, of course, a fabrication, as this book makes clear. I think I chose 1887 as the year in which to depict Holmes's revelation to me that he had an older brother because it was in the spring of that same year that my own older brother finally succumbed to the vicissitudes of his heavy drinking and perished. There seemed a pleasing symmetry, a kind of aesthetic balance, in having one sibling step into the limelight when another had just taken his final bow.

In 1880, the Diogenes Club was still in its infancy, but already it was proving a haven for the least clubbable men in England, those who sought the company of others but not the conversation, who preferred to socialise in silence and pay their fellow members so little heed they might as well have been invisible. Back then, too, there was not yet the club within a club, the secret subsidiary organisation which went by the appellation the Dagon Club.

But I am getting ahead of myself. The Dagon Club and its objectives will have to wait until the second and third volume of these memoirs.

We drove to Pall Mall, arriving at the door to the Diogenes – which stood some little distance from the Carlton – shortly after ten o'clock. In the hall we showed our cards to a footman who wordlessly led us past the glass panels through which was visible the club's large, luxurious reading room, and onward to that small chamber, the only place on the premises wherein one was permitted to speak, the Stranger's Room. There awaited a pot-bellied individual of stuffy appearance whom I took to be Whitworth.

No sooner had the door closed behind us than Sherlock Holmes said, "Come on then, Whitworth. Out with it. What is the meaning of this? Where is my brother?"

Whitworth ducked his head ruefully. "That's just it, Mr Holmes," said he. "I have no idea. That's why I asked you to come. As club secretary, I am in attendance at the Diogenes more regularly than most, but the frequency with which I visit is nothing compared with your brother. He is here, as you know, every day like clockwork, from a quarter to five in the evening until twenty to eight. You can set your watch by him. Rain or shine, he never fails to show his face. Yet for two days in a row, yesterday and the day before, he has not come."

Holmes's eyes narrowed, and his mouth tightened to a grim slit. "That is indisputable? There is no mistake?"

"You may check the register if you like. Even assuming he omitted to sign in, I was here on both those evenings and did not see him. More to the point, none of the other members saw him, and several of them drew me aside to this very room to tell so. That's how unusual they found it. We may not pay much attention to one another at the Diogenes, but by the same token we notice one another's absences. That is especially the case when someone as prestigious as Mycroft Holmes is concerned, someone so central to the club's existence, so much a part of the furniture."

"At his size, he is hard to miss."

"And concomitantly, he is more easily missable if he is not present when he should be. Since he dines in every night, the serving staff too have remarked on his non-appearance. All of which leaves me baffled, to be frank, and somewhat slightly perturbed. The other Mr Holmes is not unwell, is he? I was hoping you would know."

"We are hardly close, Mycroft and I," Holmes said. "I am not kept abreast of his daily activities. He may be unwell, he may not."

"In that case, I regret disturbing you, sir," said Whitworth, countering Holmes's curtness with obsequiousness. "I merely felt I ought to make enquiries, in case there had been some… unfortunate eventuality. I mean, the other Mr Holmes is still young, but a man of his stature…"

"Corpulence, you mean."

"And of his appetite…"

"Gluttony."

"Yes, well. One never knows, that's all. Anything can happen."

*

"And I am very much afraid something has," said Holmes as we exited the Diogenes. "Just not what Whitworth was hinting at. Not yet, at any rate."

"You believe Moriarty has abducted your brother too? In addition to Gregson?"

"Two unaccountable disappearances. Two men missing for over forty-eight hours. I cannot help but see Moriarty's hand behind it."

"But why two, when hitherto he has taken only one victim at a time?"

"The quantity of abductees matters far less than the identity. Neither of them was chosen randomly. Both of them are known to me. One is my own close kin."

"He abducted them to attract your attention."

"It is the only logical inference."

"Well, Holmes," I said, "you have only yourself to blame. You goaded Moriarty with that telegram of yours. You poked the hornets' nest. This is the upshot."

Holmes glared at me, but I discerned a flicker of guilt in his eyes. Here, once more, was the impetuous young man who had driven off to Dorking with Gong-Fen, heedless of the consequences. Now, however, he was beginning to realise that reckless actions might put others in jeopardy, not just him alone.

"That may be so," said he, "but the professor will find that I am capable of delivering quite a sting myself."

With that, Holmes stepped across Pall Mall, smartly dodging traffic, seeming to care little whether I accompanied him or not. We fetched up on the opposite kerb, before a grand townhouse. Holmes climbed the steps and rapped the knocker.

"Who lives here?" I enquired.

"Mycroft. He has a suite of rooms on the second floor."

I glanced back across the street to the Diogenes. *Very conveniently situated*, I thought. In the cab on the way over, Holmes had told me that his brother worked in Whitehall, which lay just round the corner. All in all it would seem that Mycroft Holmes preferred to confine himself to this one small district of London, leading a life both well ordered and heavily circumscribed.

A page let us in, and Holmes soon ascertained from him that Mycroft was not in residence. The page affirmed that he had not seen "'ide nor 'air of Mr 'olmes" since Wednesday and admitted that he found this a mite unusual.

"On Wednesday, did he have any guests, perchance?"

"Not as I rightly recall, sir."

"No one came to call on him at all?" Holmes pressed.

"Well now..." The young man shook his head. "I 'ave a feeling that a stranger might 'ave come by and I answered the door to him. Was it Wednesday? Maybe. Can't for the life of me say for sure. I could be getting it muddled up with Tuesday, or... or..."

"An articulate, rather charming man, albeit not good-looking?"

Holmes gave a physical description of Moriarty, but the page looked nonplussed.

"You know, I sort of remember meeting someone like that. But, oddest thing, it's like it 'appened 'ere, but also not. Almost like I might've dreamt it. D'you ever get that feeling? When you're sure you did something, only maybe you didn't, maybe you only imagined it? That's 'ow this feels."

Holmes glanced at me, his look acknowledging my own conclusion: that the page had been subjected to

Moriarty's "silveriest of silver tongues". The boy's mind had been clouded, his memory left a smeary blur, like a chalk painting after rain.

Brandishing his calling card, Holmes established to the page's satisfaction that he was Mycroft's brother and said he would like to take a look round his rooms. The page regretted that he did not have the key, but Holmes replied that Mycroft had given him a duplicate.

We showed ourselves up to the second floor. Holmes's claim about a duplicate key was not wholly the truth. He did not have one. What he did have was a set of lockpicks, the same lockpicks he must have used to gain access to Stamford's apartment on York Road. He instructed me to stand by the stairwell and keep watch, in case the page should grow curious and come to check on us, or another resident or a tradesman should happen by.

I saw little of what Holmes did with the implements, but the lock seemed to present only a minor challenge. A few seconds of deft manipulation, a quarter of a minute at most, and then, with a click, the mechanism yielded to his ministrations and the door was open.

Mycroft's habit was to be fanatically neat. That much was apparent to me the moment we stepped inside his rooms. The place was immaculate. There was not an item of furniture askew, no speck of dust visible. The curtains hung so straight and their folds were so uniform, it was as though they were marble sculptures executed with ruler and set square. Even the coals heaped in the scuttle looked orderly.

"Are you sure this man is your brother?" I could not

help remarking to my companion. "You described him a few moments ago as corpulent, and you are as thin as a rake. Now I see that he likes things shipshape, whereas you prefer a shambles."

"If ever two people could be described as opposite sides of the same coin, they are Mycroft and I," Holmes replied. "It was always so, even when we were boys. Our father was descended from a long line of soldiers and brought a martial discipline to everything he did. Our mother was different. Her uncle was Horace Vernet, the French artist, and she was altogether of a more Bohemian disposition. Mycroft and I draw traits from both genealogies, but to wildly disparate degrees. He enjoys his food, I treat it as merely fuel for body and mind. He craves consistency and systematisation, I have a bent towards creative chaos. Now, if you don't mind, I have work to do."

So saying, Holmes set about examining the spacious premises minutely and methodically. He went from sitting room to study to bedchamber to dressing room to bathroom, bestowing upon each a thorough, floor-to-ceiling scrutiny. On several occasions he took out a magnifying glass and peered at something – a section of cornicing, a chair castor, a basin tap, a doorknob – with such intent interest that it could have been a detail of the *Mona Lisa*. Nigh on an hour elapsed before this exhaustive procedure was done, and at its end Holmes pronounced himself satisfied that his brother had indeed been abducted and that the culprit was Moriarty.

"Here is a hair which can only have belonged to our errant academic," he said, holding up the tiny dark filament for me to see. "It is of the appropriate length, and it bears an odour of coconut and ylang-ylang." He sniffed it. "Yes. In precisely the same ratio as the brand of macassar oil Moriarty uses to style his hair, namely Rowland's."

"That clinches it. Damn it."

"But there is better news. I am happy to relate that Mycroft has been so good as to leave us a clue as to his current whereabouts."

"A clue? Where? Of what nature?"

"There is something out of place in this sitting room, something ever so slightly awry."

"You're joking!" I declared. "Awry? I behold nothing that would indicate anyone even *lives* here. This apartment is like a doll's house. It is too perfect and pristine to be real, let alone inhabited."

"Cast your eye about."

I did so. "The inkwell on the escritoire?" I hazarded. "Is it a fraction of an inch off-centre? No? That rug, then. A degree or two misaligned with the floorboards?"

"You are guessing."

"Of course I'm guessing. A book on the shelves? How about that?"

I scanned the bookcases, of which there were three, all made of burnished walnut and situated equidistant from one another along one wall. Mycroft's personal library consisted largely of improving novels and anthologies of poetry and essays, and was arranged according to colour of binding and size of book – folio volume with folio, quarto with quarto, and so on. All were set shoulder to shoulder, snug and gleaming.

"You are still guessing," Holmes said, "but you are getting warm. It is indeed a book, but not on a shelf."

He could only have been referring to the large King James Bible, which rested upon a lectern by the window. It sat very slightly askew on its perch. The angle of discrepancy was so small that one would never have noticed were one not looking; yet, in such a scrupulously orderly set of rooms, this tiniest of variations from true became conspicuous.

Holmes picked up the Bible carefully. It was a heavy, handsome artefact, printed on sturdy vellum, bound in calfskin, the pages trimmed with gold leaf.

"You will observe, Watson, that there is a thumb index." He gestured at the series of small round niches scooped out from the right-hand edge of the pages. "Each cut-in indentation features an abbreviation of three Biblical book names, enabling the reader to jump more quickly to a desired passage. You will observe, too, that one of those indentations bears a scoring upon it. This one, which reads 'COR GAL EPH'."

There was indeed a mark across the little semi-circular pad of black paper and gold lettering, a thin depression half an inch long.

"The book is in otherwise immaculate condition," said Holmes. "Mycroft seldom if ever opens it. He owns it more because it is a thing of beauty than for any spiritual sustenance it might afford. The scoring has been put there freshly, is incongruous, and is thus of significance. Also of significance is this scuff mark near the base of one of the lectern's legs. Do you see?"

Bending, I was able to make out a lozenge of black boot polish besmirching the veneer of the wood.

"What does all this tell you?"

"That even your brother cannot keep his home perfectly tidy?" I offered.

"It tells me that Mycroft stumbled against the lectern, scraping it with his foot, and at the same time put a mark on the index pad with a fingernail."

"By accident?"

"No, I reckon both actions were quite deliberate. He feigned clumsiness."

"You are quite certain of this?"

"Not beyond a shadow of a doubt," Holmes replied with some asperity. "I can, however, make an informed inference based on available evidence, just as you with your medical knowhow can assess a patient's symptoms and make a considered diagnosis. Mycroft would have known I would search his rooms once I learned of his disappearance, and so he took pains to shift the Bible a fraction and subtly deface it in such a way as to leave me a trail to follow. Somehow he had managed to inveigle Moriarty into revealing the location to which he was to be spirited away. That or he had applied his facility for logic and reasoning to the matter, before Moriarty's mesmerism took hold of him. In that field – the science of deduction – Mycroft is very much my equal, if not my superior."

"There is another brain like yours in the land?" I said wonderingly.

"I would say there are three, if one includes Moriarty. But in the case of Mycroft, the brain, though mighty, is untrained and unfocused. He is content to apply it sparingly and at whim, owing to an innate laziness. He allows the government to tap his intellect on demand, but the rest of the time leaves it idle. That is another way in which he and I are unalike. My brain is never idle. It refuses to be."

"But at least, *in extremis*, he *has* used it."

"Absolutely. To his and our advantage."

"I just don't see what the scoring on the thumb index is supposed to indicate."

"I refer you to its positioning. 'COR GAL EPH'."

"Corinthians, Galatians, Ephesians."

"All three form part of the Pauline Epistles."

"And what are we supposed to construe from that?"

"Think harder," said Holmes. "Try not to be such a blockhead."

"The Pauline Epistles. Paul. He who was formerly Saul of Tarsus, scourge of Christians until his conversion on the road to Damascus, after which he became an apostle and was eventually martyred for his beliefs, by Nero, or so is the general assumption."

"Go on."

"That is as far as I can take it. I am no theologian, nor any great expert on the life and work of St Paul."

"You are so nearly there, it is painful to watch. I would coax you further until you got the whole way, but time is short and so is my patience. St Paul, Watson. Remember I said it was a location. Where in London is there a place that derives its name from him?"

I slapped my forehead. "St Paul's Cathedral."

"Correct, and also incorrect."

"But it makes a perverse kind of sense," I insisted. "Follow my reasoning. Moriarty has taken Mycroft prisoner, along with Gregson. He has turned his persuasive powers on them, such that they have willingly accompanied him to a destination he has chosen."

"Yes, that is my own surmise. He enthralled and led away each one separately, like a Pied Piper."

"So why do you think he hasn't taken them to St Paul's Cathedral? St Paul's has symbolic value. It is Britain's foremost religious edifice, after Westminster Abbey. Surely Moriarty would gain a wicked satisfaction from profaning it, turning it into a place of—"

I caught myself. Holmes completed the sentence for me.

"Of human sacrifice."

"I did not want to say the phrase."

"And I appreciate your discretion. But there is no need to tread delicately around the subject. I am fully aware what fate Moriarty likely has in store for my brother tonight, and for poor Gregson."

"You seem awfully calm at the prospect."

"What you perceive as calmness, Watson, is simply fixity of purpose. I cannot afford the luxury of giving free rein to my emotions. Fear is unproductive, it will only hinder my efforts. In order that we might have a chance to save the lives of Mycroft and Gregson, my thought processes must be as clear as possible."

I marvelled at his self-control. Had it been my own brother in Moriarty's clutches, I would have been beside myself.

"I take your argument about St Paul's Cathedral," Holmes continued. "What you are overlooking, perhaps through ignorance of the facts, is that there is more than one St Paul's in London. There are several churches going by that name. Off the top of my head, without resorting to an almanac, I can tell you there is one in Knightsbridge, another in Covent Garden, and yet another in Hammersmith."

"You're saying it might be any of those three," I said, deflated. "Or, for that matter, any St Paul's in England, of which there must be dozens. Our search is rendered impossible."

"Not so. Because there is also a St Paul's in an area quite pertinent to our case, and logic dictates that it is there that Moriarty has taken Mycroft and Gregson – to St Paul's Church, Shadwell."

CHAPTER TWENTY-THREE

Forearmed Mice

"GIRD YOUR LOINS, WATSON," SAID HOLMES. "THIS is it."

We had arrived at St Paul's Shadwell, and as our hansom rattled off into the distance, we paused and took stock.

St Paul's was a Waterloo church, erected by an Act of Parliament some sixty years ago on the site of an older church, and was built in the late Georgian style, with a cupola steeple and something of the Greek temple about its lofty, portico-capped façade. It lay between the Ratcliffe Highway and the Shadwell Basin, near enough to the latter that the creak of moored ships, the groan of anchor chains and the lap of water against wharf pilings were faintly but distinctly audible. A grassy churchyard set it apart from the rest of the city, like a moat around a castle. A further bulwark against its surroundings was provided by high, spiked railings and, just within this iron perimeter, a fringe of tall plane trees.

The hour was past seven, and rain continued to fall from the darkened sky, as it had all day, in evanescent sheets. It was the kind of precipitation that chilled one to the bone in minutes, and was surely the reason why Holmes and I had marked so few New Year's Eve revellers on the streets during the drive over. The night was yet young, but it seemed as though the annual carousing would be limited this year. The weather was having a dampening effect on people's spirits.

We had spent the day preparing for a perilous

undertaking. In Holmes's case this entailed hours of labour at his chemistry bench, where he had busied himself with a number of complex, often foul-smelling procedures – mixing, straining, boiling, titrating. He had conducted these operations with reference to the notes he had taken in Sequestered Volumes in the days before Christmas. The notebooks spread in front of him contained nothing but unreadable scrawl as far as I was concerned – Holmes's handwriting was atrocious – but to him they were a source of valuable information.

For my part, I had given my Webley Pryse a thorough cleaning and oiled all the moving parts. "A gun that works properly is a gun that will save your life," as my old regimental sergeant major was fond of saying. I had also taken it upon myself to ensure that Holmes ate sufficiently, which he doubtless would have neglected to do had I not insisted upon it. Another of the regimental sergeant major's aphorisms, drummed into me by repetition, was "An empty-bellied soldier is as much use on the battlefield as a dressmaker's dummy", his personal variant on Napoleon's "An army marches on its stomach".

As we stood before the church gate, all I could think was that if Holmes and I were not now ready to confront Professor Moriarty, we never would be.

Nonetheless, I could not help voicing a concern which had been nagging at me ever since we left Mycroft Holmes's rooms. I could no longer leave it unaired, this misgiving, not when our destination loomed so close.

"We could, of course, simply be taking the bait Moriarty has laid for us," I said.

Holmes nodded grimly. "Could? There's no 'could' about it. I would say the probability exceeds ninety per cent."

"It needed to be mentioned."

"I was taking it as read. There is every chance that Mycroft did not leave that Bible clue for us of his own volition and that Moriarty wants us here."

"What for?"

"Why go to the trouble of sacrificing my brother and Gregson to his god, if we are not there to watch them suffer? It would be a concert in an empty hall. Added to that, it is highly likely Moriarty has devised some stratagem that will imperil the lives of anyone who comes to his victims' aid, which is to say ourselves."

"Is that why we have come alone? Why you have not kept Lestrade apprised of developments?"

"Precisely, Watson. Insightful as ever. We are Moriarty's target. We are the ones who must bear the brunt of any defensive measures he has put in place as we launch our rescue bid. Why endanger anyone else? We are the ones who aggravated him."

"You mean *you* did, with that telegram of yours. Had you not sent it, Moriarty would have been content to think that you and I were no threat. He dispensed with us easily at his rooms, did he not? He felt he had secured our compliance. But you had to go and provoke him."

"It was a calculated move," said Holmes.

"Not wholly."

"I admit the wording of the telegram could have been somewhat less acerbic, but the act of sending it was designed expressly to keep his attention. While we remained in his sights, there was every chance he would take a shot at us."

"You put a bullseye on our backs."

"How better to make the sniper reveal himself? What I did not bargain for — and I am castigating myself over it now — was Moriarty drawing others into the affair. I failed to estimate just how low the damnable rogue might stoop! Speaking of which, I feel honour-bound, at this juncture, to propose that you yourself do not participate in the forthcoming endeavour, Watson. You don't, as the saying goes, have a dog in the fight. Given how hazardous tonight could be, I would not think any the less of you if you were to bow out."

"Holmes," I retorted, "you insult me. I am as keen as anyone, present company included, to see Moriarty stopped before he can inflict any further horrors on the world. Nor could I stand idly by while the good Inspector Gregson and your brother are at risk of death. As your friend, and as a human being, it would be immoral, unconscionable."

"Good man. I knew I could count on you."

"All the same, I cannot help feeling like a mouse who is sniffing at the cheese, with the jaws of the trap yawning over him."

"Ah, but the difference here is that neither you nor I can be described as any old mouse. We come forearmed. Your pistol is loaded with some of the cartridges I gave you?"

"Yes." I patted an overcoat pocket. "And I have the remainder of the cartridges to hand." I patted the other pocket.

"Excellent. And I have my own unique arsenal about

my person. Well, we have prevaricated long enough."

Holmes pushed open the gate and we entered the churchyard. Many of the capital's churches were holding New Year's Eve services tonight, but St Paul's Shadwell was not amongst them – the place was deserted. We passed under the leafless boughs of the plane trees and wended our way up a gravel path. To either side of us lay a host of headstones, the majority of which marked the graves of seamen, for St Paul's had long served a nautical congregation. The original seventeenth-century building had been known colloquially as the Church of Sea Captains and could count amongst its parishioners none other than James Cook. After it was demolished to make way for its replacement, the tradition it espoused had been maintained.

As we neared the building, London's nocturnal clamour became muted, replaced by the sough of the wind and the clatter of bare branches. Shadwell itself resided on what had once been salt marsh, and on that night, in the propinquity of the church, the air smelled like it. In place of the usual sulphurous urban tang there was the reek of dampness, earth, brackish water. It felt as though Holmes and I had somehow left civilisation behind and travelled into the past, to a barren, more primordial era.

"Now to see where our friend Moriarty is lurking."

Holmes produced a stoppered test tube which held a glutinous, murky blue liquid.

"That single strand of his hair we recovered at Mycroft's has enabled me to create a lodestone solution, as prescribed in *De Vermis Mysteriis*," he said. "I only hope it works. I have followed the 'recipe' to the letter, but I am a novice chef so I cannot guarantee that this particular cake, as it were, will rise."

"Eye of newt, and toe of frog, eh?"

"Nitre of potassium and tincture of myrrh, more like. This is no magic, Watson, it is alchemy. A fine distinction, you might think, but an important one. Alchemy is the forefather of modern chemistry, and the two have a lot more in common than one might suppose. In this instance, the dissolved hair causes the solution to respond visibly when in proximity to the person from whose head it came. Skin scrapings are better, so Prinn says, and a sample of bodily effluvium even more preferable, but a hair should still yield results."

"Should? Will."

"I pray your confidence in me is well-founded. Now, if Moriarty is anywhere within range… Oh-ho! What's this?"

The lodestone solution had begun to emit a hazy azure glow. Holmes moved the test tube from one side to the other. When he swung it leftward, the glow faded; when rightward, the glow brightened perceptibly. He ventured a few paces in that direction, waving the test tube aloft and using the solution's fluctuating levels of luminosity to guide him.

Thus it was that, by trial and error, we wound up on the west-facing flank of the church, next to a bossed wooden door situated at the foot of a short flight of steps. It was the entrance to a level below ground, presumably the crypt. The lodestone solution glowed all the more effulgently when Holmes held the test tube to the door.

"There we are," said he in a low voice. "Our quarry lies within."

He stowed the test tube away and produced in its stead a plain old pocket-lantern, the candle of which he carefully lit.

"And as if to put the issue beyond question…" He held the lantern up close to the padlock which secured the door. "Do you see that, Watson?"

"See what?"

"Why, the discrepancy."

"Between…?"

"Padlock and hasp. The one is brand new, the other corroded and old."

"Is that so remarkable? One might conclude that the previous padlock rusted up and thus had to be replaced."

"One might conclude that. One might equally conclude that the padlock has been changed recently by someone who wishes to go in and out through this door but lacked the key to the original padlock. If you look more closely at the hasp, you will see a series of straight, parallel scratches directly behind the padlock's shackle. Unless I am very much mistaken, those are the marks left by the tip of a pair of bolt cutters when they were used to sever the shackle of the original padlock."

"Which does not gainsay my interpretation of the facts. If the first padlock had become inoperable, it could not have been removed in any other way but by bolt cutters, wielded no doubt by the church sexton."

"The hasp could have been unscrewed from the door instead, a simpler and more logical remedy. It has not.

The application of bolt cutters implies a desire to do the deed swiftly, with the minimum of fuss. That in turn implies furtiveness, the behaviour of someone not wishing to be caught in the act − in other words, not the sexton, nor the verger, nor any other ecclesiastical functionary. Hold this."

Holmes passed me the pocket-lantern, then produced the small leather pouch which held his set of lockpicks.

"Torsion wrench first," he murmured, inserting a slender L-shaped instrument into the keyhole. For the first time I had a ringside seat while he utilised this dexterous talent of his. "Hmmm. Three-pin tumbler. Nothing too out of the ordinary. A half-diamond pick will do. Keep that light steady, will you?" He inserted the pick as well and prodded it gently along the keyway. "Ah yes, there's the binding pin. Bit of resistance. Up you go. And the next pin. Up over the shear line. And last but not least…"

With a clunk the padlock sprang open.

"*Voilà*! Child's play."

"Don't you think that was a little too easy?" I said. "If it is Moriarty who swapped the padlocks, would he not have put more effort into forestalling intruders?"

Holmes chuckled, but then his face fell.

"Oh, Watson. How I wish you hadn't said that."

"Because it makes me sound querulous?"

"No. Because you are correct, and I have been overzealous." He pointed at the padlock as it hung loose from the shank of the hasp. "There. On the toe of the shackle. Just above the notch."

Into the rod of metal was scored a tiny elaborate

symbol. It had been etched by hand, and had lain concealed when the padlock was shut. I did not recognise the symbol *per se* but I knew it to be a magical sigil of some kind. As we watched, a crackle of bright white light coursed along its shallow grooves, there then gone in an instant, quick as a wink, leaving a crimson afterimage of itself on my retinas.

"Palgroth's Ward, if I don't miss my guess," said Holmes. "Well, at least Moriarty now knows for sure that he has guests. I hate to think what sort of reception committee awaits us."

CHAPTER TWENTY-FOUR

Magic Bullets

HOLMES EASED THE DOOR INWARD, AND WE DUCKED under the low lintel and proceeded through into the crypt with the utmost caution. The beam of the pocket-lantern picked out runs of brick columns in a grid pattern, holding up a vaulted ceiling. The floor was unevenly flagged, and dense cobwebs hung everywhere in ragged, overlapping layers. Dust and damp in the air clogged my throat, tasting of clay.

It was hard to tell how far the crypt extended, since the lantern's mirror-augmented cone of light reached no more than a few yards into the gloom before petering out. I imagined that it took up more or less the same space as the main body of the church above, which was big enough, but I had heard of crypts which spread beyond the footprint of the buildings they served, tunnelling out sideways into the grounds. I wondered if this was one of those. I hoped not. Already there was too much darkness around us for my liking, too much I could not see, too many hiding places.

"Keep your wits about you, Watson," Holmes said.

"I can go one better than that," I replied, and drew my revolver.

We ventured away from the entrance, Holmes moving the lantern back and forth in an arc so as to illuminate the broadest possible area of our surroundings. Several times I thought I detected movement in its light, a flicker such as of someone or something flitting past, and swung my gun in that direction. On each occasion it proved to be merely a cobweb wafting in the breeze from the open doorway.

"You are excessively on edge," Holmes admonished.

"Can you blame me?"

"You are jumping at shadows."

"I am afraid of shadows, with good cause."

Onward we went, deeper into the crypt, every step putting the sole available point of egress further behind us. I found myself constantly estimating, and re-estimating, how long it would take to sprint back to the door, and gauging the most direct route through the maze of columns to get there.

Then I spied a sight which sent a tingle of horripilation over my entire body. The phrase "every hair standing on end" would not be inapt.

Leering at me from the dark was a toothless, hollow-eyed brown face.

It took me several seconds to realise that I was looking at the head of a corpse. It lay in an alcove, and the cadaver was clearly very old. It had undergone a natural process of desiccation, so that it was now a set of bones encased in papery skin and the rotted remnants of clothing. Long dead, it could surely do me no harm. It had given me a fright, but it had no more agency than that.

As I composed myself, Holmes moved closer to the corpse. If he had been as startled as I by the sudden appearance of its yawning, withered features in the lantern light, he gave no sign. He shone the beam around, to reveal that the cadaver was not alone. Several dozen identical alcoves were ranked along one wall of the crypt.

Each had the dimensions of a bunk bed, and each was home to a husk of a human being.

"Sailors," he said. "All of them from the last century. Naval officers. You can tell by the uniforms, what's left of them. Look. That one is wearing a Monmouth cap. That one a tarpot hat with a 'tally' above the brim, a ribbon with his ship's name on it, although the painted letters have faded beyond deciphering. That one has the cocked hat of a midshipman. Here a neckerchief, navy blue. There a brass-buttoned frock coat, also navy blue. This fellow would have been a captain, no less. White waistcoat with gold braid, and a bicorn. One can only assume all these seamen hailed from the more prosperous Shadwell families. Not for them a common coffin in the earth and the depredation of worms. They were granted their final berth in altogether more amenable conditions."

"Fascinating, I'm sure," I said. "But shall we get on with what we came here to do?" The sooner we found Moriarty and his captives, the sooner our stay in the crypt would be over. I was resolved to spend not a second longer in that miserable place than I had to.

We turned away and resumed our search. We had gone no more than a few paces, however, when a soft scraping sound behind us drew our attention. We swung round, as one, and Holmes aimed the lantern back at the alcoves.

All was well, I thought. The corpses still lay in their last resting places. Every alcove held its cargo of decades-decayed sailor.

"Watson…"

The lantern's beam came to rest on one of the alcoves.

It was empty.

"That one was unoccupied before," I whispered.

"It was not," said Holmes with finality.

"I know. Wishful thinking on my part."

"Be on your guard, old man."

"You don't honestly believe…?"

I would have finished the interrogative by saying, "…that the corpse has got up and walked?" But I did not have to.

For the corpse had got up and walked.

The evidence was there before us, shambling into the light on rickety, creaking legs.

*

It is peculiar that I was less alarmed by seeing a corpse become ambulatory than I had been by that glimpse of an unmoving skeletal face a few moments earlier. The reanimated body was too surreal, too impossible, to have the same impact on me. It belonged in the realm of the utterly fantastic, so far outside the norm that my mind had no easy way of accepting its substance. At first glance, I was quite convinced that what I beheld was some kind of grotesque life-sized puppet, a thing of papier-mâché and carved wood, a mannequin being manipulated by some unseen marionettist. I may well have looked above its head for the strings that supported it.

Even when Holmes breathed an oath expressing incredulity and dismay, I still could not quite accept that the corpse was exactly what it was: a dead man somehow reanimated. That explanation seemed weirdly banal.

Perhaps at last I was beginning to take the preternatural in my stride. The extraordinary, to me, was starting to become the everyday.

How naïve, to assume I would ever fully acclimatise to the new world in which Holmes and I now lived.

As the corpse made its stiff, stumbling way towards us, a second corpse swung a leg out and slithered down from the alcove in which it had been shelved. A third and a fourth followed suit. None was swift. They reminded me of very elderly people crippled by rheumatoid arthritis, every joint as inflexible as a rusted door hinge. Nor did they possess any great sense of balance, it seemed. It was as though the erstwhile naval officers were having trouble reacquainting themselves with upright motion after so long a period of horizontal inactivity. They had not yet regained their "life legs", so to speak. They lurched and swayed with every shuffling step, perpetually on the brink of teetering over.

What they did have, for all their maladroitness, was an unmistakable and unshakeable purpose. They closed in on Holmes and me, and one after another they lifted their arms and stretched them out towards us. Hands that were spindly, mummified appendages, hands in which almost every metacarpal and phalange was distinguishable, hands that were in several instances missing fingers, they groped for us, and their owners seemed intent on seizing hold of us and inflicting I know not what gruesome maltreatment – tearing us limb from limb, presumably, had they sufficient strength. All to the accompaniment of the rustle of threadbare rags and the relentless grinding of bone against bone.

"Well?" said Holmes to me, as the deceased sailors, now a half-dozen of them all told, formed a rough semicircle around us. We, in turn, had begun backing away. "Aren't you going to do something?"

"What do you propose? If you mean fire bullets at them, what use will that be? These creatures are insentient. They are scarecrows of dead flesh, granted a semblance of life by sorcerous means. Surely they are impervious to harm by conventional weaponry?"

"And are you carrying a conventional weapon?"

"A Webley? Nothing could be more so."

"But what is *in* the gun?" Holmes pressed. "For heaven's sake, man, think! Did I or did I not, just this afternoon, adapt an entire box of Eley's No. 2 cartridges specifically to counter a threat such as the one before us? Did I or did I not, at some pains, daub the nose of each round with a design called the Seal of Unravelling, using a paste that numbers amongst its ingredients my own blood?"

"You did," I said, abashed.

"And you forgot."

"In the heat of the moment..."

"Shoot, Watson." We had butted up against one of the columns, our backs to its brickwork. "Six corpses. Six chambers in your Webley's cylinder. See if you can manage it without having to reload."

"Should I aim anywhere in particular?"

"As centrally as you can, for maximum efficacy."

I levelled the gun at the nearmost of the corpses, which was the one Holmes had identified as a midshipman. The *crack* of the gunshot was amplified to a deafening level in those close confines, like a skewer driven into the eardrums. The muzzle flash seemed as bright as a lightning bolt.

The round struck the midshipman in the sternum. The impact briefly staggered the corpse, but almost immediately it renewed its unsteady forward march.

So much for the Seal of Unravelling. I darted a sidelong look at my companion. Holmes's face was inscrutable, but even he must have been disappointed by the failure of the alchemy-enhanced bullet.

Then the corpse halted in its tracks, and if those shrivelled, decomposed features had been capable of forming an expression, one might have said it registered bewilderment.

That was followed quickly by consternation and then distress, as the bullet hole in the midshipman's chest began radiating lines of orange brilliance. These spread out, multiplying like cracks in shattered glass, with a sound akin to that of tinder catching alight. Dried flesh, hollow bone, even clothing – all was affected by the progress of the searing-hot orange lines, until in next to no time the entire corpse was riddled head to toe with tiny, lambent fissures. A strong whiff of burning filled my nostrils.

All at once, the undead thing lost cohesion. It had been divided into a million fragments, and these fell apart in a sudden, catastrophic avalanche. The midshipman collapsed to the floor, granules of him scattering everywhere. Nothing was left but a spill of blackened, charred debris with a clinkery texture, from whose surface wisps of smoke drifted up.

I paused to marvel at the devastation wrought by the

Seal of Unravelling. A potent device after all.

Then I took potshots at the remaining five corpses. The range was point blank. Every round found its mark. The naval officers' second lives were snuffed out, terminating in a welter of scorching fiery lines and attendant disintegration.

When it was over, my ears were ringing, but I felt a profound sense of satisfaction. A surge of optimism, too. We had faced an enemy that might have cowed and destroyed anyone who lacked our specialised knowhow, and we had overcome.

"If that is the worst Moriarty can throw at us…" I began, but Holmes cut me off with a cautionary wagging finger.

"Let us not tempt fate," said he. "We proved equal to this challenge, but there may yet be others in store."

A loud, slow handclap echoed from a remote recess of the crypt. Then came a voice: "Congratulations, Mr Holmes. You did indeed prove equal to the challenge. But then it would have been a poor show – embarrassing, almost – had a handful of clumsy, barely mobile revenants been your downfall. My expectations of you are at least marginally higher than that."

From the darkness emerged the figure of Professor Moriarty.

He was not alone.

CHAPTER TWENTY-FIVE

The Triophidian Crown

ACCOMPANYING THE ACADEMIC WAS A HOMINID with a sloping, elongated brow and a scale-covered hide. At first I thought, with a start, that it was one of the lizard men of Ta'aa. The resemblance was close. Then I perceived that, although the thing's features were reptilian, they derived from a different subgroup of that class of animals. The scales were of varying size. The eyes were lidless. Most telling of all, a forked tongue flickered between the upturned lips of the mouth. Not a lizard man, then, but a near relative. A snake man.

The particular nature of this monster and its similarity to the lizard men did not come as a complete surprise to me. I had encountered several references in the *Pnakotic Manuscripts* to ancient anthropoid races which bore non-mammalian characteristics. Some, according to more contemporary sources, existed even to this day. A New England port called Innsmouth was said to be infested with batrachian-like humans. On our own south coast a sighting or two of something similar had been recorded. Man's evolution, it would seem, had taken some aberrant turns, more so than even Mr Darwin might suspect.

The serpentine creature stood at Moriarty's side in the hunched stance of an underling. Its gaze was fixed on him as though it awaited instruction, like a gundog poised to retrieve the fallen grouse at a command from its handler.

Moriarty himself looked serenely smug, perhaps more so than when we had first met. To his sartorial ensemble of frock coat and tapered pinstripe trousers was added a new accessory; on his head he wore a diadem fashioned of bronze and wrought in intertwining plaits somewhat like a Celtic knot. At its fore arose an ornamental device which took the shape of a trio of snake heads, each jutting in a different direction. Although I had no way of fathoming the diadem's true purpose just then, I sensed it was more than a mere item of apparel. There must be some link between its serpentine aspects and those of the hominid accompanying Moriarty.

"Yes, it would have been a terrific pity, Mr Holmes," Moriarty said, "if you were to have been deterred, or even defeated, by what were after all just skeletons. Things so fragile and brittle, a puff of wind might blow them away. I should have been very disappointed, especially after Gong-Fen Shou made such a fuss about you. 'A most gifted individual', he called you."

"Gong-Fen was too kind," said Holmes. "I certainly anticipated something like that little conjuring trick of yours. What do churches have in abundance? Human remains. A supply which, in the correct hands, with the correct potions and cantrips, may be turned into a weapon." He gestured at the heaps of ash to which the six corpses had been reduced. "Zuvembies, am I right? You resurrected them and enslaved them to your will using the infamous Black Brew, in the manner of a Haitian houngan."

"You have been doing your homework, sir. I applaud you. And would I, in turn, be correct in thinking that your friend was firing bullets made not of lead but iron?"

"Iron is a known counteragent to the zuvembie,

and can cause harm to various other supernatural manifestations. But no, you would be wrong."

Moriarty frowned, then smiled, as though he had swiftly solved a riddle or some complex mathematical equation. "The Seal of Unravelling. Of course. An elegant ploy, with a host of suitable applications. Bravo."

"While we are engaged in this badinage, and before the inevitable hostilities break out," said Holmes, "the headgear you are sporting – I believe it is what is known as a Triophidian Crown."

"None other. How do you like it?"

"It certainly covers up your receding hairline. I imagine, too, that it grants you dominance over that scaly curiosity by your side."

"A Triophidian Crown?" I said.

"Do you not recall from our researches, Watson? Specifically from the *Book of Eibon*? A Triophidian Crown is an artefact of some potency, giving the wearer the ability to control all serpents – as well, it would seem, as men who have more than a trace of the serpent about them. Moriarty's appears to be brand new and homemade, not one of the original crowns, of which only three are known still to be in existence."

"All of them impossible to obtain," said Moriarty. "One is in the private collection of a vastly wealthy American antiquarian who guards his possessions so jealously that he has not set foot outside his property in more than twenty years. He refuses to see visitors, and any who approach his house, save his own domestic staff, are treated to blasts from a shotgun fired from one of the mansion's upstairs windows."

"Meaning that even you, with your exceptional persuasive skills, might have trouble gaining access to it," said Holmes.

"Not without potentially receiving a face full of buckshot. Another of the original Triophidian Crowns resides in a temple deep in the Amazonian jungle whose location is a well-kept secret. That crown is reputed to be a dud anyway. Its power has waned over the centuries through disuse, so that it is now little more than a pretty trinket. As for the third, it lies in a Persian museum, under lock and key in an underground vault. It is inaccessible not so much because the vault is secure, although that is the case, but because it is buried amongst thousands of similar relics, all in identical packing crates, without documentation or markings to differentiate them. Unearthing it from that jumble would take months, perhaps years. Making a Triophidian Crown of my own therefore seemed the most judicious option."

"No mean feat."

"It required the retrieval of numerous lesser magical objects and the siphoning off of their eldritch power, which I transferred into an otherwise inert assemblage of bronze tubing. Far from straightforward, but I enjoyed the challenge."

"Gathering those objects was the purpose of your travels abroad last year."

Moriarty nodded. "I scoured the world, far and wide, for months on end. It was tiring, but it was an enlightening experience too. Travel broadens the mind, as they say, even if it does also slim the wallet."

"Luckily not your wallet. Gong-Fen's."

"Which was so fat, it hardly felt the loss."

"And was abroad where you found this snakelike consort of yours? Was he lurking in some ancient ruined city half engulfed by desert sand? Or perhaps he was the prisoner of a travelling Bedouin caravanserai, exhibited as a freak in marketplaces to earn a few coins?"

"Oh no, Mr Holmes. My friend here is something of a local. More of a local, one might say, than any Londoner."

The snake man seemed to intuit that he was the topic of conversation. He hissed softly and swayed from side to side, still not lifting his gaze from Moriarty. There was a kind of adoration in those beady oval eyes of his, and something else buried beneath, an emotion I took to be resentment. He was a hapless thrall of the Triophidian Crown, and he did not like it.

"You are telling me," I said, "that he hails from this very city?"

"I am."

"Well, where does he live? If he has been here all this time, how has he managed to go unseen, unnoticed, for so long? Does he dwell in the sewer system? Is that it? Has he been right under our feet ever since those tunnels were dug?"

"No, he makes his home deeper than that, so deep that Mr Bazalgette's engineers would never have come across him during their excavations. He and his kind were here long before that great public work commenced. There are places in the capital about which none of its citizens has a clue. There are civilisations far older than man's that have coexisted alongside ours in secret, unbeknownst to us, from time immemorial."

"Your snake man, then, is not such a rarity," said Holmes. "There are more."

"Many, many more," said Moriarty, and he touched a hand to the Triophidian Crown. "Why don't I introduce you to some of them?"

His brows knitted, and the diadem began to emanate a soft greenish glow. At the same time it emitted a low throbbing hum which I felt as much as heard. The noise seemed to penetrate the bones of the skull and make them reverberate along their sutures. The sensation was not unlike a dentist's drill boring into a molar, and only marginally less unpleasant.

From the dark all around us, more snake men emerged. They came skulking out from behind columns. They lowered themselves from the ceiling, dropping to the floor gracefully, with scarcely a sound. A couple slid out from alcoves, where they had been lying in wait, concealed behind the supine unliving occupants.

There were a score of the hominids, and although all bore serpentine characteristics, some had them in greater abundance than others. A few could almost have passed for ordinary humans, save for their eyes, which were enlarged, round and wide-spaced, and the smattering of scales on their shoulders and the backs of their arms. Equally, there were those whose heads were simply proportionate versions of a snake's, attached to squamous bodies with slender, sinuous torsos and loathsomely attenuated extremities. One was even hooded like a cobra. There were varieties of skin colouration to be seen, too, from jade green to cinnamon red to pitch black, with bands, speckles and "eyes" providing patterning.

The creatures, at Moriarty's mental behest, moved towards Holmes and me. We retreated until we found ourselves with our backs against a wall, and the snake men closed in, surrounding us in a broad semicircle. They stood within arm's length of one another, leaving gaps through which one could not hope to pass without risk of being grabbed. There was an eerie, precise choreography to it all, Moriarty marshalling them like a child positioning his toy soldiers. Thanks to the Triophidian Crown, he had only to think a command and it was projected into the snake men's minds, becoming a compulsion to them, an irresistible inner urge.

This required effort on his part, to judge by the scowl of concentration on his face and the droplet of sweat that beaded on his forehead. The diadem was a fine-tuned instrument, demanding skill and focus from its user. Yet he appeared equal to the task.

Beside me, Holmes had stiffened. Out of the corner of my eye I spied him sinking his weight onto his back foot, as a pugilist does. He was braced for an assault.

I took my example from him, pocketing my revolver and raising my fists. The gun was spent, and there would be no time to reload. Moriarty was not about to give me the opportunity.

"Holmes…" I began.

"Just do your best, old man. That's all anyone can ask. Give a good account of yourself."

"But there are so many more of them. The odds are stacked against us."

"Then do not let them have victory lightly. Make them work for it."

Moriarty peeled back his lips in a grin, one which itself had a somewhat snakelike quality. "Such stiff-upper-lipped Britishness. But, Mr Holmes, this is your own fault. I gave you every chance to leave me alone, as I advised. Instead you sent that telegram to vex me, to declare yourself my enemy and my equal. Now you and your colleague shall reap the consequences."

He flicked a hand.

"My friends – take them."

The snake men launched themselves at us, hissing, snarling, and there followed a mêlée in which Holmes and I, though heavily outnumbered, nonetheless acquitted ourselves well. I was weaponless, and therefore obliged to rely on the boxing skills I had learnt at school and the more underhand brawling techniques I had picked up from the rugby scrimmage. Holmes, however, had brought along a singlestick, which he had been keeping sheathed in a long, specially tailored pocket in the lining of his coat, adjacent to the button hem. This baton-like implement he drew with a flourish, and instantly set about using it to belabour snake men left, right and centre, his movements as deft and controlled as any fencer's. The *thwack* of the singlestick's impacts were now and again matched by the *snap* of breaking bone and a shriek of distress from the victim, who then hobbled away in retreat. Yet the snake men were generally hardy, and those blessed with an extensive covering of scales were to some degree armoured, protected from the full force of Holmes's strikes. A blow which might have incapacitated or even crippled an ordinary human, these creatures more often than not could shrug off.

I, meanwhile, punched jaws and fended off grappling hands. There was an acrid stench in my nostrils, an ammoniac reek coming off the snake men's bodies, some kind of natural odour. It was nauseating, choking, repellent, and it gave me added incentive. I fought all the harder, simply to keep the stench and the creatures generating it away from me.

Superior numbers won out in the end, though. Not even Holmes's singlestick could tip the balance in our favour. One of the snake men managed to wrest it from his grasp, and promptly snapped it in half with his bare hands. My companion resorted to baritsu and caused a fair bit of mayhem thus, but soon enough he was overwhelmed. Snake men thronged around him, clung to him and brought him to the floor with sheer weight of numbers, as they did me. Holmes and I both struggled, but we were pinned down.

The cobra-like snake man loomed above me, and his mouth opened wide to expose a pair of fangs. They were as long as my little finger and wickedly curved, and at their sharp, hollow tips I saw globules of a clear yellow liquid welling.

Venom.

I made one last supreme effort at resistance, but it was futile. The fangs descended towards my neck.

CHAPTER TWENTY-SIX

The Onyx Obelisk

I LET OUT A DEFIANT, LAST-DITCH ROAR, AS though I might stave off death simply by bellowing at it loudly enough. It was all I could do. What sort of demise would the cobra man's bite bring? It could only be a lingering, agonising one. I had seen snake venom at work in Afghanistan when I had tried in vain to save the life of a lieutenant in the 14th Ferozepore Sikhs who accidentally trod on a Levant viper. Haemotoxia spread through the fellow's bloodstream like wildfire. His limbs swelled, his skin turned purple, and after half an hour of screaming and convulsions, he was gone.

The single pathetic hope I could latch onto was that the cobra man would surely be injecting me with a dose of venom commensurate to his size. In other words, he would be putting so much of the toxic substance into me that the end would arrive altogether more quickly than it had for the Sikh, although it would also be far more excruciating while it lasted.

"*N'rhn!*"

The cobra man halted, his fangs a mere inch from my throat.

Moriarty repeated the command. "*N'rhn!*" I recognised it as the R'lyehian for "Stop!"

The cobra man turned his head and snarled in indignation. "*K'na n'rhn?*" he said. *Why should I stop?*

"I wish them subdued," Moriarty replied, still speaking in the ancient language. "Not dead. Not yet."

"But he is my prey. I have vanquished him."

"Do not defy me!" Moriarty thundered. He had moved into my field of vision, and the Triophidian Crown on his head was aglow as never before, wreathed with coruscating emerald brilliance. "Kill him, and I will make you suffer in ways you cannot begin to imagine."

The cobra man clearly wanted to defy him. He wanted, with every fibre of his being, to strike and sink his fangs into me. But Moriarty was having none of it, and was deploying the Triophidian Crown to its fullest in order to get his way. It was a battle of wills between master and slave. The diadem fairly crackled with energy, its light dazzling.

The other snake men looked on with great interest. Several of them muttered to the cobra man, advising him to back down. The version of R'lyehian they spoke was rudimentary and unconventional, though still comprehensible. It used a dialect which was more sibilant and less guttural than the standard language – at least the version I had studied and had heard Stamford speak – and hence was better suited to the vocal cords of beings that were part snake.

In the end, the cobra man relented. He raised himself from me with a frustrated growl and sidled off. Moriarty fixed him with an imperious glare, although I noticed that the professor was wan of cheek and seemed unsteady on his feet. The mental exertion of operating the crown at such intensity must be draining. He probably could not have faced down another challenge to his authority, not in such rapid succession.

Recovering somewhat, Moriarty gestured to the other snake men and seemingly issued a silent mental command. Holmes and I were hoisted to our feet. Our arms were held fast, twisted up behind our backs so that we were forced to bend forward. The snake men were strong, exceptionally so. There was no way we would readily be able to squirm out of their clutches.

"I do apologise, Doctor," Moriarty said to me. The Triophidian Crown's glow was ebbing to its former level of luminosity. "That was unseemly and I would rather it had not happened."

"By sparing my life, Professor, you have simply given me another chance of ending yours."

"Sparing your life? Ho ho! Is that what I have done? No, sir. Prolonged it by a matter of minutes, that is all. But do not be downhearted, by all means. It's rather touching."

He stooped to pick up Holmes's pocket-lantern, which my companion had laid aside on the floor prior to our scuffle with the snake men. By some miracle it had not been knocked over during the fight and its flame still burned. Now Moriarty used its beam to light our path as he led us to the far northern end of the crypt.

There lay an area of floor that had been dug up. It was roughly square and some five yards long on each side. Flagstones lay piled neatly nearby, along with several mounds of excavated soil, atop one of which rested a pick and a shovel.

"You have been busy, Moriarty," Holmes observed. "I never envisaged you as the type to engage in manual labour, yet what I am looking at here is clearly the handiwork of just one man, else there would be more than a single set of digging tools."

"It was quite an endeavour, I must admit," came the reply. "The blisters, the backache, the night after night of industry... But it had to be done, and it seemed fitting that I should do it alone. The toil constituted an act of mild self-mortification, one might say. A libation of sweat."

The pit was deep, I had to give Moriarty that. It went down a good ten feet and must have taken at least a hundred man-hours to dig. I did not envy him the effort he had expended on it.

Its purpose was immediately evident, too, when I spied the monument which stood uncovered at its centre. This was an obelisk some seven or eight feet tall, shaped like a steep-sided pyramid. It was fashioned from smooth, gleaming black stone into which were etched numerous lines of R'lyehian text. The runic inscriptions and everything else about the obelisk struck me as incredibly ancient. Without doubt it had lain here for many centuries, embedded in the earth well before the original St Paul's Church was erected.

"You are asking yourselves, what am I looking at?" said Moriarty. "What is this thing faced with onyx, protruding from the ground?"

"Some relic," I said in an offhand manner. "An artefact dating back to the Stone Age, or beyond."

"Well, yes, but there is more to it than that. Mr Holmes? Would you care to advance an opinion?"

Holmes scrutinised the obelisk. He was battered and bedraggled from our fight, much to the same extent as I, yet his eyes retained their usual keen inquisitiveness.

"If I read the inscriptions correctly," said he, "it is some kind of gateway. A 'portal to a lower realm'. It affords access solely to 'those who utter the appropriate words'. That would seem to suggest some kind of incantation is required to open it."

"And I am just the man to say those words. Come along now."

Moriarty climbed down a stepladder that was canted against one wall of the pit. Holmes and I made an altogether less elegant descent, as the snake men holding us passed us down to others of their kind who had clambered into the pit to receive us. The manhandling was undignified and crude, and I remonstrated volubly, not that the snake men appeared to care. Once the two of us were securely pinioned again, the snake men set about assisting their brethren whose bones Holmes had broken with his singlestick. These afflicted individuals were lowered into the pit a great deal more gently and solicitously than we had been.

Moriarty, in the interim, had positioned himself before one of the obelisk's faces. He intoned a handful of lines in R'lyehian, amongst which two words recurred several times: *nglui*, meaning door or threshold, and *ktharl*, meaning unlock. His voice rose in volume as he chanted, its timbre deepened, and all at once the obelisk face swung smoothly inward, creating a triangular aperture. Steps were visible within, sinking into darkness.

"Gentlemen, after you," Moriarty said with a sweep of the arm, like a maître d' ushering diners to their table.

*

The stairs made a left turn, then another left turn, then another, at increasing intervals, and I quickly grasped that they – and we – were travelling in a widening downward spiral. Cold stone wall remained ever to our right, pitched at the same angle as the faces of the obelisk, whilst to our left there was only, as far as I could tell from the lantern's meagre corona of light, open space. The echoes of our footfalls were magnified as we descended, as though resounding across a greater and greater expanse of emptiness. It was clear that we were inside a vast hollow subterranean edifice, the stairs tracing an internal perimeter which broadened out the deeper we went.

Holmes had drawn the same conclusion, although I have no doubt he arrived at it earlier than I did. "So the obelisk is not an obelisk at all," he said to Moriarty. "It is, rather, a projection of something much larger. The tip of the proverbial iceberg."

"The pyramid in which we presently find ourselves," said Moriarty, "dwarfs any of those at Giza for height. It is also considerably older."

"May I ask how you discovered it? The *Necronomicon*, perchance?"

"Its location is hinted at in the book. I assembled the various clues and references salted throughout the pages, then applied the geomancer's art. First I dangled a crystal dowsing pendulum over a map of London to triangulate the pyramid's whereabouts. Then I investigated the crypt of St Paul's with a pair of divining rods, thereby pinpointing the exact spot. Within the first night's excavation I had uncovered the apex, a mere couple of feet under the flagstones. It was a satisfyingly quick validation of my methodology. I was perhaps a trifle surprised that a structure like this should be lying directly beneath a church, but then…"

"But then Christianity has a history of adopting sites of great pre-Christian significance for its own use," said Holmes. "It has long been the practice of the Church, and was so especially in its infancy, to flatten shrines, temples and other places deemed sacred to pagan cultures and build over them. In the same way the religion has annexed heathen festivals for its own. Hence Saturnalia became Christmas, and Samhain All Hallow's Eve. In this manner early Christianity asserted its dominance, supplanting its rivals' loci and traditions so that their worshippers were left with little option but to leave the area to find somewhere else to conduct their rites, or convert."

"St Paul's Shadwell is a perfect example of that. Before it existed, this was a Neolithic sacred site. Standing stones, dolmens and suchlike, frequented by druids for their harvest-time and equinoctial rituals. Before *that*, the ground level was lower, and what appeared to be merely an onyx obelisk stood proud of the earth."

"Its presence marking the spot where one world intersected with another, the subterranean with the surface."

"Holmes," I said, butting in, "how can you engage the man in conversation like this? As though making parlour chit-chat? He is our executioner and we are being led to our deaths."

"There is no need for incivility, Watson, whatever the

circumstances. Besides, intellectual curiosity demands to be fed. It is never sated."

"You really are a man after my own heart, Mr Holmes," said Moriarty. "Would that fate had not set us on divergent courses, that your basic temperament was more aligned with mine. We could have been tremendous colleagues. Instead we are, regrettably, obverse and reverse of the same coin, destined never to see each other's point of view."

"In that same spirit, the satisfaction of curiosity," Holmes continued, "I should like to ask about these snake men."

"*Homo sapiens reptiliensis*, as I like to call them."

"An accurate-seeming taxonomic classification." My companion gave an approving nod. "To judge by the variety of physical characteristics they present – some more humanoid than others – there has been crossbreeding with humans in the past."

"I agree. I believe there must have been. I believe, further, that the hybridisation goes both ways and that there are people walking around in the world today with some vestigial traces of the *reptiliensis* bloodline in them, entirely unknowing. Are there not individuals with an icy, aloof affect whom we think of as 'cold-blooded'? Have we not all met someone who can be said to possess a distinctly reptilian aspect?"

"One such person is not too far from me right now, Professor," I said, recalling my first impression of him as he had oscillated his head like a snake fascinating its prey.

"I shall not take that as an insult, Doctor, assuming it

is meant as one. I am in that category, yes, and I am of the view that that is the reason I am able to exercise my will over the snake men so adeptly with my Triophidian Crown. I would also submit that my ability to mesmerise, a talent I have honed in recent years to a fine degree, has its roots in a far distant serpentine heritage."

"Creatures who combine the qualities of man and snake abound in folklore," said Holmes. "It would seem that they have been less mythical than we think."

"Absolutely," said Moriarty. "Cecrops, the first king of Athens, was purportedly half snake."

"So were the Lamia and the Gorgons."

"Also the Aztec god Tlaloc, the Hindoos' Naga, the Greek god Glycon, and not forgetting the Chinese Adam and Eve, Fu Xi and Nu Wa… Who is to say that these myths do not have their roots in fact? And who is to say I am not the distant descendant of one such being?"

"Satan was a serpent too, wasn't he?" I said.

My barb, like its predecessor, found no purchase in Moriarty's hide. I was, it seemed, beneath his dignity. Compared with Holmes, whom he abundantly admired, I was a mere irritant.

"What an odd couple you are," the academic said with a chuckle. "Here is Mr Holmes, with his enquiring mind, always open to new knowledge. And here is Dr Watson, a gruff, bluff fellow who would rather lash out than learn. I could see no future in this mismatched partnership, even if it were to survive beyond tonight. Each of you hardly seems compatible with the other. Does Mr Holmes regard you, Doctor, as anything more than a pet or mascot, I wonder?"

I responded with a vicious growl, which, I will allow, might have appeared to lend affirmation to Moriarty's rhetorical question.

I would have chased it up with some sort of uncomplimentary riposte, but it so happened that just then our party's long, winding descent reached its terminus.

We stepped through a low, broad vestibule, emerging into a cave which, though nowhere near as immense as the cavern that housed Ta'aa, was of sizeable proportions nonetheless. A smattering of torches shed their light over the scene, enough of them to hold back but not entirely banish the dark. They revealed the cyclopean bulk of the pyramid behind us, which disappeared into the rock roof above like a mountaintop into clouds. Only the apex was adorned with onyx, it transpired. The rest – the vast majority – was raw, undressed stone. The torches also revealed a pool of black water in front of us. Some forty yards in diameter, its gleaming surface was so still and untroubled it looked like a sheet of pure volcanic obsidian.

Around this were ranged snake men, a couple of hundred of them in total, of both genders and all ages. They squatted on the banks of the pool, lay athwart table-like rock outcrops, or perched upon rugged shelves and projections on the cave walls. Many were gnawing upon the bodies of rats, which must have been their principal food source. Those that were not sedentary or recumbent prowled about in a slithery, undulating way. Now and then a couple of them might bump into each other and there would be an elaborate display of aggression, a baring of fangs, a flurry of hisses, sometimes even a brief altercation that ended in one or the other being wrestled to the floor and having to give some sign of submission.

For the most part, however, the snake men's attention was directed upon us, the new arrivals. When Moriarty showed his face, there was a ripple of appreciative murmuring and even a few fumbled, mangled attempts at his name: "Roffsssor Mearty. Roffsssor Mearty." He acknowledged the recognition with a regal wave.

"Sherlock!"

The cry came from a raised section of the cave floor by the pool, a kind of natural dais. From its centre rose a tall stalagmite some twenty feet in circumference. Its pointed summit reached upward to a corresponding stalactite, of somewhat greater dimensions, that hung down from above. Set into the stalagmite at head height was a large iron eye-bolt, through which were threaded a number of thick chains. These ended in manacles, and currently two of them were being used to shackle a pair of men, one of whom I knew and the other of whom, though unfamiliar, I readily identified.

The former was Inspector Tobias Gregson, who presented a very sorry sight. He sat slumped, legs straight out in front of him, arms suspended above his head by the manacles. His drooping head and glum expression spoke of incredulity, regret and resignation.

The second man, who reclined straight-backed against the stalagmite, was Sherlock Holmes, but with the addition of perhaps half as much again in weight. He shared Holmes's physiognomy, although on him it was softened at the edges, like a smudged portrait. There was the same hawklike intensity about the eyes, the same aquilinity to the nose, but he sported a flabby second chin and his brow was puffy. His attire was more flamboyant than any Holmes might have worn, too, down to a paisley silk cravat and a brocade waistcoat, the latter stretched across an ample corporation. For all that, there was no doubting that he and my companion must be close kin. I was looking at none other than the mighty Mycroft.

He it was who had called out Holmes's name across the cave, and his younger brother answered with a clipped "Mycroft."

"About time you showed up," said Mycroft. "It's awfully damp down here. Plays havoc with the sinuses."

To hear him, you might not think he had been abducted from his home forty-eight hours earlier and held captive since. He spoke as though addressing a waiter who had neglected to add a slice of lemon to his gin and tonic as requested. This was in marked contrast to Gregson, who was the very picture of dejection. The official had perked up briefly when Mycroft had spoken, but sank into despondency again upon perceiving that Holmes was Moriarty's prisoner and that his appearance in the cave did not signify salvation. I caught a look from him which was bitter in every way, and I was unable to respond with any visible measure of reassurance. I felt as pessimistic about our prospects as he.

At an unspoken command from Moriarty, the snake men forced Holmes and me towards the stalagmite and the empty pair of chains which awaited, ready to bind us

SHERLOCK HOLMES *and the* SHADWELL SHADOWS

alongside Mycroft and Gregson.

"Really, Sherlock," the elder Holmes chided as we approached, "what kept you? This policeman and I have been stuck down here for a good day or two, with barely a morsel to eat. It has been most inconvenient. Could you not have come looking for us sooner?"

"I apologise, brother. I sprang into action the moment I learned you were missing. What more do you expect?"

"You found my little clue, I take it."

"The one Moriarty obliged you to leave."

"Yes. He gave me no choice, really. I felt compelled to do as he said. Some form of hypnosis, I would hazard. Dashed hard to resist. I knew I shouldn't obey but couldn't help it. I consoled myself that you would search for me regardless, so would it hurt to make the task more straightforward? It was quite obviously a stratagem designed to ensnare you, but I reasoned that you would see through such a patent ruse in a trice and turn up with a large contingent of men, mob-handed, ready to mount a siege. Which," he added, a touch ruefully, "it is clear you have not. Instead you have brought only a single ally, and it has not worked out well for you. What a pity."

"All is not lost."

"So speaks a true Holmes. I daresay the tables may yet be turned, but you will forgive me if I don't foresee much likelihood of that happening. These snake creatures have been anticipating our demise with eagerness. Look at them. They're like Romans at the Circus Maximus, waiting for the Christians to be thrown to the lions. I doubt very much they're going to be disappointed."

"Horrible beasts," Gregson muttered. "They've no right existing. Vermin."

"Oh come along, old chap," said Mycroft. "Let us not deride them just because they are so different. Perhaps we seem no less offensive to them than they do to us."

"They stink. They're vile."

The exchange continued, but I ignored it. Manacles were being clamped around my wrists and Holmes's, and once more I did my best to resist. I thought that if I could just break free, I might somehow yet snatch victory from the jaws of defeat. If, say, I were able to reach Moriarty, might I not throttle the life out of him with my bare hands? Failing that, knock the Triophidian Crown from his head. Without him controlling them, the snake men would then become a rabble, confused, rudderless. We could take advantage of the disarray and effect an escape.

But my efforts came to naught. The snake men continued to exert their superior strength and I remained overpowered. It was damnably frustrating. The manacles were locked tight with a crude screw-like key, and there I stood, arms bent, hands hanging at shoulder height, helpless. There was sufficient slack in the chain for me to have sat down, like Mycroft and Gregson, but I elected to stay on my feet while I could. I was not beaten yet – although I was close to it.

Holmes, for his part, acquiesced in being fastened. It was almost as though he was accepting the inevitable. Yet that, to my mind, was unlike him. I might not have known him long, but he was no fatalist. I could not but think that he had some plan of last resort, that there was still an ace up his sleeve.

Once we were both secured, the snake men backed away, leaving the rocky dais and merging with their brethren and sistren scattered around the cave. The key which secured the manacles was passed to Moriarty for safekeeping.

He in the meantime had opened a casket and retrieved an object wrapped in an oilcloth. This covering he unpeeled, slowly, reverently, to expose a large, thick book. It was the size of two volumes of the *Encyclopaedia Britannica* combined, and was bound in leather so black it seemed not to reflect light, but rather to absorb it. The page edges were stained to match the binding, so that the book, taken as a whole, was a rectangular cuboid of perfect darkness, like a chunk of solid void, a three-dimensional absence in space.

There was no lettering inlaid into the leather, no tooling of any description either on the cover or on the spine. In other words, nothing at all that indicated the book's title.

Yet I knew full well what it was. There was only one book it could be.

Here, before me, was the copy of the *Necronomicon* purloined from the British Museum.

CHAPTER TWENTY-SEVEN

An Issue of Quality not Quantity

MORIARTY HANDLED THE DREAD GRIMOIRE WITH due caution, supporting it with both hands. He seemed wary of dropping it, as though the thing were made of gelignite and the least jolt or unsettlement might have disastrous consequences. He laid it on a flat-topped rock – a crude lectern for a profane Bible – and having opened the cover, began stroking a finger through the heavy pages.

Holmes spoke up. "It would appear, Professor, that you are making a final, all-or-nothing bid to appease your deity. The human sacrifices you have offered so far have failed to earn you the special favour you seek. They were insufficient."

Moriarty glanced up from the *Necronomicon*. "It is true that he has not been satisfied with the lesser souls I have presented to him. I thought if I gave him enough of them at regular intervals, he would reward me with munificence. I misjudged. The issue, I therefore determined, must not be one of quantity, but rather of quality."

"And that is where Gong-Fen Shou came in. He was the first of the 'quality'. Now we are to follow."

"I considered other candidates. It could have been a High Court judge or one of our more statesmanlike politicians. It could even have been a member of the royal family. In the end, I decided it should be you, Mr Holmes, the much-vaunted young detective whose prospects seemed considerable."

"To be set above such august company – I am flattered."

"Don't be," Moriarty said. "I chose you in large part because of that insolent telegram of yours. It may seem petty, but I really will not tolerate disrespect. I am your elder and in every regard your better, and you would have done well to appreciate that. This way, I am able to provide an offering of some calibre *and* show an impudent whelp that I am not to be trifled with."

"If I am of such value, then why not release these others?" said Holmes, indicating his brother, Gregson and me with a nod of his head. "Surely I alone will suffice. Let them go."

Moriarty gave a sardonic shake of the head. "Not a chance."

"You have me," Holmes persisted. "They are surplus to requirements."

"Dr Watson is, I admit, a man of little significance."

I bristled at the jibe and murmured a few choice words at Moriarty, even as a small, craven part of me hoped my lack of importance might just earn me my freedom.

"But," Moriarty continued, "his association with you makes your humbling that much sweeter, so he stays. The same goes for your brother and the policeman."

"Gregson and I are barely acquainted."

"That is not quite true, Mr Holmes, is it? The two of you are not merely acquainted but on cordial terms."

"Hmm. And how would you know that, I wonder. Ah yes. Of course. You observed us together at the scene of Gong-Fen's death. You were amongst the crowd of onlookers, were you not? I knew I had seen your face before we met in your rooms, ostensibly for the first time."

"Yes, I may have misled you on that front. Your powers of recall did not deceive you. I was there, witnessing the aftermath of my handiwork. And, upon hearing Inspector Gregson call you by name, I realised you were none other than the Sherlock Holmes with whom Gong-Fen had become so smitten. I perceived that you and Gregson were friendly, so when it came to enticing you here to St Paul's Shadwell, I thought why not make the inspector part of a double-baited lure? The other, juicier worm being, of course, Mycroft Holmes."

"Worm!?" Mycroft expostulated.

"Merely a figure of speech, sir." Addressing himself to the younger Holmes again, Moriarty said, "Abducting your brother in order to draw you in was my primary plan. Then I thought, 'Sherlock Holmes is an observant fellow but even he might not notice if just one member of his inner circle goes missing. Two, on the other hand, would put him on the alert and send a very clear message.' Given that you are here, my surmise was correct, and it means that I now have a splendid repast to offer up. There is the good doctor as the *hors d'oeuvre*. Then there is the worthy Inspector Gregson, an esteemed representative of the law, the piquant palate cleanser. Finally, the twofold entrée: Mycroft Holmes, peerless political fixer and manipulator, hallowed through the corridors of power, and his brother Sherlock, the budding private detective of great repute and promise. Two of England's foremost. All in all, a gourmet feast!"

"A feast for whom?" Mycroft barked.

"These snaky fiends, obviously," said Gregson. "They must be cannibals, mustn't they? Or near as. And we're the missionaries, destined for the pot."

"Fair point. Sherlock did just mention a deity. Perhaps they'll be eating us to worship him. The Holy Eucharist, only in a perverted form. Their equivalent of the Body and Blood of Christ. Transubstantiation taken literally."

At this, Gregson shuddered and let out a despairing moan. "It's not right. Eaten alive by inhuman abominations."

"Buck up," Mycroft said. "If we're facing death, let us face it like men. Besides, look at the size of me compared with you. Which of us do you think is going to take longer to consume? Skinny wretch like you, you'll be gone in no time. Same with Sherlock."

Gregson's spirits were clearly not buoyed by the joke. Yet he did at least follow Mycroft's admonition, lifting his head and squaring his jaw. I could only assume that Mycroft had been bolstering him in this manner throughout the duration of their captivity, alternately chivvying and indulging in gallows humour. Despite his soft, pampered exterior, the elder Holmes brother had all the guile and backbone of the younger. To be able to thrive in the internecine, treacherous world of Westminster, how could he not?

"The hour draws on apace," Moriarty said, with a glance at his fob watch. "The night is almost at its darkest. The new moon is traditionally the time for new projects, you know. New beginnings. The Hindoos place great significance on it, often waiting until then to hold a celebration or embark on some creative endeavour. The Mohammedans use it to determine the months of their calendar, as do the Jews. In the lore of certain much older faiths, however, the new moon is when the barriers between worlds are thinnest and one may thus more easily commune with the gods."

"In this case," said Holmes, "Nyarlathotep."

There was a murmur amongst the snake men at the mention of the name, and a rustle of activity as some of them stirred, bowing, genuflecting, even prostrating themselves.

"Oh well done! Clever chap!" said Moriarty. "When did you work that out?"

"It was a process of logic – the gradual accretion of data and elimination of alternatives. Several of the Elder Gods and Old Ones can assume the form of shadows and project themselves into the earthly plane by that means. None, however, has the protean aspect of the entity which Watson and I both beheld within one of the shadows which attacked Gong-Fen's clarence. What we saw was not formless but rather multi-formed, and while I may yet be something of a novice in these matters, even I know that there is one being who manifests in a myriad of different ways and whose core self is unfixed."

"Hence the sobriquet by which Nyarlathotep is most frequently known – the Crawling Chaos."

"Amongst countless other epithets. Is he not also the Mighty Messenger? The Black Demon? The Black Pharaoh? The Haunter of the Dark? From Cairo to the Congo, from Scotland to New England, almost everyone who knows of Nyarlathotep knows him by a different avatar. It is as though he adapts to the eye of the beholder, assuming whatever aspect he deems most suitable for the occasion, most likely to achieve the desired effect, be it awe, terror, familiarity, or any permutation of the three."

"Yes, and some occult scholars have speculated that this transformative ability is what allows him to serve as the Elder Gods' personal messenger," said Moriarty. "He can appear to each of them in a guise that is pleasing, and thus mitigate their wrath if the message he is carrying happens to be an unwelcome one."

"I knew once and for all that Nyarlathotep was the deity to whom you have pledged your allegiance when I spied his name on the obelisk, enclosed within a box. A cartouche, just as the Ancient Egyptians were wont to use in their hieroglyphs to indicate the name of a god or a member of royalty."

I marvelled that Holmes had been able to give the obelisk more than a cursory look as we were dragged into the pit in the crypt. His presence of mind, even under duress, was remarkable. Did he never stop observing, assessing, gleaning?

"Down here," he continued, "must be a point of access between our realm and Nyarlathotep's home, which is said to lie at the centre of the planet. Somewhere in this cave there is a conduit through which he may be summoned. And I would be very surprised if said conduit was not that pool over there."

Moriarty looked towards the pool and nodded. "Our serpentine friends have long been aware that

Nyarlathotep may be brought forth from those waters if given the appropriate incentive. Over the centuries they have sacrificed to him from amongst their own whenever they fall on lean times – if food is scarce, or the rate of births has dropped to a precariously low level. Nyarlathotep has petitioned on their behalf with the greater gods and restored the fortunes of their tribe. How else do you think they have managed to survive down here for so long, in such numbers? Interbreeding and a dearth of resources would surely have wiped them out otherwise."

"Divine intervention, purchased at the cost of a tribe member or two."

"And in much the same way, I intend to obtain that divine intervention for myself."

"What do you want, Moriarty?" I demanded. "What in God's name are you after? What is the purpose of all this?"

"Blunt and straight to the point, Doctor. You ask the questions that get to the nub of the matter. What do I want? Let me put it to you this way. What is it that gods have and we mortals do not?"

Holmes butted in before I could formulate an answer.

"Immortality, obviously," said he.

Moriarty laughed. "And…?"

"Power."

"Immortality and power," Moriarty said. "Absolutely. The two things which set the gods apart from us. They live for all eternity, and they possess an ineffable eldritch might which they can wield over human affairs more or less as they please."

"And you desire a portion of that for yourself."

"Who in their right mind would not?"

"In their right mind?" said Mycroft. "The description does not apply to you, Moriarty. You are a lunatic, sir. Quite mad. Do you sincerely believe any of the drivel you are spouting? Gods in pools? Immortality?"

"I do. And so does your brother."

Mycroft leaned forward in order to peer past me and look at Holmes, who was on the other side of me. "Sherlock? Is that so?"

"I believe much of what Moriarty has said."

"Really? I mean, I have listened to you and him discuss this 'Narwhal-tip' or whatever his name is, but I took you yourself at least to be talking in the abstract, as an intellectual exercise, the same way one might talk about vampires or werewolves or other such fictitious creatures."

"Would you not have previously dismissed snake men like these as 'fictitious creatures', Mycroft?" said Holmes. "The stuff of superstition? Yet their corporeality is, on present evidence, irrefutable."

"Some sort of freakish throwback," said Mycroft. "A reptilian offshoot of mankind's evolution."

"And the pyramid?"

"If the Ancient Egyptians could erect pyramids, why not our ancestral forebears too? None of it makes all this other mystical guff seem anything more than the purest claptrap. I can countenance the idea that Moriarty is going to kill us in the name of some sort of heathen deity, in return for some godly blessing. Even apparently civilised white men may fall prey to that sort of Dark Ages delusion. But it's hard to accept that you think he might genuinely succeed."

"I never said anything about him succeeding. In fact, I predict that there will be precious little chance of Nyarlathotep granting Professor Moriarty's wishes. The Crawling Chaos is no storybook genie. He is a malign menace. His gifts habitually lead to their recipients' destruction. Moriarty's dream of becoming godlike is as futile as it is tragic."

"If it comforts you to believe I am going to fail, Mr Holmes, by all means continue in that delusion," said Moriarty.

"I believe you have always failed, sir," Holmes retorted. "You have failed as an academic, for all your abundant intellect. You have failed socially, reduced to eking out a living as a tutor. You have failed, above all," he went on, clearly warming to his theme, "as a human being, incapable of cultivating friendships or any kind of relationship which does not involve your superiority and the inferiority of the other person. Ascending to godhood, in the unlikely event that should happen, will alter nothing. You will still be an abject failure at heart, and the hell of it is that you know this. You know your inadequacies, you know how great they are, and you know you will never escape them no matter how high you climb, no matter what you become."

Now, at last, Moriarty was antagonised. Holmes had cut him to the quick in a way that I had been unable to do, despite my best efforts. It was a pleasure to see colour rise in that sallow face, to watch those drawn cheeks turn choleric red, and to observe at the same time the wounded look enter those eyes – a look which acknowledged the truth of Holmes's assertions, even as Moriarty sought to repudiate them.

"Poppycock, Sherlock Holmes," he spat. "It is beneath your dignity to voice such slanders. I can only think that, in your final moments, fear has got the better of you. I held you in such esteem, too. Perhaps I should have known you would disappoint me. Everyone does, after all."

"Why don't you just shut up and get on with it?" declared a peevish Inspector Gregson, who had clearly had enough of the whole business. "Put us out of our misery. Anything's preferable to listening to you pontificate all night."

"Indeed I shall," replied Moriarty, huffing tartly. He returned his attention to the *Necronomicon*, his fingers once more turning its pages, if with less care and delicacy than before.

His anger intensified his focus on the task before him.

It also made him inattentive to anything else.

For while Moriarty was bent over the book, Holmes began to move his right arm.

In a series of stealthy, jerky manoeuvres he started hoisting something up from inside his shirtcuff. It was a small steel tube, as long and slim as a cigarette. By flexing the muscles of his forearm he was able to propel it up towards his fingers, which were doubled over, ready to retrieve it the moment it was within their reach.

I had no clear idea what the tube was or what it might do.

But I remember experiencing a sudden surge of elation as tremendous as any I have ever felt.

Holmes did, in the event, have a literal ace up his sleeve.

All he needed now was an opportunity to bring it into play.

CHAPTER TWENTY-EIGHT

The Crawling Chaos Comes!

NO SOONER DID HOLMES EXTRICATE THE STEEL tube fully from his shirtcuff than Moriarty found the section of the *Necronomicon* he was searching for. He looked up from the book with a triumphant smirk.

Holmes immediately palmed the tube, pinning it under his thumb and crooking his fingers over it in such a way that it disappeared from view and his hand seemed to be hanging loosely from the manacle exactly as before.

Had Moriarty spotted the furtive action?

I prayed not. I kept my eyes fixed firmly forward, trying to betray no hint that anything had occurred. Neither Mycroft nor Gregson was privy to what Holmes had done. I myself would have remained oblivious had I not been positioned directly adjacent to him and spotted it from the corner of my eye. I strove to maintain the sort of blank, impassive face that serves one well at cards. Whatever was in the tube, I presumed it must be an aid to Holmes freeing himself. I realised, too, that Holmes had permitted us to be taken captive and fastened to the pyramid precisely because he knew he might be able to effect an escape. He had made provision for this eventuality, seeing it as his best chance of rescuing his brother and Gregson.

Moriarty peered hard at me, at Holmes, at me again. For several terrible seconds I feared that the jig was up; that the one slender little advantage we had was about to be ripped away. All Moriarty need do was step forward and wrest the tube from Holmes's hand, thereby dashing our hopes.

To my immense relief, he did not. Clearly none the wiser, he returned his gaze to the *Necronomicon* and began scanning a particular passage there, as though to reacquaint himself with it. Then, raising head and hands, he began to recite an invocation in R'lyehian.

The opening words struck a chord of recognition in me: *"Fhtagn! Ebumna fhtagn! Hafh'drn wgah'n n'gha n'ghft!"* They were the self-same words Stamford had cried over and over in his cell. "He waits! He waits in the pit! The priest controls death in the darkness!" Stamford must have overheard them spoken by Gong-Fen at some point, or else by Moriarty, and they had become lodged in his memory. In his drugged, maddened state they had arisen from his subconscious, inadvertently exposing the truth behind the deaths by emaciation.

Here, now, was the *hafh'drn* himself, Moriarty, conjuring up death once again in this benighted subterranean domain. This time, however, that death was going to visit not some unfortunate drawn from the lower echelons of society. It was going to visit four men, at least two of whom were of great substance and standing, to consume them all in one fell swoop.

The invocation rolled on, the acoustics of the cave lending Moriarty's voice a hollow, resonant majesty. *"Nyarlathotep uln shugg. Ch'nglui shogg. Sll'ha orr'ee ah fhayak. Dlloi hafh'drn mnahn'. Y'hah."* Roughly translated, this meant: "Nyarlathotep, I call you to Earth. Cross over the threshold from your realm of darkness. I invite you to feast on the souls I offer you. Heed your humble summoner. Amen."

Meanwhile, Holmes had set to work. Turning my eyes to him, though not my head, I watched as he began to unscrew the cap of the steel tube with the tip of his thumb. He was obliged to perform the action slowly, surreptitiously, so as not to draw unwanted attention. Mentally I urged him to hurry, even though I knew he could not. Everyone else's gaze was on Moriarty, but should one of the snake men happen to catch sight of the movement, or should Moriarty himself do so, then the alarm would be raised. The only option was the cautious, painstaking approach.

Now Moriarty's hands rose aloft to his arms' full extent, in the manner of a clergyman pronouncing benediction, or a demagogue delivering some piece of rousing oratory. In R'lyehian he entreated Nyarlathotep to hear his call and bestow upon him everything that it was in a god's purview to give. He begged that his humble mortal frame be imbued with just a few drops of the Great Old Ones' essence. He asked for a share of their incandescent glory, that he might rule over the masses like an emperor and live on through aeons in a body which remained forever youthful and uncorrupted. This imprecation was not taken from the *Necronomicon*. I worked out later that it was something Moriarty had himself composed, a personal plea. He ended it with a cry of "*Iä, Nyarlathotep! Iä! Iä!*" – "Hail, Nyarlathotep! Hail! Hail!" – which he reiterated with increasing fervour and intensity.

The snake men picked up the phrase and added their voices to his. "*Iä, Nyarlathotep! Iä! Iä!*"

By now, Holmes at last had the cap undone. He

inverted the tube so that it was upside down above the manacle lock. A viscous, syrupy liquid began to drip from its interior, clear like honey but bright scarlet in hue.

"*Iä, Nyarlathotep! Iä! Iä!*"

I assumed this substance to be some kind of lubricant which might enable Holmes to slip his wrist from the manacle. I then perceived that it did not flow as any normal liquid might. When it touched the metal it divided into several smaller streams. These probed into the lock like tiny ichorous fingers. It was as though the stuff had sentience, a mind of its own.

"*Iä, Nyarlathotep! Iä! Iä!*"

Louder the chant grew, and louder still, until it was being bellowed by a couple of hundred throats at once in deafening unison. The snake men swayed. Some of them shivered as though in the throes of ecstasy. Moriarty himself seemed transported, his face fixed in a beatific leer, almost clownish in its joy.

"*Iä, Nyarlathotep! Iä! Iä!*"

As for Mycroft and Gregson, the one was scowling, the other sullen. They might not have any idea what to expect, but both knew it could not be good.

"*Iä, Nyarlathotep! Iä! Iä!*"

I looked at the pool. Its waters remained smooth and still. I allowed myself the hope that, after all, Moriarty's summons would be ignored. The Crawling Chaos would not be paying a call tonight. We had been granted a reprieve.

"*Iä, Nyarlathotep! Iä! Iä!*"

Then the surface of the pool started to vibrate. Concentric ripples spread across its glassy blackness, radiating from the middle. At the same time there could be heard the sound of distant flute-like instruments playing. The music somehow emanated from the pool itself, and was both muted and strident. There was no tune as such, just arrhythmic sequences of harsh intervals and atonalities. It was all clash and dissonance. It was the kind of music, I thought, that would be played in Hell.

The sound of the flutes, along with the perturbation of the pool, served only to excite the snake men further. Their chanting climbed to a new, frenzied peak.

As for Holmes, he was concentrating intently on the manacle. The tiny fingers of scarlet liquid worked away at the lock with all the industriousness of ants, and it was then that I noticed my companion's lips were just perceptibly moving. He was talking to the substance, I realised. Murmuring to it. Giving it instruction. He had, I could only surmise, devised a fluid which responded to verbal commands, and was using it as a lockpick. This was another of the alchemical creations that had kept him busy at his chemistry bench all that afternoon, along with the lodestone solution and the special revenant-slaying bullets for my Webley.

The ripples in the pool deepened, and then all at once they broke up, their regularity of pattern disrupted. The entire body of water was filled from bank to bank with a welter of slapping, overlapping waves. The waves' peaks intensified, becoming taller and sharper. At the same time, the music grew even more discordant, its tempo increasing and its notes skirling towards a screeching crescendo, until the unseen musicians, as though on a cue from some conductor, abruptly went tacet.

Their silence heralded an arrival.

In the black depths of the pool, something was stirring.

Something was rising.

It came up ponderously, unhurriedly from the aqueous gloom. Through the surface refractions I saw the same entity I had caught glimpses of when the shadows assailed Gong-Fen's carriage under the railway bridge. It was a creature of countless eyes and no fixed shape. It rolled and roiled like wind-driven clouds. It twisted and expanded and contracted and reconfigured. It seemed to be a thousand different beings at once, all crammed together in the same space, vying for supremacy. Now it resembled an insect, akin to a locust. Now it had the features of a woman, bloated and obscenely fat. Now I discerned something of the Sphinx about it, and then all of a sudden it was more like a bull, and then, no less abruptly, a lion. Amidst that melange of elements were also a pharaoh, a dwarf, an ebony-skinned man, an angelically glowing fair-haired white woman, a snouted demon, a winged beast.

These and others manifested and vanished, Nyarlathotep's countless incarnations and avatars, the host of forms by which he was known throughout time and space. Watching him was fascinating, and at the same time I could hardly bear to look, for his body moved too much, too rapidly, too intricately, folding in and around and over and under itself, as though it conformed to none of the known laws of biology or physics.

And those eyes. Nyarlathotep had so many eyes. Far

too many. And each was as avaricious and cruel and calculating as the next.

How, I asked myself, could something be in such constant churning metamorphosis and live? How could it hold itself together? How could it possibly be cogent? Coherent? Sane?

The rational part of my mind posed these questions, trying to make sense of what I saw. But Nyarlathotep defied interpretation. He defied intelligibility. He was pure illogic, a riposte to all the assertions of science that there was nothing that could not be codified, classified and quantified. He was an affront to everything that was enlightened and right.

As he neared the surface, I could restrain myself no more. "Holmes!" I hissed. "For the love of God, man, what is taking you so long?"

At that very instant, the scarlet liquid completed its task. With a loud click the manacle fell open.

Holmes did not hesitate. He sprang forward, pulling hard with his still-manacled hand so that the chain rattled through the eye-bolt at speed. The open manacle slipped cleanly through, and now Holmes was fully free. He continued forward apace, charging at Professor Moriarty, the loose chain flailing behind him. All this took place within the space of a few heartbeats, so rapidly that Moriarty scarcely had time to register that one of his would-be sacrificial victims was at liberty before Holmes was upon him.

In a straight physical contest between the two of them, man against man, there was no doubt in my mind that Holmes would have been the victor. He, however, had an added advantage: the chain that dragged behind him. This he pressed into service as a makeshift weapon. In a single, swift motion he swung it up and caught it with his free hand, then whipped the trailing end at Moriarty. It struck the academic in the face with enough force both to send him reeling and topple the Triophidian Crown from his head. Moriarty let out a shrill, girlish yelp that was audible even above the snake men's raucous clamour. He staggered, clutching his cheek in agony.

Holmes brought the chain back, gathering it to unleash it a second time at his foe.

That was when Nyarlathotep broke the surface of the pool. He did so by extruding a part of himself that was like a gelatinous tentacle, thick as a man's thigh and tipped with a bloodshot, unblinking eye the size of a tennis ball. The tentacle's outer membrane was a hideous yellow, the colour reminiscent of the worst kind of effluvium the human body can produce, and it squirmed clear of the water, reaching out towards the dais.

At the sight of this long fleshy protuberance, Inspector Gregson, I am afraid to say, entirely took leave of his senses. He began screaming and sobbing, and frantically pulled at his bonds as though he hoped to be able to break them through sheer hysterical force. Even Mycroft's sangfroid deserted him, and I saw his mouth shaping the words of the Lord's Prayer.

The tentacle slithered across the dais floor, leaving behind a damp trail that was part water, part some loathsome, glistening molluscan secretion. It probed towards the stalagmite, where, from long experience, Nyarlathotep knew nourishment lay. The eye at its tip radiated hunger and greed.

Holmes lashed at Moriarty again with the chain. The first time he had caught him unawares. This time, however, our enemy was prepared. He seized the end with the open manacle as it hurtled towards him. He grinned. His cheek was bleeding, a great welt rising there like a split plum.

"One free hit," he said. "That is all you get, Mr Holmes. The rest you must earn."

He yanked the chain hard, pulling Holmes off his feet.

Or so it seemed. In fact, Holmes was shamming. He stumbled towards Moriarty, as though he had lost his balance and was struggling to regain it. Then at the last instant, when he was within arm's reach of his adversary, he righted himself. He aimed a lightning-like jab at Moriarty's chin.

Moriarty surprised him, and me, by ducking aside, so that the blow whistled past his temple. His retaliation was an uppercut which caught Holmes firmly under the jaw and snapped his head backwards.

My companion reeled. He and I alike had been guilty of underestimating Moriarty's prowess as a combatant. Sickly and spindly though he looked, the academic knew a thing or two about the pugilist's art. He was no Jem Mace, no bare-knuckle champion, but he definitely looked as though he could handle himself in a fist fight.

He was devious, too. While Holmes was still recovering from the uppercut, Moriarty grasped his end of the chain with both hands and ran. Holmes's manacled arm shot up and he was tugged helplessly forward, straight into the path of a small stalagmite which rose to waist height. He collided with this at some speed, unable to avoid it. He doubled over, the breath knocked out of him.

Moriarty pressed home his advantage by clouting Holmes on the back of the head with the same manacle that had opened up his own cheek. Holmes gasped in pain, and I groaned in dismay. A couple more blows like that, and my friend would surely be put out of contention.

Holmes was harder-skulled than I gave him credit for, however. As Moriarty prepared to deliver a second swinging strike, he rolled sideways off the stalagmite. Almost simultaneously he struck at his opponent's knee with his heel. There was a distinct *crunch* which told me that the joint had been dislocated. Moriarty's anguished howl confirmed it.

All the while, Nyarlathotep's tentacle crept ever nearer the large stalagmite, groping with repugnant purposefulness. It was now so close to the three of us as to be within kicking distance, and I proceeded to do just that, in hopes of deterring it. But the thing was dexterous and possessed of quick reflexes. It danced out of the way of my foot. My kicks, besides, were weaker and less accurate than they would otherwise have been, for I was feeling again that awful debilitation I had felt beneath the railway bridge as the shadows of Shadwell had advanced, which befell one whenever one was in proximity to Nyarlathotep. The sensation seeped into my marrow, into my soul, a kind of spiritual chloroform. The Crawling Chaos must seldom have known his prey to struggle. His very presence was enough to anaesthetise his victims, robbing them of the will to live.

His enfeebling influence had spread to both Mycroft and Gregson. No longer was the elder Holmes murmuring a prayer to the Christian god; nor was the police official straining at his manacles. Passively, strung to the stalagmite like a trio of forgotten marionettes, we awaited the inevitable.

I retained enough of my sense of self, however, to understand that our one chance of salvation lay with Sherlock Holmes. While he was still in the fray, all was not lost.

Moriarty might have been hobbled but he was far from defeated. Teeth gritted against the pain from his knee, he threw himself upon Holmes, who was still somewhat winded and dazed. The two of them grappled on the ground ferociously, more like brawling animals than men. Now one seemed to have the upper hand, now the other. They rolled, clawed, pawed, grunted with exertion. Moriarty had the raw energy of madness on his side. Holmes, by contrast, fought with the fervour of a man who understood that three other lives were at stake, not merely his own, and that perhaps the entire world was imperilled if he lost this battle. For should Moriarty defy expectation and gain Nyarlathotep's preferment as he planned, then it was a sure bet that he would not wield his newfound divine power with wisdom and benevolence. He would become the worst kind of dictator, riding roughshod over his fellow humans in the same manner that he lorded it over the snake men through the auspices of the Triophidian Crown. He would be an unholy terror, a rival to Genghis Khan, Herod, or Caligula. He would be a new Napoleon.

Nyarlathotep's tentacle reared before me, and I could swear the Crawling Chaos was savouring the moment, drinking in the scent of me like a wine connoisseur testing the "nose" of a claret. His uncanny eye roved towards Mycroft, then Gregson. It was as though he was trying to select which of us to latch onto first and suck dry. He was taking his time, deriving pleasure from the anticipation, the choosing.

The fierce wrestling match between Holmes and Moriarty had been edging ever closer to the lip of the pool, and was now almost at the point where the tentacle emerged. This was no accident. Holmes had, it transpired, been propelling them that way by design.

With a sudden surge of effort he threw Moriarty from him, so that the academic sprawled across the questing tentacle.

Immediately the tip of the tentacle whipped round, curving towards Moriarty. Its eye glared at him balefully.

"Nyarlathotep," the academic gasped. "I apologise. Forgive me. I did not mean to touch your personage. It was not my fault."

He tried to push himself away, but it was a fumbled attempt. Already Nyarlathotep's will-sapping aura was affecting him.

The Crawling Chaos seemed intrigued. All at once,

with a shocking turn of speed, the tentacle moved. It curled around Moriarty like a boa constrictor, encircling first his torso, then his legs.

"No…" Moriarty protested dully. "No… This is not… not what…"

But the tentacle only tightened its grip. Nyarlathotep had taken a taste of Professor James Moriarty, and seemed to like it.

Holmes, lying prone nearby, said, "Ah-ha, Professor. Your god desires quality, and has found it. What could be more to his liking than you? A great brain wedded to a diseased temperament. Your essence will be more flavoursome than any of ours."

"No. No!"

In an abrupt burst of vigour, Moriarty grabbed the loose end of the chain, which lay just within his reach, the other end of which was still fastened to Holmes's wrist.

"I shan't go alone," he declared. "He shall have you as well as me!"

The tentacle began retracting, withdrawing into the pool, taking Moriarty with it. Moriarty, in turn, dragged Holmes after him. He had both hands clamped around the chain in a remorseless death-grip, and my companion was hauled bodily across the dais. Holmes fought every inch of the way, digging his heels in, doing all he could to counteract the pull exerted on him. But there was little for his feet to gain purchase on, and his own strength, though formidable, was no match for that of the tentacle. He even tried pounding Moriarty's hands with his fists, but could not for the life of him get the man to relinquish his desperate, vindictive hold on the chain.

Moriarty slipped over the edge of the dais into the pool. I had a last sight of his face before it disappeared under the water. It had taken on a resigned cast, as if he had come to terms with the fact that his grand plan had ultimately backfired on him. Yet there was also a strange glint in his eye, as if somehow he had also won. It was not simply that he had managed to ensure that Holmes was condemned to the same grisly demise as himself. It was almost as if he was working out how he might yet turn the situation to his profit. Even in the face of an appalling death, Professor Moriarty schemed on.

Then he was gone, pulled under, and Holmes, still gamely resisting, followed. He tumbled from the dais, slithering into the pool in an unwieldy fashion, led by his tethered arm.

The loud splash echoed across the cave, and when those echoes faded there was nothing but silence. Even the snake men were struck dumb. It had all happened so quickly. One moment, Nyarlathotep had been preparing to accept the sacrifices being rendered up to him, as he had done so many times in their history. The next, their god had rounded on the priest officiating at the ceremony, the human who had imposed himself on them as their leader, and had taken him as an offering instead, along with one of the originally intended victims. The snake men were, for a time, bewildered and bereft.

But not so bereft as I was. I stared at the pool, while the ripples caused by Holmes's immersion ebbed and petered out. I willed him to return. I waited for his head to break the surface. I expected him to reappear at any second, safe and sound.

Although we had been acquainted for only a month or so, I was convinced that Sherlock Holmes was the best and wisest man whom I had ever known, or ever would know. I could not bear the thought that he was spiralling inexorably down into those dark depths, gone for good.

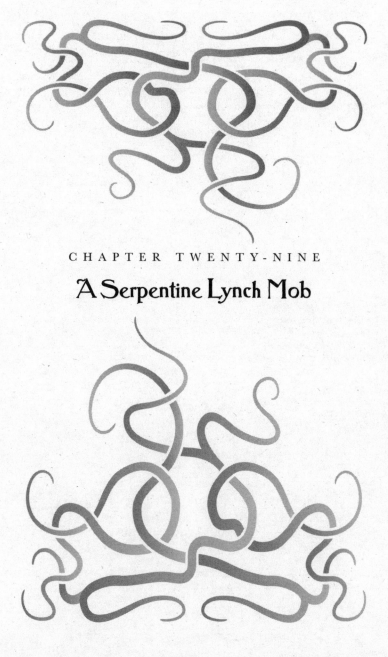

CHAPTER TWENTY-NINE

A Serpentine Lynch Mob

MYCROFT HOLMES, BESIDE ME, WAS AS APPALLED and grief-stricken as I, if not more so. He showed it by cursing volubly, telling his brother not to be "such a dashed fool", to stop "mucking around" and come back up for air.

"You can swim, can't you?" he berated the absent Holmes. "Then for heaven's sake swim!"

"You can't just *shout* him back to life," I said despairingly.

"I can and I will," Mycroft rejoined.

Meanwhile the snake men lamented their erstwhile master, keening his name over and over: "Roffsssor Mearty." They had been his hapless thralls, oppressed by the power he exercised over them through the Triophidian Crown. They had not loved him or even wanted to be ruled by him. Yet his death nonetheless left a vacuum in their lives. They had been conditioned to obey him, and were unsure how they would cope without him now.

Their period of abstract mourning did not last long, however. Sorrow curdled to disgruntlement, then resentment. I heard them grumble to one another in their lisping dialect of R'lyehian. Gazes were directed towards Mycroft, Gregson and myself, who remained locked in our manacles, shackled ineluctably to the stalagmite. The gazes became glares. The grumbling became growling. A few of the snake men prowled towards us, looking surly and vengeful.

"Well, this is a pretty pass," said Gregson, who had collected himself somewhat after his frenzied fit a short while earlier. "The wretched things are turning on us, as if we're to blame for what's happened. A mob is forming. I've seen it before, on the streets. This is how lynchings come about."

A number of the snake men were now on the dais, and others were heading in our direction. It looked as though we had been spared one manner of death, only to have another foisted upon us. The gathering throng, consisting mainly of adult males with a few females amongst them, snarled insults at us. Many of these I could not understand, but those I could consisted of uncomplimentary references to our clothing – for the snake men wore none – and to our hair, which, as far as bald *Homo sapiens reptiliensis* was concerned, was a freakish and unnatural physical attribute.

"What are you saying?" Mycroft barked at them defiantly. "I can't make head or tail of your jabber. No use speaking to us like that if it's only so much mumbo-jumbo to our ears."

The lynch mob – Gregson's description was entirely apt – loomed, and I knew at last that my time was up. I had had so many brushes with death in the past months, starting in Afghanistan. The grim reaper's scythe had swept over my head on several occasions, close enough that I could feel the chill breeze of its passing. Again and again it had narrowly missed – but now my luck had finally run out, and I was about to feel the terminal kiss of its blade. I was twenty-eight years of age. Mine had hardly been a long life, but it had not been without its pleasures, or its rigours. It had been full enough. It would have to do.

The cobra man appeared before me, the same fellow

who had so nearly envenomed me in the crypt. He seemed to be the leader of the mob, the alpha male, inciting the others to move in for the kill. I reckoned he would have been the snake men's chieftain, had Moriarty not usurped the position. Now he was reclaiming that role, and his first point of order was to resume what he had been prevented from doing up above.

With a gleeful hiss he opened wide his maw, revealing those wicked fangs affixed to the roof of his mouth.

"Go ahead then, you degenerate," I managed to say. "I hope you choke on me."

"*N'rhn!*" said a voice I knew well, a voice I had expected never to hear again.

The cobra man spun round.

To the rear of the mob, his hair plastered wetly to his scalp, water pouring from his sodden clothing and pooling at his feet, stood Sherlock Holmes.

*

In two of my published stories, "The Final Problem" and "The Adventure of the Empty House", I depicted Holmes's apparent death and subsequent miraculous-seeming resurrection. I wrote how he perished in mortal combat with Professor Moriarty, stating my presumption that the both of them had plunged into the Reichenbach Falls in Switzerland, only for him to re-enter my life three years later, having faked his death in order to evade the attention of certain still-extant enemies.

In this manner I fictionalised the not dissimilar events set forth above. I transposed them to the dramatic setting of the Aare Gorge and replaced the black, deceptively tranquil pool in the cave with the seething white maelstrom at the foot of the waterfall. It provided me with an opportunity to express the anguish I felt when I thought Holmes had died right in front of me, dragged underwater by Moriarty and Nyarlathotep, and the surprise and joy engendered by his return, all of it dusted with a liberal sprinkling of poetic licence.

There was never, in truth, any journey across Europe, with an angered Moriarty dogging our footsteps; nor was there any visit to my home by a deformed, wizened book-collector who proved to be Holmes in one of his disguises. The so-called Park Lane Mystery – the murder by air-gun of Sir Ronald Adair at the hands of Colonel Sebastian Moran – did indeed occur, but not wholly as I have recounted. The emotions conveyed in those two tales, which bookend what some have called the Great Hiatus, are sincere. The content is largely fabricated.

*

Here, at any rate, was Holmes, freshly arisen from the pool. The loose end of the chain was wrapped about his forearm, and in his hands was the Triophidian Crown, which he had retrieved from the ground where it had fallen.

He repeated his command to the cobra man and the other snake men: "*N'rhn!*" His voice carried enough authority at least to catch their attention and make them accede to his request, if only out of startlement. He had told them to halt, and they halted.

It was a temporary measure at best, however, a mere

stop-gap. While the mob of snake men paused, confusion writ large on their faces, Holmes installed the Trophidian Crown on his head.

It was slightly too big for him, Moriarty having had at least two hat sizes on Holmes. It sat askew, balanced on his ears.

That would be of no consequence as long as he could make the magical diadem work for him.

I saw his brow furrow. I saw him concentrate intensely. His grey eyes lost focus. His jaw clenched.

Tentatively at first, falteringly, the Trophidian Crown began to glow. A flicker of greenish light trembled across its tubular bronze contours. It was no brighter or more substantial than a will-o'-the-wisp, there and gone in an instant.

Then it returned, stronger, more definite, as Holmes gained mastery of the crown. Although he had never worn the device before, he fathomed its workings with remarkable alacrity. Perhaps nobody else could have accomplished the feat so quickly.

He projected into the snake men's minds his thoughts, his will, his wishes. Almost immediately, the more biddable members of the mob stepped aside, moving from the dais. The less suggestible took a little longer to disperse, but one by one they did.

Eventually only two remained, one of them being the cobra man. He and his fellow, who was possessed of yellow and black striping all over, were clearly the most independent and obstinate of the lot. They would not easily be subjugated. They stood firm, determined to finish what they had started and exact retribution on the three shackled humans. Their bodies quivered like violin strings as two opposing desires warred within them. On one side, bloodlust. On the other, Holmes's prohibition.

The yellow and black striped snake man surrendered. With a moue of rancour, he backed away from the stalagmite.

The cobra man continued staunchly to defy Holmes. My companion frowned even harder. I could tell it was taking every ounce of his mental wherewithal to operate the crown. Unlike Moriarty he had not practised with it, nor did he have any innate preternatural knack for mesmerism. He had only his wit, intellect and forcefulness to draw on. It would be enough. It must be enough.

The crown flared more brilliantly than ever, and at last the cobra man's obstinacy was worn down. Capitulating, he too left the dais. He trudged all the way, shoulders sloped, like a scolded, recalcitrant child.

Holmes hurried forward and fished in my pocket for my revolver and spare cartridges.

"The manacle key went down with Moriarty," he said, "and there is no time for lockpicking. I cannot do that and keep the snake men at bay. We shall simply have to eschew the niceties and take an unsubtle approach to releasing you."

He loaded the gun.

"Avert your face, Watson."

The report, right by the side of my head, was ear-splittingly loud.

The chain was severed.

He shot at the other end of the chain.

Manacles still encircled both my wrists, but I was free.

In swift succession Holmes performed the same service for his brother and Gregson. The Seal of Unravelling on each bullet had no particular effect on the chains since they were simply links of forged metal, imbued with no magical or alchemical force. The bullets by themselves, however, were more than sufficient for the task of shattering them.

"I shall probably be deaf in one ear for ever after," said Mycroft, grousing.

"You're very welcome," replied Holmes. "Now to make good our exit. To the pyramid! Mycroft, lead the way. Watson, help Gregson, will you?"

The policeman was ashen-faced and unsteady on his feet. The strain of all he had seen and suffered in the past two days had taken its toll. I put my shoulder under his armpit, draped his arm round my neck, and supported him as we headed for the entrance to the vestibule at the pyramid's base.

Holmes, the Triophidian Crown still glowing on his head, snatched up the *Necronomicon* and wrapped the oilcloth around it. Tucking the book under his arm, he hastened to catch up with us.

The snake men, led by the cobra man, roused themselves to follow.

We ascended. It was torturously slow going. The stairs were steep. Mycroft, at the head of our small procession, found climbing so many of them in succession hard work, due to his poor physical condition and sheer size. I myself had Gregson to deal with. He was barely able to walk, just so much dead weight leaning on me. Holmes, at the rear, devoted the majority of his energy and attention to the Triophidian Crown. The snake men were pursuing us tenaciously up the stairs. They still thirsted for vengeance. Holmes was dampening down their ardour via the crown but not altogether successfully. Without him they would have sprinted after us full tilt and easily overtaken and overwhelmed us. As it was, they only shuffled, every step an effort. I could hear them below, muttering exhortations to one another, interspersed with threats against us. Holmes was giving it his all, but the snake men were nonetheless gradually gaining on us. Their collective resolve was proving harder and harder for him to curtail, while the crown made ever greater demands upon his mental resources.

We were perhaps three-quarters of the way to the top when Mycroft shuddered to a complete halt. He planted his hands on his knees, panting and wheezing like a man with terminal emphysema.

"Can't… go on…" he gasped.

"Damn it, of course you can," I said. "You have to."

"Hardly… breathe…"

"Don't you dare give it up now. I forbid it."

"Doctor's… orders… eh?"

"Yes. Precisely."

I know not how he managed to get going again, but he did. He stirred his considerable bulk and placed one foot in front of the other, and thus we continued laboriously onward and upward. We were all but blind in the darkness, with only the Triophidian Crown affording any illumination. The susurration of the snake men's footfalls grew louder at our backs. I began to despair of ever making it to the pyramid's apex. The journey seemed unending, interminable, an uphill slog with no promise of a summit.

Then, in an instant, the triangular aperture appeared ahead. We all picked up the pace, even Mycroft. Not far now. Almost there.

One by one we passed through the doorway, into the pit Moriarty had excavated. Straight away Holmes set down the *Necronomicon*, then reached inside the obelisk, grasped the door and tugged. It would not budge. I settled Gregson on the bare earth floor of the pit and joined him, adding my strength to his. Still the door did not move.

The snake men were almost at the top now. The cobra man was in the vanguard. His eyes lit up as he saw us struggling with the door. Only a few more steps and he would have us.

Holmes pushed me back and withdrew from the doorway himself.

"Obviously it cannot be closed by conventional means," said he. "I should have known as much. It is not that sort of portal."

He proceeded to repeat the incantation Moriarty had used, word for word.

Nothing happened. The door did not move.

I groped for my revolver and the box of cartridges. Was this what it had come down to? Shooting the snake men singly as they filed out from the pyramid? Well, so be it. I would despatch as many of them as I could, in order to buy time for the Holmes brothers and Gregson to find sanctuary.

Holmes tried the incantation a second time, only now he replaced the word *k99 tharl*, "unlock", with its antonym, *tharl*.

The door duly swung shut, blocking out the cobra man's startled, thwarted face and those of the snake men behind him.

"Safe," I said, breathing a sigh of relief. "For now. But we must keep going. It will take them but a moment to reopen the door."

"I would not be so sure," said Holmes. "The inscription on it suggests otherwise. Look. Here. This part." He ran a finger along the lines of R'lyehian text, translating aloud. "'Only may one who is without become one who is within, by speaking the words enshrined in tradition.' This is a door built to keep those below in their place."

There were infuriated hisses and howls from within the obelisk, and the thumping of fists on the inside of the door, but these subsided, and in the end the snake men could be heard tramping back downward to their dismal underground domain.

And with that, it was over.

CHAPTER THIRTY

Rectifying a Desecration

OVER? WELL, NOT QUITE.

At Holmes's insistence, we set about re-burying the onyx obelisk. I would dearly have loved to call it a night and gone home. I was exhausted, near dead with fatigue. The same was true of Mycroft and Gregson, who had had a longer ordeal than Holmes and me. However, the pyramid and the underworld at its base could not be left accessible. The obelisk must be covered up before anyone else found it. There was no point putting it off until later.

From the sexton's hut Holmes commandeered an additional pair of shovels. He also broke into the church itself and appropriated a bottle of communion wine from the vestry, with which we fortified ourselves for the task ahead. This act of burglary was a crime, yes, and perhaps even a sin; but it was a desecration undertaken in order to aid us in rectifying a far more major desecration, and thus we concluded it was pardonable.

Holmes undid our manacles using his conventional lockpicks. Then he, Gregson and I set to work with the shovels. Mycroft, a stranger to manual labour in all its forms, adopted a supervisory role. Bathed in the light of candles which, like the wine, Holmes had requisitioned from the vestry, we decanted soil from the piles heaped around into the pit itself. Of the three of us, Gregson was the one who really put his back into it. Stripped to his shirtsleeves, he shovelled with machine-like regularity, his tight-lipped expression redolent of both disgust and resolve. Re-inhuming the obelisk was, to him, a way of laying to rest all that had happened below.

During a brief pause for rest, I asked Holmes how he had managed to free himself from Moriarty's clutches in the pool.

"I did not," he replied. "We were sinking fast. I have no idea whether the pool has a bottom. Perhaps it does not. I was convinced I was done for, at any rate. All I knew was icy cold blackness, Moriarty's face dimly before me like a pale moon, a sensation of pressure in my ears, and the pain of my lungs as they ached to draw air. And then... he let go."

"Let go?"

"What else do you think I mean? Took his hands off the chain."

"Yes, but deliberately?"

"So it appeared. All of a sudden I was no longer being dragged down, while Moriarty continued to plummet, still enmeshed in the coils of Nyarlathotep's tentacle."

"The deed cannot have been conscious on his part. Perhaps he simply could not maintain his grip on the chain. Perhaps he became too infected by weakness, Nyarlathotep stealing the last ergs of his strength."

"I really don't think so," said Holmes. "You were not there. You did not look at him as I did. He made a decision. He wanted me loose."

"But why? Remorse? Contrition? An attack of compassion? It hardly seems like the man."

"No, and that troubles me now. It did not trouble me at the time, of course. All I could think of was striking upwards and reaching the surface of the pool before my lungs gave out. It was a close-run thing. I almost didn't make it."

"Well, speaking for the three of us, I am very glad you did."

"I cannot shake the feeling, though, that Moriarty released me only because he knew the game was not over. He wanted me to live to fight another day. Which would imply that he himself was far from beaten."

I recalled the scheming look I had seen on the academic's face as he was being pulled down into the pool, and could not suppress a shiver.

"He is gone," I insisted. "He shall not bother us again. And good riddance, I say."

Holmes's sceptical grimace only amplified the scepticism I felt inside.

"I trust you are right, my friend," was all he said.

We picked up our shovels and returned to the business at hand. Within a couple of hours all the soil had been transferred back whence it came, and we embarked on the process of re-laying the flagstones, dragging them into position one after another and stamping them flat. Here, Mycroft came into his own, for it was like constructing a jigsaw. The flagstones were of irregular dimensions, and there was only one correct solution for replacing them in the space available. Mycroft had an uncanny knack of identifying which belonged where. Under his guidance we made short work of it, at the cost of a broken fingernail or two and the occasional squashed toe.

The bells of St Paul's Shadwell were tolling midnight as we emerged from the crypt into the night air. We were quite a sight – grimy, dishevelled, our clothing torn, our shoulders stooped with tiredness. The cold drizzle falling from the sky was a boon, refreshing and cleansing.

"Happy New Year, one and all," said Gregson with a mirthless laugh. "Let's hope eighty-one starts better than eighty ended."

That he was recovering his sense of humour, if in only limited form, seemed a good sign to me.

"I have no idea what to make of all I've just been through," said Mycroft. "It is almost impossible to take on board. Reptilian men. Monstrosities in pools. Human sacrifice. And what of you, Sherlock? What have you become? I thought you were pursuing this 'consulting detective' whimsy of yours. Now I learn that you have assumed a more chimerical role, embracing the supernatural."

"I would not have done it willingly," Holmes said, "but as you have seen for yourself, the supernatural is real." As if to illustrate the point, he held up the Triophidian Crown. He bore the *Necronomicon*, in its oilcloth, in his other hand. "Moreover, it is a threat more potent and injurious to the stability of society than any criminal activity. I cannot deny the call I have heard – the call of Cthulhu, one might say – and I cannot in all conscience refuse to heed it."

"The call of what?"

"You have much to learn, Mycroft. Many hours of revelation lie ahead of you. Because you are now a part of this. You too, Inspector."

"I am?" said Gregson.

"We all four are. We, for better or worse, have become

conscripts in a war, and it is a war we must wage in secret, without the public ever learning of it. For civilisation rests on the assumption that the universe is kindly disposed towards mankind and intended for our benefit. Imagine the upheaval were it to become widespread knowledge that that is not so."

"You believe the danger is not yet past?" I said.

"From what I know, it will never be past, not while the Great Old Ones and the Elder Gods live. They will always be pursuing their sinister agendas, whether that means seeking the total enslavement of mankind or merely wreaking havoc with the minds and souls of individual mortals. Whatever lusts they wish to slake or cruelties they wish to inflict, they will, with scant regard for the consequences. We, to these gods, are little better than flies. Shakespeare was right. They are like wanton boys, killing us for their sport. Someone must stand against them, and against the people who, like Moriarty, would facilitate their dark designs."

"And that someone is you. And us."

"Exactly, Watson. With regret, and by default, the four of us."

I tried to take in the import of what Holmes was saying. He was asking us to commit ourselves to a campaign combating the forces arrayed against Earth from beyond, from the far reaches of space, from the nether realm below, from all quarters. It seemed both an insurmountable task and an unendurable burden. It required far more than we four had to give, and the rewards it offered were paltry, if they existed at all. In fact, the only certainty about this war was that it was likely to bring us horror, madness and death.

"I cannot demand that you join me, any of you," Holmes went on, as though privy to my thoughts. "If you decline, I shall understand, and think no less of you for it. But if you search your hearts, you will realise that the choice is no choice at all. Besides," he added, "I would rather not stand alone, when I could have fine, upstanding allies at my side."

Mycroft, Gregson and I exchanged looks.

There could really be only one outcome.

In that lonely churchyard, beneath miserable rain, we all shook hands. A compact was sealed. We had become recruits.

Our army was small, pitifully so.

Our enemies were many and terrible.

Our struggle would be long and arduous.

There would be losses along the way – so many losses, of all kinds. There would be scars, too; some physical, the majority invisible but no less disfiguring for that: scars of the psyche, scars of the soul.

Yet, for the moment, as the world celebrated the passing of one year and the birth of another, I felt cause for hope.

Perhaps, with Sherlock Holmes as our general, we might survive. We might even prevail.

EPILOGUE

I TYPE THESE CLOSING PARAGRAPHS WITH MIXED
feelings. I am pleased to have purged myself of a tale I
have long kept hidden and shared with no one, not even
either of my wives. It is a relief.

Yet I am heavy-hearted, knowing that I have yet
more to do. More ground to cover, more words to write.
This self-exorcism is far from over. The events of 1895 –
which began at the Bethlem Royal Hospital at Southwark,
the "Bedlam" of renown and notoriety – will form the
next volume of this memoir. Then in the third and final
volume I must address the matter of the sea-spawned
abominations which blighted the south coast of England
some fifteen years further on.

Throughout the three decades covered in these books
Holmes and I found ourselves confronted time and time
again with an unassailable, unalterable truth. It is a truth
which contrived to sweep the legs from under us whenever
we felt we were getting the better of our foes and standing
tall, and it is enshrined in a rhyming couplet in the

Necronomicon. These two brief lines, penned by Abdul Alhazred while describing a nameless ancient Arabian city of which he once dreamed, encapsulate everything that we strove to vanquish and that strove to vanquish us in return:

> *That is not dead which can eternal lie,*
> *And with strange aeons even death may die.*

James Lovegrove is the *New York Times* bestselling author of *The Age of Odin*. He has been short-listed for many awards including the Arthur C. Clarke Award, the John W. Campbell Memorial Award, and the Scribe Award. He won the Seiun Award for Best Foreign Language Short Story in 2011, and the Dragon Award in 2020 for *Firefly: The Ghost Machine*. He has written many acclaimed Sherlock Holmes novels, including *Sherlock Holmes & the Christmas Demon*. As well as writing books, he also reviews fiction for the *Financial Times*. He lives in Eastbourne in the UK.

For more fantastic fiction, author events, exclusive excerpts,
competitions, limited editions and more:

VISIT OUR WEBSITE
titanbooks.com

LIKE US ON FACEBOOK
facebook.com/titanbooks

FOLLOW US ON TWITTER
@TitanBooks

EMAIL US
readerfeedback@titanemail.com